P: ... s:

'Fascinating to read, very well written, intriguing plot . . . I enjoyed it very much.'
Derek Jacobi

'Well-informed, atmospheric and beautifully written.'
Literary Review

The Terror of Constantinople

'Vivid characters, devious plotting and buckets of gore are enhanced by his unfamiliar choice of period. Nasty, fun and educational.'
Daily Telegraph

'Anyone who enjoys their history with large dollops of action, sex, intrigue and above all, fun will absolutely love this novel.'
Historical Novels Review

Also by Richard Blake

Conspiracies of Rome
The Terror of Constantinople
The Blood of Alexandria
The Sword of Damascus

About the author

Richard Blake is a lecturer, historian, broadcaster and writer. He lives in Kent with his wife and daughter.

RICHARD BLAKE

The Ghosts of Athens

HODDER

First published in 2012 by Hodder & Stoughton
An Hachette UK company

First published in paperback in 2013 by Hodder & Stoughton

1

A CIP catalogue record for this title is available from the British Library

ISBN 978 1 444 70971 1

Typeset in Plantin Light by Hewer Text UK, Ltd

Printed and bound by Clays Ltd, St Ives plc

Hodder & Stoughton policy is to use papers that are natural,
renewable and recyclable products and made from wood grown
in sustainable forests. The logging and manufacturing processes
are expected to conform to the environmental regulations
of the country of origin.

Hodder & Stoughton Ltd
338 Euston Road
London NW1 3BH

www.hodder.co.uk

I dedicate this book
to my wife Andrea
and to my daughter Philippa

ACKNOWLEDGEMENTS

The extract in Chapter 16 is from Gregory of Nyassa (d. *c*.394), *Against Eunomius*, Book IX, translated by Philip Schaff (1819–93).

The extract in Chapter 27 is from Plutarch (AD 46–120), *That It is Not Possible to Live Pleasurably According to the Doctrine of Epicurus*, translated by Richard Blake.

The arguments as to the Nature of Christ in Chapter 40 are adapted from the relevant articles in *The Catholic Encyclopaedia*, and from William Lane Craig, *Reasonable Faith: Christian Truth and Apologetics*, Crossway Books, Illinois, 1994.

The verses in Chapter 44 are from Homer, *Iliad*, Book VIII, translated by George Chapman (1559–1634)

1

Canterbury, Friday, 3 April 688

The present chapter in my story begins five days ago. Oh, Jarrow to Canterbury is a three-hundred-mile journey, and you don't cover much of that in five days. But I'm not starting with the day we set out from the monastery, with everyone waving us off and holding up his hands in prayer for our safety. Nor am I counting our interminable, though generally smooth, progress along the old military road, nor the changes of guard as we passed from one kingdom to another. I mention five days because it was then that I came, with young Brother Jeremy, to the silent ruins of what had, in the old days, been London, and prepared to step on to the bridge across the Thames.

'Here, what do you think you're doing?' someone cried, popping out as if from nowhere. 'I own this bridge, and I collect the tolls.' He was one of those dirty, pot-bellied creatures you see lounging on street corners in any city where barbarians have planted themselves. Without experience of his kind, you might have dismissed him as a flabby loudmouth, sliding fast into the decline of life. But I had enough experience to know trouble when I saw it.

I forced a smile and sat upright in the handcart. 'Greetings, my son,' I quavered. 'May God be with you on this glorious day. But this bridge is surely owned by His Majesty of Kent. And, as I am, you will have noticed, a monk of Holy Mother Church. I travel under King Swaefheard's protection.' I got a thoroughly nasty look for that. Ignoring Brother Jeremy, who'd let go of the handles, and who now stood looking down at the uneven stones of the road, the creature shambled over and stood between me and the risen sun. It was a nice day; correction, it had been a nice day.

'Don't you come the hoity-toity with me,' he snarled. 'I'll have you know that His Majesty himself has given me the right to collect tolls. No one – not even a bag of bones like you – goes across for free.' He stepped back and looked at the cart. An unpleasant grin now came over his face. What I'd thought at first was a sword tied to his waist turned out, on closer inspection, to be a wooden club. It made no difference to the trouble he represented. In the proper hands – especially against the unarmed – a club was as horrid as any sword.

'I assess this cart at five silver pennies,' he said with a faint sound of the official. 'Payment before you go across.'

I raised my arms in supplication. 'Five pennies, my son?' I whined. 'Five *silver* pennies? Can there be so much money in the whole of England? Assuredly, we have none. Now, in the name of God, be merciful. I am an old man of ninety-seven. I am travelling to see the Lord High Bishop of Canterbury. Let us pass freely to the other side.'

That got me another of his unpleasant grins. He set off on a walk about the cart. He made a sudden feint at Jeremy, who shrank back in terror and nearly tripped over one of the stones. Before he could right himself, his hat came off, to show his pink scalp above the ginger tonsure. The man laughed at the slightly absurd sight, and went back to his general inspection. It was a nice cart. It had been fitted out in Jarrow with leather cushions and an awning to keep the rain and sun from spoiling my ride. By the time he got back to me, he barely needed to open his mouth.

'If you can't pay the toll, I'll take the cart,' he said.

As if had by surprise, I let out a flood of sobbing imprecation. I reminded him of my age, how far it still was to Canterbury, how I'd never walk a half-mile, let alone another seventy, without falling down dead. It was worth trying – and it did amuse him. He leaned into the cart and pressed his face close to mine. 'I'll tell you what,' he sneered. 'You give me the cart, your food, and whatever money you've got. You can then have a nice little stroll to Canterbury. There, can I be fairer than that?'

I tried another reference to my great age. It only ended his show of good humour. 'What doesn't kill you makes you stronger,' he snarled, quoting an old Kentish ballad that brought back fond memories of my youth.

'My heart, my heart!' I suddenly cried, clutching at my chest. That got me another smile. 'Oh my son,' I cried again, 'I have no money. But I do possess about me something else of great value. If you will but take that, leave the cart with me and the boy.'

'Well, let's be looking at it,' he replied, leaning closer. I could smell his stomach-turning breath. I looked about – as if the escort I'd been promised that King sodding Swaefheard would provide might suddenly ride into sight. But no such luck. They hadn't been there at the border to replace the men who had turned back. They'd not be here now. Put not your trust in princes, I thought grimly. It might have been the story of my life. I fixed another senile grin on my face and took a deep breath.

Dear me! Ninety-seven is ninety-seven – that much of what I'd told him was true – and I'll not describe it as an easy, fluid motion. Still, I'll swear he didn't have time to wipe the expectant look off his face between the moment I slipped the fastening pin out of my cloak and the moment I rammed four of its six inches into the fucker's left eye socket.

He let out the contents of both lungs in one scream as he staggered back, blood and the dark fluid of his ruined eye dribbling on to his scruffy beard. I gripped the side of the cart with my left hand and gave him the best shove I could manage with my walking stick. With another wail of horror – and oh, what a stroke of luck that was! – he was straight over the low wall of the bridge. Yes, lucky day, indeed! The first blow was an admirable thing for someone of my age. The second might have been envied by a man of any age. And it saved me the trouble of clambering out to do something inelegant and possibly ineffectual with my walking stick. Given more good luck, the tide might be in, and the river would carry him away.

3

But I'd had my share of luck for that day. 'Master, he is still alive,' young Jeremy babbled as he looked back from his inspection over the wall. 'Alive, Master – he's still alive!' The boy's talent for redundancy had outdone itself. Even I could hear the feeble cries from perhaps a dozen feet down. I swung stiff legs over the edge of the cart and tottered across the six feet that separated me from the wall. I leaned on the mossy stones and looked over. Sure enough, the creature had landed at a funny angle that suggested a broken back. He was feebly dabbing at the pin still buried in his eye socket and letting out a piteous wail for help.

I straightened up and looked about me. Many years before, in Constantinople, I'd had the old tax records for London dug out of the archive. The last time an undivided and still more or less complete Empire was ruled from the new Rome, London had been the third largest city in the West, behind only Rome itself and Carthage. Its population had been close to a third of a million, and it had been a considerable trading and financial centre. Even now, it was an impressive sight. The smaller buildings were heaps of overgrown rubble. The sun sparkled on a completely silent Thames, and rabbits were scurrying about its grassy banks. But the great basilica from which all the provinces of Britain had been governed still seemed to have its roof, and most of the churches looked solid enough. There was no reason to suppose the place completely abandoned. There might even be a few inhabitants who spoke Latin and tried to think of themselves as Roman. I'd passed through here just a few months before, on my return from the East. Then, the weather had been too unpleasant for thoughts of exploration. I'd now been looking forward to a spot of tourism.

'Master, I think he will live a while,' Jeremy said, breaking in on my thoughts. 'Should we not go down and give divine comfort?'

'Divine comfort?' I asked, incredulous. 'Divine bleeding comfort? You take up these handles and get moving again if you don't want a good hiding.' I looked about again. London would normally have been well worth *some* exploration – though, sad to confess, not now. So far as I could tell, the creature had been alone. Then again, he'd come as if from nowhere. Who could tell what accomplices he might have lurking in these ruins? 'Come on, boy,' I added. 'Put your back into it.'

Divine comfort, indeed! When I was eighteen – accomplices lurking about or none – I'd have been straight down on to that river bank to slit the creature's throat and dance in the blood. But that's young people today, I suppose. Some of them just don't know they've been born. I let the boy help me back into the cart and arrange a rug over my legs. As he bent forward to take up the handles again, I managed a nice blow from my stick across his shoulders. Divine comfort – I ask you!

Stopping in London was definitely off my list of things to do. At the same time, if there was nothing ahead for another twenty miles, we'd not be turning back for the monastery where we'd spent the night. We were on a stretch that might allow Jeremy to break into a slow trot. Certainly, it was worth trying for one. The sooner the Thames was vanishing on our left as we pushed along Watling Street, the happier I'd be. Somewhere or other on the road, we'd surely meet those bloody guards. Till then, it was just me and a useless boy. I lashed out again at Jeremy and swore at him to put his back into the work of pulling me to Canterbury.

As we passed out from the last of the southern ruins of London, he slowed to a walk and looked back at me. 'You are sad, Master,' he said in a mournful gasp. 'Are you repenting the blood we have shed this day?'

'*We?*' I felt like asking. What had Jeremy done but stand there, trying not to shit himself with fright? I scowled at the sweating, spotty face and thought of telling him what sort of report I'd make to Benedict once we were back home. The Abbot might well give him the sound whipping I wasn't up to providing. But the sun had risen higher, and the day was turning out as fine as I'd expected. I laughed and found a softer spot on my travelling cushions. 'If that two-legged beast lies bleating there till the wolves come and devour him, don't suppose I'll lose any sleep over it. But that was a nice pin. I picked it up in Beirut. I doubt I'll get anything so fine to

5

replace it in Canterbury.' I hugged myself and let out a long giggle that trailed off into a coughing fit.

Yes, the day had turned out nice again. Indeed, it hadn't rained once since we'd set out from Jarrow.

2

Theodore, born in Tarsus, now Lord High Bishop of Canterbury, shifted weakly on the pillows that allowed him to sit upright in bed, and peered uncertainly at me. 'Greetings, My Lord Alaric,' he finally said in Greek. 'I trust the journey was not too troublesome for one of your years.'

I shuffled across the floor and took his right hand in mine. As I lifted it to kiss the episcopal ring, I noticed the deadness that flesh often takes after a seizure. He grunted and let the monk who was attending him fuss with the pillows. I sat myself on the hard chair that had been placed beside the bed and stretched my legs. It was probably best not to excite the poor dear with any narration of our troubles on the road.

'My Lord Bishop will surely recall that I am no longer His Magnificence the Senator Alaric,' I replied, joining him in Greek. 'I am no more than humble Brother Aelric, returned to die in the land of his birth.' I'd tried for the appropriate tone of humility; difficult, though, when, even three days after disposing of that human offal, you're still feeling pleased with yourself.

Theodore tried for a cough and made do with a groan. The monk looked anxiously at the pair of us. He was a native, and probably knew only Latin – and that only enough for praying. I turned my smile on him, and gave him a glimpse of the stained ivory that served me nowadays for teeth.

'You may leave us, Brother Wulfric,' Theodore croaked in bad English when he was sufficiently recovered to say anything at all. A look on his face of immense tenderness, the monk rose and bowed.

Once the door was shut, Theodore shifted again on his pillows

7

and pointed a weak and trembling finger at a table beside the window. There was a jug on it and one cup. It would mean getting up and walking ten feet there and ten back. But the size of the cup suggested that the jug was filled with neither beer nor water. After three hundred miles, another twenty feet was worth the risk of disappointment.

No disappointment! 'Is this from the East?' I asked with an appreciative sniff.

'It's French,' came the whispered reply.

Leaving the cup behind, I carried the jug back to my chair. I took out my teeth and had a long and careful swig. I'd had better, but this would do. I wiped the dribble from my chin and looked about the room. As a boy, Theodore had delighted in flowers. It was a love that had stayed with him through life. I didn't suppose he was up to turning his head very much since the last seizure. But he'd had himself propped where he could look straight at a mass of spring blossoms arranged on another table near the door. My wine jug aside, it was the only cheer in an otherwise bleak room that smelled of the decay that attends the very old when they have forsworn the use of soap and water. If holiness is not a force that has ever guided my own actions, I can usually take account of it. But what on earth could have possessed Theodore – already an old man – to give up his nice little monastery in Rome and spend twenty-odd years on this grotty island? In the end, I'd had bugger all choice about coming here. He'd had a first-class excuse to stay put.

'Why do you tell people that I'm senile?' he asked in a suddenly querulous tone.

That was a hard one to answer, and my response was to pretend I hadn't heard him.

'I am dying – there's no doubt of that,' he went on. 'But the reports of what you've been saying to your students in Jarrow do hurt me. I am forgetting my Latin. I sometimes find myself think-ing in Syriac. But I am not senile.'

I continued looking into the jug. In the months since coming back from the East, my renewed acquaintance with opium had been carried to a certain excess, and I had perhaps been rather garrulous in my class. Then again, dwelling on local matters had been a way of deflecting those endless questions about what I'd been up to after my abduction from the monastery in Jarrow. I could have taken another mouthful of wine and pretended that drunkenness was adding to my deafness. But there was something in Theodore's voice that reminded me of the old days – the very, *very* old days before we'd fortified ourselves from each other behind those palisades of words. I could feel a slight pressure of tears. I sighed and bent carefully forward to put the jug on the floor.

'I am, of course, most grateful for all you've done for me,' I said. 'When I first arrived here, you'd have been within your rights to send me off to Ravenna for handing over to the Emperor's agents. Instead, you overlooked all the frequently unfortunate dealings of our middle years and found a place for me at Jarrow.' I fell silent and stared at the shrivelled creature who lay before me. If he'd been ten when I was twenty-two, he had now to be eighty-five or -six. At his age, I'd still been directing the affairs of a vast, if diminished, empire. A younger man would have found Theodore enviably full of years, despite his infirmity. For me, he was a pitiable sight. I got up and pulled his blanket into place. It was the least I could do. I sat down and played with my teeth. There was a piece of bread compacted into one of the depressions in the upper gold plate. I picked it out with a dirty fingernail and put it into my mouth. I washed it down with more of Theodore's French red.

'What you say about me is of no importance,' he said with a slight show of vigour. 'In any event, I am no longer your host. The circumstances of your return have made me your keeper, and this has a bearing on the nature of our present dealings.' His voice suddenly trailed off and he closed his eyes.

I wondered if he'd fallen asleep. If so, it would be a chance for me to slope off and find what manner of quarters his people had arranged for me. A bath was probably out of the question. But I'd come to him straight from my journey, and I could do with a rest.

However, as I was thinking to get up and take my leave, his eyes opened again.

'I have summoned you to Canterbury,' he said, 'to ask a favour of you. It is a matter of some delicacy, and we thought it best at this stage to avoid putting things in writing.' His good hand twitched under the blanket, and I thought for a moment he'd pull something out. But his eyes closed again, and he went limp on the bed. I waited for his strength to come back. This time, though, he had drifted away. His breathing settled into a faint but regular gasp.

There was a gentle knock on the door and the monk Wulfric entered. He looked at the sleeping Bishop, and hurried across to rearrange the pillows. The wine jug was still half full. It was too much nowadays to finish in one go. On the other hand, taking it with me might not create the best impression. I groaned softly as I got up and made for the door.

'I'll make my own way out,' I said in English without looking back. It was a pointless utterance. If Wulfric bothered watching me leave, it was only to see when he could shut the door.

'If this is the best you've seen,' I said with what I hoped was a dismissive wave, 'it is a *very* fine city.'

Brother Jeremy nodded and went back to his eager inspection of Canterbury. Of course, when you're bumping along in a wheel-barrow, three feet above the ground, you'd think little enough of Constantinople itself. Here, I was most aware of the refuse that was the street's only paving, and the shouting of the three churls who walked ahead of us to push everyone else out of our way. I had my back to these, and was looking instead at the scrawny churl who was making a right mess of pushing me in the direction of our lodgings.

'But I never thought I'd see the like,' Jeremy cried again with all the astonishment of youth. He pointed at the leather goods hanging before one of the shops we were passing. A youngish man of darker hue than England ever produces put on an expect-ant smile and stepped out of the shop. I sent him packing with a scowl and looked back at Jeremy, who was now staring up at one of the tiled roofs. Like most other building materials here, the tiles had the weathered look that told me they were reused from London, or even my own Richborough.

'I never thought I'd see the like,' he repeated yet again, delight and wonder in his voice.

I might not think much of this place. So far as Jeremy was concerned, though, the narrow, twisting street that led from the Bishop's residence might as well have been one of the main thoroughfares in the great City that sits upon the two waters.

'I was told that the Monastery of Saint Anastasius was on the left in the square containing the Great Church,' he said, pulling himself back to the matter in hand.

I nodded vaguely. Canterbury had been my first proper stop the previous winter after I'd been dumped back in Richborough. Even I had to own that the church was a big one by Western standards. But I'd not have dignified the clearing in front of it with the word 'square'. That gave far too grand an impression of this dreadful hole on the far edge of civilisation. I was thinking of that French red, when the wheelbarrow came to a sudden stop, and I was almost pitched backwards into the waiting filth.

'Not more pigs in the way?' I muttered. No, it was people – a whole crowd of them who'd resisted every effort to be pushed. They blocked the exit from the narrow street into what Jeremy had called the square, and stood mostly still and, but for a faint buzz of conversation I couldn't follow, silent.

'Make room for the guest of His Grace the Bishop,' young Jeremy cried. He might have addressed them in Greek for all the sense he made in his Northumbrian dialect.

'Get out of my bloody way,' I snarled in the Kentish dialect, 'or I'll have my churls set about you with clubs.'

'Eat shit and die,' someone called cheerfully down at me. But the churls had taken the hint and were looking fierce. With a few protests and the dropping of something wet and foul between my feet, the crowd parted, and we moved straight into the square.

'Strike harder! Strike harder!' I heard someone cry in Latin over on my right. 'Let him suffer in this world for his sins, that he may avoid damnation in the next.' He'd called this out in a Roman accent too affected to be real. He was repeating himself, when there was the crack of a whip, and his voice was drowned out by a loud and enthusiastic cheer from the crowd. I gripped the right edge of my wheelbarrow and twisted round to see what was happening.

The voice was of an obese churchman in high middle age. Dressed in dazzling white, he was leaning forward from a raised chair as he continued his Latin harangue. There was bugger all I could make of it, though, for the cheers of the crowd. I climbed slowly out of the wheelbarrow and pushed my way to the front of the crowd. Though much decayed, I still have the remains about me of bigness. More important, I've still the air of power, long exercised, that people of this quality don't even think to question.

From the front of the crowd, I could see the naked wretch tied to a stake, his wrists pulled up so high that his feet barely touched the ground. I've never been a connoisseur of these things, but it was a most impressive beating. With all the slow deliberation you see in a church service, two monks walked round and round the beaten man. At every one and a quarter circuit, keeping opposite each other, they'd stop and land two simultaneous blows with what looked like slave scourges. Except for the regular stops and the beating, it might well have been a service – that or a demonstration of astronomical movements.

'Behold the mercy of Holy Mother Church,' someone now called out in English from beside the chair. 'Behold the penance, freely begged and lovingly given. Behold and wonder!'

There wasn't that much for me to behold in detail – not with my blurry vision, at least. But even I could see that the scourges had the iron tips left on them. To be flogged with just one of these was to be tortured. Even the first blow, laid on with the right firmness, would get a scream out of most victims. Six would tear the flesh most horribly. A dozen would lay the back open like so much putrefied liver. This poor sod must be well past the dozen. By now, his bones would be showing through, and blood, expelled from his lungs, would be dribbling through his nostrils and ears. A master with any sense of propriety would normally offer an offending slave the choice of being hanged. For a flogging of this sort always smashed a man, and I'd never seen any who survived make a full recovery. But this was a Church matter, and, once the formalities of 'choice' had been rattled through, there would be no mercy. It couldn't last much longer. The penitent's body was dark with his own blood, and there were dark splashes all over the white robes of the two monks. And this was certainly a display that pleased the crowd. Between those bursts of cheering, there was a continual murmuring of approval.

'You there,' I said, tapping someone on the shoulder who'd had the nerve to stand in front of me. 'I want to know what all this is about.'

'He baptised a dead infant,' someone else whispered into my good ear. It might have been a churl, or one of the lower trades-men – hard to tell the difference, really: the broken nose and missing front teeth told me nothing either way. 'Now Deacon Sophronius is over from Rome,' he added, 'there ain't no more laxity.' He stopped and giggled, then repeated: 'No more laxity.' He looked away to see if there was anything he was missing.

Sophronius was now out of his chair, and was holding up his arms in an exaggerated prayer. Scourges still in hand, the monks had stopped their endless wheeling, and were bent forward in obvious exhaustion.

'No, you don't baptise the dead,' the man beside me went on. 'If the magic water don't touch you when you're alive, it's the ever-lasting fire for you.' He pressed his nasty face into a broader smile. 'Oh yes, the black fires that ain't never put out, and the full view, miles above, of the blessed ones in Paradise.'

'Too right!' someone joined in from behind me. 'If a child comes out dead, it was always marked out by God for the fires of Hell. Not the Pope himself can change that. The priest shouldn't never have let the mother think otherwise.'

There was a hum of agreement all about, though I did see one or two grim faces in the crowd. Sophronius was now beginning a recital of one of Pope Gregory's more inhuman letters. I could almost hear the smacking of his lips at every pause for the translation into English. I'll not bother commenting on its inhumanity; besides, you have to accept there's a certain lawyerly neatness about the doctrine. If you want everyone to believe there is no salvation except through the Church, you can't go making exceptions for a stillbirth.

Though the penitent himself might well have been dead now, Sophronius was going at a very leisurely pace through what I knew was a letter of immense elaboration. I looked up as the dark and ominous clouds that I'd seen gathering ever since I was wheeled out of Theodore's residence now blotted out the sun, and I felt the chill of an approaching storm.

'Let's get under cover,' I said to Jeremy, who'd got himself beside me. 'If you think this spectacle is worth a soaking, I don't.'

3

I dreamed that I was young again. I was having dinner with King Chosroes. The Persians hadn't yet begun their row of shattering defeats that cleared us for what seemed like good out of Syria and Egypt. Unless you had access to the military and tax reports given monthly to the Imperial Council, this could still be seen as a disastrous war. The Persians might be mopping up the Asiatic provinces a battle at a time. They might just have been thrown back with tremendous effort from a stab at Constantinople itself. But most people out of the know expected either a military recovery on our part, or a treaty that would leave us nursing a grudge until the next war. But, as a member of the Council, I'd been fully in the know. When the Persians spoke of reversing the victories of Alexander, a thousand years before, and of recreating the hegemony that had nearly gobbled up the Greek city states, it was more than wishful thinking. The Empire was on the verge of collapse.

I saw Ctesiphon twice. The last time I was there, the Persian capital was much diminished. And the victorious army, of which I was effectively the head, left it a heap of smouldering ruins. But my dream had set me back there for my first visit – when it looked as if the Persians really would be the winners in this great struggle for mastery of the known world. How I'd managed to get there unmolested – let alone worm my way into the Royal Court at Ctesiphon – is too long a story to give as an aside. But I was there, got up as an heretical bishop, and I was having dinner again with His Majesty the Great King.

It was a jolly enough time, if you can find anything good to say about watching gory executions most days, and every single night having to shaft a pretty and inventive, but maniacally demanding, third royal wife. No, it *was* a jolly time in its own way. The Great King was tired of being nagged by his fire-worshipping priests, and, once he realised I shared his taste for opium, we'd struck up an odd sort of friendship. So, every three evenings, we'd sit in his bedroom, feasting on wild figs and cabbage he'd gathered with his own hands, and then sniffing lumps of resin wrapped in gold foil and dropped into bowls of glowing charcoal.

I'd finished a recitation of some of the lighter anecdotes in Herodotus about the King's forebears – the disappearance of their own literature always left the Persians dependent on the Greeks for their history – and was waiting for a gong to sound in one of the outer rooms. This would be notice that some eunuchs were coming in to entertain us with their efforts at wanking each other. No gong tonight, though. Instead, it was one of the royal secretaries with another list of family members accused of treason. While Chosroes listened intently to each name and mumbled punishments it needed a diseased mind to conceive let alone pronounce, I made my excuses and went out through the private door.

The Great King had just fathered something that, for the first time in twenty years, had turned out not to have three legs or a cleft palate. So the whole palace was under orders to drink itself blotto. This was my chance for another look through the Secret Archive. There had been a whole delegation of Avars in Ctesiphon. So Roxana the Lustful had whispered in my ear the night before. The generality of what had been discussed was obvious. But it was the details that mattered – and the memorandum of the joint descent on Constantinople would still be drying.

The royal entrance to the archive building was along an unwindowed corridor. There was a lamp burning dimly at the far end, and I made my way along the boarded floor without setting off any of the bells that Chosroes had caused to be placed even here. A little at a time, I got the door catch up so it didn't make any noise, and let myself in.

Oh bugger! The Pope himself was sitting in there. How he'd got here all the way from Rome – and in his most formal reception outfit – isn't something you bother asking in a dream. It was enough that he had got himself there, and was now grinning at me from the only chair in the room.

'You shifty, atheistical bastard!' he spat in Persian. 'You've a right nerve abusing the King's hospitality. I'll see you buried alive for this, an eighteen-inch stake rammed up your arse.'

I hurried across the room and tried to shush him into silence. No hope.

He now switched into Latin and began a shouted recital of my official name and titles. His voice rose and rose, until it echoed from every wall in that large room.

I suppose that, even in dreams, the Universal Bishop – Servant of the Servants of Christ, the first among equals of all the Patriarchs, and so on and so forth – deserves a certain respect. But I hope you'll not think it scandalous if I snatched up the cushion from under his feet and shoved it hard over his face. I shoved it there and held it there, while his arms flailed helplessly about, and I tried to stop up the little squeals of outrage that came through the stuffed silk . . .

All now went dark about me and I drifted, as if for many centuries, through a medium less buoyant than water, though more dense than air. I might have been very high above the earth. Or perhaps I was drifting upside down. When I did look up, I was aware of a solid blackness that might be the land. Now and again, I heard the piteous wail that might have been a child. Perhaps there was a hand dabbing at my face. Or it might have been the flapping wing of a bird, or of something larger. This was, I observed with what little rational thought I could manage, a disappointment. If its usual effect at night is a luxurious and more than sexual chorus of pleasure from every atom of the soul, opium can sometimes let you down. So it had tonight. The half pill I'd swallowed before nodding off was still at full blast, and I might now be in for a wild ride through memories best not revisited.

No, I was awake. Granted, dreams fed by the poppy can bleed into each other. Sometimes, you'll even dream that you're awake between other dreams. But, no – this wasn't a dream of being awake. Deep within me, some faint grip on reality was telling me that I really was lying on the wooden bunk where Jeremy had placed me after dinner, and that hands were pressed hard on my shoulders. Was someone shouting? Hard to tell for the moment. Beyond doubt, though, I could feel that I was being held down.

Time was when I'd have reached under my pillow for a knife – or, failing that, I'd have swung my legs upwards, and, with all the force that training could give to the heavy muscle of a northerner, I'd have got whoever was attacking me from behind. You can't do that at ninety-seven. But, as I'd shown well enough on London Bridge, old instincts don't entirely die. My shoulders were being pressed down on to the wooden boards of my cot. But my arms were still free. I clasped both hands together and rammed upwards as hard as I could . . .

'Oh please, Master, think nothing of it,' Jeremy sobbed as he sponged more water over a cut that wouldn't stop bleeding. 'It was entirely my fault for disturbing you. But you seemed so – so very agitated in your sleep . . .'

I'd got the lamp turned up in the room we were sharing, and I could see how close I'd come to smashing the boy's nose into his face.

I hobbled over and sat beside him on his own wooden cot. 'Drink this,' I said gently. He looked at the cup and tasted the stale cider I'd grabbed from the supper table before we were brought over here. It was poor stuff, but would take his mind off the pain. I held the cup while he finished its contents.

I put an arm round his shoulder. 'Listen, Jeremy,' I said, 'I do most humbly apologise.' I could have elaborated on the life I'd led, and how the habit had long since ripened into instinct of using lethal force whenever in doubt. Instead: 'It was a dream,' I said. 'That's what made me cry out – though I really am surprised if it wasn't in Latin.' I fell silent and let my bony arm rest on his bony shoulder.

I got up and went back to my own cot. I arranged the thread-bare blanket about me like a kind of shawl and sat on the rough boards. 'The Abbot here has told me,' I said with a firm change of subject, 'that Theodore wants to see me again directly after morning prayers. If tomorrow is anything like today, I don't think that will detain me very long. I suggest, then, a proper look round Canterbury. There is a lot here that you still haven't seen. We can even have food carried outside the walls for a lunch in the open. The forest that stretches between here and Richborough doesn't compare with what we passed through after London. If you can put up with holding me by the arm and keeping speed with a very old man, I'll take you to the field of Saint Maximin – it's where, when I was seventeen, everyone says I helped the most Holy Saint turn tree sap into beer.'

Jeremy looked back at me and smiled brightly. The odd turn of my last sentence had passed him by. Odd syntax, though, was the least the story deserved. So very long ago, I had started out in Canterbury as secretary to Maximin. He'd been a fat, jolly little monk fresh out of Ravenna, and I a barbarian with a pretty face who had nothing honest to sell but the Latin I'd picked up in Richborough. We'd hit it off at once, and, for five golden months, I'd gone out with him from the newly established mission in Canterbury to fish for souls. We'd faked resurrections from the dead. We'd made trees speak and stones spurt fire. I'd once even dressed in a bearskin and let Maximin teach me to pray before a whole village of gawping prospective converts. But we'd never done anything as productive as turn tree sap into beer. Still, if I'd only recently heard that story, it would never do to question it. Deny one miracle, after all, and – why – even young Jeremy might start thinking of himself.

No chance of that for the moment, however. 'I'd really like that, Master,' he said. He leaned forward and raised his hands in the way that I sometimes did in class to get attention for something important. 'When a man is tired of Canterbury,' he intoned, 'he is surely tired of life.'

He'd said this in Latin. I wished he'd stayed in English. *Taedet*, you see, is an impersonal verb. His use of it had produced the kind of sentence that, in Jarrow, would have had me tapping my cane on the ground and looking grim. But I only nodded. I leaned back and carefully swung my legs on to the cot. Trying to avoid getting a splinter through my pitiful nightgown, I stretched out and made myself as comfortable as might, in the circumstances, be possible.

I suddenly realised that the lamp was still turned up. 'Dearest Jeremy,' I said, looking up at the dark timbers of the ceiling, 'it is a sinful waste to burn oil when it isn't required for reading or prayer. So do be a love and push the wick down.' In the darkness, I straightened my legs and settled myself to wait for the opium to reclaim me.

But Jeremy was now in conversational mood. 'Master, is it true,' he asked, a hint of shyness in his voice, 'that you had to leave Canterbury after you'd killed a man?'

What *did* those boys talk about in Jarrow when my back was turned? But I didn't suppose anything could strike them as a tall story where the Old One was concerned. The only thing they might possibly have doubted was the truth. 'Oh, Jeremy, Jeremy.' I laughed. 'I had killed men before I took service with the Church. I killed any number of them afterwards. But I was on my very best behaviour in Canterbury. What did for me here was that I got the wrong girl with child.'

I laughed again in the frosty silence that resulted. Jeremy had asked me a reasonable question. Whether or not he'd like it, he deserved an answer. 'She was the daughter,' I took up again, 'of one of the chief men around King Ethelbert the Saint.' I stopped again and smiled unpleasantly. Pushing eighty years before, I'd never have thought my remote cousin Ethelbert could one day be seen as anything but the leering tyrant that he was. He'd done my father over with an enthusiasm King Chosroes himself might have respected. He'd then dumped my mother and all her children in Richborough, so he could come over as and when for a spot of rough sex. The first real notice he'd taken of me was when he'd had me trussed up one night and tried to castrate me. What a bastard he was!

'Doubtless, my young fellow,' I ended my story, giving a grand wave that I doubted he could see, 'you may think it all very scandalous. Nevertheless, I do urge you to set aside any unease or embarrassment when others talk of cock or cunt or fucking. Your vows preclude you from knowing of these things. But those who claim to be disgusted by their mention are invariably men without knowledge or honour, or courage or dignity.' I would have said more, but the gentle buzzing that Jeremy had set up towards the end of my story now deepened into a loud snore. I lay very still in the darkness and willed myself to go back to sleep.

No peace for the wicked, however! One of the reasons the old generally give up on sex is the annoyance, first of getting so uncertainly to the threshold of rapture, and then of only sometimes being able to pass across. So it now was with sleep. It didn't help that Jeremy would have kept a stone awake with his snoring.

4

But, no, I had been sleeping. Without once being other than aware of the snoring boy, I'd been back in the palace at Ctesiphon. The snoring had taken the place of flutes and cymbals to accompany the slow and elaborate gyrations of the dancing girls. With great consideration, Chosroes had told me what wines to avoid. Now, tipsy on something that tasted of wormwood, I'd been sitting with him for about a month – it may have been a year – while his chief general flopped about on the cushions like a landed fish, his face turning black from the poison he'd been fed. A good spy, you see, would have confined himself to harvesting truth from Roxana. The Great Alaric, you can be sure, had planted a few very useful lies in her mind. At last, they'd found their way into the Royal Mind, and I was now switching a complacent gaze between the fluttering, libidinous hands of those naked girls and the swelling tongue of a man who'd spent the past year studying survey reports of the walls of Constantinople.

Yet, whether I was asleep, or dreaming while awake, I certainly was back in Ctesiphon. Even as I reached out to grab lecherously at one of the firm breasts, I sensed a change in the quality of the artificial light; Chosroes and the girls were continuing as if nothing odd had taken place about us. But I looked up and saw that we were all now in the great, vaulted cellar that only the closest and most trusted companions of the Great King were allowed to see – allowed, that is, to see and be let out again. All about us, each on its own couch, lay the remains of the family members and generals and ministers he'd killed throughout his reign. Women, children, babies still suckling when he'd snatched them away, old and young men: all lay as he himself had arranged them to mummify in the dry air, each with a label pinned to the right ear that he'd written out in his own hand to remind him of names and genealogies. The couches were arranged about us in their hundreds. They reached over to every one of the far walls. In a while, Chosroes would snigger and get up, and call on me to help get this latest victim on to a couch. None would ever dare comment on his absence from the Royal Council. None would dare notice when his name was erased from every public document. His own wives and children would never dare so much as to whisper his name to each other in the dark. Once more, Alaric the Magnificent had bought time for beleaguered Constantinople, and for the drivelling fool of an Emperor who sheltered behind its walls.

And now those massed and flaring torches dimmed, and I was certainly awake in Canterbury. How long I'd lain here aware of myself I couldn't say. Never speak in the same breath of opium and any clear sense of time. Sweating in the darkness, I lay with no company now but Jeremy and the sound of his snoring. Then he stopped. As I yawned and prepared to turn over, he let out a long sicky burp. Then he farted. Then he was back to snoring.

'This really won't do!' I muttered. I clutched the side of my cot and sat up. Keeping the blanket about my shoulders, I forced myself to stand. I reached for my stick. It must have fallen down when Jeremy tried to wake me. I gave up on patting about for it, and walked unsteadily over to the window. The main shutters were bolted, and I'd have needed a chair to get at the top one – a chair and a lamp, and someone to hold me steady as I reached up to undo it. But, feeling round in the dark, I found a smaller opening about a foot square. I pulled it open. Gripping the back of a chair, I leaned forward and let the chilly night air dry the sweat from my face.

If the rain had finally let up, there was still a mass of clouds overhead, and I really might have been looking out with my eyes shut. But, if chilly, the breeze was a welcome change from the various smells that Jeremy had issued.

I thought of the brief and highly censored story I'd given to the boy. It was nearly eighty years since I'd first arrived in Canterbury.

In this time, it had grown from a cluster of mission buildings into what even I, who'd lived so much of that time in the Empire, had to admit was a city of respectable size. Five hundred dwellings, the Abbot had told me over supper. He'd gone so far as to assure me the place compared well with his native Milan. I didn't suppose he was exaggerating. Plague and the Lombards had long since finished the Empire's work of devastation in Italy.

But there was no doubt how Canterbury had grown. Eighty years was a long time to be away, and Canterbury had changed and changed again in its growth. If I looked straight ahead into the darkness, the big church was perhaps a little on my right. If so, I couldn't be that far from where the mission library had been. In a side room of this, Maximin had unpacked the boxes he'd brought with him from Ravenna and begun his dispute with the Bishop's secretary over possession.

I thought again of Maximin. For most of the previous eighty years, thinking of that name had mostly called up images of the child I'd named after him, not of the man himself. Tonight in Canterbury brought his face clearly to mind. I thought of how he'd saved me from Ethelbert, and how I'd finally avenged his death. I thought of his taste for opium – one of the few creditable things he had taught me. I thought of his wondrous ability to combine superstition and fraud, without once considering that, if his own were faked, all other miracles might somehow be in doubt. I thought of how dearly I'd loved him, and how I'd felt when I looked at his bloody corpse while the sun moved quickly down the Column of Phocas in Rome. I thought of Maximin, and I thought of them all: Ethelred, and that pretty girl and her child who may or may not have been born and who may or may not have lived, and my mother and what little I recalled of my father. And I thought of Martin and the Dispensator, and Priscus and Phocas and Heraclius, and all the others who'd gone into the darkness so long before I ever would. As I leaned there, looking out into the darkness, they and many, many others crowded back into memory as if they'd been petitioners in Constantinople, all racing to be first to touch the wide purple hem of my robe.

I stiffened and gripped harder on the chair. Was that a noise outside? I turned my good ear into the opening and listened hard. I thought at first I'd been mistaken. Behind me, the loud but even rhythm of Jeremy's snoring broke down into another long burp. As he fell comparatively silent, I listened again. Yes, there were noises outside – it was the scrape of leather sandals on gravel and the faint sound of voices.

'There was no need for you to come over,' I heard the Abbot whisper just a few yards away in the darkness. 'He ate little and drank too much. I put him and his boy to bed in the good room, just as you directed.' He spoke the clipped, irregular Latin that Italians use when they aren't putting on any airs and graces to foreigners.

The reply was a soft but disapproving sniff. 'Even so, I did give orders to be notified of his safe arrival and probable health.' It was Sophronius. You'd never mistake that rich tone, though subdued, or the exaggeratedly correct Latin. 'I haven't come all this way to deal with another drivelling old fool.'

The Abbot now had his back to me, and I didn't catch what he said.

'Yes, I could have gone to Jarrow,' Sophronius answered, filling in the blank in the conversation. 'But, if His Grace chooses to arrange things in this manner, who am I to disagree?'

With increasing gaps in my hearing of it, the conversation moved to other business. So far as I could gather, Sophronius wanted an inspection of the Abbot's school, but was being put off. 'Spare the rod, spoil the child,' he said with sudden loudness. His voice dropped to a murmur I couldn't follow. I think the Abbot was speaking about an outbreak of fever among the boys. Once or twice, I heard Sophronius laugh. There was a double repetition of 'Spare the rod, spoil the child,' and a long and anticipatory laugh. But the crunch of leather on gravel was growing more distant, and I was alone again.

Bugger all was what I'd learned from this act of involuntary snooping. I'd guessed back in Jarrow that Theodore wasn't invit- ing me over for an informal natter about the old days. He'd said as

25

much before nodding off in our meeting. Well, I'd find out soon enough what the Church wanted of me – or I might if the old dear managed to stay awake this time. Until then, I didn't think I'd burst with curiosity.

I was about to close up the opening in the shutters and feel my way back to bed, when I heard Jeremy groan and shift position till the bed boards creaked beneath him. He followed this with a fair impression of a death rattle and a return to snoring. I pulled a face, then smiled again. I pushed my face out into the fresh air and breathed in the smell of early shrubs.

Oh, Jeremy, Jeremy! Back in Jarrow, he'd not been my first choice as travelling companion. He'd not have been my first choice for anything. He wasn't bright. He wasn't brave. He wasn't at all good to look at. His lack of personal hygiene might have been notable even in the monasteries of Egypt, where soap and sinfulness were seen in the same disapproving light. I'd sat on the panel that had considered his application to be trained as a monk. My only comment then had been a joke about raising the quality of the Northumbrian breeding stock by removing him from it. I'd only given in to Benedict's urging when the boy I did have in mind had fallen out of a tree and sprained his ankle. That had left no one else strong enough to pull me all the way to Canterbury. So I'd sneered at him and poked him with my stick the whole way between Jarrow and Canterbury.

But, if he was lacking in all other qualities, Jeremy did possess a goodness of soul that you mustn't overlook. As with holiness, that isn't something I've ever myself possessed. But, as with holiness, it is something that must be recognised in others. And, unlike holiness, it is something to be valued. Tomorrow, I'd let him wake me, and dress me, and feed me, and bring me my false teeth, and comb and arrange the blond wig I told everyone I had to wear to keep my scalp warm. And I'd smile at him, and think of something pleasant to say. The moment I was done with Theodore, I'd lead him about Canterbury and show him where tree sap had been turned to beer – and I'd do nothing to persuade him it hadn't actually happened. Sooner or later, even he'd complete his training. After that, he'd be sent off to risk himself on converting the tattooed savages who dwelt in the forests beyond the wide northern sea. Before then, he might as well be shown some of the love he'd be preaching to others.

Outside, all was dark. All was silent. I might achieve a little sleep before morning. Or I might lie choking in more of the foetid smells cast off by Jeremy. Whatever the case, it was cold over here by the window. And at last, I realised, I did feel very tired.

5

I was back with Theodore. The window of his room was now fully unshuttered, and I could see that it looked over a small garden. A warm breeze came through it, and the sound of birdsong. Looking ghastly, but more with it than the previous day, Theodore had got himself propped into a padded armchair that allowed him to see out of the window.

'You will forgive me for not rising to greet you,' he said with surprising firmness. 'At our last meeting, I tried to discuss a favour that the Church would have of you. Because of the change in your status attendant on your return to England, this is not a favour that we can demand, and I shall understand if you feel that a conflict of interest prevents you from rendering any assistance.'

I smiled and took up the undisturbed wine. A bug had crawled into it and, without any consideration, died there. But I fished this out and flicked it on to the floorboards. Wulfric lifted a cup of something hot to Theodore's lips, and I waited for him to gather more of his ebbing strength.

'While you were away,' he continued, 'I had a letter from Rome. The Holy Father is involved in a matter of great delicacy with the Emperor in Constantinople. This involves the damnable heresy of the Monothelites. It is a shame that news of your own presence in the Mediterranean world did not arrive in Rome until after your return to England. It would have been most convenient had we been able to avoid all the delays of a correspondence between Rome and Canterbury.'

'Monothelitism is dead and buried,' I said, speaking carefully. 'I sealed the decree against it myself twenty years ago. We blamed everything on poor dead Sergius, and I drafted a grovelling letter of apology from the Emperor to the Pope. Why should the matter still give trouble?'

'Because it may now have been pulled, still twitching, from its grave,' Theodore gasped. He took another sip and tried to sit upright. He failed, and Wulfric had to lift him higher on to the pillows. 'You must have learned on your travels of the Emperor's great victory over the Saracens. There are hopes in Constantinople that Syria may be recovered for the Empire. Because of this, the Imperial authorities are looking again at an accommodation with the heretics in that province.'

Syria to be recovered? That was news to me. I may have spent a fair chunk of the previous summer in Damascus. But, shut away in the Caliph's palace, my news of the world beyond its gates had been sketchy at best. Still, it made sense that, if we were doing well against the Saracens, keeping Rome sweet would now be of secondary importance.

'Of course,' I said, trying for a tone of reassurance, 'there's nothing we can do to put pressure on Rome.' I broke off and grinned. The *we* in that sentence had been an entirely accidental slip. 'Do forgive me, Theodore: there's nothing *the Empire* can do to Rome. The days are gone when a Pope could be arrested in the Lateran and dragged off to some Eastern monastery. Certainly, the council you held a few years back in Hatfield was far outside the Empire's jurisdiction or sphere of influence. No one who signed its Acts can be in the slightest danger. Surely, if the new Emperor wants to go whoring among the heretical Churches of the East, all Rome needs to do is mutter a few complaints and wait for the military balance on land to swing back to the Saracens – and it will do that, I assure you.'

But Theodore didn't look much assured. He moved his head a fraction of an inch and looked at a forbiddingly large sheet of parchment unrolled on one of the tables in the room. I glanced at the tiny writing that covered it. Whoever had produced that must have done well and proper for his sight. Even in bright sunshine, I wasn't planning to wear out my own eyes on reading it. I looked back at Theodore. He was the theological expert. He'd spent half a century telling everyone who'd listen that I was just a smooth-talking fraud. If he wanted any help from me, he could at least begin by summarising whatever complaints he'd received from Rome.

But he gave me a bleak smile and went into English. 'Do me the favour, Brother Aelric,' he said, of explaining the Monothelite heresy to Brother Wulfric. It is beyond my abilities to do so in English. But you do have the advantage of being a native.'

I raised my eyebrows and looked into the wine jug. Explaining that mass of gibberish in Latin was challenge enough; why else, after all, had Rome looked so implicitly for advice to Theodore with his Greek and Syriac? Asking even me to put it into a dumpy language like English might well be seen as evidence of senility. But Theodore was in earnest. And Wulfric was looking at me with the first glimmerings of interest in two days. I sighed and drank deeply. I thought to give a summary of the account I normally gave my students in Jarrow. But that was in Latin, and the subtleties just didn't translate. If I was to get anywhere at all, I'd have to make a fresh start, and without preparation.

I think I'd lost the boy long before ending my digressive hunt for equivalents in English of Substance and Will and the various shades of Person. His eyes had certainly glazed over by the time I was able to launch into the critical matter of how the Will of Christ might relate to any of these. But he managed to keep a polite look on his face as my voice droned on and my throat began to ache from the effort of speaking for so long and with so much complexity in a language in which I might still be fluent, but in which I no longer thought.

And Theodore was highly delighted. 'Well said, Brother Aelric!' he gasped, now in Syriac. 'Well said, my Lord Senator Alaric. Age has not taken a jot of your talent for clear and shining evasion.' I smiled modestly and had another drink. I could take it as read that I'd been put up to my lecture less for Wulfric's enlightenment than to give Theodore an excuse to start ripping into me as he had in the old days. Sure enough, he shifted on his pillows and glared at me with open hostility.

'You have only overlooked your own part in bringing this gross heresy into the world, and how it was *you* who made sure it was maintained just so long as it suited the Empire's political convenience. The moment it had outlived its usefulness, *you* dropped it like a hot brick. The scandal would have been all the greater had anyone by then still believed that you had *any* religious convictions at all.'

The poor old thing had me there. Out of habit, I cast round for a politely vicious retort. As I focused on him, though, I suddenly found myself looking straight into the eyes of a ten-year-old boy. Horribly wasted, Theodore might be hovering on the edge of the grave. But, in all that really mattered, I was seeing him just as I had seventy-six years ago. Call it a spiritual burp brought on by the previous night's opium. Whatever the case, it passed. I relaxed. No vicious retort, polite or otherwise, crossed my lips. I shrugged and looked round to see if anything edible had been laid out for me.

'But where is my mother?' he now cried, still in Syriac.

I raised my eyebrows and tried to smile. 'Come now, Theodore,' I said comfortingly. 'You know she died in Tarsus. You must only have been eight at the time. I never met here, and was far off in Constantinople when the plague made its appearance.'

But he struggled back into a sitting position, and even pointed at me with his good arm. 'Don't play the fool with me, Alaric,' he snarled. 'It was you who debauched her. Everything was as it ought to be until you turned up. I ask you again: *where is she*?'

'Debauched' isn't a word I'd have thought appropriate. Fortunately, Wulfric was out of the conversation. If he was shifting and muttering behind me, it was only over the funny colour his master had gone. I turned my attention back to the wine as the boy stepped forward and fussed harder than ever with pillows. When I did finally look at Theodore, he'd nodded off again. Hardly breathing, he lay with his head flopped back on the cushions. Wulfric paid no attention to me, but sat quietly beside his master the Bishop, nursing the one good hand in both of his. 'We'll get nowhere if we continue like this,' I said to myself in Greek. Not that I was inclined to make any complaint. It was a lovely day outside. If I could fight off the slight headache the wine was producing, I could creep out of here and go off with Jeremy sooner than expected.

I'd got as far as the big stone porch of the building, and was pushing through a crowd of boys who were trying to read the inscription put up to commemorate a visit by the Bishop of Ravenna, when I heard the sound behind me of a throat being pointedly cleared.

'When one has spent all his life hearing the most astonishing stories, you will surely agree what an honour it is to meet the object of those stories.'

I thought whether I could blame it on deafness if I paid no attention and hurried out into the sunshine. It would be five yards at most before I was lost in the swirling crowd of monks and tradesmen. But all the boys had turned round from the inscription. One was pointing past me. A couple were beginning to cry. I'd have to fight my way through them to get out. I gave in to the inevitable and turned to look at Sophronius. From the first sound of that fruity, affected voice, there could be no doubt who it was. Still in white, he'd creased his blubbery face into a look of reverential respect.

'We are all so very pleased to see how well you remain, even after what must surely have been a difficult journey from the north,' he added after giving me his name. He got slowly to his knees and bent forward to embrace my feet. 'It is an honour beyond all expectations,' he intoned, 'to behold in the flesh one I have always so very much revered.'

There was no pulling back from that iron grip. I nodded and smiled, and waited for him to get up. There was a sound behind me of scared and disconsolate sobbing, and then a pattering of boyish feet as everyone ran out into the safety of the street. Lucky boys, I thought. For me, there'd be no escape.

Keeping a neutral look on my face, I stood back and acknowledged his further bow, and wondered when he'd get to the point. And there would be a point. With a man like Sophronius, there is always a point – and hardly ever a pleasant one. There'd be no escape for poor old Aelric. However bright and welcoming the sunshine might be in the street outside, I could kiss that morning goodbye.

6

'That will be all, Brother Wulfric,' Sophronius said as he ushered me back into the room where Theodore was still sleeping. 'I will have you summoned when His Grace may have need of your attentions.'

He'd spoken the English of a native. I avoided any sign of surprise, but looked harder at him. Take away the snooty expression, and he could easily pass for a stallkeeper in the butchers' market behind where I was staying. A fancy name he'd given himself on taking his vows. Then again, everything about him was fancy. It wasn't just their places in the Church hierarchy that had Wulfric bowing his way straight out of the room. That sort of commanding tone is something a man like Sophronius picks up long before he's decided to enter the Church.

He gave me another of his ceremonious bows, and waved me towards a couple of chairs and a small table in the far corner of the room. As he passed it, he took up the sheet of parchment.

'Since His Grace is overcome once more by tiredness,' I said, 'I must look to you for an explanation of his reason for calling me here. I hope it is a good one. Jarrow is not an easy journey at my age.' I had thought of announcing that I was tired. One look at Sophronius, though, and I had given up at once on that.

He smiled and arranged himself into the chair opposite mine. It creaked horribly, and I hoped for a moment that it would give way under his vast bulk. But he leaned forward on to the table, and the careful distribution of his weight allowed him to sit with all the dignity of a gloating toad.

'I must inform you,' he opened as soon as I could describe myself as comfortable, 'that His Holiness of Rome is being challenged to the point where he will have no choice but to issue a formal reprimand to the Emperor. Shortly before Christmas, a letter arrived in Rome from Constantinople. The claim that Pope Honorius, at your urging, may long ago have endorsed the Monothelite heresy is one that we have dealt with. His Holiness was deceived as to the issues, and treated them, in the manner of your presentation, as a question of Latin grammar. There is, however, a further claim that is not so easily answered. This is that, nearly eighty years ago, Pope Benedict of blessed memory knowingly subscribed to that heresy.'

I shrugged and wondered if I could ask for what remained of the wine to be brought over. But Sophronius didn't look the sort of man who could be deflected by any show of aged helplessness. There might not be a decent bath on this entire island. Not even a full century, though, since Augustine had first set foot in England, and we'd grown up our own race of Imperial churchmen. Sophronius might occasionally dream in English. That aside, there was nothing to distinguish him from the snootiest cleric in the Lateran. Little wonder these people had rolled straight over the Celtic Church a few years earlier at Whitby.

'The Holy Father is Universal Bishop,' he continued. 'Except where he has been misled, or is obviously suffering the infirmities that are natural to the human condition, he is inerrant in all matters of Church doctrine. The other four Patriarchs are due the utmost respect, but do not have the same standing before God as the successor of Saint Peter. It is therefore impossible that Benedict of sainted memory could have subscribed to the Monothelite or any other heresy. Yet the Imperial Government has had the effrontery to claim it has written testimony that he did so subscribe through his representatives.'

I was in no need of lectures on that *Thou art Peter* text. I'd spent the better part of a lifetime trying neither to endorse nor deny the meaning put on it by Rome. But I'd already guessed what was coming, and kept a polite look on my face as I inspected my dirty fingernails. I've said there was no decent bath in England. There was, however, a kind of bathing establishment close by the

Monastery of Saint Anastasius. If I could get young Jeremy to overlook that it was also a brothel . . .

'Whatever the authorities in Constantinople claim to have found in their archives,' Sophronius went on as expected, 'His Grace Theodore and you both know the truth of the matter. After all, *you were both there!*'

I looked again at the ceiling and then back at Sophronius. It might be worth trying for an attack of tiredness. No one thought ill of Theodore if he kept dropping off. But I clicked my false teeth together and put the thought finally out of mind. Some refusals, after all, are best for not being delayed. 'Look here,' I said, 'if you want me to set my name to an attack on the Imperial Government, you're asking a year too late. I'm not a refugee any more. The position now is that the Church in England is looking after me on behalf of the Emperor. There's been a grant of money for my upkeep, and I rather think I'm being written back into the official histories. In any dispute between Pope and Emperor, my duty is to remain neutral. Besides, I'm so old, no one would take me seriously. If you want an authoritative account of the Council of Athens, you should write one up yourself and get Theodore to sign it. After all, he is a bishop – and he also was there.'

'If I might be so bold, Brother Aelric,' the man pressed on, 'your rehabilitation within the Empire has given much weight to your own testimony. And no one can claim that your memory of the proceedings at Athens might be at fault.'

I gripped the table and pulled myself to my feet. 'Be that as it may, Sophronius,' I said, 'you must accept my refusal to get involved. Now, if you would be so kind as to find Brother Jeremy, I will return to my lodgings and get ready to go back to Jarrow. My life as an actor in the world is well and truly over. I can only apologise that you had to come all the way from Rome to hear this.'

Sophronius looked up at me. Slowly, he got to his own feet. Then he bowed. If he was trying for a show of respect, it was spoiled by his delay in getting up, and by his gloating smile. For the first time in our conversation, I felt a slight pricking on the back of my neck. 'You are, of course, a free agent,' he said. 'If you will not help us, Holy Mother Church can do no more than seek the best means of assisting you back to the monastery in Jarrow.'

'My dear Sophronius,' I said, keeping any appearance of strain out of my voice, 'I was brought here by young Brother Jeremy. I have the fullest confidence in his ability to take me back.' Forcing a smile on to my face, I stared back at him very hard. Though as yet with no facts to organise, my mind was beginning to work faster.

Sophronius broadened his own smile. He reached inside his robe and took out a small object. With another bow, he placed it on the table. I looked at it and sat down again. I sat down because the conversation was nowhere near ended – and to hide the trembling of my aged legs.

'Oh, Brother Aelric,' he said, in a mournful tone that fitted ill with the wolfish look now spreading over his face, 'do please examine this object, and try to recall if it might be your property.' Still on his feet, he bent forward and pushed it across the table. He watched closely as I stared at it. 'This was recovered four days ago from the eye of one of His Majesty's dearest servants,' he explained.

Not bothering to touch it where it lay before me on the table, I stared at my bronze pin. No one had bothered cleaning it. Getting the dried gore off it would take a good soaking in vinegar.

'The tollman on London Bridge was not able to say very much before he died,' Sophronius went on. 'The facts, however, may speak for themselves.' He stopped and sat down. He reached forward and pointed at the elaborate, gilded head of the pin. 'This is surely of Eastern workmanship, is it not, Brother Aelric?' he asked with a close inspection of my face. 'Are these not the Greek letters *AL*? Might they perhaps represent the name *Alaric*?'

Oh, sod, bugger, damn! I could have kicked myself. I'll grant that it's hard, in the most settled places, to tell the difference between tax-collectors and bandits. But I, of all people, should have known that you never leave a wounded enemy alive. I sat back and leaned against the chair. A mouthful of Theodore's French red would have been very welcome. I had to make do with yet another stare up at the ceiling.

'If, with the palsied hand of age,' I said quietly, 'I lost an object that should have been of great worth to me, please do accept my thanks for its safe recovery. But do also explain how its finding could disarrange the plans for my return to Jarrow?' How Sophronius kept himself from peals of triumphant laughter would normally have been worth considering. For the moment, I noted the fact and waited for the inevitable.

It wasn't long in coming. 'His Majesty, of course, is outraged at the insult to his dignity. There is no possibility that a man of the Church could be handed over to any secular authority. The agreement negotiated many years ago with King Ethelbert the Saint will stand for ever. But the young man's crime will be treated by the Church as a sin of the utmost gravity.' Sophronius paused and allowed himself an ecstatic roll of his engorged frame. 'You will surely agree that it is fitting for any who would serve God and the Church of God to maintain at all times a spirit of the utmost humility. When that spirit is lacking within, there are penances to instil it from without.' He stopped and put both hands on the table. He leaned forward and stared into my eyes. 'The nail that sticks out,' he said with quiet relish, 'must be hammered flat.'

I looked stonily back. I thought of that poor sod in the square before the big church.

'It seems, my dear Brother in Christ,' I said, 'that there were no witnesses to what may have been a sad misunderstanding. But I can assure you that Brother Jeremy was in no manner to blame for whatever may have happened on London Bridge. Though not admitting to anything at all, I do take full responsibility.'

Sophronius stopped me with a sad shake of his jowls. 'Oh, Brother Aelric, your supreme goodness of heart is famed throughout the world. Even otherwise, though, do not imagine that a man of your venerable years could possibly be credited with the blame for so dastardly a crime as the one committed on London Bridge. If any must suffer for the crime, it shall be young Brother Jeremy.'

Till now forgotten in his chair, Theodore cried out weakly in Syriac:

Abun d–bashmayo
nithqadash shmokh
tithe malkuthokh
nehwe sebyonokh
aykano d–bashmayo oph bar`o . . .

'It's the beginning of the Lord's Prayer,' I explained helpfully. Sophronius bowed. Obviously, the old dear was fast asleep, though, and this was the limit of any distraction I could expect from him. Sure enough, Theodore drifted into a stream of gibberish about his 'mother' before trailing off altogether. Sophronius was looking hard at me again. I sighed and took the pin from his hand. 'Your fluency in Latin is most admirable,' I said. 'I therefore assume that your statement about suffering was deliberately in the conditional.' His mouth fell ever so slightly open, showing the neat brown of his teeth. 'Bearing in mind the absence of witnesses within the desolation of London to what may or may not have taken place there, I might suggest that the matter should be regarded as the mystery that it surely is.

'After all, if I am to set forth in writing that Pope Benedict – neither by himself, nor by his servants or agents or any of them – never embraced the Monothelite or any other heresy, I cannot be in any sense perturbed by external considerations.' I looked yet again at the ceiling. It saved me the vexation of looking at Sophronius. Not a decent bath in England, I reminded myself. Instead, we'd raised up men like this. Since I'd been partly responsible for the origins of the system, I should have felt at least some pride.

When I looked back at him, he'd managed to contain his triumph. 'My Lord Alaric,' he said with all the softness of one who gives absolution, 'it shall, I promise, ever be our own little secret.' He breathed out softly and rested more of his weight upon the table.

Two can keep a secret, if one be dead, I thought, recalling another old Kentish song. But I'd given in to the man. He had no reason to grass me to the King.

He beamed and sat back again. 'I have taken the liberty of having your possessions moved from the Monastery of Saint Anastasius,' he said, now briskly. 'There is a suite of reasonably decent rooms upstairs in this building. I hope that you and Brother Jeremy can be made entirely comfortable during your stay. I understand that your preference for extended composition is to write in Greek on papyrus. I have commandeered every sheet of papyrus in Canterbury. More can be obtained in France. As for Greek, we can bring in scholars of sufficient learning. I am sure that, if questions of translation should arise, you will be ready to assist. In any event, as your account is to be summarised for publication to an Imperial audience, Greek will be the most convenient language.'

I moistened a finger and rubbed some of the sticky mess from the gold head of my pin. The boy who'd commissioned this for me still had no idea of my plans for him when he'd given it to me. But it can't have been by accident that he'd had its bronze body sharpened to that nasty and convenient needlepoint. I clutched the whole pin in a hand that trembled very slightly. Over in his chair, Theodore shifted again and babbled in Syriac that he'd lost his pen case. As if by agreement, we paid him no further attention.

That was yesterday. You will not believe, dear reader, how angry I've been on and off since then. If I'd but crawled down and slit that tax-gathering bastard's throat, I'd have got my pin back, and none of this would have been required. But I didn't, and it's all my fault if I'm now stuck here like some fly in a web spun by Sophronius.

Or is it really that bad? 'Since I have none of the materials I'd normally use for checking external facts,' I said earlier today when Sophronius visited me in this room, 'you will forgive me if I only describe what I personally witnessed, or can reasonably infer. Other things may not be clearly explained. Indeed, I may not give you exactly what you want.' His answer was a nod and the beginnings of another gloat. He then fussed about with a crate of papyrus and enough French red to keep a man drunk till Christmas.

He and Theodore will get their account of what is called the Little Council of Athens. And why not? How long have I been promising some account of what I did in Athens? I'll write it all down, and on the principles I stated to Sophronius. If he ever gets to read it, he'll surely have kittens.

And that *if*, I do assure you, is a big one. Sophronius may already be ordering new robes for the preferment he thinks he'll get from using me. But, if I'll need to let more time pass since that error of judgement on London Bridge, we'll see who's the spider and who the fly. Until then, here it goes: what Old Aelric – also known as Alaric – did in Athens, such a very long time ago . . .

7

If you think of it at all, my dear reader, I suppose you imagine Athens as a place bathed in the intense light of the Mediterranean. You may also think of the sovereign people, assembled in the market place, and of the matchless eloquence by which, for good or ill, they were swayed. Or you may think of the groves and colonnades where every art and every philosophy was carried to perfection. Or, if you suppose the ancients more sinful than illuminating, you may think of that scene on the Areopagus, where Saint Paul preached to a sceptical gathering about the Unknown God.

Well, that was all in ancient times. I first saw the place on Thursday, 19 October 612. By then, it was rather different ...

Oh, but I'm already running ahead of myself. Let me pull myself to order and begin at the beginning. This was early in the morning of that day. The Imperial galley on which – for what little I suspected it was worth – I was the most important passenger had been riding at anchor off Piraeus since we'd crept in the previous evening. Now, in the first light of dawn that dribbled through the window, I sat alone in my cabin, looking at myself in a little mirror. I was long since used to the continual grinding of timbers. If I listened, I could hear it. Otherwise, it no longer registered. Far above – possibly halfway up one of the masts – a sailor was into the third or fourth stanza of some sea shanty. He sang in one of the Eastern languages, and I hadn't yet made any study of these. But it had a mournful quality that was feeding my own present mood.

It wasn't vanity, you see, that had me looking so hard into that mirror. I'll grant that, at twenty-two, I was at the very summit of health and beauty. I was well worth looking at. Since the weather had turned so horribly against us, I'd almost cheered myself in this cabin by trying on every possible combination of my fine clothes, and I'd been at least satisfied by my appearance in all of them. But my attention was focused now on a spot that covered the whole tip of my nose. If I'd done as the slave suggested, a dab of paint would have covered the thing. Instead, I'd tried popping it before it was ripe, and was now paying the price of acting in haste.

I sighed and put the mirror down. I tried not to listen to that awful and probably endless dirge overhead. So far as it succeeded, the effort only made room in my thoughts for everything else. I looked again at the commission Heraclius had sent me:

You will proceed with all haste to Our most learned and famous town of Athens, it read. *There, you shall act as may be made necessary. The Lord Priscus, Our Commander of the East, shall accompany you and do likewise.*

And that was it. Unrolled and held open with lead weights, the parchment sheet was about thirty inches by eighteen. On its very dark purple background, the three sentences of my commission, written in gold, took up a single line. Because the Emperor had written this himself, and in Latin, it was surely of no importance that he'd omitted all the usual Greek formulae. Did it matter if he'd missed out all my titles and not called me his *right trusty and beloved friend*? Did it matter if he'd left off the epithet *ever victorious* from the mention of Priscus? And – far more important – what did the whole sodding document require of us? I'd never seen anything so vague – not even from Heraclius. After the ship had intercepted us off Cyprus, and turned us west from our homeward voyage to Constantinople, I'd sat looking at the parchment sheet over and over again. I'd told myself until I really believed it, that this was simply the work of someone who was at best semiliterate, even in his own language. Now the voyage was reaching its end, and we'd soon be stepping on to the Piraeus docks, every word of the commission dripped menace.

I let the sheet fall on to my desk and stretched cautiously. My official robe made a bitch of all movement, though was a refuge from the chill. I yawned. If this was the last time I ever wore it, I might as well look good when the Governor had put me in chains and taken off to Corinth. Yes, even if my career was to reach its end in some barbarian-ravaged province in the middle of nowhere, I might as well look good for the occasion. The spot aside, I could be a sight worth seeing.

'Come!' I shouted. The door opened. I should have guessed from that hesitant knock that it would be Martin and not the slave with a jug of wine. I glared at him. How he'd managed to gain still more weight on this voyage was a mystery. But he'd managed. The clothes that had fitted him reasonably well in Alexandria were now visibly bulging. In Athens, it was no comfort that he might draw attention from my spot. 'Have you eaten yet?' I asked.

Looking as miserable as I felt, he said nothing. But I saw the hungry look he darted at the cheese and stale bread I'd left untouched beside me. I grunted and waved him into the chair opposite my desk.

'When do you think we can dock?' I asked.

He shoved a wedge of cheese into his mouth and chewed without visible enjoyment. 'The Captain is still on shore,' he said indistinctly. He took a mouthful of brackish water and cleared his throat. 'I spoke with one of the sailors he sent back for something.' He swallowed and continued with a faint tremor in his voice. 'Apparently, the military situation is looking desperate.'

I shrugged again. The provincial authorities, I'd already learned from Priscus, had five hundred troops to cover the entire area south of Thermopylae. If the Spartans had once held up the entire Persian Army there with three hundred hoplites, our own people had long since given up on trying to keep out a rabble of Avars and Slavs. Thirty years of their depredations, and there really was no military situation left to call desperate or otherwise.

'The harvests have failed in Thrace and beyond,' Martin explained. I reached cautiously forward and pulled a corner off the dry loaf. I wondered if it was worth trying to eat anything at all. Once arrested, it might be some while before anyone got round to feeding me.

'Starvation is setting in everywhere south of the Danube, and possibly north of it,' he added. 'The word is that twenty million barbarians are on the move, and will sweep through the passes before the month is out.' He would have said more. But a sudden spasm of fear took hold of him, and his voice fell away.

'Make that twenty *thousand*,' I sneered, 'and then halve it.' I put the bread into my mouth and chewed with as much enthusiasm as if a priest had put it there. 'You know perfectly well that the Empire lost Britain to about that many of my own people – and not all at once. Whatever the minstrels told you in Ireland about the unstoppable flood of yellow-headed giants who dispossessed your ancestors, we weren't enough to have taken London – not, that is, if you'd done other than scuttle out of the place like frightened chickens.' I sniffed and ignored the face he pulled.

I was right in my history. The Western Provinces really had been lost to not enough armed men to fill the Circus in Constantinople. They'd crossed the Rhine into a desert produced by centuries of misgovernment, and had been quietly welcomed by the survivors. But there was no point taking issue here and now with the accounts agreed by Martin's people with the Imperial historians about those unstoppable floods of yellow-headed giants. None of it mattered any more. In the resulting silence, I reached down into my leather satchel and pulled out a small cloth bag. Its many coins made a dull chinking sound on the table. I reached down again for a sheet of parchment I'd folded over three times and sealed with my ring. I pushed both towards Martin.

'The cash is all I bothered bringing with me from Alexandria,' I said. 'I thought it would be more than enough for the journey, and it's still a decent sum.' Wearily, I lifted a hand to stop the protest. 'The draft is on the Papal Bank. It will be honoured regardless of any confiscation decree. Your job, once we are separated, is to get yourself and Sveta and your child and my child to Rome, and then wherever may seem appropriate. Go to the Lateran and speak to the Dispensator. He may not give active assistance. But you can rely on him to tell you straight if you will all be safe in Rome – or if you should make a run for where the

45

Lombards rule, or for the lands of the French King. He may even advise you to go back all the way to Ireland. Wouldn't you like that – to go home at last to Ireland? You could be a man of some consequence there. Whatever the case, you'll be far outside the Emperor's reach.'

Martin's response was to look down at the closed bag and to start crying again. 'But it's so unjust, Aelric,' he sobbed. 'None of this was your fault. You did everything possible . . .'

I smiled and patted him gently on the hand. 'You know the rule, Martin,' I said. 'When things go this wrong, *someone has to be blamed*. It can't be the Emperor. It can't be the Viceroy of Egypt – he is the Emperor's cousin, after all. That leaves me or Priscus. It's pretty clear that we'll both share the blame.'

I smiled again and resisted the urge to reach up and touch my spot. 'Now, once you've gone through the motions of announcing me as I step ashore, and of reading out my commission, I want you to vanish into the crowd. No one will pay attention to a freedman. Get away from me. Don't look back. Take the first seaworthy vessel out of Piraeus. Go to Corinth. Take whatever ship is going west. Do you understand?'

There was more sobbing and mopping of wet eyes. In the next cabin but one, I heard Maximin start wailing for his father. I told myself not to get up and go to him. It was best not to remind him that I was about. I needed Martin to make a clean getaway on the dockside. I couldn't have a child in his wife's arms, screaming and reaching out for me.

There was another knock at the door. This time, it was the wine. I drank two cups straight off, and on an empty stomach. The writing on my commission wavered slightly as I looked at it. But I could feel myself coming into a better mood since the previous night's opium pill had relinquished its hold on me, and I'd become gradually aware of the clammy bedclothes and of the damp chill beyond them. I was about to give Martin further instructions on the draft; it was too late to explain again how gold could be moved from one place to another without shipping a single piece, but I could remind him of the formalities in the Papal Bank. Just then, though, there was yet another knock on the door. Before I could call out to enter, it opened and the galley's head slave walked in. He gave what I thought the most perfunctory bow that was decent for a man of my status.

'The Lord Priscus would have the pleasure of My Lord's company,' he said as he finally looked up. Was that the remains of a smirk on his face? I pretended not to notice. I got up and walked over to the little window. This should have looked out towards Piraeus. All I could see was a mass of grey and endlessly shifting fog. There was an unusually loud scraping of timbers as the galley was jolted by a current or some shift in the breeze. Over on the table, my cup moved about an inch, but didn't tip over. Martin grabbed for safety at the back of an unoccupied chair. I thought for a moment he would start vomiting again. But it was only a single movement of the galley. I couldn't see it, but I felt a spatter of the rain that was now joining the mist that had slowed our progress through the Saronic Gulf. I pushed the lead shutter into place. Now with just the light of a few lamps, I crossed the room and pulled the door open. Maximin was still crying. It was the settled, disconsolate wail of a child too young to ask questions, but old enough to know that something was terribly wrong.

I looked back at Martin, who was staring at the bag of gold. 'Go and see if Sveta's finished packing,' I said in Latin. 'Bear in mind that most of the luggage will be impounded on the docks. Make sure that everything important is in the bags that you'll be carrying.'

8

I've said I was in an Imperial galley. This gives little notion of the size or magnificence of what the Viceroy had forced on me for my departure from Alexandria. It was perhaps the biggest vessel in the whole Imperial service. Over a hundred yards long, and fitted out with a lavish indifference to cost that went some way to offsetting the utter want of taste, it was as fine a prison as anyone could have desired. When told I'd be taking ship for Constantinople, I had insisted on something small and fast. Nicetas had smiled and nodded and given me his own official galley. I'd seen this many times in the private harbour. For a good thousand years, it, or something like it, had been kept permanently ready for those times when the King, or Governor, or Duke, or Viceroy needed to get away from the Alexandrian mob. Now, thanks to Priscus, there was no mob left, we'd all been politely bundled into it and waved off with fair cries and crocodile tears. I had to admit, though, that, once those storms had blown up near Seriphos, anything lighter would have been torn apart. If drowning would have been a mercy compared with what might be waiting for me in Piraeus, there were others to think about. As it was, we'd lost half our oars, and had been creeping forward ever since, propelled by various arrangements of sails that might, in other circumstances, have claimed my entire interest.

Once out of my own very grand room, I turned left into the wide central corridor and made my way down the length of the galley to where Priscus had his quarters. Already muffled, the sound of crying children soon faded away, and was replaced by the continued mournful sound of that sailor's shanty. As I came closer to the stern, I heard a sudden scream. I stopped and listened harder. I could just make out the hiss and impact of a whip before there was a second scream.

There was a soft voice behind me. 'My Lord is disturbed by the flogging?' the Captain asked. He'd been going up or coming down the ladder that led to the rowing decks. He now clambered easily up beside me and went through the motions of a bow. He'd taken off his boots, but still wore the fussy uniform he must have put on for his trip ashore. 'It was the black rower with woollen hair,' he explained with evident relish. 'His dream of a supernatural origin for the storms has continued to disturb the other men.'

I nodded. Just as the biggest of the storms was hitting us, I'd pulled rank on the Captain and ordered all the rowers to be unchained. Since then, rowing had been impossible, and the men had been lounging about on the lower decks with nothing to do but compete at scaring each other.

I cleared my throat and tried to look haughty. 'My secretary will need to discuss what slaves will come ashore with us,' I said.

The Captain arched his eyebrows and somehow managed not to laugh. 'I must inform Your Lordship,' he said very softly indeed, 'that my orders are to put you ashore without slaves. The local authorities will provide such assistance as may be required.' I stared back without blinking. I'd finally learned something of the Captain's own orders. Priscus and I had watched him receive these in a sealed packet. For all the questions he'd put, Priscus would have got better answers out of the Sphinx than from this shifty little Egyptian.

'Very well,' I said with a forced lightness of tone. 'Be so good as to inform my secretary of this.'

The Captain bowed again, and asked if it would please me to see the flogging.

Without bothering to answer, I turned and continued along the corridor.

Bearing in mind its natural colour on this voyage, I failed to see why Priscus had taken the trouble to paint his face green. He sat alone in his cabin, looking down at his booted feet. 'Fucking noise!'

he snarled with a look upwards. Now the flogging was over, the only sound from outside was a third or fourth repeat of the shanty. 'Can't these sailors ever keep their mouths shut?' He pushed a glass cup against his chattering teeth and took a longish sip. He burped and pushed a hand under his ceremonial chain mail for a scratch. 'So, dear boy, what's the news?' he finally asked with the ghost of a smile.

I stared up at the polished timbers of the ceiling and wondered if there was any suitable answer. Unlike Martin, Priscus had lost weight on the voyage. He'd been padded out when put into his uniform. But there was no hiding the bony wrists or the sagging wrinkles under his chin. This was my first sight of him in five days. Though the great storm had finally ended, his reaction to it hadn't. His groans and the regular bowls of vomit carried from his cabin had told me he was alive. Now, if he was up and about, he still didn't look more than the shadow of the grinning fiend who'd taken his farewell of the few persons of quality he'd somehow managed not to impale in Alexandria.

'Shall we go up on the main deck?' I asked. 'There may be sod all to look at. But I fancy some last impression of liberty.'

Beneath an awning that caught most of the rain, I looked into a wall of grey mist. Unless I'd lost all sense of direction, I was looking towards Salamis. It was now more than eleven hundred and twenty years since the Athenians had fought their decisive battle there. While he was still up to any pretence of conversation, Priscus had assured me that the figure of three million given by Herodotus was impossible. But, if you divided all his numbers by ten, they began to make sense. The Spartans had held the pass at Thermopylae longer than anyone could think possible. Even so, the Persians had come on like a charging elephant. Nothing could have kept them from eventually sweeping through the pass. Their single weakness had been the long lines of communication back to Asia. By a stroke of genius, Themistocles had got the Athenians to abandon their city and concentrate all their naval force in the Bay of Salamis. There, the crushing weight of Persian shipping had been taken completely by surprise. Once they'd lost control of the sea, their whole land force was cut off and could be destroyed at leisure.

'The problem with Herodotus,' Priscus had said to me before the storms sent him scurrying to his cabin like a monk to his cell, 'is that he just wasn't a soldier. He was fine at repeating the gossip he'd picked up from the lower class of those who lived long enough to be his sources. But he had no understanding of grand strategy. The Persian attack was a combined operation. Knock away either of its legs, and the whole mass would fall to the ground. Realise this, and the Spartan counter-attack at Plataea becomes little more than a side skirmish. For myself, I'd never have risked a battle. Instead, I'd have kept up the sea blockade, and waited for the Persians to make a dash back towards Byzantium. All the way back, I'd have followed them by sea – wearing them down without ever coming to a full battle.'

He'd gone from this into a lecture on the need to keep your forces in being, and never risking a battle unless forced, or unless sure of victory. Had he given this lecture to Heraclius outside Caesarea? Priscus had spent the better part of a year obeying his own advice. It had worked so well, the Emperor had come out in person to take the Persian surrender. Of course, the booby had no sooner arrived than he gave orders for a battle – a battle that ended in our own catastrophic defeat.

We leaned together in silence and looked out into the mist. As members of the Imperial Council, it should have been our duty to suggest mitigations for what Heraclius had brought on us – the loss of Cappadocia and the exposing of Syria to invasion. But Priscus hadn't been in Constantinople since the defeat, and I'd left before its news could arrive. Did it now matter what we thought? Were we still members of the Council?

I thought instead of Salamis, over a thousand years before. That still mattered, and always would matter. This one battle had cleared the way for the flowering of Greek civilisation. Then, after another century and a half, Alexander had gone on the offensive and destroyed the Persian Empire, and spread the light of Greece over all the East. Before that could fade, the Romans had taken up the burden of defence. Their legions, half protective, half exploitative, had given the light of Greece another seven hundred years. Now, at last, the Empire established by Rome, and inherited by Constantinople, was falling, one province at a time, to a revived Persia. This time, the decisive battle would be on land, and probably deep within Syria. Athens and the cities of Achaean Greece could have no influence in this battle. So far as their few inhabitants were even aware of it, they would await the outcome of this conflict as passive spectators.

'None of this really matters,' I said, breaking the long silence. 'The end of things is often far less important than what went before. A thousand years from now, I really doubt if anyone will be thinking of you or me or Heraclius. But they'll surely still be thinking of Salamis and what it made possible.' What I'd said made no sense in itself, and I didn't feel up to explaining the train of thought that preceded it.

Leaning beside me on the rail, Priscus continued staring down at the dark, still waters.

9

Somewhere in front of us, the sun must now be rising fully out of the sea. It might eventually burn off the mist. Or it might not. It hadn't shown itself to us in days, and might never do so again. But the sense of a new day was taking some hold in both our minds.

Priscus sighed. He coughed and spat. He sighed again. 'If only that bastard ship had missed us off Cyprus,' he said, 'we'd now be putting into the Senatorial Dock. We could hurry off to the palace and give our side of things to Heraclius. Whatever else happened there, we stopped the Brotherhood from taking over Alexandria. We stopped the Persians from invading Egypt. It's thanks to us that those seven million bushels of Egyptian corn will put in every year at Constantinople. Perhaps I did get carried away in pacifying Alexandria. You certainly fluffed your introduction of the new land law. But we did save the breadbasket of the whole Empire. No one could take that away . . .' He trailed off into a mumble about friends in Constantinople.

Perhaps he was right. I'd completed the final draft of my report a day after the Alexandrian lighthouse had vanished below the horizon. Before handing it to Martin for copying in his best hand, I'd read it to Priscus. He'd laughed and clapped his hands at its persuasive force. I'd said nothing in it of the overflowing mass graves outside Alexandria, or the plague that had drifted back into the city with the spreading miasma of corruption. I'd said nothing of the burned-out centre, or of the silent, grieving survivors. Without saying anything openly bad about the Emperor's cousin, I'd managed to throw the whole blame for what I did admit on to Nicetas. And, if the useless bastard of a Viceroy had only done his plain duty and published the new land law at once, none of this could have happened. No doubt, I'd failed miserably in my side of things. No doubt at all, Priscus had gone raving mad once he'd gathered enough force to take on the mob. But who'd let the mob go out of control in the first place? Who'd given the landed interest enough time to choose between handing over a third of their land to the peasants and calling in the Persians? It really was stupid, bloody Nicetas who'd allowed everything to go tits up. Given the slightest regard for truth and justice, Heraclius should have had him dragged off to Constantinople to answer for an incompetence amounting all the way to treason.

'We stand or fall together,' Priscus had said between reciting some of my choicer sentences in a fair imitation of Our Lord and Master's flat and whiny voice. 'Yes, dearest Alaric,' he'd said, separating the syllables of the name by which I was known in the Empire, 'we stand or fall together.'

Then we'd been intercepted off Cyprus and sent west with that sheet of utterly ambiguous parchment. If Priscus had been too overcome by seasickness to sit talking everything over with me, his mind couldn't but have been moving in the same direction.

'Do you think you were set up from the beginning?' he asked.

There was a sudden chorus of shouts behind and above us. There was none of the shifting and pitching that would suggest we were about to dock. But something was going on. I ignored this. We could wait for whatever bad news it surely meant.

I thought back to the beginning of March. I'd been called to the Imperial Palace. Heraclius had taken me to the great marble balcony that looked over the ship-crowded straits to the Asiatic shore. He'd spoken with such enthusiasm of my land law – what glorious sense it made to give land to the peasants and then arm them as a static defence force. It had worked so well in the Asiatic provinces, where a century of spreading banditry had been checked in just one season, and where, day by day, a rabble of passive starvelings was turning into a race of proud and loyal and productive defenders of their own soil. 'I can hardly spare you from the Imperial Council here,' he'd said caressingly. 'You are my one support, my choicest and most resourceful adviser. But I *must* spare you for just a few months, so that Egypt can be revived to its ancient wealth and contentedness.'

So I'd set out for Alexandria, and Nicetas had embraced me and called me 'brother'. And, then, month had followed month, and the law I'd carried out with every necessary seal and form of words sat, unpublished, on his desk. He'd given me an army of clerks and surveyors, and smiled at every land allocation I'd suggested. He'd fobbed me off with a mass of routine administration. The Lesser Seal he gave me had made me the second man in Alexandria and in Egypt. If he noticed at all, he'd looked the other way when my speculations on the future price of corn had brought me riches beyond counting. And, all this time, the landowning interest had been spinning further and further out of my control. If, by charm and gross bribery, I'd kept the magnates steady, the smaller landowners had formed a solid bloc of opposition. Every difference of race and religion between Greeks and Egyptians had been set aside as news of my intentions spread through the higher society of Alexandria. In the end, if it had appalled me – if I'd even tried to have him arrested for it – was there any real alternative to the massacre Priscus had unleashed on the streets, and the ten thousand or whatever impalings with which he'd finished his work of pacification?

'It might be,' I said at last. 'But let's allow fifteen days for a courier going by relays from Alexandria, and then another day of indecision before sending out that ship. That also fits.' I stroked my nose and rubbed thin pus between forefinger and thumb. 'Do you remember how insistent Nicetas was about your accompanying me on the galley? Letting you go back to the capital through Syria would have carried the risk that you'd get wind of the Imperial disfavour, and turn east for the army. There, you could have raised a rebellion like your late and unlamented father-in-law did against Maurice. Who knows?

Like him, you could have got yourself made Emperor. Instead, you were shipped out with me.'

'Great minds think alike,' Priscus said with a bitter laugh. 'I'm the last survivor from before the revolution. Everyone's been wondering how long the son-in-law of Phocas the Unmentionable could last in the new order of things. You might say that I'm the Empire's only half-decent general. But it's obvious I've been living on borrowed time ever since Heraclius rolled up in Constantinople and got himself crowned Emperor.' He laughed again. 'You were set up because the old nobility finally got through to Heraclius that your scheme of land reallocation would be the greatest revolution in the Empire since Constantine turned Christian. Once it was known I'd joined you in Alexandria, it was just a matter of two birds with one stone.

'Do you suppose he'll have us blinded before we're stuffed into a monastery?' he asked. 'Do you suppose we'll share a monastery? I hope you'll not take it ill. But I'd rather not have to share a prison with you. Besides, I can tell you from my own experience that there's no shortage of ghastly places of confinement in this part of the Empire. There's a particularly nasty monastery halfway up Mount—'

Martin had made one of his polite coughs behind us. 'The Captain apologises for his oversight when you spoke with him,' he said. 'But he came back from shore with a letter for you.'

Priscus and I looked at each other. I swallowed and took the unrolled sheet of papyrus in a hand that I willed not to shake.

'Apparently, the Governor is detained in Corinth by ill health,' I said without glancing up from the letter. 'We'll be met by a certain Nicephorus. He describes himself as Count of Athens.' I looked at Priscus.

His answer was a long and disgusted clear of his throat. He turned and spat again into the sea. 'Let's face it, dear boy,' he said. 'You are, when all is said and done, just a barbarian and hardly older than a schoolboy. But I am a descendant of the Great Constantine himself, and not far off three times your age. I'd have thought I was worth being arrested by the Governor.'

He took the letter from me and stared at the scruffy writing. 'I had dealings with Nicephorus when I was last here,' he said. 'There's nothing he'll enjoy more than loading me with chains. If blinding really is on the menu, he'll hold the white-hot metal himself in front of my eyes.'

I didn't care if I was seen to grip the rail and steady myself. 'When exactly were you in Athens?' I asked weakly.

He pulled himself gradually back together. 'It was in the ninth year of Phocas the Tyrant,' he said just as weakly. He stopped and scowled and repeated the hated words of kinship to the fallen Emperor. He tried to clear his throat again, but failed. He bent forward as far as his armour allowed and tried again. This time, he managed a long and thunderous burp. Then he did clear his throat. Without bothering to turn, he spat on to the deck. 'It was two years ago – just before everything went really bad for the Tyrant,' he added when he'd recovered his composure, 'and the barbarians were pushing closer and closer to the ruined fort at Thermopylae. I was sent out to see what defence could be made of the Greek cities. Unlike everywhere else north of Corinth, Athens did have a wall in nearly decent shape.' He stopped and cleared his throat again. This time, he swallowed and looked about for his box of drugs.

'I wasn't aware that Athens had a Count,' I said. I might as well go through the motions of interest. 'I thought it was under direct rule from Corinth.'

Priscus looked up from fussing with his powders and smiled bleakly. 'Because, even today, the place has a certain prestige,' he explained with a hint of the didactic, 'Athens has its own administration. Since Heraclius didn't see fit, after the revolution, to recall Timothy the Utterly Idle from Corinth, it would normally be a favour to Athens. But you haven't met Nicephorus.' He sniffed in a pinch of something dark. He laughed and leaned back against the rail as tears ran down his green paint.

'You'd better go and get everyone ready,' I said to Martin. I looked closely at him. His own eyes were heavy with tears. 'Please remember everything I told you,' I repeated.

He bowed and went below.

Priscus sniffed and coughed. He closed his eyes for a long groan of ecstasy. Then he was back with me. 'Have you told our obese friend that this galley will dump us in Piraeus before going straight off to Corinth? Does he know there won't be so much as a slave getting off with us?' His face now creased into a smile so broad, the lead underlay on his face cracked and a few specks of white and green fell on to his breastplate.

I shook my head. 'It's enough that he's ready to make a dash once we're ashore,' I said. Poor Martin, I thought sadly. Until Cyprus, he'd been counting off the days to when he and his family could settle back into my snug palace in Constantinople. Safe inside the impenetrable walls of the City, he could regard the simultaneous collapse of every frontier with an almost philosophic calm. It was now a question of whether he could avoid being swept up in a double arrest in Piraeus and, without a single slave to carry baggage, get everyone out of the Empire. Poor Martin – I felt almost lucky by comparison. But Sveta would get them all to safety. With her glowering looks and vicious temper, she might be proof of the more acetic denunciations of marriage. But if anyone could ward off a general arrest on the docks, it would be Sveta. The Emperor himself might look away from her Medusa-like stare.

'Your nose is a proper sight!' Priscus said as his drugs brought him to a semblance of his old self. 'Still, I think I did tell you that wanking was bad for the complexion.' He managed an unpleasant laugh.

I looked up at the sail. It was obvious the galley wouldn't be staying in Piraeus longer than it would take to dump the pair of us into custody. So far as I could tell, Corinth had the only shipyard in the whole region capable of putting the galley back into order. The Captain would doubtless make for there. After that, he could go about whatever else he'd been ordered. Whatever that might be didn't affect us.

The galley gave a determined pitch, and there was a renewed burst of shouting overhead. Sailors ran up and down the netting and did things with ropes. I gave Priscus a cold stare. 'Time, I think, to get ourselves ready to go ashore,' I said.

'Then you can lead the way, my big, blond stunner,' he sniggered. 'You know it takes me an age to get up and down that ladder.'

10

In ages past, Piraeus had been the greatest port in the civilised world. In those days, Athens was Mistress of the Seas and a centre of all trade. Its port was every day crowded with ships of war and with trading vessels. For all I could see through the grey mist, it might have been crowded still. But I knew it wasn't. As on everything else in this forsaken borderland of a reduced Empire, time had set its hand on Athens and smoothed away both glory and prosperity. If more than a couple of fishing vessels were lashed against the docks, I'd have been surprised.

I sat ready in my chair, Priscus sat beside me. Martin perched behind with both hands clamped on the back of the chair. From the faint smell of wood smoke and rotten fish, I guessed we couldn't now be more than a hundred yards from shore. There was a tension in the cries of the Eastern crew that told me the long voyage really was coming to its end. The white canopy that had been raised above us was already soaked by the rain. Every time I shifted position on the wet cushions, I could feel it brushing against the top of my official hat. If I hadn't felt so utterly dispirited, I'd have marvelled at the skill with which the pilot was getting us into the right docking position. I heard an eager shout and a babble of something triumphant as a scattering of beacons came faintly in sight. There was another long grinding of timbers, and now a repeated splashing of water, as the whole galley turned about and its left length bumped gently against the dock.

'Welcome to Athens, my dearest Alaric,' Priscus whispered into my ear. 'If I'm not mistaken, the city of Aeschylus and Thucydides has turned out in force to greet the Emperor's most beauteous and learned adviser. It won't be a private arrest.'

Whatever drugs he'd consumed had given his breath the smell of baked dog shit. I bent forward and squinted through the mist to try to see the figures who were gathered on the docks. Look as I might, they drifted in and out of visibility, and I was left no wiser about who or how many they were. A slave helped Martin across the plank that joined us to the docks, and he vanished within one of the thicker fingers of the mist. Then he was back to stand very carefully on a stepladder that had been placed right on the edge of the docks. I caught a look of confusion on his face. I thought of the line of armed guards ready to take us into custody, and felt my stomach turn over and over. It was exactly like the moment you get, when, riding into battle, you lose control of your horse, and realise that there's nothing you can do to avoid crashing straight into the waiting enemy.

But, though his body shook, and he had to grip hard on his stepladder to avoid falling back into the water, Martin was now going through all the correct motions. 'You will greet His Magnificence Alaric, Senator, Count of the Most Sacred University, Legate Extraordinary of His Imperial Majesty,' he cried in his grandest voice as I helped Priscus to his feet and led him on to the plank. If I had much else to think about, I was surprised at how light the man had become in the month or so since I'd last nerved myself for physical contact with him.

But Martin had drawn breath, and, with a very slight tremor in his voice, was continuing: 'And you will greet His Magnificence Priscus, Senator, Commander of the East.'

On to the carpet that had been placed there long enough to be soaked, the Count of Athens and all the other persons of secular quality who'd travelled down to receive us fell as one for a full prostration. I looked nervously at Priscus. He looked back and pulled a face. He may have been trying to look carefree and amused. He only managed to look as baffled as I felt. I looked about for a glint of steel. I saw nothing. Instead, the little gong was sounded as etiquette required, and a dozen heads splashed three times on the ruined silk. They got up, as bedraggled after their wait in the rain as if they'd been pulled from a shipwreck, and waited on my instructions.

'Gentlemen,' I said, stepping on to the odd firmness of the land, 'I do most humbly thank you for your goodness in coming down from Athens. I bring with me every assurance from the Great Augustus of his love and regard for your city and for all its people.'

No one laughed. There was even a general bowing of heads. It was now that the slaves who'd followed me across with another canopy to hold off the rain jumped back on board the galley. Their duties were at an end, and they didn't look in the slightest unhappy to be rid of us. I felt a gust of chilly rain on my face. Then, other slaves came out from behind the still bowed officials and draped some wet canvas about my official clothes.

I took the Count's hand. It was cold and slippery. There was a trickle of water from the lowest point of his black beard. 'You are Nicephorus?' I asked with an attempt at the authoritative.

He nodded and stared impassively back at me. There was no hint of welcome in his face – or of any coming arrest.

My heart was beating very fast. With every beat, though, the moment for the words of arrest was passing. 'Then, my dear Nicephorus,' I added, 'I rejoice in having made your acquaintance, and look forward to our harmonious working together.'

I stood in the rain as he hurried through his formulaic greeting in the flat Greek of a Syrian. It was all so far as it should be – and not at all as I'd been so convinced it would be. There were no other officials about Nicephorus. Instead, he'd been waiting with what may, by their manner and the look of their clothing, have been well-to-do tradesmen. These, I supposed, were the town assembly. A few of them were armed with sharpened broom handles. One of them had a tarnished sword that may have been of bronze, and might have fetched a good price in the antiques market back in Constantinople. So far as armed men were concerned, this was it.

If this was a trap, it was a good one – and pointless too. Though armed, the two of us were hardly likely to try cutting our way to freedom. The mist wasn't so thick on land as out in the bay. I could see fifty yards all about. Not one gleam of armour and drawn sword – just more of the usual formalities. I took a deep breath and made myself smile. I made as short a second speech as decency allowed. I then stood back to let Martin read out my commission, putting the Emperor's Latin a phrase at a time into Greek.

I could smell that awful breath again as Priscus leaned close. 'Isn't that my cousin Simeon over there?' he muttered.

I nodded. I'd been aware of that blaze of clerical finery from the moment I'd stepped on shore. But the dozen or so bishops had been taking shelter against the wall of a ruined warehouse, and there had been thoughts of arrest, and then the shock of our actual greeting to take all my attention. Martin, though, was now finished with his reading, and Nicephorus had turned to prod some life into the slaves, who were still grovelling on the wet stones.

'My Lord Simeon,' I cried as we hurried over the slippery, uneven paving blocks, 'I am delighted – though also a little puzzled – to see you so far from home.'

His Grace the Bishop of Nicaea gave me the sort of look that might have soured milk. 'I was told you were dead,' he grated. 'The devil himself couldn't have survived those storms.'

'But, Simeon, my dearest love,' Priscus broke in beside me, 'we *did* survive – and here we are, to keep you safe in Athens.' He reached up and wiped a rivulet of black dye the rain had carried from his hair to the beak of his nose.

Simeon arranged his face into a gloating frown and stared a while at Priscus. 'He forgave you the loss of Cappadocia last spring,' he sneered. 'But, when the Emperor heard you had abandoned your post, and gone off to join this barbarian child in Egypt, he shut himself in with his confessor for three whole days. He'll need more than your usual pack of lies if you aren't to be degraded to baggage carrier.'

'And a very full report he will have,' came the reply in the voice of a man reprieved at the last moment. 'It isn't just on the field of battle that the enemy is defeated. Isn't that so, Alaric?'

Simeon shrugged contemptuously. 'You can save your lies, the pair of you, for those more gullible than me,' he said. He turned his bearded face up at what should have been the sky, but was simply a brightness of grey mist. 'I'm getting myself back into my chair before I catch my death of cold.' Without looking at either of us, he stepped past. He was followed by the other bishops. I recognised the Bishop of Ephesus. He cut off my greeting with a haughty sniff. The others did make some effort to look charming – then again, being Asiatic Greeks, they all had the dark looks and oily manner of Syrians: if the pair of us had just been sentenced to row in a ferry boat across the Bosporus, they'd have still managed those smiles and fluttering hands.

But this wasn't the end of the matter. After a few paces, Simeon stopped and looked back at us. 'I hear, My Lord Alaric,' he chuckled, 'that you never did get your land law published in Alexandria. Such a pity, everyone in Constantinople agrees, you let Priscus burn the city down instead.'

His Grace of Ephesus gave a spluttering laugh.

Simeon raised a hand to silence him. 'You may think His Holiness the Patriarch will protect you again,' he sneered. 'The question back home, I can tell you, is who will protect the Patriarch? If Ludinus gets his way, Constantinople will soon have a new and very different Patriarch.'

'Yes, a new and *very* different Patriarch!' His Grace of Ephesus repeated in a high-pitched snigger. They looked at each other and laughed. Then they were hurrying over to their covered chairs.

Not caring who might be watching, Priscus leaned with both hands against the wall. 'So Ludinus *is* back in favour,' he whispered, going back to one of our more panicky on-board conversations. 'I could smell the old eunuch's breath all over that commission of yours.'

I looked round again. Mention of that awful name had set my insides churning again. This was just the sort of joke Ludinus would play: give us time to frighten ourselves silly – and then pounce once we'd had a moment's relief. And if he really was back in the ascendant, neither of us could expect anything better than his best ever joke. It would seal his victory and his revenge.

But I could still see no glint of armour under any of the cloaks on the wet docks. Nor could I believe the whole assembled company – not in a place like Athens – was up to playing along so well. I glanced over at Martin, who was getting things ready for the journey to Athens. Since I hadn't yet been arrested, he was assuming that my orders to get everyone safely away had lapsed.

'Not quite in the clear, I'll grant,' I said to Priscus. 'But I hope you'll agree it could be worse.' I bit my lip and wondered how to get word to tell Martin at least to stay in Piraeus. Perhaps his judgement was sound, however. Perhaps I was right in what I'd just said. There could be no fatted calf awaiting us in Constantinople. Even getting to the Emperor would be a matter of sneaking past an army of court eunuchs. But that was looking too far ahead. For the moment, we weren't under arrest. It could have been worse.

Priscus gave me one of his blankest looks. 'We stand or fall together,' he whispered so low I could barely hear him. 'Let's not forget that.'

It was now that I saw the common people of Athens. Rather, it was now that I saw about a hundred of them. Obviously sick of grovelling on their bellies, they were clambering to their feet. My heart should have sunk as I looked at them. Even making allowances for the rain, you'd have had to go to one of the lowest districts of Constantinople to find an uglier, dirtier rabble than this. If these were a fair sample of its common people, Athens was well and truly fallen below its ancient glory. One of them shambled forward, a sly look on his face. What he said must have been a kind of Greek, but I'd hardly have guessed.

I forced a gracious smile and accepted a bunch of ruined flowers that someone had produced. Speaking very slowly, and in Greek that a barbarian slave just brought to market couldn't have failed to understand, I made a little speech of thanks. I got a subdued cheer that would have pleased me more if some toothless creature hadn't started a long cackle and pointed at me. Someone else to his left was grinning and repeatedly dabbing the tip of his nose. Deeper in the crowd, I saw a couple of men dressed in the sort of dark clothing I'd seen the desert people wear in Egypt. They may have been a little cleaner than the others, but were no taller. One of them had his right hand outstretched in my direction. Normally, I'd have seen nothing through the piece of cloth he'd put over his hand. The rain, though, had soaked this along with everything else. I could see the gesture, in which middle and ring fingers were held down by the thumb, and index and little fingers were extended outward like horns.

'Since you have no wife to cheat on you, dear boy,' Priscus called from behind me, 'I'd say the locals were scared of your evil eye.'

'A shame we can't see his face,' I replied. 'But I rather think he's looking at *you*!'

Leaving Priscus to stare back, or pull faces – or just wish there had been a few properly armed guards he could send into the crowd – I turned away, and picked my way back to where Nicephorus and everyone else were standing in the full drizzle of the rain. I lifted both arms to stop them from going down for another prostration. Too late! All I managed was to dislodge the canvas from my shoulders. By the time I'd got it back in place to save my fine clothes from a proper soaking, everyone was up again. With a bow that might have looked graceful in better weather, Nicephorus stared just a while too long at Priscus. Then he pointed at two covered chairs that had appeared from somewhere.

As I parted its curtain with my own hands and fell into the dryish if rather putrid interior, I heard Sveta shouting in her native Slavic at a couple of slaves who'd dropped some of our luggage. I heard their bored excuses. Close by was the shrill crying of her child and then of my own. Now, I heard the cries of sailors and the steady splash of water as the Imperial galley that had carried us in such pomp from Alexandria set off to make its appointment in the dry docks of Corinth.

I did mention my first sight of Athens. So far, I hadn't seen much of Piraeus. But who could care about that? I looked at my shaking hands. There wasn't the hint of a manacle on either wrist. I was about to see whatever had become of Athens. And, unless my greeting really had been the cruellest trick even Ludinus could play, I'd see it as a free man of considerable status.

11

I leaned out of my carrying chair and looked at the little mounds of rubble that lined each side of the road. 'I'd have thought some effort might go into keeping the Long Walls in repair,' I said. I tried not to sound as displeased as I felt. If the rain had let up and the mist was clearing away, the sun still hadn't broken through the solid mass of grey far above us. 'Without them, Athens must surely be reduced to an inland settlement whenever the barbarians are on the prowl.'

'They were damaged, My Lord, in an earthquake during the time of Emperor Maurice,' came the airy reply from Nicephorus.

He still hadn't arrested us. But I was beginning to find something decidedly offhand about his manner. It didn't help that the common people seemed to adore him almost as much as the town assembly did not. Before getting into his own chair, he'd passed a very long time among that dirty, chattering mob. They'd swarmed about him, stroking his official robe – even kissing his hands. With a few disapproving looks at each other, the assemblymen had stood away from him. They now trudged along behind the chairs, separating us from the common people.

'The stones have all since then been carried away by farmers to fortify their homes,' Nicephorus said, finishing his explanation with a complacent leer.

I nodded and let the damp curtains fall back into place. Once the weather was improved and I had time, I made a note to walk the four miles separating Athens from its port. There were still broken inscriptions scattered all over the ground. It would be interesting to see how Greek had been carved on to stone in the best ages of the language. Who could tell what little gems of verse and eloquence might lie there unregarded?

'Pausanias says they were demolished in ancient times,' Martin whispered as he pushed his head inside the curtains. 'The walls built by Themistocles were taken down during the time of the thirty Tyrants. They were restored by Conon, but had fallen down by the time Sulla laid siege to Athens.'

'My Lord's secretary is, of course, correct,' Nicephorus interrupted from within his own chair. The man had excellent hearing – more likely, he'd been listening in on our conversation. 'But new walls were raised about three hundred years ago, after the first barbarian incursion. These were, in turn, repaired when Alaric – the *King* Alaric of the Goths,' he added as if remembering my own official name – 'invaded Greece. There were walls to shelter the road between Athens and Piraeus within living memory. I believe the earthquake was about twenty years ago.' He twisted his face into a look of polite helplessness. 'I simply regret that they fell down before I was appointed, and I have lacked the resources to rebuild them.'

'Is this a closed threesome – or can I join the history seminar?' I heard Priscus croak from behind me. A cane projected unsteadily from behind the curtains of his chair, and poked one of the carriers in the back. He was carried level with me and Nicephorus. There was now no room left on the road for pedestrians, and Martin fell back with the others. I heard the familiar click of a wooden lid pushed into place. Either that burst of ambiguous joy on the docks really had restored him, or Priscus had finally hit on the right combination of powders. He pushed a ravaged face though his curtains and looked at the desolation that stretched out on either side of the road. Athens was still a few miles ahead, and the mist hadn't cleared sufficiently to allow a view even of its high places. But, as if what he could see gave him some perverse delight, he smiled and sniffed the air.

'I think I can settle the whole dispute,' he said, now in a semblance of his usual voice. 'When I was here two years ago, there were no walls then, but I did sign an order for the erection of a line of stakes along both sides of this road. If the Lord Count ever did take note of my order, I see the stakes have now been removed as well.' He flashed a most unpleasant look at Nicephorus, who smiled greasily back.

'I regret that His Grace of Nicaea is travelling so far behind us,' I said. 'It would be useful to know the reason for his own visit to Athens.'

'Oh, but hasn't Your Magnificence been told?' Nicephorus cried with an astonishment that might well have been genuine. 'We are blessed with a closed council of the Greek and Latin Churches. In all its long history, Athens has never been so honoured.'

I composed my face into a devout smile and waited for the dramatic pause to reach its end.

'You will surely be aware,' he continued, 'of the anomalous position occupied by the Lord Bishop of Athens. Though he ministers to a Greek see within an Eastern province, he is subject to His Holiness the Patriarch of Rome. No one has been told the matter to be discussed, but it was thought appropriate that it should be discussed at a place where the two jurisdictions overlap.

'But, really, My Lord,' he now burst out with undeniably genuine astonishment, 'I was told that you had been sent to reveal the matter to be discussed and to chair the council. Surely you . . .'

So that was it! As Nicephorus prattled on, I pulled myself out of the past, and my regrets that I'd spent only one afternoon skimming the *Description of Greece* written in the old days by Pausanias, and then only for details that had nothing to do with town fortifications. It must be that Sergius had finally got the Emperor interested in our scheme of religious settlement. If so, it was to get Rome on side that this council had been called.

The missing out of titles and epithets of regard still might indicate a certain lack of confidence. Simeon's gloating mention of Ludinus couldn't be set aside. But the vagueness of the commission now made sense. You don't put this in writing and send it on a trip through the Aegean. Nicephorus might be piss-poor even in his lowish place in the order of things. At least he'd told me what I was supposed to be about. I now realised what Simeon and all the others were doing here, and why I'd had my own course diverted here. Though Priscus might still be in the shit – and, let's face it, he deserved to be there – I was in the clear. Sergius had managed to see to it that I was still a trusted servant of the Emperor – or could be again. All I had to do was get Rome to say the one word *perhaps*, and my less than triumphant performance in Alexandria would be seen by everyone in its proper context.

I had a sudden thought. Where were the Latin delegates? I'd seen Greeks and Syrians in Piraeus. But, if this council was what I felt increasingly sure it was, we'd need a few bishops from the West. Why hadn't they been waiting on the docks?

But I'd not ask more of Nicephorus. All would be made plain once we were in Athens. It was enough that I felt actually happy. For the first time in months and months, I could see my way through. It was only as it began to slide away that I realised how crushing that weight of apprehension had been: worries about the Egyptian land law, worries about being murdered, worries about that sulky but inexorable voice in the Imperial Palace.

I pulled my curtains fully aside and jumped from the chair. I took a few steps forward. After long disrepair, the paving stones were crooked from settlement into the ground. As in Piraeus, it was a little strange to be on land that didn't keep moving under my feet. Unlike in Piraeus, I was able to rejoice that I was once again on firm ground – and in more than one sense.

'My Lords will forgive me if I hurry ahead on foot,' I said to Priscus and Nicephorus. 'I'm sure that you both have much to discuss after so long apart.'

Before either could reply, I'd grabbed Martin by the arm and was hurrying him past the forward luggage bearers. If I fancied some exercise, he needed it.

'Sveta and the children are in an ox cart right at the back of the procession,' Martin explained once he'd caught his breath. 'I did try once more to impress on her the need to look cheerful. Even

71

so, it's probably for the best that she doesn't get an excuse for complaining in public. It might embarrass you.'

I grunted. So long as she didn't utter treason in front of everyone else, she could set about Martin to her heart's delight once they were alone. Until then, she could fuss about the children with blankets and warmed milk. With her in charge, they'd not catch colds.

'There is the tomb of Menander, the playwright, somewhere along this road,' he said after another wheeze. He pointed at a low structure a dozen yards ahead.

I quickened my pace and heard him stumbling along behind me. It was a tomb, though not of Menander or of anyone else famous. It wasn't even that old, I saw from the pompous epitaph. This recorded the uneventful life of Hierocles, chief pastry cook to some Emperor whose name was obscured by a scrubby bush. Bearing in mind the tactful absence of anything religious about its decoration, the tomb probably dated from the age that lay between the establishment of the Christian Faith and its being made compulsory. I kicked a stone and watched it bounce along the road. In the bleak silence all about us, it clattered like a rock fall. I turned round to look back along the road. Martin was now beside me again. Everyone else was far back behind the curtain of mist.

'There is also a cenotaph of Euripides,' he said with an attempt at the cheerful. 'Though he died in Macedon, the Athenians thought it only proper he should have some memorial in the city of his birth.' It was *very* quiet all about. Not a bird twittered in the shedding olive trees of autumn. Martin's face took on the strained look he normally reserved for an attack of the haemorrhoids – or of the nerves. 'Do you suppose there might be any stray barbarians about?' he asked, confirming an attack of the latter.

I ignored him and bent down to pull at the bush. It moved a few inches and revealed the name of the Great Constantine. I stood upright with a satisfied grunt. I'd been right about the date of Hierocles.

'Corinth is only forty miles across the bay,' Martin added with a nervous twitch. 'But the Count's letter implies that the Governor has *never* visited Athens. Could it be that only the provincial capital is safe?'

'Though doubtless past its best,' I replied in a soothing voice that only set off another twitching fit, 'I do believe Athens remains a place of some importance. You'd hardly expect all those priests to gather in a town without protection. As for present danger, we really should have faith in Nicephorus. He'd not risk this kind of journey if there were any chance of an attack.'

I tried for a real change of subject. 'I always thought I'd see Athens in better weather,' I said brightly. 'What I had in mind was an approach along a dusty road, the sun overhead, cicadas chirping from brown foliage all around.' I kicked another stone. It skipped along the road before us, coming to rest in a puddle that, judging from the lush grass beside it, might have been there all month. 'I suppose it's all rather homely,' I added. 'Kent is like this in the autumn. I imagine Ireland is like it all year.' I laughed and got a grudging smile out of Martin. Even he had to admit that it was a change from the burning deadness of Egypt. And it was Athens. Yes, it *was* Athens. It wasn't quite as I'd imagined the place – and I hadn't yet seen what time and the decline of taste and riches had done to the city itself. But I was in a good mood, and was determined to keep it going for when we'd finished creeping through the mist and Athens would finally show which of its holy charms had survived.

Yes, what *had* survived of Athens? Its ancient glories had been a thousand years before. At their beginning, Egypt was still under its native kings. Even at their close, Rome had been an obscure town beyond the pale of Greek settlement in Italy. Since then, Athens had fallen to Philip of Macedon, and then to the Romans. It had eventually been revived by the Greek-loving Emperor Hadrian. Though sacked a century after that by barbarians, it had then remade itself as the first university town of the whole Empire. But all the schools had, within living memory, been closed in the final suppression of the Old Faith. Since then, there had been another big raid. I'd been a year in Rome, and had seen little enough to remind me of Cicero and Caesar. Why should I expect more of Athens? Ever since I'd given up worrying about immediate arrest, I'd been telling myself over and over again that the Athens I was approaching wasn't the Athens of my dreams. Why, it wasn't even a provincial capital any more – Corinth had long since been given that doubtful honour. But you try telling yourself that when you are, for the first time, just a couple of miles outside the place.

I bent down again and pulled at another bush. It might be interesting to see if Hierocles had died before or after his Imperial master. It did strike me as more interesting than the story Martin had struck up of the spot, somewhere ahead, where Saint Eunapius had failed to convert nine dozen philosophers by turning stones into bread. The panel here was broken, though, and the relevant section had fallen inward. Was it worth getting my hands dirty by pulling the section out? Probably not. On the other hand, Martin's sudden fervour *was* getting on my tits. I could put up with the absurdity of stones turned into bread. That the wretched Eunapius was supposed to have done this *after* the philosophers had torn his head off was more than common sense could bear. I pushed my hand inside the tomb. I pulled it straight out again and, shaking, stood up. I looked at my hand. Unable to stop myself, I wiped it on my robe.

'What is it?' Martin hissed with a relapse into terror.

I ignored him and looked at the small area of blackness where the panel had fallen in. I nerved myself and bent down again. This time, I reached carefully in and felt about. It *was* a hand I'd touched – the cold, stiff hand of one recently dead. It was attached to a bare arm. That was as far as I could reach. I swallowed and took hold of the hand. I pulled it through the gap and stood up. I paid no attention to Martin's little scream and looked down at the bluish hand of what may once have been a woman or an adolescent boy.

12

'The barbarians!' Martin cried. 'The barbarians!'

'Shut up!' I snapped. 'Barbarians don't hide their kills.' I put a hand on his shoulder and shook him until he stopped babbling. 'Let's have a look round the back of this thing.' I stepped off the road and forced my way into a mass of brambles. I barely noticed what these did to my red leggings. I did notice, though, how the bushes still hadn't fully recovered from a recent flattening. The tomb had been built of marble only on the three sides visible from the road. Its back was of unrendered brick. At some time in the distant past, a hole about thirty inches across had been smashed into the brickwork. Its worn edges showed signs of recent disturbance. I couldn't see anything in the blackness. But I reached in and felt about. The naked body was female. It had been doubled over as it was pushed through the small hole. I felt no congealed blood beneath the chill breasts. I ran my fingers up the body. Instead of a neck and then a face, I found myself touching a nasty and roughly crusted stump. I pulled my hand straight out and stood hurriedly back. Swallowing continually, I fought against the urge to double over and vomit.

'Oh, there you are,' Priscus rasped in his most cheerful voice since, off Cyprus, we'd turned west. His chair was about a dozen yards back along the road. Emerging from the mist, the whole front half of the party had caught up and now had come to a halt. 'I was telling Nicephorus you'd not be able to resist grubbing round all these broken stones.' He got down from his chair and walked with an uncertain jauntiness to the edge of the road. He looked into my twitching and doubtless very pale face, and grinned. 'So, dear boy, will you enlighten us with your discovery? Is this the tomb of Socrates himself?' He let out a sneering laugh. Suddenly, as if reading my thoughts, he looked down at the hand that was still poking through the gap at the bottom of the tomb. He arched his eyebrows and smiled. He was getting ready for one of his more flippant comments, when Nicephorus came up beside him.

One glance down, and the colour drained from his face. 'My Lords,' he stammered when he'd found his voice, 'I do urge the unwisdom of delay on this road.' Rich that was, from a man who'd had us take half the morning to cover three miles.

Keeping my face expressionless, I stared back at him. 'What, My Lord Count, is the meaning of this?' I asked firmly. I wanted to know. I also wanted to keep Martin from looking stupid in front of everyone else with a return to wailing about the barbarians. Correction: I just wanted to know. 'Why do you suppose there is a fresh and headless body hidden just off the road?'

'Athens is safe, My Lord, only within its walls,' was the best answer I got.

Everyone else at the front of our long procession had now edged forward. I could see the cart where Sveta was looking after the children. As yet, she hadn't poked her head through the leather flaps. If no one knew what, everyone else had guessed something was wrong, and there were nervous looks on all the faces of the carrying slaves. I heard Simeon's voice raised in harsh complaint about the delay – he wanted his lunch. His earlier bounce quite gone, Nicephorus darted his tongue over dry lips and began a more insistent urging that we should get ourselves to Athens with all possible speed. The assemblymen had now crowded forward for a look at the body. They said nothing at all, but didn't look happy.

'So you are telling us this is indeed murder,' Priscus snapped. 'Don't you suppose your duty involves at least checking whose body it might have been?'

Odd that he should be telling anyone to investigate a probable killing. Then again, it gave him an excuse to be horrid to

Nicephorus. Whatever the case, I nodded. With hands clenched, Nicephorus looked up at the grey sky and then down again at the hand. He was looking for something to say, but not, it was plain, with any success.

'Well, don't just stand there, man,' Priscus added. He swore and wheeled round to look at the main party. He pointed at his own chair's carrying slaves. 'Go and do as His Magnificence directs,' he ordered.

Mouths open, they looked back uncomprehendingly. Priscus swore again. He stepped towards them, hand tightening on his stick. But Nicephorus now gave in to the inevitable and jabbered something at the slaves that bore a passing resemblance to Greek. They let go of their carrying handles and picked their way with slow reluctance through the brambles. I got them to pull at the loose brickwork until they'd made a hole big enough for pulling the body out. It had set in its doubled-up position, and getting it out was a right bitch. But a few kicks from me, and more jabbering from Nicephorus, and out it finally came. It lay huddled on the rocky ground beyond the brambles.

'Ooh, but isn't she lovely?' Priscus crooned, now beside me. He bent down and ran appreciative hands over the pale corpse. Propping his stick upright within some of the bricks the slaves had raked out, he got on to his knees and reached into the tomb. He pulled his arms out and moved closer on his knees. This time, he poked his entire upper body inside. Deeper and deeper he reached. Then, with a cry of ecstasy, he was out again, holding the severed head between his hands.

One look at the fear-twisted face, and I had to look up at the sky. I could now smell death all about me.

Priscus, though, was going into some ghastly imitation of Salome with the head of John the Baptist. Holding the girl's head between outstretched hands, he stared lovingly at the face. He brought it suddenly forward to bury his face in the dark, unbound hair. 'Perfectly lovely, don't you think?' he mumbled between long inward breaths. 'Can my darling Alaric tell me more than this?' he finally asked with a sly upward look.

I swallowed and made my own inspection. 'She was from the better classes,' I said. I'd established from one touch of the hand that she hadn't been of the free poor, or from the lower class of slave. 'Free, or' – I looked at the whole body: it had been finely proportioned – 'some rich man's concubine.' I'd have put money on the first of these possibilities; most of the slaves I'd seen had the fairish hair of Slav prisoners, and this girl's hair had been a dark and perhaps a glossy brown. I swallowed again and thought of the flask of perfume I had in my satchel. Without any breeze to carry it away, the smell of corruption was turning unbearable. How Priscus could have been rubbing his face in that hair without puking up would have been a mystery if I hadn't known him better.

I forced myself to look harder at the body. Bad weather might have kept off the flies. Nor had the rats been round to have a go at it. Even so, it might have been there four or five days. I looked at the head that Priscus was now twisting about to view from every angle. You needed some imagination to see how pretty the face had once been. It really was a ghastly thing to behold: dark where all else about the body was unnaturally pale, and damaged as if it had been dragged over the rocky ground. I looked away from the grey, sunken eyes.

'Tell me more – tell me more, my darling,' Priscus groaned as if in the approach to some powerful orgasm. He gave a quick look past me to where Nicephorus was watching in silence.

I gritted my teeth and told myself firmly who and where I was. 'No point asking if it *was* murder,' I said with an attempted smile. It was a failure and I gave up on the effort. 'With live beheading, you expect a cataract of blood. Even after death, you'd expect to see more than we can. The hair shows no evidence of wetting. But the body itself may have been washed after live or dead beheading. I'd say, however, she was hung upside down and bled to death, and only then beheaded.' I made myself step closer to the severed head and willed my finger not to shake, as I pointed at the two punctures, about an inch and a half apart, on the right side of the throat.

'Oh, Alaric,' Priscus called out, still in ecstasy, 'you really are a bright young lad! I quite agree the little dear was hung upside down and bled to death. That would explain the blackening of the face. It also explains the paleness and lack of corruption.' He shuffled forward on his knees and put the head back on to its neck. It rolled a foot away. But he took it up again and pushed it until the damp earth held it roughly in place. He bent down and put a kiss on the rigid lips. The head rolled away again. Now, he took it back into his hands and kissed it with long and passionate intensity.

Leave aside sick-making – this was embarrassing. If Priscus couldn't control himself soon, even the slaves might dare to comment. As it was, the assemblymen had all set their faces like stone. But he did control himself. He ran trembling fingers once more though the hair, then put the head down and reached for his stick. 'Sex killing or magic, dear boy?' he asked in Latin. He laughed and smacked his lips. 'What opinion might the evidence suggest to you?' he added as he staggered back to his feet.

I had to admit he'd summarised the range of possibilities. I'd let him force the legs apart to see if there was evidence of rape. Of course, that might leave us no wiser – it could be a sex killing *and* magic. But, as I cleared my throat for a reply, Priscus moved out of the way, and the slaves could now see the whole body.

'Lemmy! Lemmy!' one of them moaned, pointing at the puncture wounds. 'Lemmy! Lemmy!' he repeated, now louder, as he dashed through the brambles to get back to the road.

'Not so fast, my lad!' Priscus snarled with the full return of his old manner. Ignoring the thorns that tore at his leggings, he bounded on to the road and caught up with the slave. He felled him with a single blow of his walking stick, and started on a good, hard kicking. The man squealed and twisted on the ground, his own repetition of the word 'lemmy!' drowned out by Priscus, who was laughing as maniacally as if he were back in the days of his father-in-law, when he could torture and kill as he thought fit. But it was a momentary burst. As the slave fell silent, Priscus groaned and flopped on to the road beside him. He reached forward and rubbed his hand in the slave's hair. He held up shaking fingers that dripped fresh blood. He carried them to his lips and groaned again.

But he'd got his way. All about, order was restored. Now he'd had time for a good look of his own at the body, Nicephorus was looking merely annoyed. Obviously impatient to get back to Athens, the assemblymen were looking grimly away. Though scared, the slaves were all back in place, ready to take up their burdens. Simeon was looking out from his chair, deep in a snig-gering but low conversation with the Bishop of Ephesus. The only real noise came from Martin. A few yards to my left, he was on his knees, praying desperately in a high, sibilant Celtic.

'He says that it's a lamia,' he finally managed to say without choking, though still in Celtic. 'This is the work of a demon that feasts on human blood.'

'They can say what they like,' I hissed at him. 'But I hope you still have enough sense to recognise murder by some person or persons unknown.' It was a waste of breath, though, to try reason-ing with Martin once he'd screwed himself up to this pitch of superstitious terror. Even persuading him it was all the work of barbarians, and that they were hiding behind the other tombs, would have brought him closer to his senses.

I left him sobbing and shaking and picked my way carefully through the brambles to where Nicephorus was lounging, now with restored ease, among the trash of Athens.

'We'll need to get the body back to Athens,' I said. 'Unless you can identify it, we'll publish an announcement tomorrow morning.' I looked up at the sky. It was hard to see anything through a mist that was undeniably increasing. But the chill and general darken-ing about us indicated more rain. My clothes were already in a state that would never have been tolerated in Constantinople. But, if we could avoid a regular soaking, I might enter Athens with some semblance of pomp.

'And who will carry the body, My Lord?' came the half-mock-ing reply. He looked at the grinning crowd about him. 'Will any of you carry this thing within the walls?' he asked of them in slow and simple Greek.

His answer was a cheerful shaking of heads.

He walked out of the crowd and looked at the body from the edge of the road. 'No one will touch it,' he said. 'Surely you can accept that no one will allow it within the city walls.'

I could have tried giving the man a direct order. Since I hadn't been arrested, I was arguably still clothed in the full power of my Alexandrian commission. But I knew it would have been a waste of time. One of the assemblymen now looked at me and opened his mouth as if to say something. But he fell silent again. They'd do nothing. The slaves would do nothing. The trash were looking happy enough, but might turn nasty at the drop of a hat. Not Priscus himself, and backed by all the other agents of the Phocas terror, could have got the girl and her severed head carried along behind us.

Nicephorus was right. Though he had none in mind, justice of any kind would have to wait. Besides, it was coming on to rain again. I might already have felt one of its first drops on my forehead. My brocade really wouldn't stand a soaking.

'Very well,' I muttered. 'Let's get ourselves to Athens. We'll discuss this again later.'

'See, His Magnificence agrees!' Nicephorus cried triumphantly at the assemblymen. 'It's a dead slave and nothing more.' He repeated himself in the local version of Greek.

There was just a laugh and a few giggles from within the crowd. Someone shouted back. But his words were too fast and too twisted for me to catch even their sense. Now, they all shuffled forward, some pressing into the brambles to see what the fuss had been about. Hands bleeding where he'd dropped down on to the jagged stones, Martin was already beside me. Clutching his side and wheezing after the sudden exertion, Priscus looked as if he were in need of help back into his carrying chair. But he'd need to force himself to another burst of strength, I thought grimly. If the body was to be shoved quickly out of sight, I'd need more out of him than a token helping hand.

*　　*　　*

We hurried on, now in a terrible silence. A breeze had come up again from behind us, and I could smell the rancid, unwashed clothing of the Athenians. Martin still hadn't recovered his composure, and I'd pushed his trembling bulk out of sight into my chair. I walked beside, every so often squeezing out a few words on what we were passing. But there were no more nuggets of fact recalled from Pausanias, and I could barely recall the cheer that had felt so unshakable just half a mile back. We did pass the cenotaph of Euripides. It was topped with a statue that seemed to have weathered the past thousand years in good shape. The inscription was both long and wholly legible. But there was no chance of stopping to read it.

Now and again, Priscus pulled the curtains aside and looked out of his chair. He'd managed to lick all the blood off his right hand, and was back to looking pleased with himself. As often as he saw I was watching him, he beamed over at me and sniffed at the deathly smell that must still have clung to his damp clothing. If ever there was a lamia, it was surely him. He hadn't seen the girl die. But he had seen the next best thing, and its thrill had brought him back to more life than I'd have thought possible when we'd stood moping together over the galley side.

The mist only let us see the walls of Athens from about a hundred yards. We'd already entered the demolished and mostly cleared area of what had been its outer suburb. The walls themselves were some twenty feet high, and looked as if they'd been hastily thrown up with whatever building materials could be recovered from the demolished area. From the look Priscus gave them, they'd never have served in any region where a civilised enemy might be able to penetrate. Doubtless, they were enough to keep Athens safe should the barbarians ever show up in search of food and plunder.

'Hadrian endowed a big library when he was here,' I said quietly to Martin. 'It may still contain a few interesting books.'

No answer. I pushed my head inside the curtains. Nearly filling the stuffy, fart-laden interior, Martin was praying silently to the shrivelled tongue of Saint George that had been the Patriarch's leaving present to me in Alexandria.

No point talking about books. No point telling him how every stone we might be about to touch was holy. Still, we were at last about to enter Athens.

13

Not bothering to call for assistance, I got up to pull the side window shut. I looked out for a moment, over the desolation of what had once been a nice courtyard garden, to the far side of the residency. The stained, crumbling stucco displeased me. The central fountain displeased me. The rain certainly displeased me. I tugged at the handle and swore as it came away. Eventually, though, I did get the window shut. Its little green panes let through the fading light of a late afternoon, and it meant that the smoke from the charcoal brazier had nowhere to go but a small opening in the ceiling window that was better suited for letting in the rain. It was cold. By comparison with Constantinople at this time of year, Athens was almost balmy. On the other hand, I had just spent months in Egypt, and, this time of year in Constantinople, I'd have had the heating on at full burn. I sat down again to what passed for dinner with Priscus.

'Stewed river frog can be delicious at this time of year,' he said with an appreciative leer. He shifted position on his chair and farted gently into the cushions. I stared at the iron pot filled with a sort of grey slime and took up another piece of bread. 'Well,' he added, 'it's the best I've had in ages. Come on, Martin,' he called, '*you* tuck in if it's not good enough for His Magnificence. This at least won't make you any fatter.' He laughed happily and held out a long spoon.

Martin dipped it into the slime and stirred up an overpowering smell of garlic. At the second or third attempt, he scooped out the kind of thing you see floating belly up in stagnant ponds. As he lifted it carefully to his mouth, one of the legs came away and fell back with a soft splash into the pot. He closed his eyes and pushed what remained on the spoon into his mouth. I looked down into my wooden cup. It was filled with wine that would have started a riot on a slave galley. The pepper I'd added might now have taken away the worst of its taste. It hadn't. But I drained the cup and tried to look more cheerful than I felt.

We'd reached the end of our first day in Athens. It had been my intention, once we were settled into our accommodation, to go for a look about the city. What I'd seen of it on our way in had been more hopeful than the journey up from Piraeus might have suggested. The streets were amazingly dirty. The small crowds huddling under the colonnades had been, if possible, uglier and more degraded than those who'd met us on the docks. What I'd heard of their chattering still bore little relation to any Greek that I'd ever heard. But the new buildings in the centre had been respectably magnificent. If Justinian had shut down all the universities there eighty years before, he'd been characteristically generous with building grants. As for the ancient buildings, neither Martin nor I was up to identifying anything. But we had no doubt there was much still to be seen. By unspoken agreement, we'd avoided looking up at the great plateau that overshadowed the city. We'd save that experience for better weather.

And better weather hadn't come. Our planned sightseeing of the early afternoon had been rained off. No one had complained when I cancelled our reception ceremony in front of the Count's residency. Instead, in the absence of any slaves, I'd helped Martin unpack my clothes. These were all soaked and would need a day in the sun to dry, followed by another day of stretching and pressing. The clothes I was wearing had been damp through. Eventually, a residency slave had come in sight. As luck would have it, he was about my size. So he'd been sent about his duties in a stained silk tunic, and I was now at least warm in the padded shirt and loose trousers of a Slavic prisoner of war. I'd finally got used to the smell and had been looking forward to a dinner where I could put a few pointed questions to Nicephorus.

'You say the Count's been taken poorly?' I asked. I waited for

Priscus to suck the flesh off the whole dead thing he'd shovelled into his mouth. It was a noise that almost turned my stomach.

He leaned forward and spat the complete skeleton into a battered silver dish. 'Oh,' he said vaguely, 'the long wait in Piraeus brought back a fever he had in the summer. When I left him, he was sweating all over. He did say he'd attend on you tomorrow morning.'

I rubbed the spot on my nose. It was a fair alternative to grinding my teeth. There was no chance at all of arrest – there's a limit even to the sort of trick Ludinus might play on his enemies. This being so, I was coming over all official again. I had questions for Nicephorus accumulating like autumn leaves in a gutter, and he'd now taken to his bed.

I turned to Martin, who was coming out of a quiet choking fit from some bones he'd failed to spit out. 'Where do you suppose the rest of the slaves are hiding?' I asked.

'I've counted only six slaves in the whole building,' he said indistinctly. 'They could be the sweepings of the market on a poor day,' he added tartly.

I might have observed that, as a freed slave, Martin could have shown a little consideration for those less fortunate than himself. But I couldn't fault his estimate of their worth. *And six of them!* There must have been fifty rooms in this place – no, many more than that, once you took the three other blocks into account.

'No wonder it's all so dirty!' I sighed instead. 'And where are the clerks? You don't expect much administration in a place like Athens. Even so, a few occupied offices might be reasonable.'

Above us, the wind shifted direction. It sent a spattering of rain on to the tiled floor. I stared at the dark puddle that was beginning to make its way in my direction. A sudden draught reached one of the lamps. It went out with a sputter and a smell of rancid oil. I noticed how dark it was getting. As Martin got up to fiddle with the thing, I chewed on the hard crust.

'Why so much fuss, dear boy?' Priscus called without bothering to empty his mouth. 'Weren't you brought up in a pigsty? This must be luxury itself by comparison. But let's agree it could do with some attention, and turn to the much more interesting matter of what this place used to be. Did Plato or someone else famous live here in the old days?' He swallowed. Straight away, he slurped in another of the frogs and smacked his lips.

Plainly, his fellowship in despair act was wearing thin. I had no right to complain: mine had vanished in a puff of smoke a mile outside Piraeus. I grinned and looked down at my crust. Truth was – not that I'd ever admit this to Priscus – that a pigsty would have been one or two steps up from the hovel in Richborough where Ethelbert had dumped my mother. I stroked my throbbing nose. 'The residency is only about four hundred years old,' I said. 'According to the inscription above the main entrance, it was built as a palace by Herodes Atticus.' I could see from his blank look that I'd outpaced the man's knowledge of history. 'He was a close friend of the Emperor Hadrian,' I explained, 'and shared his taste for the very ancient. Apparently, he'd been left poor by his father's extravagance. His fortunes were only restored by the discovery of a treasure hoard under his remaining property. He built this palace on the site of the discovery, which is a shame, bearing in mind its bad position.' I glanced again at a damaged fresco of the Emperor on the far wall. Surrounded by statues of the famous dead, he was giving a speech to the people of Athens. The young man beside him was probably Antinous. But the head was missing – someone had dug into the plaster long before, possibly to get at one of the hot air ducts underneath.

Not being able to go out, and having nothing better to do with my time, I'd spent the early afternoon looking about the front block of what was now the Count's residency. You couldn't fault its original plan. The rooms that hadn't been subdivided into offices had a size and arrangement that would have pleased the modern rich in Constantinople. But I've said the offices were empty. Many were locked shut. Everything was long out of repair. It all desperately needed cleaning. And it was bloody cold. There's a limit to what you can appreciate of anything when your feet are like ice and there's a dribble of cold snot on your upper lip. Yes, I'd been glad of that slave's clothing. Even if they did smell of unwashed barbarian, I was warmer than Priscus or Martin.

Priscus broke my long silence with one of his wet coughs. 'It could be worse, my dear,' he said with a good cheer that I guessed was intended to annoy. 'Did I ever tell you about the winter I spent in Trampolinea? You soon learned to lie still at night. Then the lice would cover you thickly enough to keep you almost warm. Mind you, the days were better. You spent them darting about the city walls, throwing rocks on the barbarians who were trying to climb over to cut your throat.' He smiled at Martin, who'd now sat down and was staring unhappily into the iron pot.

Priscus yawned and poured himself another cup of wine. 'So, young Alaric,' he asked, 'do I gather right that you've been sent to Athens to conquer for Heraclius at the head of a synod?'

There are few things worse than finding a worm in the piece of bread you've been eating. Finding half a worm is one of them. I put the two halves of the bread down and brushed grey crumbs from the stained quilting of my shirt. 'I've no doubt it's waiting for me somewhere,' I said cautiously, 'but I still haven't seen his letter of further instructions. It's reasonable to suppose, however, that the Emperor has called a closed council to discuss the progress of heresy.' I tried to make it all sound very dull. Priscus suppressed another yawn and looked over at the window. The light had almost faded. Another few cups, and there would be an excuse for seeing what vermin might be waiting in our beds.

But Priscus smiled and reached for his drug box. He dropped into his wine a generous pinch of a blue powder that I knew was a stimulant. 'You may have thought your dinner of welcome here would be an elegant affair. You may even have looked forward to meeting a few men of your own age and vicious inclinations – dicing and whoring and all that, eh? Instead, we are where we are. Now, you could let me pass an evening with recollections of how I survived the final night battle in the streets of Trampolinea,' he said. 'But it would only give little Martin a nightmare.' He sipped at his wine and pulled a face. He sipped again. 'I know what, though,' he said, now brightly. 'Why don't we discuss theology? That can't upset any of us. And, just to make it even more fun, let's do it in Latin. I'm sure no one is listening outside the door. But let's do it anyway for the added challenge of discussing profundities in an unphilosophic language.'

I blinked and settled my features into complete impassivity. Martin gave me a nervous look.

Priscus laughed and this time sipped delicately from his cup. 'We're all friends around this table,' he said easily in Latin. 'Do I ever look down on the pair of you if you don't know the difference between a javelin and an artillery bolt? Of course I don't! But it does so pain me when you think me nothing but a rough soldier. I know that, when I burn or rape or hang or despoil heretics, you really do assume I have no understanding of the issues involved. Go on, my dear boys, own up – you think I regard the issues as of no more substance than the arguments between the Green and Blue factions in the Circus.'

I forced a weak smile and shook my head. The rain was beating against both upper and side window panes as if someone were knocking for entry. 'Don't you think it rather late for theology?' I asked, trying to sound bored. 'It's been a long day, and the light has gone.'

'Oh, but the night is young!' Priscus crooned. He finished his cup and giggled. I watched as his face changed from dead white to what the lamps showed as a sort of orange. As it began to change back, and his drug took proper hold of his mind, he let out a long sigh. 'Besides,' he went on in a voice that carried no trace of tiredness, 'we all know that you never go to sleep before midnight. Study, study, study, so deep into the night, isn't it? How else does a barbarian from the edge of nowhere get such fancy Greek and that formidable learning in the classics? No, my fine, young scholar, you can sit up a while longer, to hear that Uncle Priscus didn't entirely miss out on education. You just allow me to start this discussion with my own little summary of the issues. I'm sure you'll have cause to correct one or two misunderstandings of detail. But do hear me out first.'

Except when all else has failed, and it's looked as if I were moments from a grisly end, I've never been in the habit of praying for help. But, even as Priscus had his mouth open to start his 'little summary', there was a sudden rattling on the door handle.

'You finished with that yet, My Lords?' the old cooking woman rasped as she walked in. She pointed at the iron pot. 'The Master hasn't bought no other food in, and, since you ain't all dead after all, that was to be our dinner. Now, if you've had your fill, we wants the leftovers.'

I'd have said seventy. Just as easily, though, she might have been fifty or ninety – you really can't tell age with slaves or the lower classes. She stood before us, a tub of shrivelled lard in a dark dress shiny from years of cooking spills.

'Get out of here, or I'll have you flogged,' Priscus hissed at her.

She looked back at him and pulled a face. 'Please yourself, love,' she said. 'But the condemned boy was outside the walls all day yesterday picking up them frogs.'

Since she at least knew Greek, I wanted to sit her down and ask a few obvious questions about the management of the residency household. I also had a question about these persistent rumours of my death. But Priscus was on his feet and swaying about with a stick in his hand. He lashed out at the old woman, who, with surprising agility, dodged past him. He lunged again, this time tripping over the bottom part of an old dining couch. It splintered on impact, and Priscus vanished for a moment into a cloud of woodwormy dust.

'So it's just the beer for us poor slaves,' was the last the old woman said before she got back to the door. She banged it shut behind her.

I listened for the diminishing scrape of sandals on the unswept tiles of the corridor outside. Within the room, Martin had finally got Priscus free of the heap of broken wood, and His Magnificence the Commander of the East was now breathing like an enraged bull. But he controlled himself.

'I forgive the old witch on account of her cooking,' he said in a forced lightness of tone. 'Now, where was I? Oh yes, we were going to discuss the fundamental issues of our day, and in Latin.' He grinned at me. 'Even if you have heard them before, I can promise my own take on them will be interesting.'

14

The rain was getting worse. Now the smoke of the expired lamp had cleared away, I could smell my borrowed clothes. The prayer I'd been considering hadn't worked. I'd not bother with saying one. I didn't know how long it would be until I could escape from them and run a wet sponge over my body. Worse – oh, far worse! – I was stuck until then with Priscus for company.

'In the early days of the Faith,' he opened in a tone that anyone who didn't know him would have taken for reverential, 'when professing it was still a crime in the Empire, it was enough for most believers that Jesus Christ was the only Son of God, and that He had been sent among us to call us to the Truth and to redeem us for our sins. Beyond that, it was a matter of trying to follow His ethical precepts. Once the Faith had been established by the Great Constantine, however, attention shifted to investigating the Nature of Christ. What had been a minor and theoretical question now became a dispute concerning the peace of the Empire. Was Christ in His Nature identical with the Father, or merely similar to the Father? You will recall that Bishop Arius held the latter view, and Bishop Athanasius the former – and that every other bishop in the Empire, and eventually every one of the Faithful, was expected to take sides.

'That dispute was settled at the Council of Nicaea nearly three centuries ago – in the year 325 since the birth of Christ. The bishops there decreed that Christ was, in His Substance, identical with the Father, but had also been made flesh for our benefit. Arius was anathematised and his followers were driven from the Church wherever possible. The losers at Nicaea held out for a long time – not least because their position was accepted by most of the barbarian converts. But time and a great deal of persecution did eventually establish the Nicene position as orthodox.'

He stopped. 'But, my dear young fellows,' he said with what I knew was a deliberately annoying brightness of tone, 'are we not in Athens? Is this not the city of Plato and Socrates? Is this not the place where, of old, in those supremely elegant drinking parties, knowledge was reached not through dry lectures, but by the cut and thrust of debate?' He got up and smiled. 'Shall I ask you both what is the nature of the good, and how we can know it is good? Shall I call that dirty and illiterate hag back in, and, by directed questioning, get her to show that knowledge is innate by revealing some truth of mathematics? No!' He sat down again and smiled at Martin. 'So can you tell me *why* the views laid down at Nicaea are orthodox? Dear young Alaric may believe that the whole matter was a trifle got up by priests with too much time on their hands. In Greek, I know, the technical words for each of the positions have only one letter of difference between them – and, without qualifying adjectives, the same Latin word describes both positions. But can *you* tell me why the Nicene position is orthodox, and all else is damnable heresy?'

'Because,' I broke in, once it was plain that Martin was too shocked or scared to join the game, 'if the losing side at Nicaea had been more successful, the Faith itself might have fallen apart. If the Son was accepted in any sense as inferior to the Father, Christ might quickly have been degraded to the same status as the pagan philosophers gave to their many gods. Like Apollo and Hermes, He would have been regarded as one more manifestation of the Originating Principle of All Things. There would have been no establishment of *the* Faith, only an addition to the *Old* Faith. The premises being granted, orthodoxy is a logical necessity.'

Priscus nodded eagerly. 'That's right, dear boy,' he cried. 'You really have a gift for putting these things so clearly. Such a pity the Great Augustus ignored my advice to give you charge of the university at Istropolis. The world of learning lost a most remarkable scholar.'

I smiled. 'Was that before or after the place was burned by the

Avars?' I asked. I looked into the cold and glittering eyes above the bright smile. For a moment, they narrowed.

But Priscus ignored the attempted diversion and continued: 'After the Arian dispute was settled, a further question arose. If Christ was indeed God, to what extent was He also made flesh? That was discussed at the Council of Chalcedon a hundred and twenty-six years later. The majority opinion here – rather, the *orthodox* position – was that the Nature of Christ was both Human *and* Divine. These Natures were held to be perfectly distinct, but also perfectly fused in a single person.

'Unfortunately, a considerable body of dissidents has continued to claim, if in various ways, that the Nature of Christ is *single* and Divine – that, as Eutyches once put it, whatever may be Human is at best merged into the Divine as a drop of honey is dissolved in the sea. Now, these Monophysites have been largely Egyptian and Syrian, and they seem to have gained the support of most Egyptians and Syrians. What began as a theological dispute has become a source of political division within the Empire. Every mode of official persuasion, from argument to bloody persecution, has failed to impose the orthodox line, that Christ is both *Human* and Divine. Instead, during the hundred and fifty years or so since Chalcedon, the Egyptians and Syrians have insensibly thrown off a cultural domination that the Greeks had enjoyed in the East since the time of the Great Alexander. This was covered over at first by a spirit of habitual obedience to the Emperor. But, during our present and, as yet, unfortunate, Persian War, the division has progressed from running sore into a possibly fatal consumption.

'I could say more, but it would bring me to the political difficulties we face in Egypt and Syria, where the heretics await not conquest by the Persians, but deliverance. It would also involve a discussion of military issues that might be too exciting for dear little Martin. So let us turn instead to this closed council in Athens, to be attended by a select few bishops from across the entire Church.'

I looked at Martin. He looked back. Priscus laughed and paused to swallow another frog. There are occasions when you knock a glass flask over, and it rolls out of reach across the table. You know that, if you could get there in time, you could stop it from rolling straight off to shatter on the floor tiles. But you know that even trying is a waste of time. So it was with Priscus.

'Now,' he said, a triumphant look coming over his face, 'what would the most learned Alaric do about the Monophysite dispute? I know: he'd suggest an Edict of Toleration! Stop persecuting them, he'd say, and you eventually turn heretics into loyal taxpayers and defenders of their country. But we know Heraclius would never consent to the toleration of heresy. Worse, even if a more pliable Emperor could be found, you'd never silence those armies of ranting clerics. They've been anathematising each other for six generations, and have loved every day of it. Because everyone agrees that it matters, the dispute does matter, and it can't be ignored.

'So, what else would young Alaric suggest?' Priscus leaned forward. Unblinking, he stared into my face. 'Might it be a compromise? Might it be a flattening of two opposed formulations beneath a third on which both sides could agree? Shall we hope that, if the orthodox can be brought to agree that Christ has a Single Directing Will, the heretics will stop objecting to a Double Nature?'

Priscus got up and tried for a dance about the room. Even with his stimulants, it was too much, and he sat down heavily on the window seat.

I thought quickly. Martin knew everything, but he was above suspicion. There was Sergius. But the Patriarch never discussed religious policy with me other than on a boat that the two of us had to row into the middle of the Golden Horn. That left the Emperor. The four of us aside, all this was supposed to be a state secret. But there was no doubt it was Heraclius who'd been blabbing to Priscus – most likely when they'd been together outside Caesarea. I tried not to grind my teeth.

'And it is supposed to be a secret, isn't it?' Priscus jeered as if he'd read my thoughts. 'But it is one of my jobs to uncover secrets, you know. A still deeper secret, of course, is that it's *you*, and not

His Holiness of Constantinople, who is the driving force behind this compromise. You need Sergius because he's the best man to work on the Great Augustus. And, if he takes full credit in the event of success, he'll also be the one who falls if the wind ever shifts again.'

Priscus took his eyes off my face and looked out of the window into darkness. 'Well, you'll never get Simeon to go along with any of that,' he said. 'He's stupid and he's obstinate. You know he fancied himself as Patriarch instead of Sergius – and still does? And do you suppose you'll get anything at all out of the Latin bishops?'

I got up and stretched. I could have told Priscus that he'd got things wrong. But he'd got them too right to bother with denials for their own sake. 'Like every other orthodox churchman within the Empire,' I said, 'His Grace of Nicaea will do his duty. I grant the Latin bishops may be a problem. But we shall see how the council goes.' I sat down again and poured more wine. Though disgusting, it might settle my nerves.

Priscus got up again. He walked over to the iron pot and looked in. He picked up his spoon and stirred the contents. 'See, dear boy,' he took up again, 'you think that, if you can get a mob of blackbirds to sing as you direct, you'll go home in glory. I'll then be the one to pick up the blame for those unfortunate events in Alexandria.' He grinned and gave full view of his riddled teeth. 'But I wonder how easily you'll get that?' He suddenly bent over the pot and pressed hard on his belly. He gave a long burp. 'I've no doubt you'll need still more of my support before we get out of this dead or dying city.' He pressed harder on his belly and gave another burp. Then, after a moment of retching, he opened his mouth wide and, with a dull splash, something had flopped out into the slime. Priscus coughed and stood up. He leaned back and pushed the index finger of his right hand into his throat. Now, he bent quickly forward again and vomited everything he'd eaten into the pot. There was a stink of wine and corrupted stomach juices as whole lumps of clotted frog splashed back from where they'd come.

It was always hard to predict what Priscus would do next. This time, he'd really got me by surprise. Wine cup frozen an inch from my lips, I watched as he twisted his body, and burped or retched, and vomited again. But he did finally empty his stomach, and stood upright to look into the pot. To be fair, it was hard to see what difference he'd made to its contents.

'I forgot to tell you,' he gasped at Martin, 'that the blue ones can be a little poisonous this time of year. They won't kill you,' he went on reassuringly. 'But you may find yourself pissing rusty water from your arse for a couple of days.' He stood over Martin and gloried in the terrified look he was getting. 'Still, I did promise that it wouldn't make you fatter!'

He walked unsteadily round the smashed dining couch on his way to the door. As he reached the door, he stopped and turned. 'I don't know anything about Herodes Atticus,' he said. 'But I can tell you this palace is said to be haunted.' He grinned at Martin, who'd given up on clutching at his stomach and was now looking around nervously. 'Yes, there was a witch who lived here many ages ago. I'm told there are nights when you can still hear her, singing spells along every corridor.' He laughed and went out.

I listened to the slow scrape of his own sandals as he went off in the direction of his rooms.

I got up. 'I'm going to bed,' I said firmly. 'Today's been busy. Tomorrow will be busy.' I reached out to help Martin to his feet. His own hand was damp and trembling. 'Do see about a bath before waking me,' I added. 'And if you bump into him, tell that bastard Count I want a word with him at his earliest opportunity.'

15

'Open it,' the voice urged in the darkness behind me. 'You will find that it needs the key with seven hooks.'

Sure enough, the voice had urged right. Nothing I'd tried earlier with Martin had opened the big door inside the cupboard. A few centuries of damp can do wicked things to iron locks. By much oiling and rocking back and forth, we'd eventually got the cupboard door itself open. This further door, however, might have been a stone relief for all we'd been able to open it. Now, a single push and pull of the key, and I heard the grate of disengaging teeth. The door swung silently inward, and I could smell the damp, chilly air of what was assuredly one of the cellars we'd been seeking but not yet found.

'Without a lamp,' I said, 'there's no point in going further.'

The voice gave a low chuckle. 'All the light even your mind could desire lies within,' it said. 'There is no need of a lamp.'

Keeping my hands on each side of the narrow shaft cut through the rock, I counted myself down ninety-eight steps. Either they had been cut into very hard rock, or they'd hardly been used. They had none of the worn, uneven feel that I'd expected. At the bottom, I stopped and waited. It was absolutely dark and absolutely silent. 'What now?' I said. It was an obvious question to ask. I also wanted to see what echo came back at me.

There was a sudden flash of whiteness from all round me. It was like sheet lightning, but had the sort of long fade away you get from the larger dinner gongs. When I opened my eyes, I could see that I was in a chamber about a hundred feet long and fifty wide. The ceiling was a high vault of bricks or well-shaped stones. Wooden boxes had been placed perhaps six feet apart all along the left wall. As I tried to focus on these, the light faded out. But I did have time to see that some of the boxes had been broken open, and unimaginable heaps of gold – mostly ingots the size and shape of distribution bread – were spilling out of these.

'Have you never wondered,' the voice asked with another low chuckle, 'how Herodes Atticus recovered his fortune in ancient times?'

'The story is that he found an immense treasure buried under this property,' I said. 'He told the Emperor it had been put there during the siege of Athens by Sulla.' There was another flash, and I could look again at the heaps of gold. Scattered here and there among the ingots were crudely shaped ornaments and what looked like ceremonial armour. All was still of gold.

'So he told the Emperor,' the voice answered. 'But what else could he say that wouldn't provoke an immediate sequestration? Two of these boxes were as much as he dared carry away. They made him the richest subject in the Empire. The secret of the rest died with him, and the last of his posterity left this palace to the Emperor Decius in recognition of his persecution of the Church. Will you go forward and touch the gold? It is all that men desire. Have you any questions to ask? Whatever you ask will be answered.'

It was my turn to laugh. The voice left no echo, however loud it sounded. My own laugh came back at me from three walls. 'I hardly see the point in stepping forward,' I said. 'Dreams of gold are still only dreams.' I laughed again, and wondered if it might be worth turning round before the latest flash could entirely fade away. The voice might be attached to a visible body.

'And what, my little philosopher, makes you suppose this is a dream?' The question came now from total darkness.

I touched the tip of my nose. As I'd expected, there was no spot. If I reached down to my left ankle, I'd probably find there were none of the scratches I'd got from the brambles that surrounded the tomb of Hierocles. 'I know that I'm dreaming when events take place outside the normal stream of time,' I explained. 'Add to this when the events border on the miraculous. This is a dream, and you, and this room, are nothing more than emanations of my own sleeping mind. Will you try arguing otherwise?'

There was a long pause. Then, plainly displeased, the voice answered: 'I could strike you dead for your lack of faith.'

'And I'd only wake in my bed no wiser,' I sneered straight back.

'Have you not heard, that those who die in dreams die really?' Displeasure gone, the voice was taking on a note almost of pleading.

'So I'm told,' I sneered again, now louder. 'But you'll surely agree that the evidence for your claim is, by its nature, somewhat thin.'

There was another pause. Then: 'Does every truth require evidence?'

'The truths of mathematics, and a few truisms aside,' I answered, 'and even those I'm not sure about, and the answer is yes. All other knowledge begins with evidence of the waking senses, and is tested by further evidence of the same kind. What evidence can you supply that I am not at this moment tucked up warm in bed?'

'Those who will not be shown the truth must find it for themselves,' was the only answer I had. It came in a tone of quiet resignation. There was another flash of light. This time, the boxes had vanished. The vault above my head had become the roof of a low cave. At the far end of the cave, a row of faintly gleaming strands hung from the wall.

I now heard a whimpering to my right. Still expecting I'd see nothing, I looked sharply round. In the long fade out of the light, though, I could see someone. Unable to move from where I was standing, I stared until the light faded wholly away. Almost at once, there was another flash. Without any positive identification, I knew it was the dead girl I'd found outside Athens. Whole and alive, but still naked, she smiled at me with a cold and somehow glittering allure. She stepped forward. Still unable to step back, I held up both hands to ward her off. Her face twisted into a sneer of lust. She stopped. She pushed fingers between her legs and rubbed. She stepped forward again, her glistening hand held out to me.

I did now manage to step back, but only found myself against a wall that hadn't previously been there. Lips parted in a terrifying smile, the girl took another step forward. Her hand was almost under my nose . . .

I sat up in my bed. I'd woken to a flash of what was obviously sheet lightning. There was a big storm in progress above Athens. If possible, this was worse than the one that had almost sunk us all off Seriphos. The rain smashed like sea spray against the walls of the palace, and had somehow poured into the room to soak my bed. As the windows rattled from the sound of astonishingly loud thunder, I struggled with the wet linen sheet that was twisted about me and got out of bed. Even without more lightning to show where the lead had crumbled, I could feel that the rain had knocked most of the glass pieces from the window. By the time I'd found that the shutter hinges were rusted open, I was thoroughly soaked. Shivering in the darkness, I felt my way back over to my bed and pulled on the silken cord. It came away in my hand. I let it drop to the floor. There was no slave outside the room. I doubted there would have been anyone up had the cord been still attached to any distant bell. Martin had a nerve to talk about 'sweepings of the market' – trust a freed slave to look down on those less fortunate – but he'd not been unjust.

Another flash, and I could see the puddle covering most of the tiled floor. Where Martin had hung them up to air, my own clothes had caught the spray. The slave clothes I'd commandeered had fallen down and were lying in the puddle. I muttered an obscenity and wrapped the wet sheet round the lower half of my body. I then turned up the lamp that had been left beside me.

The outer room was dryish and slightly warmer. I thought of putting myself to bed on one of the larger couches. But the only covering in the room was a tapestry that smelled of damp. I could go through another door into my office. The brazier there might still be smouldering. It was hardly dignified for the Emperor's man in Athens to sleep on his office floor. But I'd known worse.

I was reaching for the door handle, when I heard a noise. I

thought at first it was a failed thunderbolt. Storms throw up some funny noises. But this wasn't an all-round crash, however muted. It was a long, low grating sound that might have come from deep within the building. What had Priscus said about ghosts? I dithered a moment by the office door. Another man might have gone back to huddle in his soaked bed. But I was His Magnificence the Senator Alaric. Old-womanish tales had no effect on me! I turned and went for the door into the corridor.

Of course, once I was out there, all I could hear was the sound of my own breathing, and the steady drumming of rain, and the dripping of yet another leak from overhead. There was then more thunder, and whatever my ears might have picked up was blotted out.

But no, there was another noise. This time, it wasn't long or low. It was instead a short and very loud click – as of some cog in a water mill that picks up a stone. Sounds in a storm, sounds at night, sounds in a palace cut up into a labyrinth – you tell me from which direction it had come. I listened hard. There was nothing. Any thoughts, though, of finding somewhere to bed down for what remained of the night were wholly gone. I hitched up my sheet and set off towards the larger rooms in the palace. The sheet was like mummy wrappings. It may have clung to me and shown the contours of my body like in the statues that lined the entrance hall of the residency. But it reduced me to a kind of aged shuffle. I put my lamp down on the floor and took off the sheet. The upper part of my body had now dried out. The rest of me was still wet, and I was aware again of the chill all about me. I folded the sheet and put it over my left arm.

As I was bending to pick up the lamp, I noticed the trail on the floor. I hadn't seen it when I was upright. It now showed plain from a different angle. It was as if someone had made one sweep of a broom though one of the puddles. It went on about ten feet until it passed beyond the outermost pool of light. I followed it along the corridor. It stopped as neatly as it had begun. I took a few more steps forward. Further ahead, the trail took up again. It glistened suddenly as bright as a stream in another flash of lightning that bounced along from behind me.

'How very queer!' I muttered. My voice was unpleasantly loud in the corridor. I fell silent and held my breath. All about was silent. I suppressed a shiver and laughed defiantly. Forget any guff about being the Emperor's man. I was Aelric, the big barbarian from Kent. I had a pair of very hard fists attached to very muscular arms. Even if I weren't completely alone so late into the night, I was a match – and more than a match – for anyone else I might find creeping about the residency. You can be sure I wasn't scared of ghosts or witches. I quickened my stride and turned a corner. A few yards beyond, I turned again.

So far, I'd been passing along one of the corridors original to the building. Ten feet wide, you could have driven a carriage there. Though discoloured by age and dirt, the walls were lined halfway up with marble, and there was a procession of naked boys painted on those stretches of plaster not completely ruined by the damp. Every couple of yards, there were niches for lamps and for polished mirrors behind. Now, I'd moved into one of the partitioned areas, and the corridor narrowed to barely a yard. Sometimes, the wall was roughly plastered. More often, the plaster had come off to show irregular lines of cheaply fired brick. The few lamp brackets I had to avoid were of rusted iron. The floor was covered in perhaps a century of unswept dust and in clumps of plaster and pieces of brick. Aelric of Richborough had mostly been a stranger to shoes. The soles of his feet had been like leather. His Magnificence Alaric was a far more civilised creature. I had to step carefully to avoid treading on anything larger than the coarse dust.

The trail came to a final halt beside one of the doors that lined this stretch of the partition wall. I went forward and looked down another corridor. Yes, it had ended. I went back and looked at the door. Now all over, I was shivering again in the cold. My throat was dry. I could hear the rapid beating of my heart. I can't say how long I stood there like a bloody scared fool. I might have been taking lessons in courage from poor Martin for all I was inclined to reach out for the handle. I laughed again and pulled myself together. I snatched at the handle and pulled it down. With a harsh click, the door swung open inwards. There was a chill and gentle breeze that took something away from what had become an overpowering smell of damp. I pushed it fully open and held up my lamp.

This had once been one of the chancery offices. The high desks were covered in dust. The ink pots were still uncovered, as if everyone had been called out suddenly and then prevented from going back. I could see a sheet of papyrus on one of the desks. Curled up and cracked from however many years of damp, it may have been half covered in writing. There was no ceiling window. Even so, a puddle had gathered somehow on the floor. It reflected the dull gleam of my lamp. There was a side window that I supposed looked out into the courtyard. Against this the rain drummed loud and rhythmically, and I could hear the distant moaning of wind.

I took a step into the room. 'Fuck!' I snarled as I nearly dropped the lamp. I'd stubbed a toe on some piece of clutter. 'Fucking dump!' I added as I sat down on the cold mosaic floor and nursed my toe. If it wasn't broken, that was no thanks to that silly bastard Heraclius and his scheme of sending me to this awful place. 'Fucking, fucking shitty dump!' As the pain faded and I began to see the funny side of things, there was a flash of lightning through the side window. This was followed by an endless peal of thunder that I thought for a moment would bring the ceiling down on me. I sighed and got up. Where puddles hadn't been able to gather, the floor was covered in dust and little bits of ceiling plaster. I brushed what I could from my bottom. From what I could see on my hand, I was probably as white behind as the lead that Priscus used to smooth out his pockmarks.

The lightning had shown me there was no dust sheet or any other covering in the room. Since I had no plans to sleep here, there was no point in staying. I went out and carried on walking along one of those endless corridors. In the last unlocked office before another turning, there was still no dust sheet. But I did find a rolled-up carpet. If I could shake the worst of the dust out of this, I might play at Cleopatra till I could get up with the dawn and kick some notion of service into the few slaves who served the civil and military ruler of Athens.

The rendered brick wall that had been made to partition a larger room cut the window in half. If you squeezed your face against it and looked right, you might be able to see into the next room. No need for that – but there was a handy ledge that was unlikely to tip over or give way. I was putting my lamp there, so I could try shaking dust out of the carpet, when I looked through one of the little panes and, far off, saw the glow of another lamp.

16

I did think at first it was just the reflection of my own lamp. The little panes were both opaque and uneven. No surprise, then, if they were, by night, to play funny tricks. But I picked at the crumbling lead framework with a fingernail, and managed to poke out one of the smaller panes. I felt the damp and chilly blast as I pushed my face close to the gap and looked out. Yes, there was definitely someone else sitting up late in the residency. This window looked out into the main courtyard. From the other side of this, there was a gentle gleam in one of the upper windows. Like Priscus and me, Martin and his family had their rooms on the ground floor of the main block. So, I believed, had Nicephorus. The slave quarters were also on the ground floor, and took up one of the side wings of the palace. I thought back to the hasty tour of the building that was all I'd been able to manage with Martin before hunger had sent us off in search of that awful dinner with Priscus. We'd found an unlocked door that revealed a staircase leading to the upper floor. By common agreement, we'd left all further exploration till the next day.

There was another flash of lightning, and more thunder. I waited for my eyes to adjust from the dazzling flash. Yes, it was a lamp in one of the upper windows. I could keep looking for somewhere dry to sleep, and see who else was in the palace come the morning. But who could have slept now? I reached for my folded sheet and took up my lamp. The carpet could stay where I'd found it. In all those corridors, I'd gone all the way round the main block of the palace. I was now only about half a dozen rooms away from my own quarters. If I remembered correctly, the staircase I wanted was through one of the undivided rooms that lay the other side of a second cluster of deserted offices. I thought of going back for a pair of sandals and some clothes. Even wet clothes might be an improvement on nudity in this chill. But I wasn't sure how long the lamp would hold up. Shivering in a draught that at least took away the horrid smell of damp, I set out along yet another corridor. In one of the partitions of what had been a very large room – an art gallery, perhaps? – I found myself looking at the cupboard where we'd earlier found the locked door – the locked door, that is, of my dream.

'I'll not be going through that!' I said firmly. My complacent laugh was drowned out by more thunder. The preceding flash of lightning, though, had shown another door that I'd somehow overlooked in our daylight tour. It hung wide open, and led up a staircase of what might once have been fine marble. I paused and looked back at the cupboard. I laughed again and pulled the door open and walked in. The door at its far end was still locked solidly shut. I'd have that open soon enough, I thought. We'd see then what was behind it. I gave the wood a hard tap. No answering echo: it must have been inches thick. I laughed, now gently. With dreams like this, I asked, who needed opium? I turned and walked from the cupboard. I took care to close the door behind me.

I felt a trickle of cold water down my back. I thought for a moment someone had touched me, and fought for much longer than that with a fit of the shivers. I tried to ignore how cold it was all about. I stared into the lamp flame, and tried to forget how, beyond a few yards in all directions, I was in pitch dark.

I told myself I'd made a mistake when I found one of the doors I had to go through to get to that staircase had been locked shut. All the doors in question had been unlocked earlier. I didn't see why the few residency slaves should have bothered with locking any of them. More likely, I'd taken a wrong turning. But I hadn't. Everything looks different at night. But I was in the right place. I had to go through this door, and then through another, before I got to the staircase. I was hurrying down another of the corridors – I thought this one might lead into the left side block of the residency – when I saw the faint glimmer from beneath a closed door.

I stopped and tried the latch. This door was only shut, not locked. Better still, it opened on to a flight of stairs that led up to a room that seemed moderately well-lit. This wouldn't be the light I'd seen from the office window. But, since I was investigating one, I might as well investigate another.

I dithered a moment at the foot of the stairs. I thought of calling up. Instead, I listened hard. No sound. I pinched the wick of my own lamp and waited for it to stop smoking. I set a foot on the first of the marble steps – and pulled straight back. Since I was now relying on the dim light from above, I couldn't see if it was seed corn or little ceramic beads that had been scattered over the stairs. But it was one of those devices I'd used back home when I needed to plot in some language a spy might reasonably be expected to understand. I held my breath and listened for any sound at all from upstairs. It was pointless with that continual drumbeat of the rain. I bent forward and let my fingers play lightly over the coating on the first and second and on every other step I could reach. It was the sort of cheap beads you put on a string and give to children – or that people wear prominently on their fine church-going clothes to show off their humility. Bare feet wouldn't crunch on this as boots or even sandals would, but would still make some noise. And little beads would most certainly hurt those ever so civilised and well-pumiced feet. I bent forward again and swept a little space where I could step. Keeping as quiet as I could, I went slowly upstairs, taking the steps two at a time.

Still alone, I stood amid the wreckage of what had once been a very fine library. One side of its hundred-foot length was taken up with a series of glazed windows. I'd looked up at these from the courtyard and guessed that they meant a library. The unrendered bricks of the big central dome had the sort of reflected gleam on them that said they were of glass. By day, the whole room must have been as light as the open air. The dome was supported by four columns of many-coloured marble. These had once been sheathed over their middle third in bronze. There was still bronze to cover the capitals where they supported the dome. There were even a few traces of gold leaf on the elegant scrolling of the capitals. The middle sheathing, though, was long since gone. Only a paler colour for the marble, and the dark peg holes, showed what had been there. Much of the panelled ceiling that surrounded the dome had come down. Where the plaster still adhered, there were elaborate painting of stars and of gods of the Old Faith, each head within a bright nimbus.

Back in the days of Herodes – perhaps till quite recently – the library may have contained one of the finest collections in the Empire. Judging from the bookracks that remained, and from where others must once have been, it didn't seem unreasonable to guess twenty, perhaps thirty, thousand individual rolls.

But I've said I was standing amid wreckage. The four-inch by four partitions in the racks were mostly empty. Many of the smaller racks had been overturned. Chairs lay broken on the floor. Tables had collapsed under various weights. As ever, pieces of glass had come loose from their lead framework, and rain had made its own contribution to the damage. The lighting I'd seen was towards the far end of the room. It was enough to be noticed from quite a distance, though not to give a detailed view of anything. But, even in the dimness, I could see the sad desolation of a grand library. Then there were the continuing flashes of lightning. Between the intense whiteness that blanks out everything, and the sudden darkness before eyes can readjust to the normal light, there is the tiniest moment of illumination. In one of those moments, I looked into what might be a good summary of what Athens had finally become.

Close by one of the good windows, there was a table that could still be used. It had a chair set to it. Here the lamps were burning – half a dozen of them in an iron holder. As I walked forward into the room, my feet crunched on an area of mosaic tiles that had come loose on the floor. I stopped and looked down to see if there was broken glass there as well. No, it was just dozens of loose stones that had once been the face of one of the Muses. There was no broken glass to worry about. But some of the stones looked sharp. I stepped back and took a longer route to the table.

There was a taper by the lamps. Cupping this in my hands against the draught that came from every direction, I carried a flame to my own lamp and pressed down the windshield. These lamps had been filled with the cheapest grade of oil, and they let off a nasty, acrid smell along with their rather dim light. But their combined light made a soft and almost welcoming glow. I stood up straight and looked across at the stained murals on the far wall. They showed Athens as it had been at some time in the past; the still unfinished Temple of Jupiter suggested the city in its grandest days. I'd come back for a proper look by day.

I stood behind the chair and turned my attention to the books that lay on the table. One of these was a roll of the ancient kind. The glue had failed, and the individual sheets of papyrus had mostly separated from each other. I picked one of them up and held it close by the lamps. The bright, aromatic smell of the decaying reeds took me straight back to the time I'd spent in what remained of the great library of Alexandria. Once I'd focused on the light and often faded ink strokes of whatever scribe had produced it, so did the text. It was from the fourth book of the life King Ptolemy had written of his friend Alexander, and this sheet carried his account of the council of war held by the Persian King just before his final defeat. I'd read the whole of this in Alexandria, and it was thrilling stuff. More than this, it had a ring of truth. To be sure, you couldn't trust any of the passages where Ptolemy himself was in action – but the King had been in a position to get at the full truth about all that had happened, and he'd mostly told the truth unless his own interest was concerned. The last few lines of the page had crumbled, and the next I could find took up the story when Alexander was approaching Persepolis.

I looked harder and compared the sheets. I'd been right. The council of war was Ptolemy, sure enough. Persepolis was in a different hand and in a more florid style. It might have been Arrian. It might have been some other late author, who'd rewritten Ptolemy and padded his effort with tales of inherent absurdity. This sheet had Alexander in conversation with an owl who was relaying a message from Athena. Vaguely interested, I pushed the two sheets together. There were of slightly different sizes. By all appearances, the reader had gathered up what he could find of Alexander and was going through it all in no particular order.

The other main work on the table was a huge book of the modern sort. Writing on parchment can be much smaller than on papyrus, and it was hard in this light to see what the book was. Noting how high it was heaped with cushions, I sat on the chair and moved my lamp so close that I had to take care to avoid spilling oil on the pages. I looked up from the wavering text and gave a contemptuous sniff. I found myself staring into a marble bust of Polybius. At some point, this had been knocked from its plinth and then replaced, minus nose and the lower part of its beard. What was left of its features seemed, in the flickering dimness of the lamps, to be twisting into the sneer I could feel spreading over my own face. I looked down again at the text and read with closer attention:

> Now these points being conceded to us, the further point is also clear to any one, that, as Moses says darkness was before the creation of light, so also in the case of the Son (if, according to the heretical statement, the Father 'made Him at that time when He willed'), before He made Him, that Light which the Son is was not; and, light not yet being, it is impossible that its opposite should not be. For we learn also from the other instances that nothing that comes from the Creator is at random, but that which was lacking is added by creation to existing things. Thus it is quite clear that if God did make the Son, He made Him by reason of a deficiency in the nature of things. As, then, while sensible light was still lacking, there was darkness, and darkness would certainly have prevailed had light not come into being, so also, when the Son 'as yet was not,' the very and true Light, and all else that the Son is, did not exist. For even according to the evidence of heresy, that which exists has no need of coming into being; if therefore He made Him, He assuredly made that which did not exist . . .

Gregory of Nyassa? I hazarded. The references to light and the nature of time were a strong indication. I turned the page – yes, it was Gregory: I'd gone through this with Martin in Constantinople.

Though one of the more ranty of the theologians we'd been pressing for the meaning I needed, he had stood out for his attack on slavery. But who the buggery could be reading this stuff for pleasure? And where was he? Even with this grade of oil, you have to be pretty rich to leave all those lamps burning away like a minor lighthouse. Had he sloped off for a pee somewhere? Had he just vanished like the chancery clerks? I stared again at what was – its inherent absurdity always granted – a most able defence of orthodoxy.

But I wasn't creeping, stark bollock naked, about the residency for a spot of midnight reading. It was worth noting that, if there was a copy here of Ptolemy's *Life of Alexander*, the library might not be completely worthless. I ignored the tangle of unrolled books that I could now see beneath one of the overturned racks. I ignored the chaotic heaps of modern books of what might have been more controversial theology or just obsolete law texts. They could all wait till the coming of daylight. The wind shifted again outside, and there was a harsh spatter of rain against every one of the windows. As in my bedroom, water splashed through the gaps in the leadwork and added to the puddles on the floor. I refilled my lamp from a flask of that cheap oil, and moved on.

17

The library was on the upper floor of the left block of the palace. To the right of where I'd been sitting was another door that led further into the block. At some time in the past, it had been locked from the other side, and then smashed open. Some effort had then been made to reattach it to the frame. Now, getting it open more than about eighteen inches caused it to grate on the broken mosaics that covered the floor. I forced it wide open and looked into the darkness beyond. There was a loud splashing of the water that made its way down from a hole in the roof. Its echo told me I was in a room of at least the same size as the library.

Time, I think, to explain the geography of the place where I was staying. I've said it was built by Herodes Atticus. So far as I could tell, he'd tried for a combination of almost Imperial magnificence with something more homely. The result was something of a muddle. The front block of the palace, where it faced on to the Forum of Hadrian, comprised about a dozen very large and high rooms where he could show off his wealth. These were lit by glazed ceiling windows. They were mostly now abandoned or divided into smaller rooms or offices with little regard to the need for natural lighting. Behind these, and facing out into the main courtyard, was a labyrinth of smaller and much lower rooms, lit by side windows or with ceiling windows, or with both. These I supposed were the living rooms for the household. A careful inspection of partition walls and the telltale pattern of the ceiling mouldings might tell what was original to the plan and what had been adapted in the conversion from palace to administrative building. So far, it had just seemed an impenetrable muddle.

The other three blocks that surrounded the courtyard were all of two storeys. The ground floors had originally been given over to slave quarters and kitchens and offices. The upper floors seemed to be smaller copies of the grand front rooms or of the living rooms. This arrangement may have been intended to match the custom in the wealthy houses in every great city where it isn't hot all year round. In the summer months, the household would have moved upstairs to catch the sunshine and whatever breeze might blow. In the winter, it would have been downstairs for the heating.

The main difference was that none of the upper rooms seemed to have been divided. On second thoughts, the place did look as if it had been looted. Chairs and other furniture had been ripped apart for their gilding, and left in heaps of dust-covered wood. Busts had been pulled from their niches and left broken on the floor. Even door handles had been cut away where they might have been of some valuable metal. The padding of my feet on marble tiles or what had once been polished wood echoed round the bare rooms that lay beyond the library. Every so often, the lightning illuminated the utter bareness of furnishing, and the sound of thunder on bare walls and ceiling added to the effect. If anyone had lived here in ages, I'd have been surprised. I was here now only because, assuredly, there was someone else up here.

I passed through what might once have been a lavishly arranged dining room, and through various other public rooms. Between the lightning flashes, my lamp threw dim and flickering shadows against the walls. In one room, a lightning flash brought me face to face with a life-size statue of Demosthenes. It was still painted, and gave me more than a momentary shock. I made myself stop and look at this, and laughed to settle my nerves. It was a marble copy of a bronze original. I could tell this from the expansive waving of both arms. One of these had needed support from a rod of painted metal that ran discreetly from hip to wrist. The eyes may once have been set with semi-precious stones. Of course, these had been prised out, and I looked into pale, empty sockets.

In another room, I found myself staring at the remnants of a mural. Most of the plaster had fallen away in sheets that had crumbled on the floor. But the central group remained of a man and woman with a young boy. They stared back at me with the big, mournful eyes of the modern style. The boy held up a waxed tablet and an iron stylus. There might have been other family members. But only these now showed. Once or twice, I was saved only by accident from stepping on heaps of broken glass or ceramic. I'd been silly, I told myself, not to go back to my room at least for a pair of sandals.

It wasn't on my way, but I let myself stop for a long inspection of a side room that had once been some manner of court. The vaulted ceiling was covered in an elaborate mosaic showing the trial of Socrates. Many of the little tiles had dropped away, and lay on the floor in heaps where someone appeared to have swept them and then failed to gather them up. Though stained now with water leaks from above, the walls had been painted a uniform dark that drew attention to the brightness of the ceiling. On a platform at the far end, the judgement chair was of cracked ebony. There had been inlays of gold or ivory. But these were now missing. The other tables and benches were arranged in the usual manner. On a low table beneath the judgement chair, I saw the faded remains of a transcript. Years of damp and sunlight had wiped the text almost clean. Only individual words and fragments of words remained to suggest that the court had last been used to try a case of testamentary fraud. So far as I could tell, the case had been adjourned so the lower-class witnesses could be tortured. If it had ever been resumed, it wasn't in here.

The Imperial bust was of the Great Justinian. That suggested things had been interrupted by a sudden appearance in court of the plague that had swept away half the Empire and permanently diminished even Constantinople. I closed my eyes and imagined the terrified scraping of chairs and muttering of the formal adjournment as all must have run from a place where someone had collapsed in the trembling fit that usually announced the arrival of plague. Until then, the palace may have been a living administrative centre, with clerks toiling in every room and a continuity of life unbroken since ancient times. After then, it may never have been the same.

What had led me out of my way was the trail of little footprints in the dust. They began just inside the door and went hesitantly about the room. They'd stopped before the judgement chair. It looked as if someone had been trying to pick up one of the cushions of dark silk that had been arranged there for the judge's comfort. It hadn't been a successful act. The cushion that was lifted out of its ancient place had burst and sent crumbled wool all over the floor. From here, the footprints led straight out again. I bent down to look at the little prints. Reasonably fresh, they showed the bare feet of a woman or a child.

I straightened up and stretched cold muscles. It was hard to say how long I'd been wandering about. Once I was out of the library, I had thought the storm was passing away. Instead, it had come back, and was reaching another climax. Except I was on the upper floor somewhere in the left block of the palace, it was hard to say exactly where I was. It was a long courtroom, and, unlike with the library, its length went into the block rather than along it. This surely indicated another mass of rooms that I hadn't yet seen. I went back out into the corridor and looked from the side window into the courtyard. A handy flash of lightning told me I was nearing the end of this block. Another dozen yards or so, and the corridor would swing right into the far block, and I'd surely be approaching where the light had been shining.

I went down a long corridor lined with doors to what had probably been individual sleeping quarters. I reached the far side of the palace from my room, and counted myself down another long corridor. At the fifth door, I paused and listened. These were thick doors, lined probably on both sides with leather. Never bright since refilling, my lamp was beginning to flicker in one of the more vigorous draughts. Feeling suddenly nervous, I lifted my right hand and knocked gently on the now brittle leather.

I thought at first I'd picked the wrong door. I knocked again, now harder. I was about to move on, when I felt the slight impact of someone pushing against the door from the other side.

'Who is it?' a woman called. It was a low voice, with just a trace of alarm. Except she wasn't likely to be a slave, it was hard to say anything through two inches of padded wood about the owner of the voice.

'I am the Senator Alaric,' I answered, trying to keep my voice steady. 'I arrived here this morning. I rather hope the Lord Count made you aware of my presence.' There was a long silence. Embarrassed, I was thinking what else to say, when I heard the scraping of an inner bolt. The door opened inward a few inches. Silhouetted against the inner brightness, a face looked out at me. 'Your husband didn't tell me he had his family with him in Athens,' I said.

The woman stood, looking out in silence. Then she pulled the door fully open. 'My Lord is mistaken,' she said. 'The Lord Count is not my husband.' She stopped and smiled shyly. 'But my late husband's brother would surely be displeased to know that I had opened my door in the middle of the night to a perfectly naked young man – Emperor's representative or not.'

She had me there. I'd clean forgotten I was unclothed. With a blush and a mumbled apology, I turned and got the sheet unfolded and hastily wrapped about my middle. I was just in time to avoid showing Nature's inevitable salute. From what I could see of her, the Count's sister-in-law wasn't at all bad-looking. About thirty, and with the faintly dark looks of the East, she was the first woman I'd seen since leaving Alexandria. Sveta, of course, didn't count – nor the elderly cook Priscus had tried to beat. If she'd been a slave, I might have honoured her with a request before setting down to business. But you don't begin an acquaintance with free women of the higher classes by suggesting a quick jump into bed. On the other hand, she hadn't squealed and made all the usual fuss. Now, she stood in the still open doorway, plainly inspecting the uncovered upper parts of my body. I was suddenly aware that my last depilation had been in Alexandria. I was showing areas of blond stubble on my chest and lower arms that suggested anything but my exalted station. I resisted the urge to unwrap the sheet and rearrange it in the semblance of what the Greeks had worn in ancient times. Unless I turned round again and showed the comical whiteness of my bottom, it would have revealed my interest far too plainly.

While I was thinking of anything to say that wasn't ludicrous, I heard within the room the staccato sound of a child's coughing. 'Your child is sick?' I asked.

Again, she smiled. She stepped back from the door and motioned me into the room. There was a strong smell of something aromatic in the little brazier that kept the room warm.

'Not my child,' she said. 'Not, at least, my own child.' She led me over to a small bed, where a child was twisting and spluttering in its sleep. 'My husband left me with a son from his first marriage. I am all the poor child now has.' She sat down beside the bed and fussed with the blankets. 'You might say he is all I now have.' She smiled sadly and stroked the boy's dark hair. As there was more lightning and I waited for the answering thunder, he groaned and threw off the blanket that had been tucked underneath him.

I stood back from the bed and looked about the room. Though large, it was plainly furnished. There were some book rolls of the old kind and a box of toys. There were a few unmatched chairs and a table. I took it that this was the child's room. His stepmother must sleep in the next room. There was another door in the room that probably led through to this.

'There are no slaves to assist?' I asked.

Her answer was a shake of the head. It was a final and, so far as I could tell, an entirely reasonable denial. I could see it would be worthless to ask if she'd heard anything in the main block. It was too far away. Plainly, she'd been wholly involved with caring for the sick child.

'The Lord Count has long lamented that his budget leaves him without means to afford such comforts. The household slaves do what they can to help. But they are now assigned to guests of considerably more importance.' She got up and crossed the room to play with the wick of the single lamp.

'I do most earnestly apologise,' I said, 'for disturbing you so late at night. But Nicephorus did give me to understand that we were the only other residents here apart from himself.' I paused and chose my words. 'If you will allow me to speak with the Count, I will ask for you and the boy to join us for meals. I'm sure no scandal would be caused. I have no doubt you had the freedom of the residency before we arrived. It would sadden me to think that you were both confined now to these rooms.'

The woman looked back from attending to the lamp and smiled more brightly. 'The Lord Count is my only kinsman,' she said. 'That does not make him my keeper. I am a widow, and am free to come and go as I please. I have stayed up here only because my presence might have been thought an inconvenience to yourself. And it would please me to be able to eat in comfort.' She came and stood again beside the bed. 'I do believe I heard young children crying after you had entered the residency. If so, Theodore would surely delight in their company. He sees no children of his own age. Even much younger children would be a joy for him.'

I took a few steps backwards in the direction of the door. You can always be sure when you think you fancy someone rotten. You can usually be sure when you think someone fancies *you* rotten. I was pretty sure on both counts. For the moment, it wouldn't do to outstay my welcome. Besides, there was something faintly unpleasant about that aromatic smell. There was a hint of beeswax about it, and of something much dryer and sweeter that I couldn't place. The woman seemed unaware of it. But if it was intended as medicine for young Theodore, she'd long since have grown too used to it to notice the smell.

I turned various stratagems over in my mind. 'I regret that I didn't catch your name,' I finally said. There was a very white flash of lightning.

She laughed, now happily. 'Then you must forgive my want of manners,' she said once the thunder had done its work. 'I am Euphemia, born and married in Tarsus, widowed in Hierapolis, now transplanted to Athens.'

'Then, My Lady Euphemia,' I said with a bow, 'I am delighted to make your acquaintance.' Without bothering to die away, the storm seemed now to have stopped. I could hear the rain, no longer driven by wind, pattering gently on the window panes. A perfectly irrelevant thought crossed my mind. That disembodied voice in my dream had addressed me not in Greek, nor even in Latin, but in English. How very peculiar!

18

The storm really had ended, and ended as abruptly as a water jet is turned off. Now, as I went back through those desolate rooms, the clouds vanished and the still and silvery light of a fullish moon streamed through every window. Now in what would, but for the continued splashing of water from a dozen entry points overhead, have been complete silence, I padded over floors of various covering. The relative silence and the new patterns of light and shadow made it seem I was in a different place entirely. The family mural shone with a brightness that bleached all colour from the faces. Except for the outstretched right arm, Demosthenes stood in darkness. Every statue that remained and every moulding on the ceilings and walls threw still and impenetrable shadows.

I felt comfortable only when back in the library. I'd left the lamps burning away, and these, plus the light of the moon, showed the room to better effect – and to worse. I'd been right about the glass bricks of the dome. They gave the ceiling a greenish translucency. Though still not enough for easy reading, the combined light allowed me to see still more books. They lay in abandoned jumbles beside the racks that had once housed them, and in untidy piles against the far wall.

It was now that I saw the remains of a small bonfire in the middle of the room. It wasn't worth asking how I'd missed it before. As said, the light was completely different. I picked up a chair leg and poked the embers. They were long since cooled, and all covered in dust. In better light, I could have tried looking at the charred scraps of writing surface to see what had given such offence. But I really couldn't be bothered. It was enough to wonder if there'd once been a riot in the building. That would explain the chaos in the library.

I went back to the table and sat down again. The pages of Gregory of Nyassa shone an unearthly pale in the moonlight, the ink showing a kind of red that it would never possess in normal light. I pushed the heavy volume to the other side of the table and waited for the cloud of dust I'd thrown up to settle. Theology was the last thing on my mind at that moment. I was thinking hard of Euphemia. Watching her bob up and down in that tight robe, all loving concern for the sick child, had set off any number of pleasing reflections. I squeezed my eyes shut and tried to think of something else. I only saw Euphemia more clearly. No effort of will could shut off the slow removal of clothing and the look of cool desire on her face. I opened my eyes and tried to focus on the bust of Polybius. He sneered back at me to no effect. I leaned forward and tried to look at Gregory. The tiny writing danced and wavered and blurred to bars of blood redness.

'No,' I croaked, 'no, not here!' But I was already lost. As if I were watching someone else, I wriggled myself into a comfortable position within the cushions that padded the chair. I raised my legs and reached about until my feet made contact with the inner legs of the table. I pushed hard. The table was too heavy to move from its spot, but the chair moved back a couple of feet until it made contact with the window seat. Now trembling, I squeezed one of my very firm nipples. From far off beyond the pounding in both ears, I heard a groan of lust. What remained of my willpower gave way entirely, and I could see that wanton and now fully unclothed body as clearly as if it had stood before me. Even as it merged into the naked girl of my dream, horror only added to the arousal.

Since my intention here is to write a kind of history, I see no value in giving close description to the act of self-pleasuring that followed. Writing about sex of any kind is rather like writing about eating. No matter how skilfully it's done, it doesn't make a hungry man full. You do it. You enjoy it. You put it aside. I'll not deny that I enjoyed myself about as well as anyone could with no assistance but his own hands and a fevered imagination. What little sense of time I'd managed to possess now vanished. In total self-absorption, I sprawled for what may have been an age in that chair. At last, in full exhaustion, my body chill with sweat, white flashes of ecstasy still going off behind my eyes more intense than any lightning, I slowly untensed and came back into the normal stream of time.

I opened my eyes. The light was good enough for me to take everything in at once. I doubt if the slight contracting of muscles, to reach for the broken chair leg was even noticed. I relaxed fully and squirmed against the rough cushions. I smiled and reached up to brush a lock of hair from my eyes.

'Hello, Martin,' I said lazily. 'Have you shat the bed?'

Martin swallowed and looked about for words. 'What are you doing?' he eventually gasped.

I laughed softly and lay fully back. 'Haven't you ever seen a man having a wank?' I asked. It was an odd sort of question to ask of a man who'd once, in his days as a slave, been put to work in a brothel. I laughed again and reached for the sheet to wipe away the mess that covered my belly and chest. I did think of making some comment on his early life. But it would have been cruel. I sat up and looked past him. There was a shaft of moonlight coming through the windows. It seemed for a moment that a whole cloud of dust was dancing about within it. But I blinked and looked again. Whatever I thought I'd seen was already fading when I looked. Now, it was gone. I put forefinger and thumb together and noticed how sticky they were. I could almost have done some absent person a favour and glued those papyrus sheets in a loose order. But Martin's face was now relaxing, and he was looking more his normal self. He'd put on a dressing gown that was far too small for his bulk, and I could see the tangle of what I knew were ginger hairs that covered his lower gut. It required some effort of imagination to see what had once possessed whoever had finally sold him to the Church to set him to work as an object of pleasure. It was an effort of imagination I didn't currently feel inclined to make.

'But why are *you* here?' I asked. There was a dull and pleasurable ache in every muscle. If Martin hadn't been scowling at me from across the table, I might have set about myself again to settle things entirely. Already, though, I was beginning to feel stupid. Giving way like that in an unknown place – even if I had believed I was alone – hadn't been an entirely sensible act. But it was only Martin. There was no harm done. I looked at the pattern of veins that stood out on my left forearm. The lamps showed the covering of tiny golden hairs, and I was aware again of how uncouth I was beginning to look. Had Euphemia noticed my spot? I wondered. I hoped the light hadn't been good enough for that.

'I saw the light from downstairs,' he said. 'I thought you might be up here to look for something to read.'

I smiled happily and touched my left nipple. Sure enough, it set off more flashes in my mind. But I sighed and pulled myself fully together. I supposed Sveta really had kicked him out of bed – that, or he'd run away from more of her private nagging about the cobwebs and general absence of comfort. I thought of dinner and saw the pained look on his face. Perhaps he had shat the bed!

But I was wrong. 'The storm sent Maximin into one of his crying fits,' he explained. 'Sveta kept him from waking everyone with his screams, but she sent me to find you. She thought it would be necessary for you to comfort him back to sleep.' He broke off and looked nervously about the room. 'Don't you think this room has an evil atmosphere?' he muttered.

Letting the crumpled sheet drop under the table, I stood up and arched my back. I looked at the wreckage of the library and shrugged. Martin had a talent for reading emotions into arrangements of stone and glass and wood. If he chose to announce this place was evil or friendly or supremely good, that was his affair. I could see that it was a question now of finding something to put on and then going off with him to see if my child was still sobbing disconsolately in Sveta's arms.

I took up my lamp and made for the door leading to the staircase. Suddenly, I stopped. I listened hard. Far below, in the main block of the residency, I could hear voices. They were argumentative but too low for me to catch any words. I was about to step forward again, when I heard the scrape of sandals on the stairs.

Normally, I'd have stood there and waited to see who else was wandering about this place in the middle of the night. I might even have learned something. But I was stark naked. Worse than that, I had another stiffy that I didn't think would go down in time. All that, plus Martin for company, might be made a reason for comment by whoever was coming up the stairs. I put the lamp on one of the window seats and pinched hard on the wick. I hurried back to where Martin was frozen to the spot. I put out his own lamp and took him by the arm and forced him silently over the less crunchy areas of mosaic to where a couple of bookracks had fallen together. If we took refuge here, we'd be out of sight until the library was clear again.

'Oh, get down, you fool!' I whispered as I pushed hard on the top of Martin's head. I took a final look across the littered floor of the library to where the moon shone back at me, distorted to twice its normal size by the little panes of window glass. I had an irrelevant thought about what use I might somehow make of glass shaped with better order. Then I heard the renewed sound of much closer voices to my right, and forced myself down into the shadow of those bookracks.

As I'd already gathered from the voices, it was Nicephorus and someone else. 'How should I have guessed it would be found – and by the young barbarian?' that someone else insisted in a tone of finality as he paused just outside the door to the library. 'Just be thankful it was done in time.' I heard him walk in and stop. He breathed in and gave a long and satisfied sigh. 'But I tell you again, My Lord Count, this room is a place of the greatest potency. When, at the beginning of time, Athens was appointed as the centre of the world, two lines of the Primal force were set running through your palace. They meet in this very room. Was it not here that Plato was visited by the spirits that revealed their fundamental wisdom?' He breathed in again, and now mumbled a few words of gibberish.

But he took up again. 'The power invested in this building is enough to contain every evil,' he said with a thrilling descent.

'Properly harnessed, it can protect against every evil. And, after this one, I promise, we have just six more nights till the stars are again in their long-awaited place. Then, once more, shall be the time of greatest strength and greatest weakness.'

I really couldn't help myself. When a man comes out with this sort of thing in a combination of bad Greek and a fancy accent, how can you not poke your head up for a quick look? I did for just a moment, and then dodged back down to where Martin was twitching and shivering beside me. I'd seen a tallish man – far taller than any of the local people I'd seen that day – probably in late middle age. I think the mop of dark hair beneath his hat was a wig. Under his cloak, he wore a robe of dark linen painted all over with stars and moons and astrological symbols. Beside him, silent and looking angry beyond belief, Nicephorus was slowly hopping from one foot to the other.

'You promised he'd never get here,' Nicephorus now said accusingly. 'You said the storms you'd raised would sink his ship. Yet here he is, safe under this very roof.'

I pricked up my ears at this. Martin's whispered prayer might not reach all the way over to the door, but was getting on my tits. I silenced him with a quick elbow to one of the fleshier parts of his back and listened harder.

'The Great Goddess serves those who are pure of heart,' the other man replied in a tone of still greater superiority. 'But who can divine her ultimate purpose? If she has allowed him to survive the perils of the sea, and return to the site of his previous outrages, it is assuredly for a good purpose.'

Return? I thought. With a stab of disappointment, I realised it was Priscus they were discussing, not me. But never mind this, I told myself. I still might learn something. Even deliberate spying, I knew already, can be a gamble. You often learn nothing at all – what you overhear makes sense only in terms of what you haven't heard. Sometimes, though, you do get lucky. This might be one of those latter occasions. Already, I gathered that Nicephorus was an accomplice to murder. I'd see what else I could learn.

I heard the two men walk past me. They continued left until

they must have reached the ring of lamps. I looked up again. Yes, they were both by the table. Arms outspread in some gesture of reception as he breathed in the air of this allegedly *potent* room, the other man had his back to me.

Nicephorus was looking down at the open book. 'I want you to make him go away,' he said, for once managing to sound like the civil and military ruler of Athens. 'If you have any real powers at all, Balthazar, *you must get rid of him*!'

Immediately, as if on cue, came the quavering voice: 'Is that you up there, Nicephorus?'

I heard Priscus call from the bottom of the stairs. I heard the uncertain scrape of indoor sandals on the beads as he set one foot on the stairs, and then another.

19

Here, in the library, there was a moment of panic. 'You must hide,' Nicephorus cried in sudden though soft despair. 'Look, just go over there.' Luckily, they were a long way over to my left, and the fallen bookracks where Balthazar now took cover didn't allow him to see the pair of us.

'Isn't this wonderful?' I whispered happily. Things were turning out better than I'd even dared to hope.

Martin gave a strangled sob beside me and let himself down fully on to the loose mosaic tiles. As they scraped a little under his belly, I thought he'd fallen dead with fright. But he breathed again finally, and, now in Celtic, started another whispered round of prayer.

And it really was wonderful! I'd been rained out of my bed in a filthy mood. Now, if I'd believed anything at all, I'd have been muttering prayers of my own – but, in my case, prayers of thanks.

Priscus came into the library. I heard nothing for a moment but the gasping of a man who's had trouble with a dozen steps. But he pulled himself together soon enough. 'Ah, dear Nicephorus!' he called, now in a tone of nasty enjoyment. 'I thought I'd find you up here. Even if you aren't much of a reading man, this always was your favourite place for skulking away by night.'

I didn't dare look up this time – Priscus had eyes in the back of his head, and at the sides. But he'd paused again, and I could easily imagine how he was looking about. I was right.

'This building is still more of a dump than the last time I was stuck in it!' he spat. I heard a scrape, followed by a spattering of mosaic tiles, as he kicked viciously at the floor. 'That hovel of a room you've given me is cold enough for making ice.' He kicked again at the floor. Then he laughed. I heard him walk quickly past where we were hiding as he made for the table. There was no glow of lamplight on the glass bricks overhead. Trust Priscus to be wandering about in total darkness. He stopped, and I think he now kicked at an unravelled book on the ground. 'But I can see that, even if you've turned from peculation to wholesale embezzlement, you still haven't been found out by that duffer in Corinth.' He laughed again, and I heard the faint crunch of cushions as he reached the good chair and sat down in it.

'I never thought you'd dare return,' Nicephorus said with a recovery of nerve. 'What do you want now?'

'Oh, don't flatter yourself I'm here by any exercise of free choice,' came the reply. 'I just happened to be with bastard Alaric when he got sent here to chair that fucking Church council. Believe me when I say that Athens was the last place I fancied dropping by on my way back to Constantinople.'

'So who is that blond boy we're all supposed to grovel to?' Nicephorus asked. 'The letters I had gave me to expect someone much older.'

The reply now was a long and contemptuous chuckle. 'The *Senator* Alaric,' he added, 'is the current apple of Caesar's eye. If I didn't know the fool better, I'd have said he fancied the boy. But Alaric really is just a eunuch with balls. He's one of those men without deep connections, who do as they're told and can't raise any challenge, no matter how they're promoted, nor how they're pulled back down. Yes, he's the current apple of Caesar's eye – and the fly in my own ointment. He's some barbarian from God knows where in the West. He rolled into the City two years back, and has stuck about ever since like a bad smell.'

There was another long pause, during which I took a chance and looked up again. I put my head back down at once. Priscus was turned away from me. But I could see Balthazar looking up from behind his own cover. One look right, and he'd need to be blind not to see me.

I think Priscus swung his feet on to the table. 'But let's not be so dismissive about dear little Alaric,' he said gloatingly. 'He's not so bright as he thinks himself. But don't be deceived by those pretty boy looks. Neither is he a fool. He's been pissing in my bathwater these past two years, and I still haven't managed to bump him off. That, you'll appreciate, needs either great skill or great luck – let's just say it needs both. If you think he isn't already suspicious about your accounting, you're a bigger fool than you look. Tomorrow, he'll get hold of you and start asking questions about the use of that direct grant you've been thieving. Give him one look at your accounts, and he'll turn very nasty. And you'll be bleeding lucky if he stops his enquiries there – yes, bleeding lucky, I can tell you.'

'And what, pray, do you mean by *that*?' Nicephorus asked with a failed attempt at sharpness.

There was a long moment of silence, broken finally by a low and menacing chuckle from Priscus. 'You don't need me to tell you he's a tow-headed barbarian,' he said. 'Well, my darling little Syrian, jumped-up clerk that you are, you look hard enough past that fancy diction and those finicky ways, and you'll see barbarian right the way down. He has a very strong moral sense, that young lad. He'll do you for bloody murder, and hand you straight over to me for execution. Don't expect me to put in any pleas for clemency.'

Was that my name I heard from Nicephorus? He'd broken down rather fast, and was now reduced to faint whispers of protest and supplication.

Priscus gave one of his more villainous laughs, and I heard a loud scrape and a creaking of wood as he got up from the chair. 'And you give me one reason why I should even try saving your worthless hide,' he sneered. I heard what may have been the thud of knees on the floor, and then the muffled voice of what may have been a face buried in clothing. Now, I heard a yelp and the sound of scattered mosaic tiles.

I couldn't resist the urge. I tried, but couldn't resist. I held my breath and darted my head up for another look. There, in the moonlight and the glow from the lamps, I saw Nicephorus grovelling on his belly a few yards from where Priscus stood with his chin jutted forward. Looking straight forward, Balthazar wasn't even trying to keep his head down.

'Did you ever see a man crucified?' Priscus asked.

The answer was a terrified squeal and a babble of pleading that trailed off into Syriac.

'Let's ignore the details,' Priscus went on in a conversational tone. 'But I was crucified for half a morning when I was a cadet. It was a good lesson. Pain in itself can be handled. It's the fear of lasting and even fatal damage that breaks you. Once he's finished his inexorable questioning – and it's amazing what he can learn without even the threat of racking – that blond boy will condemn you for false accounting and sorcery. He'll not come and watch when I have you nailed to a shithouse door in this place. But he'll get pissy drunk with me after it's all done.' I was looking again. Priscus threw his head right back and laughed softly. He laughed so much, he staggered slightly. He steadied himself against one of the overturned tables and sat down again. 'It was a shame, let me tell you, when the Great Constantine banned crucifixion after he converted to the Faith – such a fine penalty withdrawn from the arsenal of the state!'

He paused in mid-laugh. 'But have you been playing with yourself in this chair?' he asked accusingly. 'Look' – he lifted his right arm – 'there's wank all over my sleeve.' Like some reptile, he shot out his tongue and licked at the crumpled silk he was wearing. 'Yes, that's wank,' he sneered. 'You disgust me!'

Beside me, Martin suddenly let out a long fart. It was too gentle to be heard above the loud babbling, now in Syriac, from Nicephorus, who was back on his knees. But the frogs had definitely made their way to the relevant area of Martin's insides, and the smell would have startled a dead fox. If I had to suppress a coughing fit, though, the smell didn't seem to reach across the room to where Nicephorus had caught Priscus by the lower legs and was now trying to kiss his feet. Priscus sneered something also in Syriac that sounded awful. He kicked out, and laughed at the no longer subdued cry of pain.

He got up and followed Nicephorus as he tried to crawl under a broken table. He stood over him and gloried in his power. 'But, my dear, dear Nicephorus,' he said, now at his most charming. 'There really is no need for unpleasantness. We parted as friends. It is as a friend that I return to Athens. Of course, I'll stand by you when Alaric gets round to questioning you. I'll take him off any path that leads to suspicions of a capital offence. I'll not ask what you've done with *all* the Emperor's money. But I can see the deal you made two years ago is holding. You keep reporting back to Governor Timothy that Athens is too poor to tax. The locals don't complain about your total filching of the budget. So long as Timothy remains too lazy to get himself over here, you can spend your ill-gotten gains as you please.' He laughed, and I heard what may have been the scrape of a hand on dust-covered wood. This may have been followed by the rubbing together of dirty hands. 'Oh, Nicephorus, Nicephorus.' He laughed. 'I said I'd not ask what's become of the money. But I can wonder about the lack of slaves even to keep this place habitable.'

'What do you want?' Nicephorus asked pleadingly. 'Just say what you want – I'll do it.'

There was another long creak as Priscus sat down again and made himself comfortable. 'Don't ask me why the Great Augustus has called this bloody council together in Athens,' he drawled. 'The man's a right fool – you can take that from someone who knows him very well. But why Athens, when all his reports tell him the place is a heap of ruins? No point, though, trying to understand the workings of a mind far below even yours. It doesn't suit your convenience to have the place crawling with nosy priests. It certainly doesn't suit mine to have them reach agreement with Alaric at their head.

'So do be a love, Nicephorus, and have the boy killed for me.'

There was an explosion of horrified protest. I heard the scrape of more loose mosaic tiles as Nicephorus got to his feet, and another creak as Priscus got up.

'Oh shut up, you fuckwit Syrian!' he snapped. 'I'm not asking for much. Just kill the little shit. I imagine that loser Balthazar is still leeching money out of you? Well, it's about time he and his friends did something tangible to earn their keep. Just make sure that, when it is done, there is nothing that a full commission of enquiry can pin on me.

'Do that, dearest heart, and you can shuffle, unaudited, round this glorified cowshed till you retire – or your "researches" reach some triumphant conclusion and I have to grovel to you.' Priscus laughed. He may have picked up another of the fallen book rolls.

I pulled my head right down as he turned and walked in my direction. I didn't breathe – Martin didn't breathe – as he hovered just inches from where we cowered. I heard the crackle of papyrus and a snort of contempt. I heard the book hit the floor and unravel. Then, Priscus was walking quickly back to the door. I heard him stop just beyond it.

'I'm doing you a mighty favour, Nicephorus,' he said. 'Do as I ask, and I'll stand by you all the way to Hell and back. Fail me, and I'll put you there myself.

'Yes, my dear little man,' he said after more whining from Nicephorus, 'I'll get myself to sleep by composing his funeral speech. It'll be the finest thing Athens has heard since Demosthenes topped himself. I'll deliver it with a ripe onion cupped in my hand.' He paused again and sniggered. 'I really am counting on you, Nicephorus – don't let me down!'

I heard the sound of his feet on the beads as I counted him down the stairs. There was a loud sobbing over by the desk. For the first time, I noticed the loud splattering of water from a broken downpipe outside the window. But Balthazar was now clambering out from behind his hiding place, and he was trying to jolly some appearance of manhood back into Nicephorus.

'Those were most ungracious comments,' he said when Nicephorus had finally unclamped both hands from his face, 'particularly, I might observe, as they applied to me! Nevertheless, you can be sure that I looked fully upon His Magnificence the Senator Priscus, and I saw the Hand of Death on his shoulder. Did you not see how old he has become in just two years? He will not trouble us much longer.'

'That's what you said about him at the beginning of the month,'

Nicephorus sobbed. 'But he's here.' He went down on his knees again. 'And you haven't seen the blond boy. He's read all the public wisdom of the ancients. He's big and strong enough to crush a man's windpipe in one hand—'

'Silence!' Balthazar cried with a dramatic upward sweep of both arms. 'Can you not feel it? Are you not aware of the Presence in this room? I tell you, Nicephorus of Tarsus, *we are not alone!*'

Beside me, Martin froze. For a very short moment, I thought of getting myself right down again on the floor. But it was just more fraud to silence the Count. Balthazar was uttering another stream of gibberish in what I knew must be a made-up language.

'I watched the boy's arrival in Athens,' he said with a dismissive wave. 'Using powers that are allowed only to me, I have looked into his mind. He is a dirty savage, fit only to smear butter into his yellow hair. Before you waste time on killing him, let us call on the Goddess to take him and his vicious debauchee of a friend together out of this world.'

A dirty savage, I can tell you, would have been straight out from where I was hiding, to crush a windpipe in each of his hands. I, of course, merely noted that the deal Priscus had offered wasn't to be taken up.

Now Balthazar was walking away, towards the far door that led into the upper depths of the residency. He stopped and looked back at the Count. 'I have told you that so many bishops in Athens are displeasing to the Goddess,' he said. 'Their endless praying to the Jewish Sun God has caused a disruption in the Force. Let us, then, pray as arranged for Priscus and the blond youth to be destroyed, and for the council never to meet. It will please the Goddess. Surely then, she will crown all our long efforts with success.'

I could see Nicephorus looking up at him with a face that glistened with tears in the lamplight. He didn't seem terribly convinced.

But Balthazar was now setting to work with the tones and gestures common to the ministers of every religion when confronted by less than total conviction. 'Come with me,

Nicephorus, Count of Athens,' he declared thrillingly. 'Let us consult the Goddess while the heavens are still washed clean.' He reached out for the door handle. There was a loud scrape as he pulled it back open, and he vanished into the darkness.

I pulled my head down as I heard a soft moan and what may have been a prayer from Nicephorus. I could see the moving reflection on the glass bricks overhead as, lamp in hand, he hurried after Balthazar.

20

Martin and I huddled together a while longer in the silence that resulted. At last, when it seemed clear that the door wouldn't open again, I got up carefully. 'Well, come on,' I whispered, taking him by the arm. 'Don't you want to know what they're about?'

It was a worthless question. Martin sagged forward over one of the bookracks and farted again. His face was in shadow, but I could hear his terrified whisper about the need to get out of here. He pulled his face out of the shadow and reminded me that Sveta was still waiting with Maximin.

'Very well,' I said impatiently – if she couldn't get a frightened child back to sleep, she wasn't the woman who could sometimes frighten even me – 'you stay here and wait.' I hurried over towards the door. I kept to the side of the room, ready to jump under cover if the door opened again.

As I stepped into the renewed darkness of the corridor, I heard a padding of feet behind me.

'You're mad, Aelric,' Martin groaned. 'What do you think you'll say if we're caught?'

I stopped and spread my arms. I slapped my now dry chest. 'I *am* the Emperor's Legate,' I announced. 'If any explanations are needed, they won't be mine.' I hurried forward.

Trying to control his heavy breathing, Martin tagged along behind me. We had no lamp with us, and it was a matter of relying on the moonlight and on my own recollection of what was about us.

I didn't suppose they were heading for Euphemia's room. Hadn't Balthazar said something about an appeal to the sky? Sure enough, opposite the niche where Demosthenes continued his burst of silent eloquence, a door was now open. I looked up about a dozen steps to another open door that led on to the roof. I crept up and looked quickly out. This part of the building was covered by a double roof. The door opened on to a path of nailed lead sheeting that went, in deep shadow, between the two roofs. To my left, the path terminated in a wall of crumbling brick. I stood and listened. I could hear a gentle sigh of wind on roof tiles, but nothing more. Leaving Martin to follow at his own pace, I darted to the right, making sure not to step in any of the puddles or disturb any of the heaps of shattered tile that covered the path.

It was hard to match the roof to the corridors and rooms that it covered. There should have been a turn right at the end of the path. This would have taken us on to the roof covering the back block of the residency. Instead, after the beginnings of a path, progress in that direction was closed by another wall. I could only go further if I went back and climbed a ladder that went all the way to the top of the left-hand roof. As I set a foot on the lowest rung and tested its strength, Martin clutched at me.

'Let's go back,' he pleaded. 'Can't you feel the evil all about us?'

'Oh, shut up!' I answered. 'Stay here and be ready to make a dash if I hurry down.' I tested the next rung, and then the next. The ladder had been here a long time, and the wood was rotted through in places. Though reinforced with iron bars, these too had rusted, and one of the rungs sagged under my weight. Even as I was ready to pull myself to the top and look over, Martin clamped both arms about my middle and pressed a hot, sweaty face into the small of my back.

But I also had heard the noise. It was a low obscenity, followed by another man's laugh, and had come from back where we'd come out on to the roof.

'O Jesus!' Martin groaned. 'Sweet and merciful Jesus!' He'd probably have dithered there till he was caught. But I was straight off the ladder and dragging him into the dead end that may once have led to the far block of the residency.

It was just in time. Even as I got him down to the ground, from where he'd have trouble bolting, the voices grew louder. 'The

Leader said it would stop raining,' someone insisted in a poor but comprehensible Greek. 'And it rains no more. The Force burns strong within him tonight!'

The response had a tone of piety about it, but was too peculiar in its intonation for me to make out the actual words. I hadn't been in Athens a day, and I still couldn't make much sense at all of the local dialect. But something told me these weren't Athenians. There was a muffled but anticipatory laugh as the ladder creaked under someone's weight. Though I'd have been in deep shadow, I didn't dare look out from where we were hiding. My hair alone would have shone like a beacon in the darkness. I kept my breathing under control and counted perhaps a dozen men up the ladder and on to the roof. It was only when I heard no more sounds from the passage between the roofs that I allowed myself a single quick glance. We were now quite alone again.

'Let's get out of here,' Martin whispered pleadingly.

I reached down to push him into silence, but got him on the stump of his missing ear. By the time I'd finished apologising and hugging him, there could have been no one at all dawdling near the top of the ladder. I took hold of it and prepared to step as noiselessly as I could back on to the lowest rung.

'You aren't serious . . . ?' Martin gasped. I laughed softly and stepped on to the ladder. Trying not to make any noise, I climbed to the top and looked cautiously over.

The moon was behind me. Its pale light shone over a large expanse of lead that rose in its centre to a low dome that I guessed was the roof of the courtroom. I couldn't see Nicephorus or the other men. But I could see Balthazar; rather, I saw his head just beyond the leaded dome. From its angle and the waving arms that shone silver in the moonlight, I could imagine that everyone else was down on his belly for a superstitious grovel.

'Have you no faith in the Goddess?' Balthazar cried. Though he must have been twenty yards away, his voice had the unnatural closeness of sounds at night. He bent forward out of sight, and I heard a general groan of terror. Balthazar came back in sight, his arms still raised. 'O men of little faith,' he said, 'behold now the power she gives to her servant!' He rubbed his hands together. As he pulled them apart, they both caught fire. He clapped them together again, and they went out.

My weight, pressing forward on the ladder, was already causing one of the roof tiles to crumble. Add to that an almost irresistible urge to burst out laughing, and I thought I'd crash sideways. But I shifted position and the ladder stabilised. I could see the shadow of my head on the damp and pitted sheeting. I was suddenly aware of how cold I was, now I was standing still in the breeze of an autumn night.

'What can you see?' Martin croaked from below.

I freed my left hand from the ladder and waved at him to shut up. His response was a spluttering fart and a smell that almost knocked me off the ladder. I looked again across the bright expanse of lead. I could see that Balthazar had put his arms down. I knew from my early days in the Church, where I'd assisted in the production of 'miracles' to bring over the Kentish heathen, that he'd need to piss on his hands soon if the skin wasn't to peel off them. But Nicephorus was getting over his earlier fright. From behind the dome, I could hear the firm cries for enlightenment of a man who's pretty sure of getting his way.

'I tell you,' Balthazar cried with another dramatic wave, 'that the woman knows nothing. The child knows nothing. The intruders know nothing.'

Unless she was fast asleep, Euphemia must have been deaf not to hear all this wailing. We couldn't have been that far from her rooms, and the sound really was carrying. But Balthazar and his whole congregation were now raving back and forth at each other in some stupid but long-practised litany about the Goddess and her Force, and the wondrous things she would soon assure to her followers pure in heart. I heard the voice of Nicephorus raised above all the others. Leave aside the sorcery charges I was now determined to throw at him for that girl's murder, anyone who could have been taken in by this shite for at least two years deserved immediate removal from office and transfer to a monastery for the insane.

I could have remained there until they all set out on their return. I could then have cowered with Martin in the shadows, and followed them about whatever other business they might still have. But the breeze was now become an insistent, frigid wind. My teeth chattered. I could feel my nipples tighten to painful dots, and a shrinking in my crotch to the dimensions and probable appearance of a prepubescent boy. Over on the roof, everyone had joined hands and was dancing in and out like girls at a wedding feast. The only words I could catch in this had no meaning. More important was who these people were. There was Nicephorus, of course, and Balthazar. With them, though, I could see perhaps a dozen men in the same dark clothes as the men I'd seen at the back of the crowd in Piraeus. I really wanted to see more. However, I was now shaking uncontrollably. It was as much as I could do to get silently down the ladder and fight to stop myself from curling into a ball.

'Hold on to me Aelric, hold on,' Martin cried softly. He put his arms round me and shared some of his blubbery warmth. 'There is evil all about us,' he said, pulling away to make the sign of the cross. 'It ripples from that damnable group in freezing waves. Come quickly, or be drained of the life they must extract for their Hell-bound blasphemies.'

I might have giggled through chattering teeth at his belief that the night breeze was other than a nuisance. But I was badly in need of the heat from his body. I'd noticed how the cold was reaching deep inside me as Balthazar had done his conjuring trick with the powder on his hands. From that, I'd gone in moments to the edge of collapse. Without Martin to keep his body against mine and drag me back along the path, I can't say how I'd have got back to the comparative warmth of the residency.

We stopped for a moment in the library, where Martin shook out the crumpled-up sheet and got it over me like a cloak. 'What did you see?' he asked with a nervous look at the reclosed door. 'I heard enough. But tell me what you saw.'

'Not very much,' I said, fighting off another attack of the shivers. I pulled myself together. 'Martin,' I said firmly, 'I don't want you to breathe a word of this, not even to Sveta. Do you understand?'

Shivering himself, he looked about. 'I told you this place had an evil atmosphere,' he said. 'Can you really not feel it surrounding you like a fog?'

My answer was a non-committal shrug. Still cold all over, I was coming out of the fit that had almost downed me on the roof. So long as he kept his mouth shut – and I knew he would – he was welcome to his fancies. I looked again at the closed door. It might reopen at any moment, and I was unarmed. I waited for Martin to get both our lamps lit. This time, we were entirely alone. I let him go first down the stairs, noting with tired approval that he managed to step without making any noise. I looked briefly back into the library. Outside the pool of light from the lamps, the moon was back to playing funny tricks with the dust.

21

'For a man who says he's too sick even to leave his bed,' I said in Latin, 'His Excellency in Corinth is a wondrously busy correspondent.' I eased myself down a few inches into the lukewarm water, and looked again at my face in the mirror I was holding. The spot on my nose was now definitely ripe. The bitch was it had been joined by another. I turned my attention back to Martin. He was sitting in the glow of sunlight that was reflected down on us from the high, unglazed windows of the bathhouse. I'd been right about the Governor. His letters had come over unrolled, and formed a heap of papyrus several inches thick. It was a short dash across the water from Piraeus. But he must have worked like a demon to get all this over to us. Martin coughed politely and reached for what he considered the most important of the letters.

Beyond the first intake of breath, however, I heard nothing of whatever he read. With a force that reminded me of a heretical baptism I'd once attended, the slave pushed down hard on my shoulders and sent me so far under water that I felt the sudden chill as my legs rose into the air. I felt the mirror land on my belly and then slide off until I heard it scrape against the leaden bottom of the bathtub. As I came up again spluttering, he set about my hair as if it were potter's clay. By the time I was able to go back to any kind of conversation, Martin had put the letter down and was back to chewing on his stale crust. He'd farted while I was under the water, and the smell was almost worth a brief comment.

But, 'I'll read his military update myself,' is all I said. I really hadn't the patience to sit through another attack of the vapours when he read about the barbarian flood gathering north of Thermopylae. 'Then you can summarise anything else that isn't a waste of time.' I sat up and reached for the cup of ginger cordial that Martin had set for me on the little table that was attached to the bath. Heated and with a dash of some local stimulant, it was an improvement on all the wine I'd so far been served. 'You know, I'm wondering about the value of a trip over to Corinth. If the Governor really is ill, it could be made to look as if I actually cared for the man. And, though you and I have business in Athens, Sveta and the children might be more comfy in the provincial capital.'

I was expecting some reaction from Martin to this very diplomatic admission that Athens might not be completely safe. But it was now that the slave spoke. Rather, he giggled and let out a sentence of what sounded like Egyptian while poking at my nose. I frowned and gripped the sides of the bath. He repeated himself and gave me another poke. Would it be unreasonable, I wondered, if I stood up and boxed his ears? Or might it show a certain want of dignity?

'I think he's asking if you'd like him to suck out the pus,' Martin explained, seemingly unaware of my admission.

He was right. The slave had spoken in the local dialect. Now I bothered listening, it did have a Greek base, but was so corrupted, and so mixed in Slavic words and grammatical forms, that it might have been a different language. Sad, I thought, that Athens had come to this. I nodded and tried to ignore the blast of stinking breath and the scrape of teeth against my nose.

'Have you seen our host yet?' I asked as the slave pulled momentarily back and spat a mouthful of goo into the water. Even if he was rather an unlikely spy, I might as well avoid any mention of names or titles that had meaning in Greek as well as Latin.

Martin nodded. 'He was up before me,' he said. 'He got the big slave to heat your bathwater. He said he'd not be able to join you for breakfast, but would arrange a tour for you of Athens. He had a black eye,' he added.

I waited for the slave to suck again on my nose. 'I choose to assume he's off on some official business,' I said. 'For sure, with no one employed to copy letters, or even deliver them, he must be running about Athens like a blue-arsed fly.' I closed my eyes as the slave attached himself still harder to my nose, and thought about possible departure times for Corinth. I had no great wish to see the Governor. But I did want Sveta and the children safe behind the walls of the provincial capital. Also, I was short of cash. What Martin had handed back to me might have got him and my other people to Rome. But, now I'd be in Athens for some while – and now I'd heard it plain the whole official budget was embezzled – I needed some Jewish or Syrian banker to cash a draft for me. If I wanted any degree of comfort, I'd need slaves of my own to clean up my part of the residency. I might even get some of the heating back into working order.

The slave finally pulled back from my face, and I watched his pink spittle dissolve in the bathwater. I resisted the urge to put a finger to my nose. I sat up again and reached forward for the mirror. I wiped it clear and looked at the bright swelling. Had this been, in any sense, a worthwhile treatment? I put the mirror on the table beside my cup and changed the subject.

'There is,' I said to Martin, 'a summary of the issue that I prepared for the orthodox and heretical Patriarchs of Alexandria. I believe you packed it in the smaller document box. You'll need to make certain obvious cuts. But I'll be most grateful if you could translate it into Latin for me to read out to the Western delegates. If they've arrived yet, and if there are no contrary instructions from the Emperor, I think I'll convene the council the day after tomorrow. We'll have a nice Sunday service, where everyone can be sworn to secrecy. Then we'll proceed to whatever place of meeting Nicephorus has been ordered to make ready for us. The clearer we can make the issues, the sooner we can get everyone to agree the manner of their future discussion.'

'What are you going to do about what you learned last night?' Martin asked suddenly in Celtic. 'The tongue of Saint George will protect us from satanic spells, but—'

'Oh, do shut up, Martin!' I laughed, joining him in Celtic – you can never be too paranoid where even idiot slaves are concerned. 'I've told you many times there is no such thing as magic. You control the forces of Nature by the uncovering of facts and careful reasoning from them. There's no short cut to be had from incantations, or chance resemblances of tree roots to body parts, or whatever. Be aware that the Count is a murderer, aided and assisted by some local charlatan and his agents or servants. There really is nothing more to be said.'

I smiled and reached forward to pat Martin on the back. I noticed too late I was putting a wet stain on his tunic and apologised. 'Look, Martin,' I said earnestly, 'there is no magic. All that chanting does no more harm than the twittering of some bug at night.' I stopped and waited for the look of strain to go out of Martin's face.

Of course, it stayed put. 'And you're not going to act on what we learned last night?' he asked, his mouth dropping open. 'Even if you're planning to overlook the girl, Priscus did say he wanted you dead.'

I stretched and yawned. 'Oh, Martin,' I said, 'what do you suppose I should do – arrest the Commander of the East?' I laughed. 'In the first place, there's the question of where to hold him. Then, there would have to be a trial before the Emperor. Even if we managed to throw in a few accusations of sorcery, the Great Augustus would require *some* evidence – and we really have nothing to offer at present. I hope you'll agree that our only option is to take reasonable care and to wait on further developments. Besides, you may remember that, if our friend did request a murder, his request doesn't seem to have produced anything other than a few more of the magic spells that didn't stop us from getting here in the first place.'

I smiled reassuringly and had another look at myself in the mirror. That gave me an excuse for saying nothing more. Martin did have a point, I had to allow. If sorcery itself is nothing, sorcerers can still be dangerous. The rotting corpse we'd found the day before was proof of that. I changed my train of thought. Murder is murder. Sooner or later, that has to be punished. But I thought again. There was, to my knowledge, neither civil nor military government in Athens. Nicephorus had seen to that. I'd need at least a few days of caution. Balthazar had dismissed me as of no account. Of no account I'd therefore be. I'd make a few ineffectual enquiries about the state of affairs – do less than that, and I'd raise suspicion. Today was Friday. On Monday, I'd be off to Corinth. There, all being well, I'd take charge of things and come back with fifty or sixty armed men. The only shame was that I'd not be able to include Priscus in the arrests. But I really would try every one of those bastards for murder, from Nicephorus down, and throw in a sorcery charge to justify the executions. Even without the brilliant success I had in mind for the council, Heraclius would wet himself with joy as he read my account of the proceedings in Athens.

Or perhaps I'd do nothing at all, I told myself with yet another change of thought. I might not even make a trip to Corinth. I could send Martin over with letters. He and the others could stay there. The money I wanted could come back by courier. The most important single job in hand was getting that bloody council under way. Could I afford any time at all outside Athens? And what might be the effect of a full-blown sorcery investigation on those already skittish priests? Murder is murder. You don't walk by on the other side when you see it. But I'd been sent here under a cloud. My one chance of redeeming myself was to get agreement on the importance of that Single Will argument I'd fabricated out of nothing. Murder is murder. But there was a religious dispute to be settled here in Athens. Back in Constantinople, there was an interlocking set of crises brought on by disaster in the war with Persia – and who else was there but me who could even understand them, let alone resolve them? My own interest aside, perhaps I should just keep all focus on the job in hand. Would justice in the main really be served by making a fuss here? *Fiat iustitia ruat caelum* is a fine motto for lawyers with no wider duties to consider. But would the skies not fall everywhere in the Empire if I insisted on strict justice here in Athens? Might they not fall on *me*?

Martin suddenly leaned forward and pushed the mirror aside. 'Listen, Aelric,' he urged, 'why don't we just get out of here? If we're all going to Corinth, why stop there? We can all get away together. You say the Governor is useless. He won't even notice if we take ship back to the West. We can—'

'We can do no such thing!' I snapped. 'Since I don't seem to have been dismissed from his service, that oath I swore to Heraclius still holds. My duty is to do what I can for the Empire.' I looked into Martin's drawn face. Surely he could understand the concept of duty. After all, wasn't he also a barbarian? Honour, duty, courage – even a *cowardly* barbarian couldn't set those aside. Or could he?

I sighed and went back to the previous matter. 'Until further notice,' I said firmly, 'last night didn't happen. Trust me, and keep a stiff upper lip.' That was an order, and I expected no more about any supposed magic in Athens, or any more about running away from our undoubted duties. I stood up in the bath and looked across what had been a cavernous steam room. No general heating, of course, meant no steam. But having the lead tub moved in had at least reminded me of the comforts I was missing. I climbed carefully out and stood shivering on the unheated tiles. I took the towel Martin passed me and rubbed myself dry. The rain that had gone away when the big storm ended didn't look as if it would return for a while. If so early in the morning was any indication, we had a fine day ahead. Already, there was a bright patch of sunlight inching its way down the plain bricks of the domed wall.

'You,' I said to the slave in very slow and simple Greek, 'take up this mirror and hold it while I shave myself.' Whether or not he'd sorted out my spots, he could help get that shameful blond bristle off my body. I stared back at a thoroughly idiotic smile on his face. I tried him in one of the Slavic dialects that I knew was spoken south of the Danube. It didn't help. 'Oh, go away!' I groaned. 'Go and report for cleaning duty.' I stepped out of the pool of sunlight that had now just reached where I was standing and grabbed both oil and razor. I pointed at the door. 'Get out!' I roared.

The slave finally understood me and scurried out, leaving the door wide open.

'Martin,' I said, once he had returned from closing the door, 'I don't like to remind you of less pleasant days. But I do believe you once did bathroom duties when you were a slave. If I can do the rest myself, do be so kind as to shave my back.'

I was inspecting the underside of my crotch in the mirror when the door opened again. It was the idiot slave come back. He capered about, shaking his head and pointing at my crotch. He laughed and clapped his hands and let out another burst of nonsense. This time, I made an effort to listen. He *was* speaking a kind of Greek. The main problem was that he was defective in the head.

'I gather the Western delegates have now arrived,' I said to Martin. 'Am I right in believing, however, that the Pope himself is outside?'

'Not His Holiness in person,' came the reply in a voice I'd never thought – or hoped – I'd hear again. 'And, I assure you, there is nothing immediate about our arrival. We have been kept waiting here longer than we might have wished.' I'd put my question in Latin, and I'd been answered in Latin.

I looked over at the door. A monk beside him, who was trying his best to pull the front of his hood over his eyes, there stood my old friend the Dispensator.

'The head of the Roman delegation offers his deepest respects,' he said, 'and would have an audience with the Lord Senator.' He ignored the fact that I was standing naked with my legs apart and showing every appearance of trying to sodomise myself with the handle of a bronze mirror. In both general and specific circumstances, a prostration would have been out of the question – at any rate, from him. But he did manage a very stiff bow.

22

'My Lord Fortunatus!' I cried. I hurried across the room, hardly noticing that the towel Martin had tried to wrap about me fell off after two paces. 'This is a most unexpected honour.'

He raised his arms for an official embrace. Our lips met without touching in a way that might have impressed a geometry teacher. As soon as decency allowed, I took my hands from his stiff, bony shoulders and helped him into the only chair in the room.

He'd aged a little in the two years since our last meeting. The parchment of his face was paler and more withered. He might have been a touch smaller. But it was the Dispensator, sure enough – chief servant of the Servant of the Servants of Christ. He was the man, that is, who, formally charged with handling the Papal charity, was in fact governor of the Roman Church. So long as he took the trouble to get addled old Boniface to stamp his seal on whatever writing surface embodied it, his word was law in spiritual matters over the whole of those vast regions, mostly now unknown to Constantinople, that looked to Rome.

'My Lord will forgive me,' I said with all the smoothness I could find, 'if I am overcome for the moment by the joy of an acquaintance that I never thought would be renewed.'

He stared back at me while Martin made a better job of getting the towel tied about my waist. It had its convenient side that he'd chosen to come out as head of the Western delegates. No one would ever dare question what agreement we might eventually reach about the questions for a future council. At the same time, someone more junior – and more pliable – would have been more immediately convenient.

The Dispensator settled into his chair beside the leaden bath. 'The Lord Count did assure me,' he said, with a hint of what might have been quiet pleasure or disapproval, 'that you had been drowned on your journey from Constantinople. I rejoice in the knowledge that rumours of your death were an exaggeration.' He fell silent and looked down to where I'd sat before him on the floor. He managed a chilly smile. 'But please do accept my congratulations on your rise to such eminence as you have achieved. I did not imagine, when I asked you to represent us in Constantinople, that your career would so blossom – and at so young an age.'

There was a slight emphasis on the word 'blossom' that I could have taken for insolence. But the man had put up with far worse from me in Rome when our positions were reversed, and I contented myself with a smile.

'Still, God does move in mysterious ways. Even you might appreciate the Divine Providence when it is so plainly displayed.'

I smiled again and reached forward to pour two cups of wine from a tray that the idiot slave had now found the initiative to carry in. The Dispensator tasted it and put his cup on the floor with a finality that indicated I'd have to share the ginger cordial.

'But I must also rejoice,' he went on with a look at Martin, 'to see your secretary in such good health.' Probably, he was looking at the gap where Martin's left ear had been. Priscus had eventually apologised for the 'untoward circumstances' that had compelled him to slice this off. He'd even promised a replacement in red leather just as soon as we were all back in Constantinople. For the moment, Martin was hiding the gap as best he could by combing his few remaining locks of red hair over it. He blushed and covered his embarrassment with a polite bow.

'If you can have that translation ready before lunch, I'll be grateful,' I said to Martin. He took the hint and bowed again. He was followed out by the Dispensator's secretary. As the idiot slave danced after them, I got up and closed the door. I emptied both cups back into the jug, then pulled the napkin off the ginger cordial and refilled the cups. The Dispensator sniffed at his and tasted. He nodded and put it down, this time within easy reach. I sat down.

'I must protest – and I am aware of your status as the Emperor's representative – at the shocking treatment I have been subjected to during the ten days since my arrival in Athens.' He scowled and looked across at the wall behind me. 'I must remind you,' he added, 'that any offence given to me is an offence given to His Holiness the Universal Bishop.'

I got up again. It had been a mistake to sit on the floor where he could look down at me as if at a boy in class. I perched carefully on the edge of the bath. The lead bent slightly under my weight, but didn't buckle and send a flood of cold water over the pair of us.

'In particular,' he said with as dark a scowl as I'd ever seen cross his face, 'I take exception to my not having been informed of your arrival yesterday morning. I had given appropriate orders to all the Latin bishops to mourn your loss at sea. I am most provoked at having not been told that, even as we were tearing our second best robes in lamentation, the Count and all the Greek bishops were welcoming you in Piraeus.' He stopped and turned his mouth down. I put the image he'd suggested straight out of mind. If I didn't, I knew I'd not resist the urge to dissolve in helpless laughter. I might even fall backwards into the water.

He leaned down and recovered his cup. 'Please accept, on behalf of the Universal Bishop, my formal complaint against the Lord Count and against Their Graces the Bishops of Nicaea and of Ephesus. Their joint behaviour, since my arrival in Athens, has been a disgrace. I have no doubt there would be still graver reason for complaint if they were able to speak a word of Latin, or I of Greek.'

He finished his cup and held it out for a refill. 'But let me turn to the matter of interpreters,' he carried on, with a move from the chilly to the frigid. 'The only one of them who is not utterly deficient in Latin showed every appearance, four days ago, of having gone mad. Since then, he has displayed a progressively smaller regard for our comparative positions in the world. This morning,

he did not even see fit to attend on me at dawn. The other interpreters are both insolent and incompetent. One of them was
caught yesterday examining the contents of my writing box. When
my secretary put a knife to his throat, he had the effrontery to
plead direct orders from the Lord Nicephorus.

'I see no point in addressing myself further to the Lord Count.
I now see that, when I spoke to him yesterday, he was already
preparing to hurry off without me to the port. I therefore ask you,
My Lord Alaric, to take such steps as may be required to assert
and maintain the dignity of His Holiness of Rome.'

I slid down from the side of my bath and walked over to
where I'd let the mirror fall. I picked it up and put it on a ledge.
I turned back and tried for a reassuring smile. I caught the look
on his face and thought better of the attempt. 'My Lord
Fortunatus,' I said very smoothly, 'do be assured that, as representative of the Emperor, I regard any affront given to His
Holiness of Rome as an affront to the Great Augustus himself.
It would have pleased me more than I can say to see you on the
dock yesterday morning. I am certainly pleased to see you now,
and do believe that I look forward to a return, in this consulta-
tive meeting, of all the harmony and friendship of our old
dealings.'

Harmony and friendship? Well, that was pushing matters more
than a bit. All I got was a look that might have turned wine to ice.
'The last time we met in Rome,' he said with stony calm, 'you
asked us, on behalf of His Imperial Majesty, not to anathematise a
set of formulations that may not be heretical, but that do not strike
us as fully orthodox. We complied with your request. I now find
that His Holiness the Universal Bishop is required to subscribe to
these formulations. We do, of course, understand the difficulties
the Empire faces within the Egyptian and Syrian Patriarchates.
Even so, the settled position of His Holiness in Rome is that no
clarification of what was agreed at one ecumenical council can be
made except by another ecumenical council.'

I nodded solemnly and managed a second time not to burst out
laughing. An ecumenical council, indeed! When did Rome ever

stand up for Church democracy unless it thought there was some benefit to be had for Rome? Within its own branch of the Church, it had long since allowed less consultation than a drill sergeant does with new recruits. If it was now demanding full consultation, it would only be so Greeks and Syrians and Egyptians could be set against each other and still more concessions of primacy could be extracted for Rome.

'My Lord is surely mistaken,' I said smoothly, 'if His Holiness the Patriarch of Rome is required to subscribe to anything.'

The Dispensator scowled at the implied demotion of Boniface to equality with the other heads of the Church.

I smiled and pressed on. 'The function of this present meeting is merely to explore the possibilities for what may be discussed in future at some wider and more formal gathering.' There was no point wondering how he'd guessed what we were about. Even if I hadn't blackmailed him at our last meeting into avoiding any statement about a Singular Will for Christ, the Roman Church had its spies even inside the Imperial Palace. I could be surprised that Priscus had got wind of my scheme. I'd have been more surprised if Rome *hadn't* known.

I sat back on the edge of the bath and tried to look earnest. 'This is not a regular council of the Church,' I said, 'where hundreds of bishops have been called to reach a conclusion. Rather, it is an almost private seminar, in which only the very best men have been called to a place where they can speak freely – to express their innermost feelings – and from where they can take back a fuller understanding of questions that will be put at some future gathering of the whole Church. I do assure you that no one here is required to subscribe to any new formulations of the Creed.'

'Then perhaps you should tell the Lord Bishops of Nicaea and Ephesus,' he snapped, 'that the best men of *both* Latin and Greek Churches have been invited. The last time that demented interpreter did anything worth calling work, they insisted through him to my face that our liturgies were translations from the Greek rather than coordinate texts. If that is really the opinion nowadays of the Greek Church, I fail to see the benefit of our remaining in Athens.'

'I will see what I can do,' I said emolliently. 'It is certainly the wish of His Holiness of Constantinople, and of His Imperial Majesty, that our Roman Brothers in Christ should be treated with all proper respect. We come together in the fullest love and fellowship of Jesus Christ.' I stopped. I could see that I was wandering across the line separating moral earnestness from parody.

'Can I ask if you have been accommodated to your satisfaction?' I asked with a sudden change of subject. I'd speak to Simeon – yes, buggery Simeon, the worst choice even Heraclius could have made as head of the Greek delegation. Trust a fool to send a fool, I thought. I had another thought that sent a chill straight through me. I put that out of mind. I'd speak to Simeon. I'd know more then. I'd also have Martin cast a look over the interpreters. Otherwise, I could at least ensure that everyone was fed properly and kept warm. I put on a sympathetic face as I heard the complaints about the rats and pigeon droppings in the monastery that had been assigned to the Western delegates. If Rome itself was a heap of stinking ruins, the Lateran kept up certain standards. I'd see what improvements could be made to the accommodation.

'My Lord,' I said, standing up, 'though I am not a churchman, you will appreciate that I am fully aware of all the issues under discussion. I have the greatest confidence in the ability of His Grace of Nicaea to represent the Patriarch of Constantinople. But please do bear in mind that I represent the Emperor, and that he has every reason to ensure that all discussions are as smooth and productive as they possibly can be. The things that are of God must always be left to the men of God. At the same time, you will, I hope, regard me as wholly at your service in all matters that can make your stay in Athens to your complete satisfaction.'

The Dispensator nodded. He even allowed himself a neutral smile.

'I think it would be fitting,' I added, 'if you and your fellow delegates could accept the Count's hospitality for dinner tomorrow. It is a while since I last rejoiced in the Latin spoken by natives of the old Imperial capital. All else aside, there are so many mutual friends of whom I should like to hear.'

That wasn't enough, so I continued: 'Naturally, you will sit at my right hand for dinner.' Still not enough, I could see. Well, I was here to chair things, and it was my decision entirely how they should be chaired. 'I am also able to confirm that, as representative of His Holiness himself, you will, of course, occupy a bishop's chair.' That got his eyes wide open. He might in effect be head of the Roman Church. Formally, he was still only a deacon.

'The moment you first stepped into my office with Father Maximin – but I correct myself: with *Saint* Maximin,' he said with a look of growing ecstasy, 'I knew that you were a most remarkable young man, and that you were destined for greatness.'

That wasn't my recollection of things. If he'd waited a few days before turning openly nasty, neither had it been all love and kisses at our first meeting. But no matter that. I was here to get Rome on side, and this was a good beginning.

I still had no clothes to put on, so I hitched my towel a little higher about my waist and led him from the steam room. I escorted him across a courtyard not yet reached by the sun, and that was still unpleasantly cool, and back into the close-smelling corridors of the residency. They looked better than they had in the night, but were still decidedly smelly from the soaking. We stopped in one of the undivided rooms.

The Dispensator nodded at what had once been a gilded statue of Hadrian. 'Is this where the Emperor stayed on his celebrated visit to Athens?' he asked in a pretty good attempt at the conversational.

'It might have been,' I answered. I guided him round a puddle that had formed under one of the ceiling windows. I gave him a potted history of the building. I might have shown him the chapel, had I known where it was. But the Dispensator had long since rumbled my lack of faith, and pretending any now would only ruin the amicable tone on which we were parting. I led him to the main entrance hall, where his secretary was waiting. Though I must have looked a strange cross between wrestler and bathhouse slave, I followed him out into the Forum of Hadrian and made sure to embrace him again.

'A further matter we shall need to discuss,' he said as he stepped sideways to avoid a pool of mud, 'is the grant you purported to confirm, when last in Rome, of the title of Universal Bishop made to His Holiness.' He stopped and squinted at me in the sunshine. 'You are surely aware that the initial grant was defective, and that your confirmation of it may be void. Our new head of Legal Affairs is assured on both these points.'

I pulled a sympathetic face and spoke of a letter I'd be sending straight off to Heraclius. I'd been wondering if – no, when – he'd get round to that. I'd known all the time, on my last visit to Rome, that my confirmation of the grant was beyond my authority. It had been made by Phocas in his last days as Emperor. All his acts had then been cancelled by Heraclius, and, though exalted, the status in which I'd been clothed for my visit to Rome was nowhere near sufficient to revive a grant cancelled under the Great Seal of the Empire. But it had suited Heraclius for a grant made by Phocas to be taken as binding in Rome, though deniable everywhere else should it ever get us into hot water with the other territorial branches of the Church. Since then, I'd been sitting on letter after letter from the Dispensator. Bearing in mind what was probably going on seven hundred miles away in Constantinople, I'd rather not have to take notice now of his complaints – even if I did possibly have the authority to settle them. If I did have to take notice, though, it would only be at the right moment, and after some very hard bargaining. I'd certainly not be notifying the Emperor of anything until I could get myself alone with him.

I watched as he vanished behind the big sundial. Before going back in, I gave a long sideways glance at the two men in black I'd seen skulking behind a bronze urn that had been anciently set up to receive anonymous denunciations. As in Piraeus, they were covered up from head to toe. With the return of good weather, they must have found so much clothing a very sore trial. They saw me, and dodged fully out of sight. A whole party of local women shuffled past now. Also dressed all over in black, they turned for a moment to look at the residency. A few put out their right hands in the same gesture I'd seen in Piraeus. The woman in front shouted something in the shrill voice of the aged, and everyone hurried across to the other side of the square.

All considered, my stay in Athens was turning out more interesting than I'd expected.

23

I paused on the wide, stepped incline of the Sacred Way, and looked at the Propylaea. We were slightly past noon, and the sun was behind me. If now rather creamy from its great age, the marble of the columns and its unadorned pediment were as crisp today as when it served as gateway to the spiritual heart of the nation that had caused it to be built.

'It was a gift of King Solomon himself,' Nicephorus struck up again in an annoying whine that he might have hoped would be taken for erudition. 'It follows the exact plan of his temple in Jerusalem,' he continued in blithe ignorance of both history and Scripture. 'For its everlasting security, angels fashioned an image of Moses that will come to life and smite the first barbarian to desecrate its sanctity.' He pointed at a statue of what, even without the inscription on its plinth, was obviously the Emperor Julian.

'Do you suppose he's making this up as he goes along?' I muttered in Latin. 'Or does it represent some modern consensus in Athens?'

Martin's answer was a scared look at the men in dark clothes who'd been tagging along ever since we'd left the residency, and were now trying to conceal themselves behind any convenient statue base.

'Don't worry,' I whispered. 'I don't see how he'd dare make a move in broad daylight – not in front of the whole town assembly.' I smiled a reassurance I didn't really feel and led him by the hand within the darkened interior.

I listened to another comment of jaw-dropping stupidity and suppressed a snort. I smiled politely at the Count, whose response was to strike a pose and cross himself with dramatic emphasis. He'd recovered all his nerve since the previous night, and was now basking in the full worship of the great mob of the unwashed who'd also followed us from the residency. I still hadn't made the effort to get him alone. Until then, I might as well play along. I nodded my thanks as he stood back for me to go before him through the gateway.

The day had ripened into a most glorious afternoon. There was still a faint chill about the shadows – this was an autumn day far north of Alexandria. But the previous day's appearance of a Kentish winter had been followed by the warm brilliance of the civilised world. If I looked down from the Sacred Way, the lower part of Athens lay within the clouds of steam that rose from the narrow streets. But, however briefly, we'd had sight of a few glories. My first impression had been of how small everything was. I knew Rome and Constantinople. I'd spent a few months in Alexandria. These were, or had been, immensely large and wealthy capitals. I could now realise that every building there inspired by the ancient styles was something of a fraud. The porticos and various orders of column were simply adornments to vast structures of brick faced with marble. Truly ancient buildings were generally smaller. On the other hand, even when porticos were bricked up and buildings had been converted to unintended uses; even after two devastating barbarian raids, and the other ravages of time and depopulation, what I'd seen was still of astonishing elegance and fineness of proportion.

It would have been better had I been able to know in every case what I was seeing. I'd spent two years in Rome before the Dispensator had jollied me into my fateful trip to Constantinople. Two years, and endless questions of anyone old enough to have heard his grandfather speak of better days – and still there was much I hadn't been able to identify. Book illustrations of a city usually come with little captions to identify the main buildings. In cities still at their best, you learn pretty soon what is what. Such you'll find if you ever make your way to Constantinople. Had I really stood on the Unwrought Stone from where Pericles and

Demosthenes had once addressed the Assembly? Or had this been part of some ruined foundation? There had still been an inscription over the door of a monastery to tell me this had once been the complex of buildings from where Aristotle and his followers had spread their uncertain light over the world. Nicephorus hadn't been able to identify the Garden of Epicurus, and had spent more time talking rot about the *many visits* of Saint Paul than explaining the colonnade that ran along the side of a very impressive building where every inscription had been cemented over. Even Martin, with his encyclopaedic if uncritical reading, had been vague about most of what we'd seen. He might have been no better even if his guts hadn't been playing up from a combination of stewed river frog and funk.

Nevertheless, I'd been dreaming of Athens ever since, back in Richborough, I'd first heard second- or third-hand descriptions of its wonders. Now, if I had to put up with a guide whose ignorance was matched only by a possible intention to murder me, I was finally here in the great City of Human Enlightenment.

It really was a shame about the common people. You might, by thinking hard enough, forget about those men in black. I had come out armed, after all – and there were monks wandering about as well as all the town assemblymen. But you couldn't forget that stinking rabble. I could doubt if any of them stood above five feet. This wasn't the smallness of the Egyptian lower classes – though ugly, they were at least in reasonable proportion. These creatures seemed to have neither thighbones nor necks. Where not in filthy, matted hair, their faces were covered in pockmarks or livid sores. You could almost see the vermin on those nasty bodies poised to hop off on to your own. Jabbering softly and pointing, they'd come after us at first at a respectful distance. Every so often, when the breeze shifted, I'd had a whiff of garlicky breath and unwashed clothing. But I'd managed to ignore them on and off. As we'd reached the Sacred Way, however, they'd increased in numbers and proximity. Plucking at his clothes and stroking his back as if he'd been some large cat, they'd flowed about Nicephorus. He'd alternated between indifference and benign smiles. Though still a few yards away, they were now doing their best to spoil what illusion I'd managed to create of being in Athens.

'Do you suppose these parodies of humanity have *any* blood relationship to the ancients?' I whispered to Martin, now in Celtic.

He said nothing and looked at a marble statue of someone called Arrhidaeus. The inscription told me he'd been an Archon back in the days of Augustus. There were still traces of blond paint on his hair, and he looked rather English. If the answer to my question was no, it was worth asking how these people had got here. They all looked as if they were loosely related, but couldn't have been descended from any of the barbarians who'd been raiding and settling ever since the collapse of the Danube frontiers. The assemblymen did mostly have the size and ruddy colouring of Slavs. One or two of them might – given a year of diet and exercise – even have resembled the ancients. Certainly, when they tried to speak it properly, their Greek had a Slavic intonation. These locals, though, looked neither ancient nor barbarian. I do assure you, they looked still more degraded than the 'Greeks' I'd had to deal with in Alexandria.

But I now did put these thoughts from my head and looked resolutely forward. I thought nothing of the stinking crowd behind me. I thought nothing of those men in black. I even put aside thoughts of what I would, eventually, do to the murdering swine who was making such an astonishing show of ignorant piety. Here, beyond all doubt, were the matchless buildings of the Acropolis designed by Ictinus and Callicrates and adorned by Phidias, and still praised as fresh and perfect five hundred years later by Plutarch. And fresh and perfect they seemed mostly to be. As my eyes adjusted to the darkness inside the Propylaea, I could see holes on the walls where Hadrian had set up pictures of the victories he and Trajan had won beyond the Danube. It was a shame these had been taken down and shipped off to adorn the Imperial capital. But they were late additions, and I'd seen them, or good copies of them, in the Central Law Court in Constantinople.

Nicephorus opened his mouth again as we emerged blinking into the sunlight on the other side. 'My Lord will see the Church of the Virgin,' he cried with a good stab at the enthusiastic. 'It was cleansed of the last stain of devil worship by command of the Emperor Justinian, and returned to its ancient purity.'

I found myself looking right, at a high wall covered in reliefs from which all traces of paint had been washed away by time, but which still showed in their original crispness the meeting of the Assembly that had sanctioned the rebuilding of the Acropolis temples after the Persians had left them in ruins. I paid no attention to the commentary and looked hard at the perfect realism of the figures. Each one might have been sculpted from life. Even now, it might have been possible to identify the leading figures. Yes – either the ancients had been consummate liars about their own appearance, or there had been some disruption in their bloodline. Or perhaps the muttering crowd still pressing in from behind was their posterity, and there had been some spontaneous degradation. Though not now, this was worth considering. There might be a whole book in it – assuming I lived long enough to write it.

I would have stayed to look more at those reliefs. But when you are passing for the first time through the treasure house of the Muses, you barely know where to look. You barely feel the urge to look too long on one masterpiece when there are so many others all about. The wall was topped with bronze statues that gleamed darkly above their marble bases.

'That must have been the pediment for the big statue of the demon Athena,' Martin said, pointing directly ahead.

I smiled at the slight emphasis he put on *demon*. Of all the arguments we'd had to while away loose moments, one of the more pointless was whether the gods of the Old Faith had been demons come to deceive the ancients, or had been figments of the ancient imagination. Doubting the existence of the old gods may have said nothing either way about the True God, but only ever set Martin into a sweat about my general beliefs. Saying nothing, I followed his pointed finger. Yes, the pediment must have held the statue of Athena. Like everything else that was beautiful and could be moved, this had long since been taken off to Constantinople. There, I think, it had perished in the big riots against Justinian. Unlike the Hadrian pictures, this was a decided loss. Now I was looking at the massive pediment, I could see how the absence of its statue robbed our carefully planned surroundings of complete perfection. Far over on the left was a cluster of low buildings. Normally, I'd have been straight off to look at them. But, as I said, I was in the treasure house of the Muses. Between the high wall on my right and another on my left, there was an approach to the east. This terminated in a group of more buildings of a magnificence that I now realised I'd seen duplicated in one of the central squares of Alexandria – duplicated though not matched.

I hurried forward through the forest of statues that narrowed the path. Though often ancient in their own terms, these too were mostly late additions to the original plan. One of them, indeed, had the fussy robes and porcupine hairstyling of an official from barely a generation back. I hurried forward. Martin puffed along behind, the Count behind him, the modern Athenians now some way behind us all. Nicephorus had expected me to spend time on looking at the statues, and was still spouting gibberish about how they represented a visit in ancient times of the entire Senate from Rome.

Even without the deliberate shaping of the plateau to make it obvious, I already knew that the great Temple of Athena was best viewed from the east. As I emerged at the far end of the approach, I kept looking forward. On my left were buildings that would have crowned the whole composition – but, that is, for what was on my right. I forced myself not to look. I quickened my step. I could hear Martin beginning to wheeze again. If we'd been alone, he'd surely have complained about the hurry, or just hung back to follow at his own pace. If I even bothered to note his lack of condition, it was only to blot out the far worse noise of the Count's commentary. I circled what had been the small Temple of the Roman Majesty built by Augustus. My right foot on its lowest step, I looked up and stared west.

You need to bear in mind that conversion to a church imposes change on a building that even a skilled architect can't fully reconcile with the original. You should also consider the altered effect of allowing the ancient paintwork to fade, and its replacement within the portico by a set of mosaics in the modern style. But, though it's hard to find much good to say about Justinian – every disaster we now faced, after all, was an effect of his schemes of Imperial reconquest, and of his demands for uniformity of faith – he had employed good architects in Athens. And nothing short of complete ruin could have taken away the miracle worked in ancient times. I looked and looked. It doesn't do for a member of the Imperial Council to be seen weeping in public. So I sat down on the steps of the temple Augustus had built and took off my hat. I fanned my sweating face and waited for Martin and Nicephorus and everyone else to come over and stand beside me. About a dozen hooded monks shuffled over and stopped between me and the west pediment of the temple. Their faces were hidden, but you could tell from their height that they weren't locals. One of them pointed at the mosaic. Now, they all hurried over to stand under the portico. They might have wanted to assure each other how the mosaic had improved on the original scheme. Perhaps they just wanted to get out of the sun.

But no – they had trouble in mind. They joined another group of monks in a different style of horrid clothing and started an argument. I didn't bother straining to hear what they were shouting about, though it did have the rhythm and confidence of proper Greek. But one of them suddenly stepped forward and jostled another. In no time, they'd set about each other with sticks and leather satchels. I rubbed my eyes and looked up at the blue sky.

'You'd never think it, dear boy, but there's not a straight line in the whole building.'

Oh, no! I thought. What was he doing up here? I stared to my right. Over by a wooden shrine of Saint Prolapsius the Unthinking, Priscus was reclining in a chair carried by four sweating slaves.

24

This was the first I'd seen of Priscus in full daylight since just west of Cyprus, and there was no doubt how he'd aged and shrunk within himself in so short a time. Balthazar was probably as wrong about him as he was about everything else. But he might have had a point. Priscus jabbed with his cane at the chief carrier's head, and the chair came properly over. He smiled brightly and waved a satchel that was doubtless stuffed with drugs.

'When I was last here,' he cried in a voice as bright as his smile, 'the bricked-up entrance still hadn't been rendered, and it was all an untidier thing to behold. I'm glad it looks so much better now.' He got up unsteadily and waited for Martin and Nicephorus to help him down from the chair.

Now he was showing himself in full view, the local trash had set up a low and sinister mutter. Before his arrival, they'd been edging closer and closer to where I sat; one of them had even reached out a short and rather dark arm to touch the damp robe in which I was trying to look grand. Now, they'd all withdrawn to stand a dozen feet away. I can't say I'd been glad to see Priscus. But I wasn't displeased by the effect he was having on the Athenians.

He tottered past me and sat down heavily on my left. He sat a while in silence, absorbed in the shouting, wheeling monks over by the temple. Then he stretched his legs with a groan that showed his real state of mind. But he gathered himself almost at once. 'I guessed you'd be up here the moment the weather permitted,' he said with a forced return of jollity.

He bent forward and looked past me to the right. 'Ah, there you are, my fine young man,' he said. 'Come on, don't be shy. If *I* haven't bothered eating you, the Lord Senator Alaric will do you no harm.' He laughed and waved at a darkish boy whose lack of size was only emphasised by the amount of clothing in which he'd been swathed. 'Well, come on, Theodore,' he urged, 'the Lord Senator is waiting for enlightenment.'

The boy blushed and stood up straight. He gave a slight bow of greeting to Nicephorus, who stared back without movement or expression. 'Every line is curved to give an impression of straightness,' he said in the harsh but correct Greek of a Syrian. He pointed at the western portico and stammered slightly from shyness. 'The centre point of the base here is two inches higher than the outer points. The centre point of the long base is four inches higher. On this, the columns incline inwards. If you extend the lines of the outermost columns, they would meet a mile and a fifth above the base. Because they incline in diminishing proportion to their distance from the edges of the base, any two pairs of the inner columns also form a triangle, though of progressively shorter base . . .'

An encouraging smile on my face, I let the boy go through his lesson. I paid no attention to Nicephorus, who'd finally shut up and was watching the fight with vague interest. There was nothing I didn't know already – this much about Athens I'd read and reread – but he was a sight more accurate than his Uncle Nicephorus had been. I pretended not to notice the increasing volume of what was on its way to a small riot, and listened to the boy. I'd thought, when I saw him asleep, that he was only about six. But, if he was undersized, Theodore must have been ten, or even twelve. Whatever his age, he was a scholar of some precocity. It was plain he must have been the person who was reading Gregory of Nyassa in the library. Those cushions now made sense. So did the lamps that had been left burning. He must have read until his chest had given up on him, and then staggered off to be put to bed by Euphemia.

I thought of Euphemia. At some time since he'd gone off to compose my funeral eulogy, Priscus must have made or remade her acquaintance. I felt a stab of jealous anger. I'd find out sooner or later what could have got her to lend him Theodore's services as a guide.

I turned my attention back to the building I was having described to me. The western pediment, I knew, had been sculpted by Phidias himself, and showed the contest between Athena and Poseidon for guardianship of the city. The long sides carried an immense and glorious relief of a Panathenaiac Festival. Even in old times, I'd have been too far away to see much of this. As it was, the sculptures had been cleaned of their paint and gilding and then covered over with a uniformity of what may have been plaster, but that I hoped was only white paint. In the next few days, I'd give orders for a wheeled viewing platform to be built. This would let me see everything properly. If it was plaster, I'd see if I could get it taken off. Because he was subject to the Pope, I'd make this approach to the Bishop of Athens through the Dispensator. If that didn't work, I'd offer him my tongue of Saint George. That would surely be enough to set the workmen in motion.

A loud and final scream from one of the monks drew me down to the riot under the portico. Things had now turned openly bloody. One of the monks was on his back, and a couple of his rivals were jumping up and down on his chest. I could have taken this as an excuse to get up and intervene. It would have saved me from the trouble of being pleasant to His Magnificence the Commander of the East. But, since Nicephorus himself was taking no active interest, I failed to see any reasonable excuse for noticing the fight.

I glanced a little to the right. A boy had climbed on to one of the statues and was rocking backwards and forwards on it. Now I was getting used to the local dialect, I could hear his repeated shout that he was taller than all the Prophets. Someone in the shabby crowd called back what might have been an obscenity. The boy rocked hard and shouted something that was too fast to catch. If he didn't get down soon, he'd have the head off the statue. Again, Nicephorus said nothing.

I got up and walked towards the nearest edge of the Acropolis. I could hear everyone else follow me over. I looked down to what had been the Temple of Hephaestus, though it was now a shell with a church built within it. I knew that this had once been close by the centre of Athens. Now, there was a huddle of silk weaving factories for about a hundred yards between it and the modern wall. I scanned the rest of the old centre. It made as little sense from above as it had from the ground. Perhaps if I spent a while in the residency library, looking at that mural, I might get some idea of what was down there . . .

'You are welcome to disagree, dear boy – your taste in art is perverse enough, I'm sure,' Priscus broke in behind me. I only noticed that Theodore had continued his explanations as he halted for another stammer. 'But I can't say any of this compares with even the Church of the Apostles back home. Would you like to comment, by the way, on its conversion to a church?' He turned and pointed back at the astonishing little Temple of Athena.

I might have taken this as an excuse to leave the edge of the Acropolis and walk right over to the temple. But the scuffle of the monks had passed through riot into a small pitched battle. Instead, I focused on the pediment. 'I imagine it was damaged at some time in the past – perhaps in the barbarian attack of three hundred years ago?'

Priscus nodded.

'That may be why the original roof is gone. The new roof is based on the inner wall, into which I can see windows have been cut for the church. That leaves the outer colonnade redundant. But I'm glad the architects had the good taste to leave it in place.'

'You're a clever boy – I'll give you that!' came the reply. 'But let Uncle Priscus assure you the barbarians never got up here. There's too little damage to indicate that. I'd blame fire or some other accident of time for the loss of the ancient roof.' He turned and raised both arms at a couple of boys who'd crept up behind us.

One of them screamed softly and made a complex sign with his hands. A warning voice from within the crowd called them away.

Priscus watched complacently as everyone shuffled back another few feet. 'I still don't think much of these old buildings,' he said. 'Certainly, this one pales to nothing beside the Great

Church in Constantinople. Even so, I'll grant it all has a certain elegance for those who like that sort of thing. Didn't some Roman general think so in ancient times?'

'You are surely thinking of Sulla,' I replied with a sly smile. I leaned against the warm stones of the boundary wall and looked at the Temple of Athena. If I ignored the dark figures still darting about under the portico, it had a nobility about its shape that no scowling mosaics of Christ could take away. 'I'm surprised you could forget the man who set the precedent for every later reign of terror. Those who don't compare your late father-in-law to Caligula often compare you to Sulla.'

Cheering by the moment, I smiled into the sneering face. 'Yes,' I went on, 'it was Sulla. The Athenians had, with a regrettable want of common sense, backed Marius in the first of the civil wars that ended the Republic. So before he could get home for his big killing spree in Rome, Sulla rolled up here at the head of an army. Just before the city fell, the whole city assembly went out to beg for mercy. They wasted every trick of Greek eloquence on the old beast. Finally, they fell silent and pointed up here. Sulla followed their pointed fingers and stood silent for what everyone thought an age. Then he turned and, without looking at the scared assemblymen, walked off to his tent. "I spare the living for the sake of the dead," was all he said before going in.'

'Well said! Well said, my dear young fellow,' Priscus jeered at me. 'You've a talent for dramatic narration – such a pity you weren't sent off to Hippopolis. But you have left something out. The real drama in the account is that Sulla's engineers had already got part of the wall down, and the first wave of soldiers were through the breach and getting stuck into the customary massacre. It was a devil's job to call them off. No one but Sulla could have done that.' He stopped and flashed a nasty look at Martin. 'Do you suppose the barbarians will show such taste and restraint when they push down the heaps of rubble that pass nowadays for the walls of Athens?'

I saw Martin jerk slightly as if he'd been prodded from behind.

Nicephorus unfixed his gaze from the monks, who might now have succeeded in kicking someone to death.

Priscus leaned closer to me. 'Shall we go somewhere a little more private?' he whispered. 'Even in Latin, what I have to say is not really for an audience.'

25

There was a time when you could stand anywhere on the high end of the Acropolis and look down to Piraeus and the sea. Then the whole plateau was levelled to make a regular platform for the temples, and was surrounded by walls. After that, you had to go back into the Propylaea and through a side door to climb on to the roof of what had been the Temple of Victory for the sea to be visible. This was where, so legend said, King Aegeus had stood and waited for the return of his son Theseus from Crete; and from where, when Theseus had forgotten to show he'd not been eaten by the Minotaur by replacing black sails with white, the old man had jumped down and killed himself. That may have been two thousand years earlier. Now, I stood in much the same spot, with the nearest equivalent I'd yet seen to a man-devouring monster a few paces to my right. Groaning from a very gentle climb, Priscus had clutched hold of a sturdy but dead bush that had poked through the roof, and was trying his best not to look worn out.

'I didn't suppose tourism would be your motive for coming up here after me,' I said.

Four miles away, the sea was a sparkling, blue carpet, broken here and there by dark islands. Just below me on the left was the theatre built by Herodes Atticus – a most generous benefactor, second only to Hadrian himself. If I looked right, there was the head and upper torso of yet another statue of Hadrian. This time, he was patting the head of his boy Antinous. An ancient city is a place of many layers. There's a continuity of building from earliest times into the fairly recent past, and it takes much forgetting and a lot of squinting to see things as they must have appeared at any specific time in the past. Up here, though, I could almost think myself into better times, when Athens still mattered as other than a defensive point in a game that spanned the known world. Certainly, the shining sea, far off, and the deep blue of the sky were as they'd always been in Athens, and always would be.

I pulled myself back into the present and stared at the Governor's letter that Priscus held in his free hand. 'I'll admit I came out before I'd bothered opening it,' I said. 'I don't suppose it's a cheerful read.'

'Cheerful, dear boy, would be an unfair description,' came the reply. Priscus tightened his grip on the bush and reached inside his robe for a lead flask. Holding the letter under his arm, he pulled out the flask and handed it to me.

I unstoppered it and sniffed the contents. Most of it was wine. The rest was unlikely to kill me – Priscus was still expecting others to do his dirty work. I took a swig and passed it back. Whatever of it wasn't wine hit me as if from behind almost before Priscus could take the flask and pour most of it down his throat. Heart racing, I tried not to fall off the roof, and waited for the pattern of colours behind my eyes to settle into a reasonable blur.

'It's an infusion of yellow bugs that are gathered from the slopes of a volcano somewhere to the east of China,' he said. 'Mix it with sea mandrake, and your balls will explode with lust.' He fell silent, and joined me in peering into the distance.

At last, he let out a long and despairing sigh and cleared his throat. 'We can forget about his numbers,' he said. 'They make no sense, even in terms of what the land will normally support. If I weren't out of area, I'd have the useless toad scooped off his bed of alleged sickness and flogged round the walls of Corinth. But I won't question the generality of the Governor's information. There's sod all to eat anywhere south of the Danube where a grain ship can't be landed. In the occupied territories, every barbarian without a sword who's still alive is a walking skeleton. Those who are armed have stopped gambling over what food can be had, and are cutting each other's throats. It's only because rainwater has blocked all the passes that they haven't turned up here already.'

I looked away from the horizon and waited till I could focus on another part of the city wall. At some time in the distant past – it might have been in the great days of Athens, or after the first real incursion in the chaotic times before Diocletian had steadied the Empire – there had been a much more substantial wall, enclosing a larger space. I could now see where it had been from a few courses of dark stone, or from a gap in the ruins that stretched out beyond the present wall. I'd not have dismissed this as 'heaps of rubble'. Then again, I had no military experience. The walls about Constantinople were so thick, you could drive two chariots side by side along the battlements. Even the sea walls had never been breached. These walls, for all they seemed high enough, had no thickness at the top; mostly, you looked over them from a wooden platform that needed its own supports. From the other side of the Acropolis, I'd stared down at a wall without even this kind of platform.

'No regular soldiers to guard the walls?' I asked. I had no doubt that, whatever he said in his reports to the Governor of Corinth, Nicephorus had long since embezzled his military as well as his civil budget. If he was happy to live in a slum and even deny medical care to his nephew, I didn't suppose he'd spend a clipped penny on guarding the city walls. But I'd see what response I might get out of Priscus.

He gave a contemptuous sniff and let go of his support. Leaning carefully to avoid slipping, he found a stable place on the tiles where he could stand without risk of falling off the roof. 'You've always been rather keen on citizen militias,' he said. 'You may get a chance to see how good they are.'

I looked at the weathered bronze of the roof tiles on which we were perched. I waited. He gave a weaker sniff. Then he cleared his throat. I looked again at the distant sea. Now Priscus laughed.

'Forget old temples,' he said. 'You should go and look at those walls. If they don't fall inward at some barbarian child's first push, we'll see how long they can be held by whatever civilians we can trust not to impale themselves on their own makeshift weapons.' He pulled out his flask and drained it with a sound halfway between a gasp of pain and a laugh. 'But never mind that, my dear,' he said at last. 'We have a few days until the fun begins. Why don't you call your priests together and send them all off to Corinth? If they can't all be housed in proper comfort in what I gather is a somewhat crowded city, you can ship those of lower status across to Aegina. Unless the Avars have discovered how to work a ship, everyone will be safe enough there.'

So that was why he'd brought me up here! I had expected better of Priscus. Perhaps his health really was collapsing, and this was his best plan for making sure that, when he stood before Heraclius in disgrace, I was hanging my head beside him. 'We'll have to take our chance on that,' I said. 'So long as the walls don't actually fall inward, the council must go ahead. And, with so many bishops gathered in one place, I'm sure we can rely on them to pray for an avoidance of another Trampolinea.'

Priscus made no answer at first. Then: 'Have you forgotten about our child?' he asked.

'Not at all,' I said. I stepped halfway down the roof. I held out a hand for Priscus. The tiles were pitted from a thousand years of rain. The soles of my boots gripped them as if they'd been pumice stone. I could help Priscus down to me with one hand, and let him down with the other to where the roof flattened out. 'Unless the Governor sends more dispatches,' I said, 'the Corinth boat comes in on Monday. My plan is to get Sveta there with the children.'

'The bitch Sveta and her spawn can take their chance with the rest of us,' he spat. 'But I do feel increasingly paternal about dear little Maximin.'

Silent again, I helped him down the big final step from the temple roof. We were now on a broad platform below the roof that was probably for maintenance slaves to store materials. Priscus had lost all right to paternal feelings when he cut the mother's throat and caused the boy to be dumped outside that church in Constantinople. I'd adopted him. I'd given him his name. He was mine by custom and by law. Still, if Priscus too wanted the child out of danger, I'd not object to any belated stab of duty. It would be a cover for my own trip to Corinth.

He stepped into a patch of shade and rubbed his eyes. 'If you have any sense, Alaric, you'll have your clerics out of Athens at the same time. Can't you go with them?' he asked with a change of tone. 'If you took them all off to Aegina, you could still have your council there. At least, the city would have lost a few of its useless mouths.'

The soldierly reasonableness of his tone was almost convincing – or might have been if I hadn't known perfectly well that he knew what I knew. Several dozen bishops and other dignitaries, plus any number of secretaries and servants and other hangers-on, made about a hundred and fifty. Getting them out of Athens, and then settled *anywhere* else and ready to do what I wanted, wasn't a matter of shouting some religious equivalent of 'About turn: quick march!' One breath about approaching barbarians, and half of them would bolt for Corinth in search of a safe trip home. Getting the rest moved would be like herding cats. No, I had them all in Athens. Here they'd stay until I'd got from them what I wanted. If the walls did fail us before then, and we all got butchered, that was a risk worth taking. It was certainly better than going back home, tail well and truly between my legs.

Priscus didn't even wait for me to put my refusal into words. 'Oh, do let's go down,' he wheezed. 'It's time we rejoined everyone else. I suggest we let them think we were nattering over the good old days in Alexandria – the good old days of last month, when at least I had a few hundred armed men to lead against the mob. Yes, let them enjoy their sightseeing. It'll be the last fun they have before General Pestilence turns back the barbarian horde.'

We'd got to the roof by climbing a ladder that had been left against the temple wall. As I helped him down its final rungs, and we stood, looking at one of the blank outer walls of the Propylaea, there was a sudden noise of shouts and howling. It was as if a stag had rounded on a hunting pack and was goring everything within reach. The noise echoed about the enclosed space, and it was hard at first to guess from where it was coming. But there was a flight of steps up to a rampart on one of the new defensive walls. We'd avoided this earlier, instead choosing the highest point we could find. I now bounded up the steps and leaned over the wall.

The noise was coming from the Theatre of Herodes Atticus. When I'd first come up here, it was empty. Now, it was crowded. The upper semicircle of benches was mostly ruined, and covered with what remained of its collapsed roof. But the lowest benches were filled with more of the rabble. They squeezed together on the marble seats and spilled on to the stairways between. Some even stood together in the large orchestra before where the stage had once been. As I shaded my eyes from the glare of the white marble, I gradually saw that the audience had rounded up what may have been every stray dog and cat in Athens. These were now being killed with sharpened sticks and some of the smaller building blocks that had come loose over time. Dogs ran madly about the rubble of the stage. But all escape was closed off, and the whiteness was already covered with little splashes of blood. Men and boys danced and cheered as they set about the work. Though taking no part in it, more of those dark figures hung about on the margins of the slaughter.

'Oh, but isn't that senseless, fucking cruelty?' Priscus called softly. 'Such wasted effort when there are people here just calling out to be massacred.' He sighed and looked into my face. 'Disgusted, are we, dear boy?' he asked. He began another sentence, but broke off with a long cough. He turned pale and clutched at his side.

I was wondering if I'd have to carry him off for help. But he steadied himself and looked down again at a new sound of decidedly human screaming. From where we stood, the remaining wall that enclosed the theatre hid part of the action. By craning my neck and squinting, though, I could now see that there was someone tied to the other side of the furthest column on the stage. I could see only both naked arms where they were stretched halfway round the column. But I was sure it was a woman. There were a couple of old men just in view. It looked as if they were jabbing sharpened poles into her body. It was because the slaughter of animals was coming to an end that I heard her own despairing cries.

As I shifted position to try to see more of this, I looked right. Somehow, Nicephorus had got himself up on to the rampart without making any noise. He now stood beside me, smiling indulgently at the proceedings a few hundred feet away. 'Athens, I am told, was anciently a democracy,' he said with gloating politeness. 'If this be the will of the people, who are we to interfere?'

Priscus cleared his throat and spat over the wall. 'Why don't you just fuck off, Nicephorus?' he said without turning.

Nicephorus stared back for a moment, then put his face into an oily smile and touched his forehead. I looked over the wall again. Someone had pulled all his clothes off and was dancing about like a madman before the bound woman.

'I suppose you find these people loathsome in every respect,' Priscus went on, now turning his head very slightly in my direction. 'Not at all like your wonderful ancients, are they?' He laughed. 'I, on the other hand, must confess myself rather impressed.' He shaded his eyes and leaned further over the wall. 'I'd never realised these people had such white skins.' He pointed at the naked man and at the arms of the bound woman, and laughed with soft menace.

I looked down into the theatre. He was right about the colour of the local skin – hardly surprising for people who never took their clothes off, possibly not even to wash. Whatever the colour, though, it was less than a pretty sight. I was glad of the several hundred yards of separation. They blurred the worst details, and allowed me to forget about the smell.

I stepped back from the wall and looked down to where Martin was now standing with Theodore. They must have heard the noise, but were deep in conversation about something that took their whole interest. Priscus, though, wasn't finished.

'Can you tell our young friend,' he asked, 'why these two-legged animals are so ugly?' He now looked at Nicephorus and waited expectantly.

The Count bit his lip and tried to lick moisture on to his dry lips.

'Come on, Nicephorus,' he added with cold and silken charm. 'You may be Count of Athens. But we both stand far above you in the Imperial pecking order. You'll do well to answer when you're spoken to.'

Nicephorus now managed a sickly smile. 'There is a story,' he said, 'that, in ancient times, the common people of Athens and all their posterity were blighted with a curse of ugliness. They are said to have offended a being of great power.' There was a loud scream from within the theatre. He stopped and looked over the wall. 'Is My Lord not satisfied with his tour of Athens?' he asked with desperate politeness. He waved vaguely over the jumble of ruined or converted buildings that spread below us all the way to the new wall and beyond.

'Your stewardship of Athens is most impressive,' I said blandly. Indeed, so far as Athens had been left with any machinery of justice, this was probably it. If Nicephorus chose not to pay attention, it wasn't my business to act in his place. I put those increasingly horrible screams out of mind and smiled easily back at him. Our eyes met. Still smiling, I looked long into his strained, sweaty face. I thought for a moment that he'd stand up to my stare.

Then, just as I was about to be really impressed, his eyes took on a renewed shifty look, and he looked away. But he recovered fast. He laughed and stamped his foot. He looked at Priscus, who was momentarily out of action with more of his Eastern bug juice.

'Then all is excellent!' he said with another forced laugh. 'Shall we not make our way back to the residency?' Except his whole manner dripped beast and weakling, you'd hardly have recalled the shrill, supplicating figure of the night before.

I stayed behind to help Priscus down. As his grip loosened on the top stones of the wall, he ignored my outstretched hand. 'Alaric,' he said through suddenly chattering teeth, 'I hope you'll take advice from a somewhat older man who's had more experience than you of the civilised world.' He stood upright and put his flask away. 'Don't think any more about these local customs.

Believe me, dear boy,' he added with sudden earnestness – he even dropped his voice as if someone might be listening, 'Athens is an ancient city, filled with ancient sins. Things happen here that are often best overlooked. Your capacity for overlooking what everyone else can see is legendary. You should now hope it doesn't fail you.'

26

I sat down at my desk and fished inside my tunic for the bronze key that I'd hung about my neck. I pushed the chair back and bent down to look at the pattern of bright scratches round the lock. I pulled again on the handle of the compartment. Holding it at the proper angle, I pushed the key firmly in. It failed to engage. I muttered an obscenity and pushed it in again. Standing on the other side of the desk, Martin opened his mouth to speak. This time, though, the teeth of the key did engage with the teeth inside the lock. With a gentle click, the lock moved out of position. I pulled the handle and got the compartment open.

Like everything else in the residency, my desk was long past its best, but had been made in the most luxurious style. It was of cedar wood and ebony, with ivory inlays and the remains of a silver inkwell that had been built in. It had one cupboard underneath, that went right down to the floor and, now the legs were a little rickety, gave useful additional support. Between where this started and the desktop was a curious sliding compartment. It was a kind of box that pulled out. This is what I'd now opened. I lifted it fully out and put it on the desk.

'The gold . . .' Martin whispered.

I took out the heavy cloth bag and emptied its contents on to the desktop. Martin snatched at one of the more circular pieces before it could roll on to the floor and added it to the shining heap. In silence, I scooped the gold closer and arranged it into stacks of twelve. I scattered it again and rearranged it in tens. I added the tens together into twenties and then into forties. I moved them all into a narrow circle and stabilised them by placing a waxed tablet on top.

I looked up. 'Nothing missing,' I said.

Martin swallowed and sat down. I lifted the tablet off and took a few coins from the highest pile. I added these to the lowest. The tablet no longer wobbled back and forth when I replaced it. Though a decentish sum – especially in a place like Athens, where all prices were lower than in the great cities – this was, until we got over to Corinth, all we had. When drawing enough in Alexandria for reasonable travelling expenses, I'd specified good, current solidi. Even so, about half of them had dated from the reign of Phocas – some of them from the unfortunate Maurice who'd been done in so horribly by the Tyrant – and a few had been clipped and sweated to the point where they'd never pass again other than by weight. But, if the bag had undeniably been moved from where I'd put it, none of the gold was missing.

'I think it's my commission he was after,' I said. I picked this up and showed where it had been rolled up again from the wrong end. 'I think we can rule Priscus out. He admitted he was in here to read the Governor's letter. And, if he had stopped for a full search, he'd not have made this mess of it. Nicephorus left with us and came back with us. I'll eat their cooking if you can show me that the slaves can read, or could resist pinching at least a few of these coins. That leaves us with some person or persons unknown. I might lay money on Balthazar. Or I might not.' I picked up the gold, one pile at a time, and dropped it back into the bag. I thought and took some out again. I put the bag into the compartment and pushed this back into place. I locked it.

I glanced once more about the office. Martin still hadn't found the time to arrange my things properly, and the closed and opened boxes of documents lay more or less as we'd left them in the morning. But, if nothing seemed to be missing, it was reasonably clear that everything had been touched. The following day, I decided, I'd get a key made for the lock to my whole suite of rooms. And that was all I could say for the time being. I twisted in my chair and picked up the long and venomous letter of complaint from the Dispensator. I'd found this lying on the floor just inside the main entrance when I returned from looking about Athens. 'A most slovenly way to deliver letters,' I'd said to Martin while bending to pick it up. 'Whoever brought it might at least have set foot inside the residency.'

I skimmed down the letter, looking for the relevant passage. 'I believe the Western delegates have been accommodated by the Bishop of Athens,' I said. 'Since he is subject to Rome, this is an internal matter in which I don't propose to get involved. It seems, however, that the interpreters have been provided by us. Not surprisingly, Nicephorus has got them on the cheap. The mad one, I think, is called Felix.' I looked again at the letter. Yes, his name was Felix. The Dispensator's pen had spluttered on the irregular surface of the papyrus as he wrote it. He'd underlined it three times, then had appeared, from the smoother writing that followed, to have paused to sharpen his pen. I could easily imagine the cold stare down at the name. 'We need to get this sorted. I propose a visit to wherever Felix lives at dawn tomorrow. We'll catch him in bed and give him a good talking to about his duties.'

I stared up at nothing in particular. The answer to all these complaints seemed to be that no time or planning had been put into this council. This wasn't an ecumenical council, which can take years and years to call together. But nor was it a dinner party. It must have been called with barely enough time for everyone to get to Athens. Not surprisingly, everything was in chaos. I'd not have credited even Heraclius with that level of stupidity. In this, if in nothing else, he'd exceeded all expectations. I might have taken the Dispensator aside and explained all this to him. Behind those cutting phrases, though, was the anger of a man who'd been called away from where his word was something like law, to where he was dependent on others – even down to communicating with most of these others.

I was about to speak again, when there was a faint scratching on the door. I quickly dropped the letter on to the exposed gold. 'Come in,' I called.

The door opened, and what can be best described as a poker topped with a black wig looked in. 'Oh, there you are, dearie,' said Irene. She opened the door wider and stepped into the office. Still wearing the old military cloak that had let me take her at first for a man, she looked as if she'd come straight from the market where I'd bumped into her earlier that afternoon. Without stopping to bow, she came forward and sat herself lightly on one of my unopened packing boxes. 'If you'll pardon my advice, that slave of yours is in need of a good whipping. He led me twice all round the world in the place, then let me find my own way here.'

'I did suppose, madam, that your husband would be attending on me,' I said coldly.

Irene gave me a flash of brown teeth. 'Oh, he don't come out no more, dearie – not with his legs.' She looked about the room and frowned. 'I wouldn't like to say when this place was last cleaned,' she said with a downward turn of her mouth. She leaned forward and ran a fingertip over the desktop. She rubbed forefinger and thumb together and grunted. 'The Good Lord did you a favour when he made you trip over those fetters. You could fill a wine barrel with the cobwebs I've seen.' She sat back and smacked her lips. 'A big wine barrel,' she added with a glance at the tray on a side table.

I nodded to Martin, who got up and filled her a cup of wine. I waited for her to drain it and hold it out for a refill. She took a more delicate sip now, and then reached inside her robe for a sheet of papyrus. She smiled again and pushed it at me across the desk. The sheet had been reused more than once, and the imperfect cleaning, together with the crossings out and other amendments to its present listing, was a proper mess. I got up and took it over to the side window, where a shaft of late afternoon sunlight gave me a better view.

'I want twenty-five slaves,' I said eventually. 'I want all males except for five experienced lady's maids – and everyone fit for heavy cleaning work.' I paused. 'I don't want anyone who was born in Athens. If it means some of them have to be unbroken prisoners of war, I'll take a chance.'

Irene tipped her head back and laughed. 'O mercy, mercy!' she cried. 'You won't get no local-born slaves in this place – not with all them stories.'

I looked up. 'What stories might those be?' I asked sharply.

She laughed again and finished her wine.

Ignoring his scared look, I nodded once more to Martin, and watched as he poured out most of the jug.

'Oh, witches and ghosts and all that, lovey,' she said vaguely. I waited for her to go on. She leaned forward and put the cup on my desk. 'But don't you go worry yourself with those old stories,' she said. 'It was all a long time ago, and I'm a woman of business.'

'These ones have Slavic names,' I said, putting the list in front of her and jabbing at a whole block of listings. 'I want those. These others have names I can't recognise, but are listed as experienced in houses of quality. I want them all cleaned up and given a change of clothes. I need them here at the latest by noon tomorrow. I'm giving a late dinner, and I want everything ready for that. If they aren't here by noon, I'll come looking in person for your husband – bad legs or none.'

She peered uncertainly at her list. 'If it's money you're short of, dear, I'm sure we can reach some agreement,' she said. 'It's not every day we gets to deal with the Emperor's man.' She put the list down and cleared her throat. I thought for a moment she was looking for somewhere to spit. But the moment passed, and she swallowed the gob. 'These ones you've chose isn't fit for nothing better than the mines. If I might suggest—'

I cut her off with a blank stare. She shrugged, and we turned to the matter of pricing. That took up about as long as I'd expected. There's a limit to how far you go with the Emperor's Legate, but Irene went right up to that limit, and then a little beyond. We got there in the end, though.

'I can't say how long I'll be in Athens,' I said. 'But I prefer to buy slaves. I've never known hiring to go very well.' I uncovered a few of the gold coins. Her eyes widened, and she smiled eagerly.

I got up. Irene remained seated. 'Martin, do give the lady a tour of the residency,' I said. 'Make it clear which parts will need attention and which can be ignored. If it seems that more slaves will be needed, I leave that to your own discretion.' I looked down at

Irene. 'You can give me your account after I've had a look at the slaves.' I paused and waited for her to get up slowly. 'I'd rather not have to send any back,' I said with quiet emphasis.

'Now, Martin,' I went on in Latin, 'I'm sure this dear lady came over with the same retinue of thugs we saw with her in the market place. Do borrow some of them for protection and get yourself over to where the Dispensator is staying. I think it's the big monastery halfway up the Areopagus Hill. Give him my regards. Add whatever else may put him into a better mood than he had when writing his letter. Ask him to meet us tomorrow by the Column of Theodosius. He can then take us to where Felix lives.' I handed the letter to Martin.

He looked at the return address and nodded.

'And, while you're in the area,' I went on, 'drop in on the local Bishop. I didn't see him yesterday in Piraeus, but he should be in town. Present my most loving compliments and all the rest. Above all, see if he's done more than our friend the Count to get this council under way on Sunday. It will, I very much think, be where the Areopagus Court used to have its meetings. I can at least hope he's made sure there will be enough seats there for everyone.' I had a further thought. 'Oh, and do check if everyone has been invited to dinner tomorrow afternoon.'

He nodded again. I'd given all the dinner invitations to Nicephorus. There was no certainty any of them had been delivered. 'I'd like you to stay for as long a gossip as it takes to see if those priests have done *anything* since they arrived except bitch to and about each other. Our job is to see that the right seals get fixed below the right form of words to flash round Constantinople and the Eastern Patriarchates. It will help if our council doesn't go as badly as that act of clerical love we witnessed on the Acropolis.'

I crossed over to the door. I opened it and waited for Irene to take the hint. As she passed through with Martin, I plucked at his sleeve. 'And do try to be back while it's light enough for a proper look round this building,' I whispered. 'I'd like to see it by day – and all of it. We also need to make an inventory of the kitchen. I want to see how bare the cupboards are before I start ordering in supplies. We can't serve up another dinner tomorrow of stewed river frog.' I grinned at the pained face Martin pulled. I'd avoided mentioning it at the time. But my nose had told me that there was some place behind one of the Caryatids that would – bearing in mind how often it was cleaned – be for ever Ireland.

Alone, I sat down again and nerved myself for what was left of the wine. I stared at a wall painting that may have copied the *Venus Rising from the Sea* by Apelles. Some patches of blue had fallen off with the underlying plaster, and been replaced with rough grey. Otherwise, this may have been the best surviving painting in the residency. The sun was dipping down in the west, and would soon disappear behind one of the towers of the rear block of the residency. For the moment, it shone through the side window and made my uncovered gold glitter as if it had been alive.

I stood up. I had no idea how long Martin would be. Might it be worth restarting my tour of the building alone?

27

I bumped into Nicephorus as I emerged from a long gallery that had busts of all the emperors to the time of Arcadius. He was sweating from the weight of a large wooden box he'd been trying to push all by himself along the corridor. He gave me the shifty look of a man who's been caught in some questionable act. Then he straightened up and grinned back at me. 'My Lord is satisfied with the glories of Athens?' he asked as his eyes darted everywhere but into my face.

'They'd have been a sight better without you or your bloody friends!' I might have said. But this would never have done. I could instead have mentioned the interpreters. Again, that would have led into areas I didn't yet choose to visit. So I smiled happily as if I still hadn't noticed the stinking slum he'd made of the residency and asked if he needed a hand with his box.

He bent straight down again and hugged the box. He looked up at me from the corners of his eyes. 'Oh no, My Lord,' he said with a hint of triumph. 'I'd not dream of spoiling your fine outgoing clothes.'

I looked harder at the box. From the sound it had made on the dirty tiles of the floor, it was rather heavy – but was too big to be wholly filled with gold. That would have needed more than one man to push along. I wondered briefly if it might be worth waiting till he'd pushed it round the corner, and then sneaking after him. But I put this thought out of mind.

'It is as you wish,' I said. 'Please be aware, though, that I've arranged a few dozen slaves of my own for my stay here. When you have a moment, I'd be most grateful if we could sit together and work out their accommodation and duties in the residency.'

He shuffled from side to side in the little corridor like a cornered crab. Much more of this, and I'd really have no choice but to ask something relevant. But he let go of his box again and stood up. He nodded and bowed. He looked up at the sunlight that streamed obliquely through the ceiling window.

'Very good,' I said in a final tone. 'Since nothing has come here directly from Constantinople, I'd be most grateful if you could look again through your own correspondence from His Excellency the Governor of Corinth, to see if there is anything forwarded to me. My commission gives me a free hand with the council. But I did expect at least one supplemental letter from the Emperor.'

As soon as he decently could, he ended the conversation and went back to pushing his box along. He vanished round the corner, and I stood listening to a diminishing sound of long scrapes and grunts of exertion. I found myself looking at the cupboard within which was the door set in the wall. I did remember pulling this shut the night before. It was now ajar. I resisted the urge to open it and walk in. That could wait until the following day, or even the day after. I turned and walked back into the confused layout where the grander rooms at the front of this block gave way to the main living quarters. I'd not bother with exploring. The smell of damp and unswept dust was getting on my nerves. Instead, I'd make my way out into the main courtyard garden. There, I could sit until the sun went altogether. Until dusk came and turned the wild flowers a uniform pale, I could sit by myself and try to put my thoughts in order.

As I passed by the staircase that led up to the library, I heard the muffled, rhythmical sound of someone reading.

I'd been right about the palace library. It was, in its basic plan, as fine and elegant by day as I'd imagined. It even had a few dozen books that might be worth reading. The other few hundred were forbiddingly theological. Gregory of Nyassa was light reading by comparison. In my view, they were all fit at best for cutting up and pasting on to the spines of cookery books.

Young Theodore was plainly of a different opinion. He'd been so absorbed in one of Gregory's sermons on the infinity of God that he hadn't noticed the crunch of my feet on those beads, and then across the loose mosaic tiles, until I was standing on the other side of his table. 'Please don't get up,' I'd said as he finally caught sight of me. I'd insisted he should carry on in his bright, childish and faintly Syrian voice while I made my own inspection of the place.

Now, I was sitting opposite him in an unbroken chair I'd pulled over from one of the corners of the room, a battered scroll of the historian Dexippus open on my lap. Theodore was less shy than I'd seen him in the afternoon. He was larger than I'd seen him in his bed. He was now just a very clever boy, making the best of a dreadful time by reading everything in sight.

'But how can My Lord read without speaking?' he asked with less of a stammer now we were alone.

I smiled and let the book roll shut. Even then – yes, back then, at the very opening of my days of glory – I had the makings of a schoolmaster. It wasn't an inclination I could practise on Martin. Though I'd now exceeded him in whole areas of ancient literature, it was only a year since he'd really left off being my own master. Here was a little boy, though, on whom I could impose to my heart's content – and on whom I had my own reason for imposing.

'I believe Syria is a place where reading is considered a communal activity,' I said grandly. 'It's the same in Constantinople.' I paused and waited for his eyes to widen at the mention of the City. 'Where I come from, though, it is considered rather common to read aloud.' That was a lie. If I'd got into the habit of reading to myself, it was only because that nature of what I was reading half the time in Canterbury would have got me straight into trouble if I'd recited it for all to hear. But I smiled as if silent reading were the most natural thing in the world. 'It also allows you to read much faster. You'll find that, once you've got out of the habit of reading aloud, you can go ten or twenty times faster.'

'Then I will endeavour, My Lord, to still my own tongue when reading,' came the grave and implicitly trusting response.

I felt a sudden stab of shame and took up Dexippus again. I unrolled him to the place where he described how he'd got everyone on to the Acropolis for his final defence of Athens against the Gothic raiders. That had been under three hundred and fifty years earlier. But his refusal to call any weapon or place or people by its modern name – indeed, his refusal to mention any building that wasn't already built by the time of Demosthenes – made his account incomprehensible in places. To be sure, it left me no wiser about the fate of the buildings on the Acropolis. I twisted the spine of the book in my right hand, and watched as the glued pages scrolled further and further towards the probable climax of the work. There was a two-inch hole in the antepenultimate page. It wouldn't stop a determined reading. But I was already going off a man who'd been so universally praised by later historians. I put the book down on the table and watched as the stiff papyrus rolled back on itself.

'How long have you been in Athens?' I asked in a more normal voice.

'We came here just over three years ago, My Lord,' came the reply.

I nodded and waited.

'It was after my father died,' he went on, now squeezing his eyes shut as if to remember the chronology of events. 'There had been a poor harvest in our district. There was little food for the authorities to requisition from the country people, and want among the poorer classes brought on a plague in which many died throughout the whole city.' He stopped and tried not to look confused. 'My mother – I mean the Lady Euphemia – applied for help to one of her own relatives. But he refused to accept me into his household. So my Uncle Nicephorus offered us a roof. He was unable to pay for our journey. But my mother sold some of her jewels, and we took ship from Zephyrion.'

'That would have been while Phocas was Emperor,' I prompted.

'Yes, My Lord,' he said, more eagerly. 'I'd been in Athens a whole year, when officials came over from Corinth and threw down the statues of the Tyrant and announced the beginning of a new age of freedom and perfect justice.' He stopped and looked down at the table.

I could see he'd covered all his waxed tablets in notes from what Gregory had told him. I had no wish to discuss theology – not with a boy, at any rate. I smiled and leaned carefully back in my chair. Though unbroken, it had the rickety feel about it of old furniture on the turn. Theodore stared up at the sudden creak of old wood. 'So how do you find the Glorious City Crowned with Violets?' I asked. 'I suppose Tarsus was hotter – and less past its best.'

The boy looked cautiously back. 'It is a privilege, My Lord, to stay in so famous a city,' he said. He stopped and looked down again.

I leaned forward and tried to see what was on one of the loose papyrus sheets he'd had stacked up on his left. It was more about Alexander, but the writing was too stained and faded for me to see from upside down where Theodore had reached in the story. He saw my interest and passed the sheet over. It was Ptolemy again; he was describing how he'd seized possession of Alexander's body on its journey back to Macedon and brought it to Egypt, which he'd just grabbed in the dissolution of the Empire.

The boy screwed his face up as if for some great effort. He stammered a little. Then: 'Is it true, My Lord, that you were in Egypt?'

I nodded. Egypt wasn't a subject I'd have wanted to discuss, given any choice. But I was eager for any conversation that went beyond extracting one sentence at a time from him.

'I did see the mummy of Alexander when I was there,' I said. I thought of that ghastly riot in Alexandria, in which the mob had laid hands on the thing, tearing it in pieces – and even eating parts of it. 'You don't often set eyes on a genuine hero,' I went on with a laugh. Couldn't the boy have asked about something that brought back more welcome memories? Priscus might see the suppression of the Alexandrian mob as one of the high points in his career. I couldn't see it as other than part of the disaster that had made my job here essential to succeed. But I'd now managed a look at the sheet that had been underneath the fragment of Ptolemy. This was one of the attacks that Plutarch had made on Epicurus.

'Have you read any of the pagan philosophers?' I asked.

'No, sir,' he answered. 'They have nothing to add to the truths given by the Holy Fathers of the Church.'

I tried to look devout. By much squinting, I now managed to read a few bits of Plutarch:

And, when the lower classes see their loved ones die, they would rather think them still existing, though in Hell, than utterly erased. And they like to hear it said that those they have lost are in a better place ... But they are stricken dumb with grief to hear about the dissolution of atoms. They cannot even understand it when told that someone is no more ... Behold, then, how the philosopher of bodily pleasures really takes away the sweetest and greatest hope of the lower classes ...

What could I say about this to make conversation? I wondered. That facts are facts if true? That wishful thinking doesn't affect whether they are true or not? Best not get involved in that. I looked up at the glass dome directly above where we sat. The sun was now low in the sky. But the glass bricks still shone as if with their own light. 'Good writer, Plutarch,' I said, keeping up my school-master act. 'But Epicurus is also worth a read. Though lacking the same inspiration, he does fit in to some degree with Gregory of Nyassa on the infinity of things. He takes issue with Plato on the nature of the world that we are able to comprehend. His universe has always existed, and always will exist. It is boundless in all directions. His streams of hooked atoms combine and recombine in endless sequence.'

The boy frowned. 'But the atoms are surely an impious fraud?' he asked – or perhaps he asserted. 'Does not Plutarch say that Epicurus was the meanest of thinkers?' he went on in similar tone. 'He was a man of loose morals and had feeble powers of analysis.'

I smiled and leaned forward on the table. 'Ah, but were similar claims not made by the philosophers about our own Christian Faith?' I pushed the scroll to one side and pulled up my sleeves to avoid the dust on the table. 'I do agree that there are problems with the atomic theory – the "swerve", for example, to rescue freedom of the will, the infinite divisibility of whatever has extension, the paradox of physical movement. Against all this, however, is the compelling evidence for a world beneath our senses that is comprised of very small particles. Surely, we can rescue the hypothesis of the atoms by allowing that God created them, and that He has determined their motions, and that we can, by patient investigation, use the reason that God has given us to order the atoms to our own convenience?'

If I'd finally got the boy's interest, preaching even a bastardised version of the truth hadn't been my intention. But I had got his interest. Trying not to show how pleased I was beginning to feel, I waited for him to smooth off his previous notes with the wide end of his stylus.

'I think the reason Epicurus is so unpopular with all the other pagan philosophers,' I continued, 'is not his openness to refutation by logical paradox, but his claim that government is fundamentally unnecessary. He asserts that a viable human society can exist on the basis of free association of its members – no slavery, no taxes, no lies. Does not our Gregory here also deny the legitimacy of slavery . . . ?'

And so, as the sun dipped lower and lower, and the glass bricks overhead turned various shades of pink, I settled into my first long dialogue with young Theodore. Looking back, I can regret that it wasn't our last. But all those shouting matches and pamphlet wars were still so many years in the future. I could have no premonition of them here in the library, as I set out my case, and filled it with just enough weaknesses for a clever boy to best His Magnificence and think well of himself.

I looked up finally as the last reddish tinge faded from the glass bricks. 'But you must forgive me, young Theodore,' I said as if startled by how long we'd sat here together. 'It will surely soon be your bedtime.' I paused. I let my face break into a friendly smile. 'The lady Euphemia tells me that you have been deprived, here in Athens, of the company of other children.'

'But, My Lord,' he cried, 'I was playing all day with the children of your secretary. They are delightful creatures.'

I smiled. He could find out for himself that one of them was mine. 'Then I must arrange,' I said, 'for you to spend one or two nights in the nursery. My secretary's wife is a most charming woman. She would like nothing better than to let your mother sleep free of cares. And I'm sure she would appreciate your help in getting the youngsters to sleep. Her own singing voice is more determined than pleasing.'

Theodore nodded. I managed to avoid biting my lip as he explained that Euphemia had come up with exactly the same suggestion.

'Then I must arrange it for this very evening,' I said. I got up and straightened my clothes. I could already feel a pleasurable tingling in my loins.

There was an approaching crunch on the stairs. I heard the telltale cough. 'You were quick about your business, Martin,' I said without turning. 'Come in – you will find me less – er – less preoccupied than on your previous visit.' I looked over at Theodore, who'd now turned back to the Alexander sheets and was trying not to move his lips as he read. 'You have met young Theodore already. I've no doubt you'll both get on very well indeed. He has a request from his mother to discuss with you.'

'My Lord,' Martin said in his most formal voice, 'His Grace the Bishop of Nicaea would have a word with you in private.'

I barely had time for a scowl, when I heard another crunch of steps outside the library.

28

Simeon walked in and gave a long sniff of disgust. 'You, boy,' he snarled at Theodore. 'If the Emperor's Legate can stand for a bishop, you have no business sitting in my presence.' Ignoring that the boy had been making every effort to climb from his chair, Simeon sniffed again. 'Get out,' he said, speaking either to Martin or to Theodore – perhaps to both. 'Come back with something fit for me to drink.' He looked down and glared at one of the areas of mosaic that still held firmly in place. It was the bare breast of one of the Muses. Avoiding a shattered reading stand that lay in his path, he walked over to where Theodore had been sitting. He picked up one of the cushions and beat the dust out of it. He sat down heavily and looked steadily up at the last glow of light from the dome. It was just enough to bring on a sneeze. By the time he'd finished blowing his nose, Martin and the boy had gone off together, and we were alone.

I walked over to the mural of Athens in its best age. The Acropolis had been painted both higher and smaller than it really was. There were obvious inconsistencies of perspective that told me the painting was fairly modern. This was less interesting, though, than further evidence of burning in the library. At some time, there had been a series of bonfires in the room. The heat in several areas had been so intense that the mosaic tiles were lifted and the underlying concrete had cracked. Looking up, I could see that some effort had been made to clean smoke from the glass bricks.

I turned to Simeon, who was now muttering over the text of Gregory. 'My Lord,' I opened with a smooth and diplomatic smile, 'I cannot say what a pleasure it always is to see you.'

'Then it's not a mutual pleasure!' came the immediate and spat reply.

I caught sight from where I stood of a reasonably complete book roll within one of the fallen racks. I bent and picked it up. Big disappointment: it was complete, even to the firmness of the glued sheets, but someone had washed it in vinegar or some other corrosive, and all the lines had faded to a pale grey.

I walked back over to the table and sat down again. 'It would please me much to learn the reason for My Lord's intemperancy of mood,' I said, still very smooth.

Simeon glared back at me like some caged beast. 'I have just discovered,' he said, rising towards another snarl, 'that I shall not be sitting on your right at tomorrow's dinner. That place, I am told, is promised to some gross and vulgar barbarian out of Italy.'

I raised my eyebrows. 'But, surely, Simeon, you will appreciate that the Lord Fortunatus represents the Universal Bishop,' I said. 'As for his origins, he comes from a most illustrious family that has produced great men ever since very ancient times. I do even think he is related, on his mother's side, to the Great Augustus himself.' *Gross and vulgar barbarian* – eh? I could be glad the Dispensator was half a mile away in his rat-infested monastery. I could think of no words better calculated to have him calling for his packing boxes.

'If it doesn't know Greek, it's a barbarian!' Simeon snapped.

I looked back at the twisted face and thought quickly. I could have lectured him on the continuing status of Latin, even now that I'd got Greek established as the official language of the Empire. But you'd have to be a bigger fool than Simeon was not to be aware of this. I gave him a long and very cold stare.

'My dear Simeon,' I said quietly, 'I can see from the slight blueness of the powder under your left nostril that you've come straight here from a meeting with your dear cousin Priscus. Doubtless, he told you about the seating arrangements for tomorrow. He may also have told you certain things about the reason for the council that has been summoned to Athens. But do please allow me to give you the full story.' I could have waited for someone to come back with wine. I could have waited for the effect of the drugs he'd been given to fade. But, if that made him less personally unpleasant, it would have done nothing to shift what I could see was his settled view of things. There's a time for jollying along, and a time for turning nasty. I could see it was time for the latter.

'Simeon,' I took up again, 'you were appointed to your see with the express consent of the Emperor. By the Emperor's grace, you are permitted to spend part of the year amid the joys of Constantinople. You undoubtedly have certain advantages of wealth and learning over your brethren of Rome. The Scriptures were composed in your own language. You may claim primacy in certain spiritual matters. But the real difference between you and the Lord Dispensator is this.' I leaned forward over the table and snapped my fingers into his face. I took hold of his beard and pulled it. I pushed him gently in the chest and watched as he nearly went backwards.

'You presume too much, Alaric,' he finally cried back at me. 'Just because the Great Augustus—'

I silenced him with a crash of my fist on the table that knocked all Theodore's waxed tablets out of order. When he'd finished jabbering back at me, I leaned forward and pushed my face close to his.

'Don't talk back to me about the Emperor,' I said with quiet menace. 'So long as he keeps the army sweet, and doesn't let the Circus mob get out of hand, Heraclius can declare for any Eastern heresy that takes his fancy. He can announce that Christ appeared on earth as nothing more than a ghost, and that it was by a continuing miracle that those round him thought he was other than a direct Emanation of God. Or he can resurrect the Arian heresy. Or he can declare that Christ had a bald patch two inches wide, and got seven children on Mary Magdalene. He can do all of this, and your interest will be best consulted by assenting to what he says and preaching it to however sceptical a people. And if you breathe so much as a word about his orthodoxy or sanity, a file of guards will march straight into your church and arrest you at the very altar. If you still refuse to see sense, you'll be lucky to drag out the rest of your days in some monastery on the edges of Scythia. Shall I take you through some of the precedents? Or can we take them as read?'

When he was able to look back at me, I continued: 'Those Western clerics you've spent the past ten days or whatever insulting, and over whom you've now insulted me and the Emperor himself, are in a very different position. They don't ultimately give a toss about us or our difficulties with the Eastern Patriarchates. They don't need to. Between Ravenna and Bari, I don't think we have a single armed man in Italy. Certainly, Rome is both governed and defended by the Church. For all we can do anything to those he represents, the Lord Fortunatus might as well be from China.

'We can do nothing to him and his,' I said, now with savage ill-humour, 'but they can fuck us over good and proper. That deacon from Rome has more power in his little finger to hurt us in our Syrian and Egyptian dealings than you Greeks have in your collective loins. And I know that he will use that power if he thinks he or the Roman Church has not received the total respect he believes appropriate. And I'll do whatever it takes to keep him absolutely sweet – even if it means dragging you by the hair into the dining room tomorrow and setting about you with a cane until you offer him your clerical kiss of peace.'

'And what makes you think Heraclius really wants your settlement of the Monophysite heresy?' Simeon now got the wind to cry back at me. 'How much confidence do you think he's still got in Sergius? If anyone is at risk of being shipped off to Scythia, it's surely His Present Holiness the Patriarch of Constantinople – a Patriarch, I'll remind you, appointed by the tyrant Phocas against the wishes of every Greek bishop.' He laughed bitterly, and even managed to stare me in the face.

'And I know exactly how much confidence he has in *you*, My Lord Senator!' he went on. 'You failed him in Alexandria. You've made trouble for him among everyone of quality with your land confiscation project. You want to give land to the peasants, in the hope that they'll do more to defend the Empire than their betters have. More likely, you want to reproduce the same chaotic spirit of independence as among your own dirty barbarians! Can't you see how you've been set up to fail? Oh, you can lay violent hands on me. But it doesn't alter the truth of the matter.'

Whatever drug Priscus had fed him was working miracles for his courage. But, if he really thought I'd set about him with the cane he deserved, he was wrong. I made my mind up and smiled calmly back at him.

'Dear Simeon,' I said. 'The workings of the Imperial Mind are far above both of us. Let us not argue what they may or may not have resolved before you took ship for Athens. But I will remind you that we have a most important council starting the day after tomorrow. Your duty there will be to judge such issues as may be raised purely on their theological merits. If I find reason to think that you are following some other agenda, I will see to it personally that Heraclius is made aware of certain facts that will not stand to your credit. I assure you that your truest interest lies in acting as a bishop of the Church and not as some third-rate politician, dabbling in affairs that are beyond your understanding.'

I waited for this to impress itself on his mind. The thing about intelligence information is that it should only be used when all else has failed. Even then, it should, in the first instance, be used allusively. This was now one of those first instance times. Possibly, Heraclius *was* out of sorts with me. Possibly, he was tired of Sergius, and was interested in some purely local deal with the Greek Church. Whatever the case, all I could do was press on as if the words of my commission were explicit instructions to do as I'd resolved. And, if I gave him that on my return, he might even decide it was what the Great Augustus had wanted after all.

'Simeon,' I continued in more earnest tone, 'I will assume Priscus has told you what you may already have suspected. This being so, please do consider that nothing in the Acts of the Council of Chalcedon, nor officially declared since by way of explanation, rules out the possibility of a Singularity of Will for Christ. If you can agree with the Westerners that this is not ruled out, we may bring the Eastern Churches, little by little, to full orthodoxy. The main council may still be several years off. But do consider that you have been spoken about as the next Patriarch.' I paused and waited for that lie to sink in. 'We know that Sergius has weak lungs, and that the smoke of last winter in Constantinople was a sore trial for him. Who knows what advice the doctors may give him this winter? Who knows what gratitude Caesar will feel for a man who has done more than any other senior Greek churchman to enable a reconciliation with our separated brethren in the East?'

I got up and stretched out a hand for Simeon. Silent and thoughtful, he took my hand. I led him from the library and down to the main body of the residency. I put him with my own hands into his carrying chair, and followed him into the street.

Back in my office, I sat down and unlocked the sliding compartment under my desk. I took out twelve of the better coins and transferred them to a leather purse. When it came to shopping, Athens plainly didn't compare with Constantinople. It didn't even compare with Rome. But, if none of the silk factories I'd seen from the Acropolis existed for any purpose of tax or regulation, I might see what they could do for me. I smiled and thought how, by doing nothing at all, Nicephorus might unwittingly have done this place quite a favour. If you could only find the right mix of neglect with a dash of civil justice, the whole Empire might be saved yet.

That brought me back to thoughts of my duty here. Unless Nicephorus was far more effective than he'd so far appeared, and Priscus did get to deliver my funeral oration, I could handle things in Athens. As for Constantinople, that was out of my present control. So long as there was no overpowering emergency in Church or state, Heraclius would remain irresolute in all things. If only I could get back home before Christmas, and give him that provisional settlement on a plate, he might well forget all the poison Ludinus had been dripping into his ear. At the least, it would remove any excuse for turning openly nasty. Give me that, and I could give another few months to sorting out the Imperial finances. Give me that, and he might persuade himself that I was irreplaceable. I might even find myself basking again in the sun of Imperial favour.

I stared at the scroll of Dexippus that Martin had carried down from the library and left on my desk. Even if the single lamp he'd set out for me had been enough, this wasn't a book I now fancied. What it described had been the greatest crisis Athens had faced since the end of its long war with Sparta. The ruin it left had closed one chapter in the city's history and opened another that wasn't yet ended. Given the lack of any Imperial assistance, Dexippus had managed the best defence possible in the circumstances. It was a shame he'd written it all up so badly. A month of carefully walking over the ground might illuminate the story as he'd told it. Or it might only deepen the confusion of his text.

Since there was nothing else to read, I decided, I might as well change out of these clothes. I took up the lamp and made for the door. Though it was covered with a thick cloth, there was a smell of unemptied chamber pot in the outer room. If I could have trusted for it to be collected, and not simply kicked over, the next morning, I'd have put it out in the corridor. Instead, I put it on the window seat. Still half pleased with myself, half nervous about what might be happening seven hundred miles away in Constantinople, I opened the door into my bedroom.

There was a sudden smell of beeswax. I heard the creak of leather bed straps. I looked at the dim but smooth shape on the uncovered bed. 'Your secretary's wife was most pleased to accept Theodore's offer of help in the nursery,' Euphemia said with a slightly nervous giggle. 'He will sleep there until further notice.'

'He's a good boy,' I said. My fingers shook slightly as I untied the cords that held my outer tunic in place. It couldn't be seen in this light, but I reached up automatically to tap the much reduced swelling on my nose. 'You must let Martin direct his reading. He can be a most excellent schoolmaster. His father was the best in Constantinople.'

She giggled again as I pulled my inner tunic over my head. 'You must think me a most abandoned woman,' she said.

'I've been hoping no less all day,' I replied. I turned the lamp full up and stood beside the bed.

29

I looked up from my prostration into the blackest face imaginable.

'You failed me in Alexandria,' Heraclius whined. 'All I then asked was that you should get Greek and Latin Churches to agree that probably manifest heresy might be orthodox. And you failed me again.'

I tried to speak, but no voice came as the Emperor got up from his throne and stepped over me. Court protocol didn't allow me to get up yet. Instead, I crouched on all fours, looking at a mass of purple cushions.

The gong struck, and I could finally get up. Heraclius now sat on the far side of the Great Hall of Audience, every bishop he'd called to Athens ranged about him. I felt the blockage clear from my throat and was able to speak. 'If I was never meant to succeed, how can you blame me for failure?' I shouted.

My answer was a burst of laughter that went on as if without end.

Acquittal was beyond hoping. Perhaps I could beg for mercy – if not for myself, then at least for mine. I hurried over and fell down for another prostration, and tried to think of the best form of plea. Should I be the manly young Alaric? Or should I just squeal and babble? What was most likely to move these bastards?

I heard the grind of machinery as I raised my face from the carpet. The throne had now been raised about six feet, and all I could see when I finally stood up again was purple flesh bulging over the red leather boots.

'Who are you to question the workings of power?' Heraclius

asked from aloft. 'If I command you to do something, I expect it to be done – even if I command others to frustrate you.'

There was more laughter. The bishops had now been joined by the whole of the Imperial Council and what may have been the whole of the Senatorial Order. Already large, the Great Hall of Audience had expanded somehow to the size of the Great Church. The laughter came in massed bursts, and echoed from the impossibly high ceiling.

I put aside all thoughts of protocol. The hall had expanded still further, and contained everyone in Constantinople above the lowest class. It even managed to contain people who'd died years before. Every one of these was dressed in white, and had a nimbus about his head. I stepped forward to approach the distant throne. As I came close, I saw the bishops shrink back as if I'd carried a sword. I looked up at Heraclius.

'I could have you shut away in a monastery,' he sobbed. 'I could have you blinded. I could have your tongue slit in two to make you resemble the serpent that you truly are. Behold, however, the Mercy of Caesar!' He looked down at two heralds. There was a sheet of parchment held out for them by one of the black eunuchs.

'It is the judgement of our Great Augustus,' they read in unison, not trying to keep the laughter from their voices, 'that you be taken to the topmost roof of your palace, there to look down for the space of one hour at the manifold glories of the Imperial City; and that you be taken thence to the land of endless night and of endless cold that was once the fruitful Province of Britain; and that you there be turned loose among the filthy and unlettered savages who are your rightful people; and that infamy attend your name in the Empire, and that death attend your return to the Empire.'

As they ended the sentence, there was wild applause and cheering. I wanted to stand upright and look defiance into every face. But I was only pushed from behind for another grovel. The laughter and the cheering went on and on. It left off any echo, and I felt a chilly breeze on my exposed neck, as if I were now in the Circus, and my sentence were being pronounced before the whole assembled people of Constantinople . . .

I woke in my bed to the sound of wolves howling in the distance. I had the impression that Euphemia had been shaking me for some while, but was only aware of this as I came fully back into the present.

'You were crying in your sleep,' she said. 'Were you dreaming?'

The lamp was long since gone out, and there was no sign of dawn. But I sat up and reached to where I knew there would be a cup of water. I drank and wiped my sweaty face on the sheet. 'It was nothing,' I said, 'just a dream.' I pressed my eyes shut and put it all out of mind. Of course, it had been just a dream. All else aside, when did the real Heraclius *ever* finish a sentence? If he'd managed that even once since he came to power, there might have been less doubt regarding his actual wishes. I opened my eyes again and listened. 'But how have wolves got into Athens?' I asked. Even before she began her soft laugh, I realised the answer. Though awake, I'd still been in the vastness of the Imperial City, where a man could walk for days and never see the same street twice. Here, in Athens, you were never more than a quarter of a mile from the walls. If some shortness of food in the mountains had brought them down early to prowl about the plains of Attica, it stood to reason they'd sound close enough to be just outside the residency.

'Were you dreaming?' she asked again.

I made a non-committal reply and drank more water. It was rather brackish. But Euphemia was now sitting up and had her arms about me, as if to protect a frightened child. 'Do you believe that dreams are a communication with some higher force?' she asked.

I put the dream itself out of mind and gathered my thoughts. 'Dreams are nothing more than a distorted continuation of waking thoughts,' I said. 'They contain no new sensory impressions. They can suggest new ideas that might otherwise have remained overlooked. But they are generally so connected with waking concerns, that they cannot be regarded as other than unshackled trains of thought. If not that, they are just inexplicable fancies. There is never any outside cause to them.' Because I was still not fully awake, my self-control hadn't its usual rigidity, and I found myself wondering about the balance in this dream between fancies and new ideas.

Euphemia smiled and sat a moment in silence. 'The howling disturbs you?' she asked with a change of subject.

The short answer was that it did. Even if wall after wall stood between us, the sound those black and vicious creatures made took me back to my earliest childhood in Kent. Perhaps a year after my mother had been dumped with us in Richborough, there had come a winter as cold as anyone could remember. Then, the wolf packs had streamed through every breach in the city wall, and I'd lain awake every night, hearing their snuffling and scratching outside our barricaded door. We were among the lucky ones. We might not have had much of a roof, but we still had four walls. Almost every night, I'd heard the wild screaming of those who were old or manless and whose defences had failed, and who were devoured in their beds. Had this somehow been the cause of that stupid little dream?

I got up from the bed and felt my way to the brazier in the centre of the room. I got hold of the poker and jabbed at the invisible embers. As they came back to life, I put oil into the lamp and got it alight.

Euphemia lay naked on the bed. She sat up and looked back at me. 'I haven't seen you properly in the day,' she said. 'But your eyes are so light here, they must be a very pale blue.' She looked harder at me. 'How old are you?' she asked.

'Twenty-two,' I said. I felt a tremor of renewed lust and sat heavily beside her. 'Shall we – shall we do it again?' I asked.

'Again?' she cried with mock alarm. She laughed. 'Have I not yet satisfied My Lord?' She laughed again and pushed me gently back. 'Twenty-two,' she said, now thoughtful. 'Except for your exalted status, I'd surely have thought you a little younger. There must be an interesting story behind your progress.' I said nothing and she dropped that line of questioning. 'But were you not sad to leave Constantinople and come down to this shrivelled husk of a city?'

I nodded, and wondered how she could have come so close to guessing what my dream had been about. But I said a little of the vastness and beauty of the City as it might appear to anyone who couldn't see the deadness and corruption at its heart. As she prompted, I spoke on about the teeming streets, and the crowded docks and markets, and the museums and galleries, and the mass upon mass of statues and monuments plundered from an empire that embraced every city that had been great and famous long before Constantinople itself had been other than the mediocre town of Byzantium, notable only for its position at the end of a finger of Europe where it almost touched the shores of Asia. If no longer the capital of an empire that reached from north of York almost to Babylon – though pressed on every one of its reduced frontiers, and giving way on all of them – there could be no doubt of its place in the world. I tried, and now succeeded, not to doubt my own place within the City.

'Oh, to be in such a place,' she breathed with a desperate longing, 'a city so large that you can walk about in freedom and never be recognised. It is surely a place of dreams – a place where every dream is able to become real.'

I nodded again and put my own dream finally out of mind.

There was a renewed howling. I froze instinctively and looked about for my sword.

'Do they really frighten you?' she asked.

I tried for a smile and reached out for her.

'But you grow used to them in Athens. They are not even the worst that Athens has to offer.' She put a hand on my stomach, and drew a sharp nail over the ridges of muscle.

I shivered and drew her into my arms. The smell of her perfume was overpowering. Everything began to fade out of mind but the closeness of our two bodies.

She laughed, now very softly. 'Like us,' she said in a dreamy voice, 'they are the children of the night. Their hunger is as our own. And who shall deny the feeding of that hunger?'

Once more – and I can't say how many times it had been already – I lay back and arched my body as those unbelievably powerful hands took hold of both my wrists, and I gasped and bit my lips almost to the point of drawing blood in the beginning of another ecstasy that I knew would pass, but that would, throughout its entire duration, seem infinite in both time and nature. Before I passed out of all rational perception, I felt her scented, unbound hair brush against my face. Her lips pressed suddenly against mine, and I felt all her weight upon me. I could hear the wolves still howling, but no longer cared about it, or was properly aware of it.

30

Back in ancient times, the streets of Athens were as mean and crooked as of any modern city resettled by barbarians. In the massive improvement works he'd commanded, Hadrian had flattened everything in the centre not hallowed by recollections of the past. But that had been four centuries ago. Since then, we'd had two – perhaps three – devastating raids; and the rebuilding of a now depopulated area had restored much of the original squalor. The sun was peering across from above one of the lower houses when the Dispensator came to a sudden halt.

'Can this be the house?' Martin asked uncertainly.

The answer he got was another disapproving look.

I had to admit that, in the labyrinth of streets that lay between the derelict Temple of Apollo and what was now the Monastery of Saint Paul, one box of rendered mud brick appeared the same as any other. In illustrations to the better class of books, Athenian houses are always shown as miniature palaces. If you bother to read the *Dialogues* of Plato, or any other ancient literature that mentions how even persons of quality lived then, you'll know that the pictures are not a fair reproduction of ancient ways. Bring him forward a thousand years, and Socrates wouldn't have felt at all out of place in these surroundings. Of course, he'd have been stoned to death the moment he opened his silly mouth. But he'd have been quite at home otherwise.

'I have had cause more often than I care to admit,' the Dispensator said at last, 'to make my way here. If I have not so far left in any mood of satisfaction, this is most assuredly the house of Felix.' He sniffed and brought the iron tip of his walking staff down with a gentle thud on the compacted earth of the track between the houses.

I looked pointedly at the step to the door of an abandoned building, and waited for Martin to take the hint and spread his cloak. I waited for the Dispensator to grunt his reluctant thanks and sit down in a shaft of sunlight.

'You go in,' I said to Martin. 'Since the man really does appear to have gone barking mad, it'll be better if you put him at some ease before we start instructing him in his duties.' I stood in the shade and stretched lazily. There were some children playing on the other side of a wall. A few late bluebottles were about already to make a nuisance of themselves to a dog who was still trying to sleep. Otherwise, this district of Athens had all the silence you'd expect of a middling slum before everyone is up and about.

I was thinking of the previous night, and of all its endless pleasures, when the Dispensator coughed and looked at me across the narrow street. 'I was visited yesterday evening by the Lord Priscus,' he said.

I nodded. Getting Martin out of the residency for our tour of Athens had taken everything short of a slap to the face. Getting him off to the Areopagus had taken a few hard looks. 'We're as likely to be murdered in our beds as anywhere else,' I'd told him. 'Besides, Nicephorus has no orders, so far as we know, to set hands on you.' That had given him very little cheer – and could have given him none, bearing in mind the repeated assurances of what Priscus had in mind for him in the event of my fall from the Imperial Grace. Now, if it seemed that Priscus was simply working on the fears of all the delegates, we might be safe enough. After all, what he probably wanted most was me to share in the disgrace back home. Doing away with me might give him an intense if momentary pleasure. But he surely knew that having to explain a dead Legate to Heraclius would only add to his eventual embarrassment.

'For a Greek nobleman, his Latin is most fluent,' the Dispensator added.

I nodded again. Unless he made a particular effort, Priscus

spoke neither language with much delicacy. I had to grant, though, he had as great a talent for languages as my own. Indeed, I'd now discovered he knew enough Syriac to follow Nicephorus in his more unrestrained moments of terror. Give credit where it's due – Priscus was a cut above your normal modern Greek.

The Dispensator brushed off a small feather that had settled on his outer robe and cleared his throat. 'Something I have long wondered, however, is how the son-in-law of the Unmentionable Tyrant could have survived the revolution.'

I smiled. The Dispensator never broke bread without a stratagem. And here it was! The Lateran had its spies everywhere, but still hadn't fully made sense of the snake pit that lay at the heart of politics in the Imperial capital. I walked over and sat beside the Dispensator. For a moment, our calves met. Then he shifted a little to the right, and there was an inch of space between us.

'He did switch sides before Heraclius turned up outside Constantinople,' I said. 'He betrayed his own defence plans for the City, and made sure that, when the gates swung open, there was a minimum of fighting.' Since Phocas had bullied me, once Priscus had flown, into making his last stand – and I'd been overwhelmed by the professionals Heraclius had picked up on his journey from Carthage – I'd not go into details here. 'That earned him a high place in the new order of things. Besides, he is the Empire's only decent general. Without him to slow their advance, the Persians would already have reached Antioch.' I paused and spoke carefully. 'Certainly, but for Priscus, we'd already have lost Egypt.' No one could deny him that. With or without his arrival in Alexandria, I'd never have got the Viceroy to publish the land law. But Priscus had drawn the Brotherhood into Alexandria, before flattening it. He'd then stopped any invasion of Egypt from across the Red Sea. Without him, I'd have been taking very bad news back to the Emperor. There'd not have been even the pretence of a second chance in Athens.

'He's also the head of the old nobility in Constantinople,' I added. I changed the subject. 'Did he bring you any alarming news last night?' I asked, as if I didn't already know the answer.

Now, the Dispensator gave one of those smiles that verge on the friendly without ever quite getting there. 'He made me aware of the situation north of Thermopylae,' he said. 'This did perturb His Grace the Bishop of Messina. My own response, however, was that we were called here for a purpose that no merely secular difficulty could serve to interrupt.'

I looked up at the very blue sky. Trust the Dispensator to send Priscus away with a flea in his ear. If it meant that Nicephorus and Balthazar might now be pushed into arranging a sad accident for me, that was easier to deal with than standing in the way of several dozen clerics, all on the bolt for Corinth.

As I looked down again and waited for the Dispensator to get to the subject of the defective Universal Bishop grant – and this was plainly uppermost in his mind – I heard the door open to the interpreter's house.

'You'd better come in, Aelric,' Martin whispered in Celtic. 'It isn't very good.'

I stood in the larger of the two rooms in the house. Though bare, it was neat and clean. There was an icon of Saint Luke on the longest of the walls. Beneath this were a writing table and the pens and many inkpots of one whose living is words and their exact equivalents in another language. Felix himself sat in bed, a threadbare blanket wrapped about his shoulders. It took a while for my eyes to adjust fully to the darkened interior. I could see at once, though, that this was an old man. He might or might not have been as old as he seemed from his unkempt white hair and beard. There was no doubt his wits weren't all that were needed of someone employed for his job.

'But where is she?' he asked as if repeating himself. 'She went out with letters for the Lord Count. She should have been back long before evening. Where has she gone?' He looked up into my face.

I caught the haggard despair in his eyes. Much truth is got from strangers by a course of questioning and observation. Sometimes, like a flash of lightning, it will cross from one mind to another.

One look at the face is then enough. I swallowed and ordered myself not to let my shoulders sag.

'Please stay where you are,' I said gently. I sat down opposite the old man and took his hand in mine. 'Tell me – when did your daughter go out?' Getting a meaningful answer did now take questioning. She might have gone out seven days before. It might have been five. If I really needed to know, I could turn and ask the Dispensator exactly when the man had gone from eccentricity to apparent madness. But the description Felix gave me confirmed what Martin had also guessed.

How do you tell an old man that his only child – a daughter he'd loved, and who'd been his one reason for staying alive in this ghastly world – has been murdered in some obscene and utterly worthless ritual, and then dumped like a scraped-out melon husk? I could have taken the easy path and pretended ignorance. I could have made smooth promises of a search and left the news to be broken by someone else. After all, without a positive identification, I could have told myself, I might be mistaken, and that there was no point in giving what might have been an unnecessary shock. But the birthmark he'd mentioned on the right forearm was undeniable identification. I told the man as gently as I could what had happened.

I was trying again for some words – *any* words – of comfort, when the Dispensator got up and stood beside the icon of Saint Luke.

'Felix,' he said.

The old man looked up bleakly.

The Dispensator raised his arms and stretched them out to the old man. 'Felix, it is the settled conviction of our Faith that the end of this life is no more than a gateway through which all must pass into a new life. Whether you had gone before your daughter, or she has now gone before you, is a matter of the Divine Providence that it is not for us to question. It is enough for us to know that whatever happens must assuredly happen for a purpose that is ultimately good. Your daughter is with Jesus, and you will, it is the promise of our Faith, see her again on the latter day. I tell you this from my own conviction. I tell you also as representative of the Universal Bishop.'

The old man wept as the sermon continued. But he was no longer looking wildly about. In matters of faith, as in all other matters, you might as well have argued with the waves on Dover Beach as with the Dispensator. Odd to say – and he'd never dressed otherwise, or acted other than as chief functionary of the Pope – but I'd never thought of him as any kind of priest. Now, as I heard that irresistible flow of comfort, I realised what a good missionary the Church had lost when the Lord Fortunatus first took possession of his mean little office in the Lateran. Given that mood of bleak despair, even I might have drawn comfort from his words. A reasonable man must face facts as they are, not as he might wish them to be. Equally, there are times when no reasonable man will challenge false consolation. There is something in what Plutarch said against Epicurus.

'She will be forgiven her sins?' the old man asked.

'There is not the smallest doubt, my son,' came the reply.

Trying for a devout look of my own, I listened to the conversation. Once or twice, when the poor old creature lapsed into Greek, I had to give a whispered translation to the Dispensator. I was glad he'd come along, to show me the house and join me in the act of bullying I'd had in mind. I could never have managed this flow of commanding comfort. Even Martin could only have had the authority of a firm but untonsured believer. I listened, impressed – and I worked hard to make sense of the incidentals of what Felix had let slip about the nature of his daughter's dealings with the Lord murdering Count of Athens. They were broken. They were repeated. They were contradictory in their details. The senility that despair can throw like a blanket over an aged mind is one of the few mercies in life. If he was never to recover his wits, and if his days would not now be prolonged, the old man's suffering would not be all that it might otherwise have been. The bitter despair of the old has no other cure. But I'd learned something.

31

'You have no choice, Aelric,' Martin whispered beside me. 'You *have* to act.'

Still silent, I looked again at the icon of the Risen Christ. He glared disapprovingly back at me from the wooden panel, the Virgin clutching at His left hand, the tomb broken open beneath His feet. I had to grant that, once you accepted the glitter all about us of jewelled relic boxes, and the endless profusion of bright colours, Justinian had employed architects and workmen of great ability to convert the Temple of Athena into a church. You really couldn't tell that the main structure had been turned round, so it was now entered from the west, nor that the internal columns had been removed to make room for worshippers to stand inside. I'd seen the gold and ivory statue of Athena in Constantinople; it had been placed in the covered Theatre of Oribasius, so the seats flowed round it. Here, it must have been placed behind me, where the main door was now located. I looked up at the ceiling. This had been replaced at some time during or before the conversion, its weight now supported by a couple of brick arches in the modern style.

But there was to be no more thinking about architectural details. Martin drew breath to carry on in his whispered Celtic. I almost wished he could have gone back to insisting on a dishonourable flight from Corinth. I sighed and got in first. 'He was fucking the girl,' I conceded. 'I have no reasonable doubt of that. He was fucking her, and leading her along with all the usual promises. What happened next, though, may be doubted. We might assume this was a sex killing. A man in the Count's position is able to develop and indulge some questionable tastes . . .'

'You know perfectly well it was sorcery!' Martin hissed. 'We both heard that he sacrificed her to whatever demon was being asked to drown us at sea. Why else his behaviour when you found the body?'

I could have thrown doubt on all of this. What we'd heard in the library was at least ambiguous. All that Nicephorus had said and done beside the tomb of Hierocles could make sense on the assumption of a mere sex killing.

The Dispensator, though, had now finished his own long prayer for the soul of the dead, and was standing behind us. 'God understands all,' he said in a voice that, however softly he spoke, echoed from the curved ceiling. 'But I choose to think it both unfriendly and a sign of guilt if your conversation is in a language that neither I nor any other worshipper here can understand. You know, Alaric, that the poor girl was murdered. Will you resist me if I claim the right to *all* the information you have about her death?'

I certainly would resist him, and I did. Not so buggery Martin. After a few promising evasions and shifty looks, he gave straight in and told the lot, probable sorcery and all.

The Dispensator got down again on his knees, this time beside us, and prayed for what seemed a very long time. 'We have been called to Athens,' he finally said, now very grim, 'to agree some process by which heretics may be reconciled to the Faith as laid down at Chalcedon. I now learn that the Count of Athens himself is in communion with the demons of the Old Faith, and that this communion has not stopped short of human sacrifice. Might I ask His Magnificence the Lord Senator Alaric why this fact has not been reported?'

The plain answer I could have given was that Nicephorus was the normal authority to which these things should be reported. Since that was out, I was the next authority, and I already knew all about his crime. What I did about it was a matter for me alone to decide. I turned and looked nervously about. We weren't alone in the church. But the five monks behind us had the dark beards and eyes of Easterners. The old women who'd probably come in out of the sun, and were muttering to each other as they carried on with their knitting, also could be trusted not to follow any of the Latin in which we were speaking. The previous day, I'd fixed myself like a cart in some ancient rut. There was justice in its widest sense to be served here. If murder was murder, there was also an empire that had to be saved. We'd save this most effectually by sorting out the Monophysite heresy – not by setting everyone in a twitter with allegations of sorcery.

'Look, Fortunatus,' I said, trying to sound reasonable, 'the moment I'm ready, I'll have that bastard Count clapped in chains before he can squeal the name of his goddess. He can then be shipped off to Constantinople for trial before the Emperor. But there are, for the moment, other things to consider . . .' I fell silent and began to feel dirtier than ever. I looked back at the icon. You don't expect a few daubs of paint on wood to give advice on how to govern Church and state. I got no guidance whatever. Like a fool, I turned and stared into the pitiless face of the Dispensator. At once, I felt myself back in his office in the Lateran. I might be His Magnificence the Lord Senator to everyone else. But here was someone who knew just as well as Martin who I actually was. Unlike Martin, the Dispensator would never back down from that knowledge. I looked straight down at the limestone tiles that must have been laid over the ancient floor, and tried to focus on a mean-ingless graffito someone had scratched there.

'Alaric,' the Dispensator said, 'when Constantine established the True Faith, the demons who had previously deceived mankind were not destroyed. Instead, they were simply displaced from their temples and from the general regard. Ever since then, they have lurked in every dark place, ready to be called back into power by the appropriate words, and given new power by offerings of blood. Sometimes, they will take over the minds of the weak with gifts of carnal knowledge; demons, you will be aware, can assume living forms of great beauty and allure. Sometimes, they will remain invisible, but offer power over things. Christ Himself will not combat their wiles, but has resigned that task to those who freely use their own will and the secular power of the Empire. You are the highest secular power in Athens. I charge you with the duty to act in defence of right, truth and justice.'

I might have tried for a bitter laugh. But you really didn't try interrupting the Dispensator.

'At the very least,' he went on, 'our duty is to go out and recover the body of that poor child. She deserves a Christian burial.'

I made no answer, but left him to prose on to his conclusion about our duties to the dead and to the living, and to God in His Heaven. I'd never shut him up. All I could do was start persuading myself, with a desperate lack of conviction, that he was jogging me into a combination of justice with convenience.

He turned to Martin and glared his burst of twitching and muttering into stillness. 'She was sixteen,' he spat. 'How would you feel in that old man's position? How about losing *your* only child?'

I looked again at the icon and wondered. Even if I left Nicephorus at large, and had to send all my people off to Corinth without me – even if I had to lie alone at night, with a sword under the bed – I *couldn't* afford the risk of going public with sorcery charges. Then again, if I acted not alone, but at the behest of the Church . . . ? A thought was stirring at the back of my mind.

'Very well,' I said when the Dispensator finally stopped to collect his own thoughts. 'We'll go out and recover the body. Before you can have it for burial, I'll shove it under the nose of Count bloody Nicephorus. He doesn't look the sort who's up to denying apparent proof of his actions. I'll charge him with sorcery and treason and misappropriation of funds. We'll see if we can also lay hands on that fraud Balthazar. After all, he probably killed the girl.' I thought again. 'We might even consider arresting our dear friend and companion in our travels the Commander of the East. If we can shock a full confession out of Nicephorus, we'll have the evidence we need for that. After all, any failure to report sorcery and treason *is* sorcery and treason so far as the law is concerned. We'll hang the lesser trash, and drag the other three off to denounce each other black in the face before the Emperor. They can then be taken off to be eaten alive by pigs or boiled in lead. The Circus mob won't have seen the like of their execution since wicked old Phocas was Emperor.

'No,' I went on, giving way, I could tell myself, to the inevitable, 'I'll produce that body in the residency, and start the wheels and pulleys of justice. I'm sure the Bishop of Athens can lend us a holding dungeon until we can all take ship for Constantinople. Until then, we can see how well our dear friend can support the prospect of having his own eyelids peeled, and starved rats shoved into his own wide-stretched arse, before the big day in public. You know that, where accusations of sorcery are concerned, the Big Boss makes up laws on the spot.'

I got up and scowled. That icon of Christ, I vaguely noted, looked at its best from a kneeling position. Modern artists might lack the realism of the ancients, but were no less skilful at producing whatever effects they wanted. I looked about at the colours that glowed on every wall. I'd give in to necessity. But for Martin, I'd surely have found some pleasing lie to keep the Dispensator quiet. But what was done was done. I suddenly wilted inside myself. Was it really policy that I'd given in so easily? Or was it just anger? Was this Aelric the barbarian, acting from outrage? Or was it Alaric, the subtle politician? I felt confused. I felt dirty. I felt confused again. But I steadied my thoughts. Whatever I finally decided about my own motives, this was now a Church matter. In theory, the Dispensator was as much in charge of these matters here as in Rome. The Bishop of Athens took his orders from the Pope – which meant the Dispensator. Regular armed men would have been better. But a few dozen of those vicious monks would be a fair alternative to the civil power. Give them a whiff of sorcery, and they'd tear Athens apart to get at Nicephorus. I could no more stop what had to happen than Felix had been able to stand up to the Dispensator's flow of comfort. Perhaps I no more wanted to. I could still hope I'd get up to address my council to a burst of applause. If I merely unsettled every mind still further, that was something I'd have to take into account as and when.

I looked at the Dispensator. 'Very well, My Lord Fortunatus,' I said again. 'You can have your way. But we need to move fast. For evidential reasons, it would be useful to have a witness with me in the residency whose sworn declaration must be taken seriously by any court. If you can oblige me in this regard, I can promise that justice will be served as fully on earth as it will be in Heaven.'

The Dispensator pursed his lips, but nodded.

'As soon as you can manage, I'd like four strong men from your monastery, and a stretcher with heavy blankets. Please do this quickly and without explaining any purpose. I'll be waiting a few hundred yards along the Piraeus road.'

We'd been walking slowly back to the main door of the church. Now, we stepped out into the impossible glare of the late morning sun. 'You can't be thinking of a trip outside the walls *now*?' Martin groaned. 'Shouldn't we go back to see if Irene has delivered those slaves?'

I opened my eyes and stared down at the steps. If I were to lie down on them, I'd be able to see for myself how they curved along their length to produce the effect they gave to the whole of great lightness. But I sniffed and gave Martin a frown of annoyance. That was all his fault, I could have reminded him. But for his loose tongue, we'd already have been back to have our slaves strip naked and show their teeth for a last-minute inspection and possible haggle over whether they came up to the stipulated health and fineness. I waited for him to turn his eyes away from mine. 'I'm not risking a trip back to the residency,' I snapped. 'Since we can't agree to wait, speed and secrecy are of the essence. If you saw that we were followed when we came out, you didn't tell me at the time.' I touched the sword I was carrying about my waist. I could, of course, go back and arrest Nicephorus, and then go outside Athens for the evidence. But, if I wanted Priscus too, I'd have to observe all the forms, and make sure they were witnessed.

I stared back inside the dark interior of the church. You kill for defence. You kill someone who's guilty of something that merits death. You kill those for whom death is an occupational hazard. No one but a beast kills like this. Where the lesser accomplices were concerned, I'd probably not go beyond hanging. But that would be the only mercy they could expect.

I rubbed at my nose. A final look in the mirror before coming out had let me think the spots were going. But was there now a third coming up? 'Do remind me, Martin,' I said, 'to arrange a pension of the eighth grade. I will seal the order myself, though search me how it will be paid. You can also see if any of the remaining interpreters is worth promoting.'

'I must assure you, Alaric,' the Dispensator said as we paused for a moment within the Propylaea, 'that you are doing the right thing.'

I didn't bother answering.

But, now there was no one to overhear us in Latin, he raised his voice. 'You must consider,' he said, 'that every stroke of what you are vulgar enough to call luck has come your way precisely because, when called upon to do the right thing, that is what – however protestingly – you have always done.'

I could have laughed in his face. Instead, I wished I'd stayed in my bed the night before last. Better still, I wished I'd never got out of my chair on the Piraeus road. There's much to be said for ignorance, especially of facts that only get in the way of what absolutely has to be done.

32

I stood looking at the cenotaph of Euripides. Except that the continuous rains of the summer had left every plant an unautumnal green, the Piraeus road was now as I'd first imagined it. Giving up on the residency slaves, Martin and his wife had finally got all my fine clothes into order, and I'd come out to see the interpreter in one of my thinner tunics. Athens was far north of Alexandria, and the heat even of a good noonday in October didn't compare. Despite the moderate freshness, though, I was happy to stand here hatless and without any cloak. Though not many, there were now passers-by. None recognised me, and the few looks I got were simple interest in the incongruous match of my colouring and the finest white silk.

'Do you remember the game we used to play in Alexandria?' I asked in Latin. 'I mean the one where we'd stand ourselves in such and such a place, and try to imagine what it must have looked like at such and such a time in the past?'

He left off his nervous inspection of the few passers-by on the road and nodded.

'Well,' I went on with the artificial brightness of a man who needs to jolly someone out of total funk, 'I tried to play it yesterday on the Acropolis. Then, worse luck, I had Priscus beside me, and it didn't quite work. Here's a fine place for the game, though – don't you agree?'

I got another abstracted nod, and took this as an assent.

'The monument would have gone up after the Spartans had been eased out and the Long Walls were being rebuilt. So far as I can tell, the city walls then would have been about a hundred yards back along the road, rather than their present quarter mile.

If you looked back, you'd surely have seen scaffolding on some of the Acropolis buildings, and their marble, if still unpainted, would have shone much whiter than it does now. The crowd here must have included Plato. Xenophon too might have been here – or would he then have been in exile? I can't remember the dates.'

Martin opened his mouth, and I waited for some authoritative correction. Instead, he fell back into glumness.

'Everything back then would have been fresh,' I pressed on. 'All the words spoken would have been in a natural and unlaboured Greek – neither the gibberish of the modern locals, nor the stilted and almost paranoid Attic of the educated moderns. Wouldn't it be a grand thing to speak a civilised language that was also natural? Try to imagine your Celtic or my English, but able to express all the subtleties of Greek. Native fluency in a perfect language: hardly surprising, wouldn't you agree, that the ancients excel the moderns in all composition – indeed, in all thought?'

No answer.

'What would have been most different, however, was the *spirit* of those gathered here.'

That got me one of Martin's pained looks. He turned and, taking care not to trip over one of the ruts left by a thousand years of cartwheels, walked diagonally across the road. He knelt before a very recent shrine and raised both arms in silent prayer. I stood behind him and waited for his devotional fit to pass.

'I've been thinking about the locals,' I said.

Martin didn't look round.

'Let me put this to you. We know that all animals have more young than survive to maturity. This includes human animals. We can suppose that those who do survive are better fitted to their surroundings than those who don't. We can further suppose random variations in every generation – sometimes deformities and weaknesses, sometimes improvements that mean better chances of survival and reproduction. Granting that people show some resemblance to their parents, we may conclude a gradual adaptation of whole groups to their circumstances.'

Martin did now look round. 'And how does this fit in with the known story of creation?' he asked in a low mumble. 'Every form that God created in the first six days he surely fixed until Judgement Day.'

Another hypothesis, I thought, not for setting down in writing. I smiled reassuringly. 'It is as you say,' I replied. 'However, since the lower classes we've seen shuffling about Athens bear no resemblance to the ancients or to any barbarian race we know to have passed by in the past few centuries, it's worth asking if these people are an adaptation to changed circumstances. Adaptations can surely be degenerations as well as improvements. Let us assume that heavy taxes and a drift of the more able into distant military service or the Church . . .'

I trailed off. Martin had gone back to his long prayer. I heard a dry cough behind me. I turned and looked at the Dispensator. He'd now put on his best robes and a hat with a very wide brim. 'You really didn't need to come out with us,' I said. 'Once I'd got her inside the walls, it was my intention to give the child over for burial.' I could have asked what had taken him so long. I must have read every inscription five times as I stood here in the sun. But I didn't ask.

'Your voice carries far along this road,' the Dispensator said in his chilliest, most disapproving voice. 'It is fortunate you speak in Latin, and there are so few in any event to hear your bold speculations.'

I shrugged.

He looked at the Euripides monument. 'I take it this is the grave of someone from the famous past?'

I nodded.

'Well, if I lack your ability to read these men in their own language, I will remind you that their minds were no more "rational" than those of the moderns. They were both bloody and superstitious. Even if you choose to mock it, the Christian Faith is an improvement on what they believed. A single, omnipotent God the Creator is less childish than the ludicrous pantheon of the Old Faith. You know that Plato believed all manner of nonsense, and his preaching of reason only served to promote deliberately muddy thinking among his followers.'

I smiled and suggested that we might start about our business, now we were all together.

But the Dispensator stepped closer to the monument and traced a few words of the inscription with his forefinger. I saw a faint movement of his lips – whether of recognition or disapproval I couldn't say. But the name Euripides is much the same in Latin and Greek characters, and it was repeated in many grammatical forms. He sniffed and stood back. He now stared thoughtfully at Martin, who had stood up for a respectful bow. 'Even if they hadn't rejected Him,' he said, 'Christ wasn't sent for the Jews. He wasn't sent for the Greeks and Romans. He came as Messenger for a universal faith. And, whether or not you like His message, you are still one of its beneficiaries. You're a barbarian, Alaric.' I tried not to frown. 'A good head and an eye for the main chance have got you further than I'd ever have supposed when you first presented yourself in my office. But you're a barbarian – *Aelric*,' he said, relishing the difficulty of sounding my real name. 'A thousand years ago, neither learning nor intellectual brilliance would have let you cross the line these people drew around themselves. My own ancestors – may God eventually take mercy on their damned souls – might have granted you citizenship, and then forgotten your origins for the sake of your grandsons. So far as *these* ancients were concerned, you would at best have been a beautiful but inferior object of use. It is Christ, and Christ only, who has blurred what otherwise would have been an absolute line.'

Anyone else who'd dared say that would already have been picking his teeth off the pavement. But this was the Lord Fortunatus, Dispensator of the Universal Bishop. No – forget the title and office – this was Fortunatus. The Emperor himself would have shrunk before that withering stare. I set my face into a smile and suggested that we might care to make a start.

'My own very words,' he replied. He stared at the scowling, dark little men who'd followed him out of Athens. He frowned and looked back at me. 'You will forgive my lateness,' he said with icy control. 'The one person in the monastery where I have been lodged who speaks Latin was absent. On his return, he answered my request with an impertinence that has caused both him and my secretary to retire to bed for the day.'

No answer needed to that, nor possible. His walking staff clicking on the stones as he kept pace with me, we set out along the road.

It was undeniably a cheerful day. Birds twittered. A breeze sighed gently in the bushes. I could feel the sun making its way through my clothing. There weren't many others on the road. But these were all monks or from the better classes, who had largely avoided the degeneration of the rabble. Some of these latter, it was pretty clear, were of barbarian stock. Still, no one recognised me. A few took note of the Dispensator, and bowed to him. Our previous journey along a silent, fog-bound road might have been in a different world. Even if Martin weren't dragging his own personal cloud a few yards behind us, it would have been nice to walk the whole distance to Piraeus and back. The monuments had much to commend them. It might also have been interesting to sit on the old docks, looking across the bay to Salamis.

But it wasn't for a stroll in the sun that we'd left the walls of Athens far behind. In bright sunshine, the tomb of Hierocles was much closer than it had seemed two days before. With a muttered apology to the Dispensator, I hurried over the last few dozen yards towards it. Everyone else could follow along at his own pace. Bearing in mind the ghastly, rotting thing that awaited us, it was worth getting this whole business out of the way as quickly as possible.

I heard his faint panting as Martin caught up with me. 'Priscus was with us when she must have been killed,' he said. 'How do you suppose he can be an accomplice to murder?'

I sighed and kicked a stone along the road. This time, there was no mournful echo of its skipping. It made a bright, cheerful sound and sent up a little cloud of dust. 'Oh, Martin,' I said, 'let's go through this. Priscus knows Nicephorus from his previous visit here. Balthazar spoke of "outrages". I'll guess that Priscus tried his own hand at magic in the past. He had nothing to do with this particular outrage. But we may get an accusation out of Nicephorus that allows an arrest. At the worst, I can induce Priscus to a greater prudence in his dealing with our clerical friends.' I looked at him. He'd not taken off hat or cloak, and was sweating with heat and exertion. His face was taking on the strained look that suggested he was about to be taken short again by those horrid frogs. 'The body may be still less pretty than it was,' I said. 'Can I tempt you to some of my oil of roses?' I reached into a leather pouch that hung from my sword belt and took out a stoppered glass bottle. 'It cost its weight in gold in Alexandria. Let's see if it was worth it.'

The Dispensator now came up beside us. 'I have been thinking further about the possibly defective grant to His Holiness that you purported to confirm,' he said.

Anyone who didn't know the man already might have assumed that this had just happened to cross his mind. For myself, it was a surprise he'd taken so long to come out with it. I doubted he could have entirely lost sight of it even when giving comfort to poor old Felix.

He actually swallowed and had to wet his lips before continuing. 'I took the trouble, when he came to see me yesterday evening, of questioning Martin about the precise nature of your authority in Athens.' He paused and licked very dry lips again. 'As chance would have it, I did bring a fresh grant out with me from Rome. You will see that it is drawn in exactly the right form according to law. It needs only your own seal—'

I smiled and broke in: 'Naturally, I shall have to take my own legal advice before I can do anything at all.' I looked at him from the corner of my eyes. He was now sweating very slightly – and not from the heat. 'Martin's opinion is always to be respected. But I do remain a little unsure of my authority. All else aside, if the grant made two years ago should turn out to be valid, we need to consider whether a *second* grant would not simply confuse matters. Can I suggest we wait until the council is over before sitting down to discuss the matter properly?'

I glared Martin into silence and commented on how cheerful the day had turned out. Indeed, it was much improved. I'd walked out of Athens still unsure of myself. Now I was committed to a double arrest, I could appreciate the desperate need for my seal on that very clean sheet of parchment the Dispensator must have been fretting over three times every day since he'd set out from Rome. No one but a fool would have sealed it before the council began. I'd need excellent reason to lift a finger till after the council had finished. I looked up at the sky – still not a cloud in sight.

'I might add,' the Dispensator went on, strain evident in his voice, 'that my summons from the Grand Chamberlain himself did touch on a possible resolution by you in Athens.'

It was my turn to fight for control. I stopped and covered my shock by looking at all that remained of a very old funerary statue. 'Are you telling me,' I asked with an unnaturally steady voice, 'that your summons was sent by His Excellency *Ludinus*?' Anyone else would have thought nothing of the fact. It is the job of the Grand Chamberlain to correspond with foreign powers on behalf of the Emperor. But Heraclius was the Emperor. Though he'd devolved them straight to me and Sergius, he had taken all religious matters into his own hands on coming to power. Unless there had been a total revolution in Constantinople since I'd left in the spring, it was unthinkable that a eunuch could be summoning delegates to any sort of Church council.

'I believe the man's name is Ludinus,' came the reply in a tone that showed my own mood had been noted. 'His communication was most gracious, and even friendly. He said more than once that nothing less than my own attendance in person would be satisfactory to the Emperor.'

We covered the last few yards that separated us from the tomb of Hierocles. In proper light, it looked shabby as well as derelict. The Euripides monument looked more recent, though was a good seven centuries older. That's what you get when money is saved on a funeral. I turned and waved at the monks, who'd been drifting along far behind. I hid every doubt that had crowded suddenly back into my mind – every doubt, and every new prickling fear.

'Come, dear brothers,' I cried cheerfully in Greek. 'There's sad work to be done. The sooner it's over, the better.'

As the monks put on leather gloves that reached all the way up to their shoulders, I opened my perfume bottle. I shook it over a napkin and stood where I could take what advantage might come of the very gentle breeze. The Dispensator ignored my offer and looked down in quiet prayer. Martin was already on his knees and had his arms raised in a prayer of his own. I took my thoughts off Constantinople – they brought no profit – and wondered again what funeral rites Hierocles had been given. The Old Faith wouldn't have been made illegal till about fifty years after his probable death. Enforcement in a place like Athens would have come perhaps a century after that. The absence of anything specifically religious probably meant, then, that he'd been a Christian. A Christian burial here – or one so prominent – would, until quite recently, have risked immediate violation. Even now, the rabble gave no appearance of more than formulaic devotion.

I looked up at the commotion from the monks.

'My Lord,' one of them cried, 'the tomb is empty!'

33

'It was surely wild animals,' I said again. 'Didn't you hear the wolves last night? They came right up to the walls.'

Martin shut up and looked ready to start crying again. A disappointed look on his face, the Dispensator had taken off his hat and was fanning his face. Now they realised what we'd had in mind for them, the monks had cheered up mightily where they sat with their cheese and bread, pleased they'd got off so lightly. I looked away from the scrap of black cloth that hung on a strand of the flattened brambles. No body meant no excuse for an arrest – rather, it meant an excuse for no arrest. Sooner or later, justice would have to be done. The balance of convenience, though, had just swung decisively against any action. If Ludinus was even in part behind this council, it was plain that Simeon was right. I'd been set up to fail. My only salvation was in *not* failing. Arresting the Count of Athens, and getting everyone into a sweat about sorcery charges, had suddenly become a luxury I couldn't possibly afford.

I stepped forward and planted a booted foot over the scrap of cloth. 'Since it has been taken away,' I said, trying not to sound as relieved as I felt, 'we'll have to reconsider our plan.'

'My experience of wolves,' the Dispensator said with a close look at the flattened brambles, 'is that they devour their food where they find it. Also, they fight over it.' He looked at the odd position of my right foot, and watched as I shuffled forward to stand more naturally. 'I see no evidence here of wolves or any other wild animal. I am surprised, Alaric, that you – of all people – should come so quickly to your conclusion.'

I shrugged and ground my foot hard through the brambles to

the stony soil beneath. I stepped forward again, and kicked gently at one of the bricks that had been pulled again from the hole in the back of the tomb. The body had been taken away by some person or persons unknown. That much was plain. Also plain was that it had been taken not long before – that strong a smell of corruption shouldn't have lasted beyond the clearing of the morning mist. I looked about. Once off the road, and past the straggle of tombs and other monuments that lined both sides, it was an endless wilderness of green and of jagged white rocks that may have been put there for some human purpose, or that might just always have been there. So it was as far as the eye could see. Nicephorus had mentioned farmers who'd carried away all the stones of the Long Walls. There was no evidence of agriculture that I could see. There was, however, any number of places where a body might be hidden. The real question was who had taken it, and why? If I could fob the Dispensator off with talk of wild animals, I'd be back later for a proper look round.

I was drenched in the oil of roses Martin had jogged over me in his first shock. I raised a sleeve to my nose and breathed in slowly. I looked up at the sun and sneezed. 'The body has gone,' I said firmly. 'This being so, I can only suggest that we return to Athens and consider our next move.' If this meant having to dangle the Universal Bishop title much earlier than I'd intended, it might be worth the loss of pressure in the actual council. Then again—

My thoughts had been interrupted by a squeal from one of the monks.

'O Jesus!' Martin breathed with a tight clutch at my arm. 'The barbarians.'

And this time, he was right. It was indeed barbarians. How none of us had seen them did little credit to our watchfulness. But we had been focused on the tomb and its expected contents, and then on its lack of contents. And this was anything but the unstoppable flood of humanity everyone was shitting himself over. These were three children. The eldest was a boy of perhaps fourteen. With the shambling movements you read about in the reanimated dead, he and his sisters were picking their way through the brambles on the other side of the road.

'Eat! Eat!' the boy was croaking in Slavic as he stepped forward and almost fell on to the road. I looked over the expanse of stones from where they'd come. They were alone. I put my sword back into its scabbard and stepped towards the boy. He fell on his knees and raised outstretched arms. The girls had flopped down on the paving stones of the road and were beginning to cry weakly. If they'd eaten in days, it would have surprised me.

'Where are the others?' I asked in the Slavic dialect I thought the boy had used. I looked about again. But for the chirping of cicadas and Martin's renewed urgency of praying, we were gathered in silence. Unless there was an army of dwarves hidden out there behind the stones, they really were alone. I wondered how they'd got here.

'In the name of Christ, we starve,' was the only reply I got from the boy. 'Food, I beg – food, if only for the girls.' He spread himself on the paving stones in a kind of prostration.

Priscus was right about my knowledge of the military arts. One thing I did know, however, was that you don't feed your enemy. I gave a ferocious look at no one in particular and stood back. 'These unfortunates,' I'd once said of the poor in Constantinople, 'are numbered among those for whom no place has been set at the feast of Nature's plenty.' That had got me a murmur of applause in the Imperial Council when I nagged Heraclius to cut the bread distribution. But I caught the look on the Dispensator's face. 'These savages have no proper business on Imperial soil,' I answered him. 'Their wasting is to our benefit. Give food to any of them, and you feed the enemies who would kill us in our beds.'

'Even if they beg in the name of Christ?' the Dispensator now said. 'These are children. They can do no harm at all.' He leaned on his walking staff and frowned at me. 'Does your concern about the young extend only to the dead?' he asked with a slight look round at the empty tomb.

I was thinking of a suitably firm negative. The Dispensator might have some religious duty to feed the starving. I had an empire to think about. But I looked again at the barbarians. The boy hadn't moved. I looked over at his sisters. I found myself staring into a pair of very big and pleading eyes. Ten? Twelve? You really couldn't tell – certainly not with that degree of emaciation. I told myself to ignore her. It doesn't matter how few of them there are, or how weak they look: *you don't feed barbarians*. Give food even to that girl, and her first thought would be to ask how and when to get a knife into my back.

I drew a deep breath. 'Be off with you!' I was intending to shout. I found myself looking again into those eyes. I looked away. I gritted my teeth. I turned to face Martin. 'Put what's left down there,' I muttered. 'I've no doubt there is plenty left over.'

I avoided looking at anyone as Martin dropped a still bulging satchel on the ground and danced back. The boy ripped it open and pulled at its contents. He paused in the act of shoving half a loaf into his mouth and called the girls forward. The Dispensator now had another of the satchels open and was distributing cheese. He'd come out to pray over the dead. Now, he was feeding the starving. That, plus comforting the bereaved, and someone at least was having a good day.

I watched them gorge themselves. There is something unpleasant about watching the hungry eat. It may be in itself the rapid, suspicious movement of food to the mouth. It may simply be the pity of it all. I was getting ready to question the boy properly, when I heard a scrape of stones behind me.

I looked round just in time to get out of the way. Dressed in black, the small, darting figure missed me and stabbed viciously into thin air. He landed noiselessly and wheeled about to face me. I had my sword back out and went into a fighting pose. From the far left, I saw another dark blur. I lunged forward and then round in a wide, cutting move. Even in broad daylight, you don't stop and count your attackers. But I was aware of five of those dark, rapid creatures. I stepped back against the tomb and raised my sword again. Almost too late, I heard the scrape of clothing on weathered stone, as someone jumped on to the roof of the tomb and tried to get me from behind. I leapt forward at the nearest of the attackers before me. I felt the point of my sword make contact with something solid, and heard a high squeal of pain. But there was no kill – not even some disabling injury.

I turned again and lunged with another cutting movement at the man still on the tomb. This one I did get. I took him by surprise, and felt the reassuring crunch of expensive steel on the flesh and bone of the man's neck. He went backwards off the tomb with a bubbling scream. I turned and stared at the four who were left. Now together, they hung back. I could see they were dressed wholly in black, even down to the masks on their faces. Each had a short sword in one hand and a knife in the other. In a moment, they'd fan out again and close in like flies round a drop of spilled honey.

'Run for it!' I shouted in Latin. I had a momentary glimpse of Martin, who'd pulled out a length of dead bramble and was trying for a weak flourish. 'Martin, fuck off!' I shouted again. 'Run and get help.' This was no place for him. I slashed at someone who jumped at me from the left, and then at someone who tried getting at me from the right.

'Look out – behind you!' I heard the Dispensator cry.

I looked round in time to see him hurry forward, his walking staff raised as a weapon. One of the attackers had climbed on to the bloody roof of the tomb. The other three were closing in. I heard the whizz of the Dispensator's staff as he knocked the man from the tomb. With a rapid lunge, I struck out at the attacker who was trying to get him from the side. I missed, but he and the others fell back again. I felt the Dispensator's back press into mine, and we moved into the middle of the road. So long as no one managed a lucky slice against that walking staff, we now had some advantage. The attackers shouted rapidly at each other. One of them made a dash at me, sword arm fully extended. Stupid move! I stood head and shoulders and part of my chest above any of them. I had another six inches at the least in my own sword arm. I had him skewered far short of where he could have done me any harm. As the dying man fell to his knees, I kicked him back into the path of one of the two survivors.

Behind me, I felt the Dispensator press into me as he swung his staff. Leaving me for the moment, the attack was now focused on him. I jumped forward to avoid being caught by the staff and picked up one of the fallen swords. I threw it at Martin, who was waving his piece of bramble and screaming like a terrified woman. The Dispensator's staff was now cut off just a few inches from where he'd been holding it. As he stepped back, I went past him and, holding it in both hands, swung hard with my sword. I missed where I'd been aiming, but still managed to take a sword arm off at the elbow. I had a brief glimpse of the arm, still clutching its sword, bounce on the paving stones.

The attackers were now down to one. As he stepped cautiously back from me, Martin rushed him from behind. Still screaming, eyes shut, he slashed feebly and at random. It was a marvel he didn't crash straight into me. But the attacker looked round for a moment. I took my sword again in both hands and went at him. I took the top of his head off as if it had been a breakfast egg. He fell to his knees, his sword clattering on to the road. I didn't bother to watch him drop forward, but turned to finish off the man whose right arm I'd taken. But he was now running for it. Screaming with fear and pain, staggering from loss of blood, he was already off the road. I could have followed him on to the stones. But, injured as he was, he darted away with more speed than I thought I'd manage.

Keeping my sword up, I looked round. Within a ten-foot radius, all the paving stones were red and slippery. The monks had bolted. Far along the road, I could see their dark blur as they made for the safety of Athens. Towards us, coming from both directions, I saw the approach of other travellers, the sun glinting on their drawn swords. There was a distant sound of shouting. Close by was the sound of the Dispensator's loud breathing and Martin's return to frantic prayer. No birds sang. In place of the merry chirping of insects was the buzzing of flies as they gathered to feast on the blood that I'd shed. Probably cowering behind some of the larger stones, the children had vanished.

I forced myself into a calm I didn't feel. 'You are hurt, My Lord?' I asked.

The Dispensator shook his head. One of his sleeves had been ripped all the way down, but the sword hadn't touched his arm. He bent and picked up the remaining length of his walking staff and tested it.

Farting and sobbing, Martin sat like a man who'd been stunned. His own worst injury was where he'd ripped his hands on the brambles. As I watched, he clutched at his stomach and began rocking back and forth. As the excitement faded like the echo of a voice in church, I could feel a shaking fit coming on. I willed myself not to give way to it.

'Alaric,' the Dispensator cried sharply, 'this one is still alive.'

I made myself look round. Still dazed, the man the Dispensator had got with his staff was sitting with his back against the tomb. I tightened my hold on a sword now slippery with blood and sweat and stood over the man. His masked face turned up in my direction, he pulled a small knife from his belt.

'That won't do you any good,' I said through chattering teeth. I could hear the rapid approach of the other travellers. I stepped back and transferred my sword to my left hand. I wiped my right on my tunic and took the sword back into it. I pulled myself together. The man had now scrambled forward on to his knees and was looking at me through his mask. I lowered my sword. 'Punishment in Athens,' I said with desperate control. 'But questions first.'

He turned his face up to the sky and laughed. It was the mad, exultant laugh of a gambler who, given up by all as broken, has managed a sudden lucky throw. Cautious of a sudden rush at me, I stepped back further. The man said something I couldn't catch and, taking it in both hands, raised his knife above his head. With a shrill cry I'd normally have taken for sexual pleasure, he brought it suddenly down into his belly. Still holding it hard, he ripped the knife upward all the way to his breast bone. With a babble of ecstasy, he tore the knife out and threw it aside. Somehow, he got to his feet. I heard the ripping of cloth as he pulled the gash wide open and pulled at his entrails. There was a scream of horror from behind me. I may have cried out myself as, holding out those bloody things in both hands, he stepped heavily towards me. I stepped back again – but not fast enough. With a final, extreme effort, the man threw himself at me. I overbalanced as he hit me and fell back on to the road. For a long instant before they dulled, two eyes blazed triumph and hate from behind the mask.

But now many hands were pulling the body off me, and were lifting me back to my feet. Someone put a wet cloth to my face. I watched it come away red. I looked down at my sopping, red tunic. I wanted to sit down again. But I was hurried instead over to a wooden box that had been unloaded from one of the carrying slaves. Someone shoved the bone spout of a wineskin into my mouth. I sucked on it till I thought I'd be sick. Looking through the jostling, admiring crowd, I saw the Dispensator. He had his back to me, and was reaching down to help Martin to his feet.

34

Priscus lifted the sheet again off one of the bodies and smacked his lips. 'If you can stomach a little more praise, dear boy,' he said without turning, 'consider me impressed.' He bent for a closer inspection. 'You killed three of these, and disabled another, with just Martin and an old priest for help? Well, I suppose you'll make a soldier yet.' He pulled the sheet right off the body and nearly overbalanced. He gave up trying to laugh and sat down with a groan, and went back to nursing his left arm. He'd got back here slightly before me. About the time I was fighting for my life outside the walls, he'd been jumped on his way back from an apothecary. There could be no doubt of the main facts: they'd been seen, if at a distance, by the Bishop of Athens.

'Of course, my little darling,' he went on with forced brightness, 'yours was more a glorified street brawl than a battle. If you look at the harvest from the attack made on *me*, you'll see that each was felled with a single stroke from the front. So much delicacy of language – and you still fight like a barbarian drunk on cider.'

I ignored the obvious reply, that I'd come through my own ambush without so much as a scratch, and took another sip of beer fortified with a half opium pill. We were sitting in one of the larger abandoned offices in the residency. The tables had been cleared of writing materials and other old clutter, and now supported six variously carved-up bodies. Though the windows were all closed, the still air was filled with the smell of ingrained human dirt and with the buzz of those ever-present flies.

Priscus got up again and chased the flies away from one of the cleaner kills. He sniggered and pointed at the crotch. 'No wonder that one of yours was so pleased to do himself in. Just imagine how you'd feel if you'd cut off the organ of pleasure, but left the organs of desire untouched.'

I forced myself to look once more at the tangle of black hairs. Where the shaft had once emerged, a gold ring was half-buried in the hair. The hairy ballbag hung between parted legs. The mutilation – rather, the *self*-mutilation – was repeated on all the other bodies. I swallowed and sat back in my chair.

Priscus laughed. 'It's all a bit like that wog Brotherhood we smashed up in Egypt – don't you think?' He cupped the ballbag in the hand of his good arm and went into a coughing fit.

There was no denying that these weren't your ordinary bandits. If I hadn't known better, I might have put them down as Christian; there's no limit, after all, to what some of the wilder heretics can read into Scripture. I thought of the text about those 'which have made themselves eunuchs for the kingdom of heaven's sake'. But I'd seen them, or colleagues of theirs, with Balthazar in that invocation of 'the Goddess'. These were all debased remnants of the Old Faith. I've said Athens had come late to the Established Faith. It had also come rather imperfectly.

'Now, it might be relevant to ask,' Priscus added in the tone of one who's desperately at war with the need to go and lie down, 'not just who these buggers were, but who sent them, and for what purpose.' He tried for a sweet smile, but failed. 'Any thoughts of your own, My Lord Senator?'

'How about your good friends Nicephorus and Balthazar?' I asked. As his face turned blank, it was my turn to laugh. 'I should hope by now you've finished writing my funeral oration. Any chance of reciting its exordium? You can dispense with the onion.'

He played with his wine cup and gave me a long and thoughtful look. Then he smiled. He put his cup down and stretched. He leaned forward for another look at the nearest body, and clucked happily as he pulled at the gold ring. He pulled harder and fought to suppress another cough as a peak of dead flesh poked through the hair. He let go of the ring and turned back to me. 'I really must be getting old,' he said with a sorry shake of his head. 'I knew that

239

old fraud Balthazar was spying on me the other night. But I didn't even consider you might have been there too. Oh dear!'

He paused and thought. He brightened and lifted his cup. 'But you surely know all about my often odd sense of humour. Come, dearest Alaric, we're two very old and very dear friends!' he cried with a wave of his cup so expansive that wine splashed over the floor tiles. He leaned forward and smiled. 'You surely know that I'd never lift a finger against you – not after all we've been through. Haven't I often said that we stand or fall together?'

Not blinking, I stared back at him. Should I give him a list of the times he *had* tried to kill me? Best not – it might show there were times I hadn't noticed, and encourage him to try harder. At last, I could feel the warmth of the opium spreading out from my stomach. Another few moments, and my remaining jitters would be smothered beneath great waves of serenity.

Priscus sat back and gave me a sly look. 'Besides, dear boy,' he went on with smooth charm, 'there's fuck all you can do about whatever you may have seen the other night. Let's admit that Nicephorus hasn't just made himself scarce – he's scarpered. Without him to bully into a confession, it's your word against mine in any trial before Caesar. Even with Martin to back you up, Heraclius will have to pretend not to believe you. Bear in mind, he does need *someone* to face down the Persians when they start their march into Syria. Believing any charges you care to make just wouldn't be convenient.'

'Oh, Priscus, my dearest friend,' I cried satirically, 'how could I doubt your word?' And the pity was it didn't suit me to doubt his word. I'd not tell him about Ludinus and my now desperate need to get the right answer out of that council. Without having to make any actual promises, I'd managed to swear the Dispensator to inaction. There'd be no wave of arrests – no superstition-crazed monks combing Athens for Nicephorus and Balthazar. I'd take whatever risk that entailed and keep an unwavering gaze on the main action of this particular story.

There was a soft scraping on the door. Priscus looked up, a bright smile on his face. He pulled down the one blind that had been left to let in the sunlight and wiped off a rivulet of hair dye that had run down his face. 'Come in, my dearest,' he called.

The door opened and Euphemia walked in. Wearing a hooded cloak that must have been sweltering, she bowed modestly in my direction and began fussing with a bowl of hot water. She didn't acknowledge that I'd stood up for her, and I sat down again.

'A most splendid woman is the Count's sister-in-law, don't you agree?' he said, holding up his bandaged arm for her attention. 'We can rely on her not to miss Nicephorus.'

She looked sharply over at me.

Priscus laughed happily. 'Yes, my dear, he's buggered off at last,' he said to her. 'That means you can go now where you will – so long as Alaric makes it possible.' He gasped as she undid the bandage and began sponging at the long wound on his arm. There was a long pause as she finished her work and tied on a clean bandage. Priscus twisted his face into another smile and opened his mouth to speak. Instead, he went into another coughing fit. By the time this was over, Euphemia was halfway to the door. 'But, my dear young woman,' he finally managed to cry in his jolliest tone, 'have you got him yet between your legs?' He suddenly turned and looked into my face. He laughed again. 'So, it's all as good as agreed,' he said to Euphemia, now softly. 'If it ever comes to pass, I'm sure you'll find much to amuse you in the Capital. You might even be useful to young Alaric.'

As the door closed, and we were alone, Priscus got up and went back to the bodies. He tugged again on one of the gold rings. This time, he took out a knife and cut it free. He went over to a window and pulled up the blind to inspect the ring in a shaft of sunlight. He bit the gold to test its fineness and held it up again to look at the tooth marks. 'You can believe what you please about my instructions to Nicephorus,' he said. 'You can be sure, however, I didn't commission my own death. And, now our bird has flown, don't expect me to call him and Balthazar off.'

No answer to that. I'd get the Dispensator to order a discreet search of Athens, though didn't expect his monks to find anything.

'Do tell me, Priscus,' I said, 'what Balthazar could have meant when I heard him refer to your previous "outrages" in Athens.'

He slid the ring on to the little finger of his left hand and sat down. He raised his hand and looked at it from several directions. 'Since I wasn't a party to that conversation,' he said, 'don't expect me to interpret anything said by Balthazar. But it may have referred to a certain attempt I made – an attempt soon called off, let me add – to obtain a blessing that you now seem to have taken for yourself.' He giggled and went back to admiring his ring.

There were other questions I wanted answered. But these could wait until I could get them fully clear in my own mind. Priscus got up again in the silence that followed and stroked one of the dead chests. I haven't said that the nipples also had been cut away, leaving jagged pits in the dark, hairy flesh. He poked at the square of stained cloth stuck just over the heart.

'Do you know what this is?' he asked with another snigger.

'I'd say it was part of the cloth a woman has used to contain her menstrual discharge,' I answered. I got up and yawned in the heat. I stretched. I picked up the knife Priscus had used and pried the cloth loose. Using it to hold the cloth, I lifted it into the sunlight. 'Since it's old blood, we can assume it had some magical purpose – a talisman against danger perhaps.' I ignored the reply about its effectiveness. 'It's the same with all the bodies.' I took a long sip of drugged beer and thought. In all investigations, the enemy is less often lack of evidence than settled but false assumptions about the evidence you have. But there was no doubt of a connection between theatrical sorcery and a gang of desperate assassins. For the moment, I wouldn't ask myself what Nicephorus had done with all the money he'd embezzled. Nor would I assume anything of the town assemblymen beyond complicity in tax fraud. Something I did need to know, however, was how anyone had known I'd be going off in search of that girl's body. It might well have been moved because of me. It can't have been by chance that those men had jumped me right beside the tomb. It was important to know exactly when Nicephorus had last been seen in the residency. The slaves I'd questioned had been utterly useless. He might have disappeared when I set out for the house of Felix. Or it might have been while I was outside Athens.

But I was now feeling lazy from the opium. I tried to glare at Priscus. 'You will, of course, stop trying to make trouble for me in Athens,' I said.

He smiled and patted his bandage.

I grunted and looked into his cold and glittering eyes. I'd have got more from staring at an icon of the Risen Christ. I looked at my hands. A hasty scrub in cold water had cleaned all the gore off my body. But I'd need to get a scraper under my fingernails before dinner. That reminded me of other business. 'You'll be glad to know that I've had no choice – unless Nicephorus shows up for dinner – but to place you beside Simeon,' I said.

Priscus grinned. He even kissed his new ring.

'I hope you can restrain yourself from any further discussion of the Trinity.'

'So our friendship remains unscathed?' he asked with mock eagerness. He flashed his ring at me, then groaned with the sudden pain of the movement.

'I have business elsewhere in the residency,' I said. 'I'm sure you can find your own way to bed for a couple of hours.'

He was still laughing softly as I walked from the room.

35

'What's in that box over there?' I asked, pointing at the far corner of the office.

Martin looked up from a set of accounts that even he could see were crooked. 'I think they are the Count's ceremonial clothes,' he said. 'They've been left to get wet, so all the colours have run on the silk, and everything is creased.' I looked down again at the only two documents Nicephorus had left behind that had any relevance to me. Martin had already been more than once through a place as dirty and chaotic as I'd expected. If this was all he'd found, there might still be more – but it wouldn't be easily found.

'Well, this one,' I said, holding up a sheet of folded papyrus, 'mostly explains itself. The names listed correspond with my understanding of who was included in the main writ of summons. There's no mention of me or Priscus. Instead, Sergius is named as convenor.' I looked again at the date. It had been sent out from Constantinople just days after my departure for Alexandria. Ludinus couldn't possibly have got himself so quickly into the sort of favour that would let him take over religious affairs. At the same time, why hadn't I been told about this before I left – or at least notified in one of the endless messages of regard Heraclius had been sending me? Since the letter carried the Patriarchal as well as the Imperial seal, why hadn't Sergius sent me news of the council?

I put the letter down and turned to the other one. This had been sealed by Ludinus. From the unpractised formation of the characters, and one substantial crossing out and marginal correction, he may have written it in his own hand. 'I can understand that some *financial* provision should have been made for a place like Athens to feed all the delegates. But I fail to understand why notice should be sent of a grain ship of the second class to unload at Piraeus. If it was even half-laden, there would be enough grain to keep the entire city through the winter months.' I wiped more sweat from my forehead. A bright morning had turned to a stifling afternoon, and there wasn't a breath of air in the whole residency. I shut my eyes and opened them again. I waited for the writing to come back into focus and regretted the opium. Like water on dust, it had settled my nerves. The dose I'd taken, though, was also making me sleepy. It was clouding thought processes that needed to be much clearer than I was able to manage.

I put this letter on to the rickety desk and looked at Martin. 'How are your hands?' I asked. Martin had been carried back to Athens in a chair. If I hadn't needed his immediate help, I'd have left him with Sveta. I felt a slight stab of guilt for having paid so little attention to his own shattered nerves.

'You could easily have been killed,' he said quietly. He got up and came over to the desk. He held up the letter that Ludinus had sealed. 'Look, Aelric,' he said in Celtic, 'we aren't safe in Athens. I'm not even sure about the residency. You've admitted you have no idea what's been happening in Constantinople. Why don't we just go back to the plan you made before we landed? This time, you could come with us. We can take the ferry to Corinth, and then go west. You could get to England before anyone knew where you'd gone. You could even come back with me to Ireland. My father's brothers would take you in without questions. You've had three good years in the Empire. You must see that it's time to move on.'

I frowned him into silence. 'I've decided that you will get everyone over to Corinth once the ferry comes in,' I said very firmly. 'I am thinking to send you to Rome to wait on further instructions. But, Martin, do you really suppose I could turn up in Corinth without being spotted at once? Let's agree the Governor there is a prize idiot, but even he wouldn't just sit on his arse while I obviously made plans to run for cover. I'll stay here. If I get all these bishops and what-have-you properly on side, we'll see how it plays with the Emperor. In the meantime, you just get Sveta packing for Monday.' I leaned forward and picked up a small box that had been puzzling me. It had been lying in the congealed mess of the Count's inkwell. 'Pills for a stinking breath,' it said in faded ink in the underside. I shook the box. It was empty.

But Martin wasn't finished. 'Do you remember the story in ancient times of the fall of Seianus?' he went on, still urgently, though now in Celtic. 'He could have made a run for it the moment Tiberius got up to make that interminable speech in the Senate. He could have used his still intact power to commandeer post horses and get out of Rome. Instead, he sat there, waiting for his Emperor to wind up with a full denunciation. You're in a better position. The Emperor's seven hundred miles away. No one appears to have any instructions to arrest you here. Unlike Seianus, there really is somewhere you can go where you couldn't be dragged back. Let's just go. This city isn't really Athens – it's a rotten husk. The residency almost throbs with an evil even you must be able to sense. The Empire itself is falling.' Though still in Celtic, he looked about and dropped his voice to a whisper. 'Priscus is the best they've got. And you know he's useless for anything but massacring civilians and stabbing everyone round him in the back. You've done everything you could for the Empire, and there's no one in power who likes it or even understands it. *Let's just go!*'

There was a sudden rattle on the door handle, and I was saved the trouble of further argument.

'I heard you was round abouts here, my love,' said Irene. She kicked the door wide open, scattering a pile of old reports, and walked in. She was now wearing a much taken-in military tunic. She might even have had a sword under her cloak.

I scowled at her. 'I did specify slaves before noon,' I said harshly. I looked out of the window. 'That was some while ago.'

She smiled and gave a dismissive wave. 'Oh, don't you worry yourself, dearie,' she said. 'There was problems with the lady's maids – I had to flog a couple into a proper view of their station in this life. But they're all ready and waiting for you. If you'd like to follow me into that big room with the statue of Sappho – lovely girl she was, too, if you'll pardon the digression . . .'

I sat on a raised chair in one of the less tatty halls of audience, and looked at the huddle of slaves who stood before me, their heads turned down in misery and respect. I took another long draught of beer and handed the mug to Martin. I burped into my sleeve and got slowly to my feet. Perhaps I had overdone the opium, I thought yet again. But I took a deep breath and put myself into a semblance of order.

'If you were born to be warriors,' I opened in what I hoped was the right dialect of Slavic, 'it is by the fortune of war that you stand before me. I will not have you chained up at night, nor made to wear iron collars by day. I will not beat you, or subject you to other humiliations. In return, I expect total obedience to my commands and total devotion to my interests.'

I paused and steadied myself. All who could understand me were now looking up at me. Their pale, slab-like faces showed no emotion. I suppressed another burp and went on: 'You may be aware that I have bought you outright from the Lady Irene, your former mistress. Unless detained here by the onset of winter, or by some other untoward circumstances, I do not expect to be long in Athens. But I promise that those of you who serve me well I will free before I leave. You can then return to your homes or go where else you may please. Those of you with whom I am not satisfied I will sell back to the Lady Irene, who will dispose of you at market as may suit her convenience.

'Can I expect the devotion I seek?'

You can put that choice to any rational being and get exactly the same answer. I'd paid ready cash for these creatures, and they knew they were mine as absolutely as the clothes I was wearing. But I stood with right arm held out as each took his turn to come forward and take my hand between both his own. It did no harm to add the semblance of fealty to a freely chosen lord to the duties prescribed by law. And it wasn't just heavy cleaning and other household work I had in mind for them. If Priscus might have the good sense not to try poisoning me as we sat together at meat, Nicephorus and Balthazar were still on the loose. I might well have need of those big men for much else beside.

'Do make the same offer to the female slaves,' I whispered to Martin as I stepped past him. I turned to Irene, who'd thrown her cloak off and was indeed wearing a sword. 'If you can get everything ready for dinner, I'll be in your debt,' I said.

She gave another flash of brown teeth and turned to clap her hands at the slaves for attention.

I was now aware of a newcomer to the room. I took him by the shoulder over to the main door. 'Any luck?' I asked in whispered Latin. The Dispensator's secretary shook his head. As ordered, a few dozen monks were unobtrusively combing the city for Nicephorus or anyone dressed all over in black. A dozen more were lounging by the two gates that were opened by day. Nothing so far to report.

'Then I want you to keep looking,' I said. 'If it means pulling me out of bed before dawn, I want to be told the moment anyone is found or even seen. Do you understand?'

He bowed and confirmed that the Dispensator had given no reason for his orders.

'Excellent,' I said. The opium was pressing hard on me, but I smiled. 'I look forward to seeing His Lordship your master at dinner.'

'I'm going for a lie down,' I said to Martin. 'Since you'll need a good voice for the readings, I advise the same of you.' I looked at his torn hands. 'No, Martin,' I said with soft insistence. 'After what you've had to go through already today, I command you to go and lie down.' I might have patted him on the shoulder. A Greek would have kissed him in recognition of his attempted defence. But there is much to be said – in public at least – for a stiff upper lip.

36

Naked, I stood in the library. This wasn't the shattered wreck that I knew. It was instead the luxurious, well-stocked house of books that it must have been in ancient times. Elegant in blue silk, her toenails shining with gold leaf, a young woman reclined on one of the window seats. She'd fallen asleep in the sun, a scroll open on her lap. I stared down at my hairy nakedness, and was ashamed. I wanted to step forward and see what the young woman had been reading. I wanted to stand closer to her and see her face, which was turned away from me. There were no loose tiles or other debris on the floor. It would be simply a matter of walking forward a dozen feet and looking down. But that disembodied voice was speaking again from behind me.

'Do you want to know what happened in this room?' it asked in English.

I smiled and turned round. There was an old man fussing over what may have been the library catalogue. I stood just a few feet from the desk where he muttered over an open scroll of listings. I looked at the wall painting of Athens. Its colours fresh and vivid, it showed the city in much greater detail. Though I could see no captions above any of the buildings, I now recognised what everything was. There was the Garden of Epicurus, and there the spot in the old market place where the speakers had once stood to address the Assembly. As I stared, everything made more sense than it had, either in Dexippus or in my own tour of the modern city. But the voice was repeating its question.

I laughed and waited to see if the old man would look up. Of course, he didn't. He picked up a book sleeve and squinted to read the parchment tag on it. He put it down and made a fresh entry in his catalogue scroll. He picked one of the books on the desk and unrolled it a few inches. He put it down and took up another. This time, he pushed it gently into the sleeve. He got up from the desk and walked towards me. I stood my ground and strained to feel any trace of disturbance as he walked straight through me on his way to one of the bookracks at the far end of the room. It was, I could see, as if he'd walked though a column of smoke from a bonfire. I saw myself disintegrate and then come back together – but I felt nothing. I turned and watched him pass down the room. He stopped before the unbroken bust of Polybius and bowed in silent respect.

'Do you know what happened in this room?' the voice asked for a third time. As a few nights before, there was a trace of annoyance behind its calm urgency.

'The answer you want,' I answered in an English that sounded as utterly barbarous as I knew that I appeared, 'requires me to make up a story based on all the facts and rumours and hints of rumours I've heard since I came into Athens. For what it's worth, I'll say that young woman over there is a witch. She's fallen asleep over a book of incantations. In a while the low murmuring that I think I can hear will become a roar of anger, as the mob breaks into the palace and makes for this room. The woman will be seized and held while the library is torn apart for other allegedly magical texts. They will be heaped up, and perhaps she will be burned on top of them. Her ghost will then haunt the palace, appearing before those who have the sensitivity of soul to perceive it.'

No reply. I stepped towards the desk and looked at the catalogue. At first, the writing made no sense. It was just the dark squiggles you see in cheaper mosaics that show a book. As I looked harder, though, the squiggles resolved themselves into one of the antique scripts I'd occasionally had to puzzle out in the University Library in Constantinople. The one sheet that showed where the book hadn't rolled back on itself was a listing of what could only have been works by Gregory of Nyassa.

I snorted and wheeled round. There may have been a slight shadow in the place where the voice had spoken. But it had dissolved before I could say it was there. I laughed again. 'That was shit opium,' I sneered, 'if this is the best library catalogue I can imagine.'

'And why do you say that?' the voice asked, annoyance giving way to a reluctant interest.

'Because, except in Egypt,' I explained, 'papyrus rolls had gone out of fashion in libraries of quality some while before Gregory was born. Even otherwise, I might add, his works wouldn't have been an obvious choice for any educated Athenian.'

'You really are a fool, Aelric,' the voice said. 'I can only speak to you in dreams, and then in riddles determined by your own imagination. But I am trying to warn you of a terrible danger. Can you not reach for once into your deeper self and try to see things as they really are?'

'Not really,' I answered. 'There is much to be said for a keen and lively glance over the surface of things. You pick up a lot of truth on the surface. If you must look below, it should only be to uncover laws that regulate the visible world. Everyone who's ever tried going deeper has only come up again barking mad, and with ideas of setting the world to rights with a spot of murder.' I sniffed and thought of Plato. I turned back to the window and tried to step forward.

'Even if it has to be in riddles,' I sneered, 'can you tell me why I'm not able to go close to that woman? Why can't I look out of the window? Have I worn my imagination out with recreating this library?'

'You might better ask why you are worth all this trouble,' the voice answered, now in disgust. 'Oh, go on, then,' it spat. 'Have your look into the garden. See if you like what you see.'

The soft and universal pressure that had kept me back was suddenly lifted, and I nearly tripped forward against the nearest window. I looked out through the glass pieces and tried to focus. It was as if I'd woken in a strange room before the dawn was fully up. I knew that all could make sense with a little effort, but wasn't up to making that effort. I can say I didn't like what I saw. I stepped quickly back into the main part of the library.

* * *

Covered in sweat, I sat up in my bed.

'Aelric, it's me,' Martin whispered in my ear. 'Everything's all right.' He relaxed his hold on my upper body and pushed a cup of water to my lips.

I drank and opened my eyes. I'd had a leather curtain hung over the window against night draughts and any further rain. But I could see from the red glow coming from behind it that the sun was going down.

In the gloom, I focused on Martin. 'Was I crying out?' I asked.

He nodded. 'It was just the opium,' he said. 'Everything is really all right.'

I looked at him again. He'd got over our battle on the Piraeus road in better shape than I might have expected. Everything wasn't all right. But it would have to do. I threw the damp cover back and swung round to sit on the bed. Soon, it would be aired and changed every morning. For the moment, I was aware of the faint smell of beeswax and sex. The drug was fading, and I could feel a slight thrill of lust. But I put this out of mind and sat upright.

'The Bishop of Nicaea has been here a while already,' Martin said with an urgent look at the window. 'I saw him in conversation with Priscus. I've had some of the new slaves carry the bath into your dressing room. Can you bear cold water? Irene says the boiler can't be repaired.'

I stood up and stretched. 'I'd like to see Maximin before whatever bath you've managed.'

Martin looked thoughtfully at the lengthening shadows outside, then nodded.

'Now do help get this sheet arranged round me. I'm young enough to be a sight worth looking at. But we can't have naked encounters with Auntie Irene – not, at least, on our first day!' I stretched again and laughed.

Coming out of the nursery, I bumped into Euphemia. 'I've been with Priscus,' she said urgently. She had another bowl of bloody water in her hands. That settled my stab of jealousy. 'He told me everything,' she whispered. 'You were a fool to go looking for that body.'

I bent forward and kissed her. I waited for her to put the bowl down, and pressed my body against hers and moaned with a suddenly overwhelming lust. 'I do – I do assure you,' I said thickly, 'that my own encounter was less unfortunate than the Lord Commander's.' I stood back from her and forced myself into a semblance of order. 'But is there anything you can tell me about where Nicephorus might have gone, and what he was doing with the interpreter's daughter?'

She stepped away from the bowl. 'What I will tell you,' she said, looking me straight in the eye, 'is that the Count Nicephorus is a good man. People may think him strange. But he was the only person in the whole world willing to give a roof to me and his brother's child. If he was stealing the Emperor's money, do you think he would keep his own nephew short of medical help? As for murder, you don't know him at all.'

I could have told her that, if he ever did get a hearing before Caesar, I'd be the main prosecution witness. But hadn't Balthazar said very clearly that she knew nothing? She might know more than she realised. But there was an appropriate time for everything. Despite the lingering charms of my opium, I felt a sudden need for sex so desperate, I could have taken her there and then. But she twisted out of my embrace.

'Not here, not now,' she said with an attempted laugh.

'Then come back with me,' I pleaded. 'I left Martin with his wife. She'll keep him for ages yet.' I stretched out imploring arms.

Euphemia stared back at me in the fading light. She pursed her lips and tried to look away.

'Oh, come on,' I urged. 'There's nothing like a bit of killing to get the amorous propensities going. Just a quickie before dinner – you surely can't deny me that.'

Nor could she. Nor did she. The question I found myself asking afterwards, as she whimpered softly in my bed and I splashed cold water over my body, was not whether but *how* I'd manage to take her with me back to Constantinople.

37

Miracles of the Christian Faith usually astonish most when heard at fourth hand. What a little gold can do anyone may see for himself. We'd begun the day with an empty kitchen and a dining hall probably not used since the accession of Phocas the Unmentionable. Well before the coming of darkness, my new and reasonably clean and attentive slaves had begun serving a dinner that would never have passed in Constantinople, but that no one else could have despised. In one respect, it was an improvement. Because this was a partly ecclesiastical function, we could do without dining couches. Instead, I could sit at the head of an open square of tables arranged as Nature and Scripture agreed was most fitting for human convenience.

I waited for the Bishop of Athens to finish a very queer sermon on the text 'If I find in Sodom fifty righteous within the city, then I will spare all the place for their sakes.' As he finally came to a close, and sat down with a look about him as queer as his sermon and a tight clutch at a jewelled relic case, I let a couple of slaves lift my chair a foot back from the table and stood up. There was a massive scraping of chairs and grunting as a hundred diners got to their own feet and went into a long and respectful bow. I motioned with my arms for everyone to be seated – this really wasn't Constantinople, and the niceties could be overlooked – and stared round the table at which I had to sit, and at the two long tables that ran at right angles along the length of what had once been a magnificent room, and that was now respectably clean.

'Most learned and reverend Fathers of the Universal Church,' I began, 'O men of Athens.' I'd been working on this speech between bouts of frenzied copulation. It can best be described as a kind of warmed-over Demosthenes, with long allusions to Scripture and the Fathers. It rolled out with an appearance of unprepared fluency, and my only need to think was in choosing where to stop for Martin to put it into Latin for the sake of the Western delegates. It allowed me, while on my feet, to have a good look at everyone. The Athenians were easy. Most of them were town assemblymen, and I'd seen them shuffling twice about Nicephorus. The others I had no idea about – Martin had got all the names out of Nicephorus on our second day – but they looked of much the same quality. Their Greek was better than that of the lower classes, though I soon realised that my speech was still somewhat above their understanding. Nodding in what they thought the appropriate places, they stared back at me with the tight, sweating faces of provincial tradesmen whose uppermost thought is to worry that I might take it into my head to notice their fine clothes and sound the fiscal equivalent of the Last Trump. If any of them might wonder, or might know, the whereabouts of their Count, no one had commented on his absence from the seat beside mine, and I'd not trouble myself with commenting.

The clerics were a different matter. Again, Martin had got their names out of Nicephorus. Comparing that list with the one supplied from Constantinople showed a few and sometimes odd alterations. But the world is a big place. People die, or move on. Others come to notice. Overall, though, much as I hated the flabby eunuch, the correspondence of the names on both lists showed a very brisk efficiency in Ludinus – all the more admirable, given how quickly the council had been arranged. What struck me most on looking about, however, was what a strange gathering they were. It's one thing to look at names on a list, and when you have other things uppermost in your mind. It's another to look at actual faces. I'd been calling these people the 'best minds' of the Church and trying to believe it. Some of them were remarkably fine theologians: when they did speak as one, it might well be for the Church as a whole. What bound the Greeks most together, though, was that they were nearly all prize troublemakers of one kind or another. Simeon – well, Simeon *was* Simeon. But Ajax, deacon in the Metropolitan Church of Aphrodisias; Soterius, thrice enthroned and twice removed Bishop of Nicopolis; Creon, Bishop of Saranta; and so on and so forth: this was as rich a cast of nit-picking fanatics, drunks, fornicators, office-peddlers and general villains as could ever be assembled.

As for the Westerners, I knew very few of them even by name. But the Dispensator was enough trouble in himself for the lot of them. Ludinus was too far away to be pulling any actual strings. But it wasn't hard to imagine how he'd be sniggering every night into his pillows as he thought of the mob he'd called together for me to try somehow to whip into the right order. Yes, intellectually – and, where not that, socially – this was the Church in miniature. But what I'd thought the previous day about herding cats would apply in force to this lot.

I ended with a fancy peroration cribbed from a speech I'd written for the Emperor at a banquet in honour of the goldsmiths of Constantinople, and sat down to a few desultory acclamations. 'I want beer,' I muttered in Slavic to one of my attendants. 'Bring it in the biggest cup the Lady Irene can find.'

I held up my hands for wiping by the slave who stood behind me, and smiled at the Dispensator. I'd had Simeon placed on my left, with Priscus next to him. It was turning out rather convenient that neither Simeon nor the Dispensator spoke a language the other could understand, and that, with no interpreters present, all conversation had to pass through me. In the intervals of a long and mind-rottingly dull argument with his cousin about a stolen pomegranate when they were at school together, Simeon had tried a few stilted pleasantries with the Dispensator. I'd touched these up in Latin till they could have served as the flattery of someone fishing for a legacy.

The wine was still putrid – better had been located, though not in time for the lees to settle – but, if they had spoiled the grain harvest, the endless rains of summer had given us a fine choice of fruit juices in which to dissolve whatever drugs took most fancy. I waited for the slave to finish with my hands, and reached for my cup of honeyed melon pulp.

'It is often sad news that friends must exchange after so long apart,' I said in what might have passed for a mournful tone. 'If the Gospels report that he frequently wept,' the Dispensator had told me near the beginning of our acquaintance in Rome, 'Our Lord never once laughed.' Whatever was in his lemon juice was now testing this imitation of Christ to the limit. Still glowing with the holiness and excitement of the day, he was far into the news from Rome. The last plague had run a scythe through the upper reaches of the Church there; and, if one or two of those carried off were to be regretted, we could both privately admit that the others wouldn't much be missed. The Dispensator took a long and diplomatic swig from his cup. I looked across to where Martin was getting ready to start another of his readings. Above us, I heard the scrape of a vast chandelier pulled up again. It was loaded with candles all of the finest local beeswax, and it cast a gentle glow over the company.

'I'm just a rough military man, as you know,' I now heard Priscus say quietly to Simeon. 'The councils of the Church are quite beyond my understanding. But I have picked up a little Scripture in my time. Doesn't Matthew report Our Lord as having said: "Not every one that saith unto me, Lord, Lord, shall enter into the kingdom of heaven; but he that doeth the will of my Father which is in heaven"? Something I don't quite understand is how this statement can be reconciled with any hypothesis that, while Christ has two Natures, he has only a single Will.'

He caught my scowl and raised his voice. 'Can you explain this, My Lord Senator?' he asked with a devout raising of eyes to Heaven. 'I do know the further text from John: "Then said Jesus unto them, When ye have lifted up the Son of man, then shall ye know that I am he, and that I do nothing of myself; but as my Father hath taught me, I speak these things." This shows a *uniformity* of Will. But does it show any *singularity*?' he asked with another pious raising of eyes.

'If you don't shut up at once,' I answered in Slavic, 'I'll have my slaves put you in chains, and I'll take a chance with the Emperor.'

He grinned and carried on in Greek. 'A most complete and elegant response!' he cried. 'A shame, though, you choose not to give it in either Imperial language. Of course, Scripture itself can only be understood as interpreted by the infallible councils of the Church, and who am I to venture into such complex areas?'

Simeon had set his face like stone. One of the Asiatic Greek bishops was beginning to look thoughtful over his wine. I put my face into a friendly smile and nodded to Martin, who was waiting for silence. I pretended to listen intently to Saint Augustine's sermon on the virtues of continence. If Priscus thought he'd got me with a few random tags of Scripture, he could think again. I'd long since made up answers to those questions – and answers to whatever supplementals might be raised. The Latin version still had a few edges I hadn't yet managed to blur over. But, given the absurd premises, the Greek original followed as unshakably as any demonstration in Euclid. However, this wasn't the time and place for showing exactly what I had in mind. Even if word of that had gone round – and had done even without Priscus to leak it – it could wait for my opening speech to the council.

'Was the Commander of the East quoting Scripture?' the Dispensator asked as Martin came to a dramatic pause in his reading.

'Augustine is his favourite Latin author,' I lied irrelevantly. I looked up to the circle of glowing lights. Priscus aside, the dinner had gone rather well. No one had commented on the smell of damp that drifted in from the rooms that hadn't yet been cleaned and aired, nor on the slight jerkiness of the service, nor on the audible savagery with which Irene had directed things from just outside the door. Even better, no one had still uttered a word – not, at any rate, in my hearing – about the missing Nicephorus. The arrest warrant, plus the direct rule order, that I'd got Martin to throw together could both remain unsealed until further notice.

I'd agreed a set of readings between courses where Greek and Latin alternated. We were now coming to the end of the Augustine.

There would, if I recalled correctly, be a course of dormice stuffed with beans soaked in fish sauce, followed by Basil of Caesarea in Greek on the need for religious correctness; then cabbage stewed in wine, followed by prayers in both languages. After that, I could kiss the whole company a very good night and take myself off to bed.

No one else, I'd already observed, seemed inclined to sit the night out, cup in hand. With a minimum of conversation, the food had been scoffed down as quickly as served. Now it was properly dark, I got the impression that everyone else would be much happier the sooner he could be out of the residency.

Martin was finished with Augustine. The Dispensator leaned towards me. 'I'm still wondering,' he whispered, 'how those men could have crept up on us so effectually.' He smirked and gave himself a little hug. We'd agreed not to discuss these things fully over dinner. But it's not every day even a Roman cleric gets into a fight for his life – and gets out of it without having to commit the sin of drawing blood.

'Oh, I think I can answer that,' I said. And I could. I'd had a thought in my bath, and had gone straight off for another look at the bodies. The different patterns of dirt on the clothing of those Priscus had killed and my own kills had been decisive. I'd been labouring under one of those false assumptions. 'Based on a very rapid look on my journey up from Piraeus,' I explained, 'I'd supposed the tomb of Hierocles was nothing more than an unburied stone coffin. But our attackers were covered in brick dust. That suggests a larger chamber underneath the tomb, where they'd lain in wait. It could even be that the dead girl was down there. Unless you positively insist, I'll not trouble you with another trip outside the walls. But I do intend going out myself tomorrow, once the first session of the council is over.'

'Then I will certainly come with you,' he said firmly.

No arguing with that. I ignored the loud crash behind me. If that was the dormice, I'd be rid of this lot in no time at all. I also ignored the Dispensator's praise of my ability to observe important facts. If I were right in this supposition, it only raised further questions. Those men hadn't followed us out to the tomb, but had been waiting there all along. How could they possibly have guessed movements I hadn't myself known until I was about to make them?

Far down one of the side tables, one of the tradesmen had switched out of proper Greek and was jabbering softly away in the local dialect. Someone opposite had raised a titter at whatever joke was being told. I looked up again at the candles. Far above them, there was a flickering redness that came in through the windows to play on the ceiling. It was as if the Northern Lights were suddenly visible from Athens.

Though I still avoided looking round, it hadn't been the dormice that had crashed on to the floor. Three of the things had been dumped before me on a clean silver plate. Whoever had cooked them hadn't known they should first be skinned and gutted. On my left, Priscus had left off theology, and was now explaining how he'd sat out the final massacre in Trampolinea by burying himself in a cesspit and breathing through a piece of lead water pipe. On my other side, the Dispensator was speaking to a French bishop whose plaited blond hair about his tonsure and giant moustache indicated a shift of power in the Church beyond the Alps. I settled my face into an expression of polite boredom. Nothing is forever: even this was coming to its end.

As Martin reached what I thought as fine a turn of phrase in Basil as any of the ancients might have envied, Simeon leaned over and burped into my face. 'Even if this doesn't go as badly as you deserve,' he whispered with a drunken leer, 'do you really think it will be any better for you in Constantinople? I thought even barbarians knew when they'd been set up to fail.'

Priscus looked down from his own inspection of those red and flickering lights. 'You'll do as you're fucking told, my dear kinsman,' he said without turning round or moving his lips. 'There's always room for a third set of squirting bowls before the Wrath of Caesar.'

Simeon looked as if he'd been slapped hard in the face. 'But Priscus . . .' he whined. He tried to say more, but fell silent after a few words of protest.

Priscus stared up again at the ceiling. 'I gather you've been putting yourself between those trembling white thighs,' he said to me with a turn into Slavic. I ignored him. 'Still, so long as she has strength to change my bandage, you go right ahead and fuck your brains out. Even you won't tire her out that much.'

He laughed oddly and nodded upwards. 'Do you see that flickering from the north?' he asked with a change of tone. 'Unless I'm seriously mistaken, that will be Decelea burning.'

I looked up again and thought. Decelea was about twenty miles due north. Given a clear night, its fires would be visible on the horizon.

'Well before morning,' he went on, 'there'll be streams of terrified survivors banging on the gates. You'll also see a better class of Athenian than the city trash, as the farmers drive in their animals and carry anything else that can be moved.'

With a great clearing of his throat, Martin was about to begin his bilingual recitation of the Sermon on the Mount. In Greek or Latin, I might have added: 'Blessed are those who wait on events – their enemies shall be turned.'

38

'I must thank Your Grace for having had the goodness to stay on for a while after our most enjoyable dinner,' I opened with my smoothest charm. Simeon sat in the library, looking nervously between me and Priscus. 'What we have to discuss is a somewhat delicate matter, and I hope you will agree that this generally unfrequented place is most appropriate for our discussion.' I smiled and looked at Priscus.

'You reorganised the Intelligence Bureau, dear boy,' he said. 'This is best coming from you.' He switched for a moment into Slavic: 'Besides, my darling, I'd only spoil things by enjoying myself too much.' He walked over a few yards and leaned nonchalantly against one of the bookracks that was still in place.

I sat down at the desk and looked over at Simeon. His face had now turned pale in the lamplight. If he didn't know any Slavic, he knew Priscus well enough to follow his tone of voice in any language.

'Very well, My Lord,' I went on. 'I thought we had reached agreement when we sat here together yesterday evening. Perhaps, as a foreigner who only learned Greek when already mature, I was mistaken as to the extent of our agreement. I do hope you will forgive me if I must now speak with a bluntness that I never thought would be required.'

I paused and waited for Simeon's face to change to a paler shade of white. 'Allow me to enquire, My Lord Bishop, if that patch of rough skin on the inside of your throat is giving you pain tonight?'

As I'd expected, his face sagged as if I'd killed him with a single blow to the back of his head. He swallowed and gave a scared look over at the mural behind me. I was still smiling as feet sounded on the stairs and Martin came in with cups and a jug of wine. I nodded for him to leave at once, and poured three cups. I waited for the footsteps to die away and sipped at my own cup.

'The Baths of Anthemius are very big,' I said with a friendly smile. 'You can get ten – sometimes fifteen – thousand people in them at the right time of day. That may be why so many people think they are anonymous. Whatever the case, that feeling of anonymity is something the Intelligence Bureau does everything to foster. The days are gone when your dear cousin Priscus could send his Black Agents into private homes to arrest people and drag them off for arbitrary torture and killing in one of his dungeons.' I turned to Priscus.

He grinned at us and even gave a little bow.

You can be sure I'd kept him well away from my reorganisation of the security services. If Heraclius could turn as nasty, given the right provocation, as Phocas had ever been, I'd got my way about purging every last agent of the Terror, and a return to some kind of due process.

I turned back to Simeon and waited for his choking fit to pass. 'But the Intelligence Bureau still keeps a careful watch on persons of quality as they disport themselves in ways that a reasonable third party might not think entirely dignified.'

Simeon turned his eyes upward. He glanced back at my polite but implacable face, and put up both hands to cover his own face.

'What would you say,' I asked softly, 'if I mentioned sworn statements about a certain person of the *very highest* quality who was in the habit of offering his lips, even to the lowest bathhouse attendant, every Sunday afternoon? Is it necessary to add how this certain person has a peculiarity about his throat that a doctor – or even the Emperor, should he be made to feel inclined – could easily investigate for himself?'

Hands still clamped over his face, Simeon began swaying from side to side.

It was now time for Priscus to have his turn. 'We're all men of the world in here,' he said with his broadest smile. 'And none of us is entirely without sin. But you do know how the Great Augustus feels about what he insists on calling "male vice". With anyone else in charge, you'd be tried by a committee of the Imperial Council. Its members would surely accept that sucking wasn't the same as fucking, and the penalty would be only degradation and confinement on relatively easy terms in some local monastery until your friends could work on Caesar. But Heraclius will certainly try you himself, and his ignorance of legal procedure is famous all over the Empire. Having established the lesser offence of sucking, he'd take the greater offence for granted. It would then be a matter of having you paraded round the Circus, with sharp reeds inserted into the pores and tubes of most exquisite sensibility, followed by amputation of the sinful instrument. If that doesn't kill, there is always burning, or the teeth and claws of wild animals.'

I took over again. I leaned forward and patted Simeon gently on the shoulder.

He whined and pressed hands harder to his face.

'But, My Lord Bishop,' I said, 'none of this is necessary. You know that Priscus would never wish for a scandal in his family. You know my own regard for the honour of the Church. Let us suppose that the Emperor may have allowed one or two ambiguous comments to pass his lips regarding a supposed resolution of the Monophysite controversy. But Emperors say many things. Don't imagine that anything Ludinus may have whispered at you through those gold teeth of his amounts to an authoritative clarification. The great difference between us and the Persians is that we take notice only of what our Lord and Master has expressed in the appropriate form. Heraclius the Person may speak now and then without full thought or proper advice. That is why we give our fullest attention to what Heraclius the Emperor says on a sheet of parchment bearing the Imperial Seal, or from the Imperial Throne in words that can be given clear legal effect.'

I got up and walked round to where Simeon was sitting like a cornered hedgehog. I bent down and embraced him. Priscus came round and helped get the man to his feet.

'Come, dearest friend,' I said. 'Your chair awaits you, together with torchbearers and guards. It will never do to keep them waiting. It would never do to keep you up when tomorrow must be such a long and responsible day. As I said in our last conversation here, this will be a council where arguments must be judged purely on their theological merits. I have no doubt that, when I explain the provisional thoughts of His Holiness our Patriarch, you will give them the fullest and most unbiased consideration.'

I looked up at the glass bricks of the dome. The red flickering was more pronounced up here than it had been in the dining hall. It gave a pleasantly warm glow to the library, smoothing out the worst of its desolation.

I walked back with Priscus through the darkness of the residency. The new slaves hadn't been instructed yet on the need to place lamps in all the corridors likely to be frequented at night. We passed in silence through what had once been the proper dining room, right up to the threshold of the old audience hall that I'd had cleaned and perfumed for the dinner, and made to give some impression of Imperial wealth and power. Here I stopped. Irene was hard at work with getting the slaves to clear up the mess that had been left behind.

'I wish Your Grace Godspeed through the streets of Athens,' I'd said to Simeon as we finally bundled him into his chair. I'd drawn breath and continued in oratorical tone: 'I think we can both agree on desiring a homeward voyage before the sea lanes become really impassable. Can I therefore count on your assistance in getting this council over and done with before the month is out? My enquiries suggest that you have a certain closeness with His Grace of Ephesus. I will leave you to arrange matters with him as you see fit – with him and with the other Eastern bishops. You know the council will begin tomorrow, after Sunday service. If our next Sunday service can celebrate a smooth consensus of opinion between Greek and Latin Patriarchates, you may be assured that neither I nor the Commander of the East will forget your own part in bringing this about.'

Priscus had confirmed this with a great slobbering kiss, and then a parting kick at the biggest of the carrying slaves. 'If there is a "next" Sunday service,' he'd giggled into my ear, 'even you might join in the prayers of thanks.'

We'd watched as the flaring procession made its way through the Forum of Hadrian. Then we'd watched as slaves had closed and barred the only gate into the residency. Now, in darkness, we were walking through its dark interior.

'They might have been strays,' Priscus now said, referring to the children I'd seen out by the tomb. 'But, if you saw one family of them, it does mean the passes are open. It's a matter of time.' He stopped suddenly and doubled over for a long coughing attack. We'd moved into a shaft of moonlight from one of the overhead windows. In this, I saw the dark streak on his bandage.

'You need a doctor,' I said. 'Don't try telling me again this is seasickness.'

Priscus stood up and leaned against one of the locked doors. 'If you have any sense in that pretty young head of yours,' he whispered, 'you'll not go round telling people how the Commander of the East is indisposed. I was able to inspect what passes here for a militia this afternoon. With me at their head, those duffers might just hold the walls. Do you want them in a panic?'

I swallowed. In Constantinople, in Alexandria, in Egypt, and on the whole voyage to Athens, I'd done everything short of pray that Priscus – as much my fly in the ointment as I was his, my sworn enemy, my backstabbing opponent in every measure I could urge on poor, stupid Heraclius – might fall down dead of something. Now it was looking as if I'd get what I wanted, I really would make a point of praying in church for his recovery.

We continued along the corridor. After a few paces, Priscus stopped again to clear his throat. He spat into the darkness. He laughed and took my arm to help him forward. 'When will you officially notice that Nicephorus has abandoned his duties?' he asked.

'He seems to have done bugger all when he was about,' I answered. 'Unless anyone important makes a fuss, I think we can overlook his absence for another few days.'

We'd now come into a long room that had a side window at the far end into the courtyard. Through this came another hint of distant red. 'I know that Martin's been urging you to scarper since before we got here,' Priscus said with a recovery of strength. 'We can agree that Nicephorus had no orders to arrest you on the docks. But you really can't deceive yourself that you're in the clear. All that guff you spoke to dear Simeon about the Imperial Constitution doesn't touch the fact that you serve an absolute and arbitrary despot who may still have something nasty in mind for you. So do tell me, dear boy – why hang about when you could be straight out of here?'

'Because I swore an oath to Heraclius,' I said. 'And because I have an overriding duty of service to the Empire so long as I'm in a position to do any good at all.' I was saved the trouble of continuing by a sudden explosion from Priscus that was part laugh, part sneer.

'Duty?' he gasped when he was able to speak again. '*Duty* to that shambling wretch in Constantinople? I have duties to family and class. You have a choice.' He waved at a mass of damp cobwebs overhead that hadn't yet been cleaned. 'This whole Empire is no better than Athens itself. Whatever it may once have been, it's nothing more than a ghost of what the old poets and philosophers laid down for it. If it's any better than Persia, or even the less chaotic barbarian kingdoms, I haven't yet noticed. You tell me what lies between savages like me and those lunatic priests that is worth saving.'

I didn't break the silence that followed.

'Oh, well,' he took up again, 'it's so nice that we're working together again. Even if I am thinking back just one month or so, to when we did so well in Egypt, it will be just like the old days – don't you think?'

'Yes,' I said. Since he was no longer holding on to me, he didn't feel my shudder.

39

'I said I wanted *every* door opened,' was my curt reply. The slave bowed and looked again at the door in the cupboard. 'If you have to break it open, please do. However, I want every effort made first to pick the lock.' Martin tagging along behind me, I walked back along the corridor towards one of the courtyard doors.

Out in the courtyard, and once I was used to the dazzling sunshine, my first sight was of Maximin. He was cackling like a mad thing as young Theodore pushed him higher and higher on a swing that had been lashed to a tree branch. I stopped and smiled at the happy scene. Theodore's clothes were too big for him, and he was sweating in the morning sun from an effort that, even slightly increased, would pitch my son straight out of his enclosure on to the dried mud.

'This place is a stinking hovel!' Sveta hissed in my direction. She'd spoken in a Latin that I could be sure none of the slaves could understand. Still, I chose to assume she'd been directing herself at Martin.

'Please, my dear,' he quavered back at her. 'We did agree—'

She silenced him with a blow to the side of his face that still had an ear. 'Don't you "please dear" to me!' she snarled. 'The whole place stinks. And, now we're at least unpacked, your lord and master is sending us to Corinth – no doubt to somewhere ever dirtier.' She drew breath. Then, with the lack of reasoning ability you get in women, went back to complaining about the residency. 'If he was half the man you think he is, he'd have got us moved right out of this slum. It's too dirty even for the rats.'

I was pretending not to have heard this – though she'd had a point about rats: why were there none at all? – when I was almost knocked over by a smell that took me back to the mass graves of Alexandria before they'd been covered over. I poured half a bottle of scent on to a napkin and clamped it over my nose and mouth.

'Ah, the latrines are being cleaned out,' I said with a muffled attempt at cheer. Their unopened smell at twenty paces had been quite enough for me, and I'd so far avoided a direct visit, making my own offerings into a brass chamber pot. But these were, I had no doubt, civilised latrines. Once in working order, they'd be flushed by as continuous a stream of water as could be arranged from what remained of the aqueduct. Then, we could have oiled and scented sponges, and try to imagine ourselves in a place for persons of quality.

I was thinking of the possibility of getting water into the bath-house, when Sveta pushed a reddened forearm in my direction. 'Not a rat to be seen or heard,' she went on in grim fury, 'but more bees than you'll find in a hive.'

'But Sveta, my dearest love bucket,' Martin managed to get in while she drew breath, 'Athens is famed for its honey.'

'Honey?' she said with a flat menace I'd heard only once before, when she'd learned that I was proposing to take Martin out of Alexandria into the south of Egypt. 'Don't talk to me about honey. Don't you care if your own child is eaten alive by nasty little bees?' She dropped her voice and looked in my direction. It was to no effect. I'd have heard her clearly enough from deep inside the residency. 'And don't you think you can tell him *something* about that bloody witch?'

With his own nervous look in my direction, Martin tried to put his arms about her.

But she broke free and raised her voice again: 'Oh, I should have listened to my mother, God rest her soul. If she could see me now . . .'

I heard the warning cry just in time to avoid a shower of sweepings thrown from one of the upper windows. I stepped aside and took the opportunity to get as far out of hearing as I could manage.

'I trust you are feeling well this morning?' I said to Theodore, who was still pushing on the swing.

'Oh, yes, My Lord,' he cried, bowing just low enough for the now unattended swing not to knock him dead on its recoil.

'Excellent,' I said. I paused and put the napkin back to my face as a shift in the wind sent invisible but dizzying fingers of sewer smells in our direction. 'I trust the Lady Euphemia is happy with the attendants I have assigned to her,' I said finally.

Seemingly unaware of the smell, Theodore bowed again and smiled. 'Indeed, My Lord,' he said. 'My mother will thank you in person, but regrets that the full daylight is bad for her eyes.'

I smiled. She'd crawled out of bed to splash water over herself shortly before dawn. If she now stirred from her own bed before noon, she'd confirm I hadn't been sufficiently inventive in the night. Even thoughts of the fallen Decelea hadn't taken the edge off my lust. Now, the mere recollection of all we'd managed set off an entirely delicious twinge in my loins.

I nodded and left Theodore at play with Maximin. Careful not to trip over the ridges of dried mud, I picked my way across the main part of the courtyard. There had been a sizable lawn here, and flower beds, and a nice marble fountain in the middle of it all. The fountain remained, though silent now, and choked with years – perhaps generations – of rotted-down compost. Still holding the pitcher on his shoulder, the naked boy who was the main part of the fountain stared back at me with the blankness the ancients had generally preferred in their art. I stopped about a dozen yards from what I took to be Euphemia's window. It had been opened outward a few inches to let in air, and the blind was fully up inside. Impossible, of course, to see anything by day through those thick, greenish pieces of glass. But did I have the impression of being watched? I gave one of my charming smiles and bowed. A shame I had no excuse for going into the building and upstairs to continue what I regarded as unfinished business. Far behind me, I could hear Sveta's voice rising to one of her cold furies, and Martin's answering wails of embarrassment. Maximin was laughing again fit to burst.

'Oh, there you are, dearie.'

I turned and looked at Irene.

She made a sort of bow and stepped away from what had turned out to be a soft patch of ground. 'This cleaning doesn't have no end,' she said. She swore and snatched at a bee that had flown too close by her. She held it between forefinger and thumb of her right hand. With her left she pulled off its wings and legs. She popped it in her mouth and chewed thoughtfully. 'It does the rheumatics a power of good,' she explained with a smile that showed pieces of black on her teeth.

I patted a lock of hair back into place that had fallen down when I nearly tripped over a bush. I frowned. 'I thought we had agreed,' I said, 'only to clean the places that will definitely be used. I am most grateful that you have chosen to move in and supervise the slaves. But there is a limit to how many more of your slaves I wish to buy.'

She came over beside me and looked up at the window. 'She's a right peach of a girl, don't you think?' she asked. 'I've given meself a room near to hers – in case she gets lonely, like.' She pursed her lips and only just managed to stop herself from nudging me with her elbow.

I coughed to hide a smile I didn't think I could suppress. Loneliness would be the least of Euphemia's problems. 'But Irene,' I asked, 'surely your husband will be missing you?'

Her reply was a disapproving sniff.

I had a sudden thought. 'You told me the other day you didn't believe any of the stories about this place,' I said. 'Any chance of a few details?'

I waited for her to take the bait. But all I got was another sniff and a comment about the overriding importance of business. Without any pretence of a bow, she walked off to continue her shouted instructions. There was an answering cry from one of the upper windows and another shower of dirt. I looked up again at Euphemia's window. I heard Sveta's voice raised in another shrill rebuke.

I turned and made my way towards the happy couple. Sveta had run out of insults, or at least of breath to voice them, and was contenting herself with a vicious look in my direction. I walked past her in the direction of one of the secondary courtyards where I might have a carrying chair waiting for me.

I was about to round the corner, when Priscus stuck his ghastly face out of a window. 'Ah, young Alaric,' he croaked with better cheer than I might have expected, 'if you can spare the time, I've something *wonderful* to show you!'

'We thought it was a door leading to some storage rooms,' the slave explained in one of the more northerly Slavic dialects. 'It was only when we got it open and found the other door that we realised it was something else.' He stood back and motioned at the blackness within the opened door. We were on the ground floor of the left block. The library was directly above us. I've said that the glass dome was supported by four columns. The combined weight, plus that of the floor and its bookracks, I could now see, was supported by a set of brick arches. Every other of the arches was just a storeroom. This one really was different. I walked towards the far door that had now been opened and sniffed at the stale air. There was a smell of damp brick dust and of undisturbed cold. I stood back and examined the door. It was of heavy wood, reinforced with bands of rusted iron. The heavy bolts that had secured it from the outside were also rusted, and must have required the strength of two men to force them back. How many other doors concealed by doors might there be within this building?

'Needless to say, the lazy bastards wouldn't go in,' Priscus added in Latin. He grinned and leaned on a broomstick he was using to get himself about. 'It takes someone of proper nerve to explore those hidden delights.' He switched into Slavic and called for pitch torches. He turned back to me. 'Shall I go down first?' he crooned. 'It will, after all, be my second visit. Or would the Lord Alaric take his turn to show he wasn't afraid?'

How I avoided sliding straight down those crumbled steps isn't worth narrating. But I stepped at the bottom into a six-inch depth of cobwebs and nearly sprained an ankle on what felt like a brick floor. Priscus barked another order, and two slaves moved reluctantly past me. They stood each side of the little chamber and held up flaring torches.

'Every palace has one, wouldn't you agree?' Priscus asked, now back in Latin. 'Doesn't even your dear nest in Constantinople have one for those slaves who don't pay attention to your words of gentle admonition?'

I ignored the laugh that turned into an attempt to clear his throat. I ignored the splatter of doubtless bloody phlegm on to the cobwebs, and looked about.

Just because nearly everyone of importance has endorsed it, and just because I've never deprived myself of its practical advantages, doesn't make slavery other than a disgusting institution. Yes, I hadn't made use of such a place as this. I can say that I've *never* done this to a slave. But there's no denying that the good behaviour of your own slaves rests ultimately on the knowledge that these places do exist, and are sanctioned by the laws and customs of every civilised race.

This end of the dungeon was so low that I had to stoop to avoid knocking my head. Its other dimensions were about eight feet by twelve. Still in their manacles, two of the skeletons lay where death had overtaken them. The others had been pulled apart, and it was only from the manacles that I could tell there had been another three. I bit my lip and stared at the closest of them. Half concealed in the mass of filth that lay over the cobwebs, the skull might have been of a child or a small woman. I looked further along the wall, at one of the skeletons that held together. It still nursed what looked like a gnawed wooden pitcher.

'What bastard could just have left them here?' I breathed as if to myself.

Priscus heard me and laughed, now with more success. 'Why ask questions that can't be answered?' he said in a firm and mocking voice. 'How often have you used these very words?' He suppressed a cough and stepped forward. I heard the dull tread of his velvet shoes as he hurried over to the skeleton in good order.

I followed him into the overpowering smell of must. All dead matter had long since decayed into its constituent atoms. Even so, I made sure to breathe in through my mouth.

'Just look at this, dear boy,' he cried. He twisted round to see me and beckoned me eagerly forward. 'Come and see what refinements the ancients knew and we have forgotten.'

I took a deep breath and took another step. I tried not to think of my ruined shoes. I did manage to avoid looking at the two slaves, who stood unmoving with bowed heads, torches held out before them.

Priscus tugged one of the manacles free of the wrist it had enclosed for what may have been centuries. He tossed the bones into the dirt and stood up. 'This really is lovely, don't you think?' he asked.

The manacle was of a design I hadn't seen before. What I'd always seen was essentially a broken ring that was screwed or locked together round a limb. This was something much more complex. It can be best described as a hinged bracelet welded to a chain. When fully outstretched, it resembled the antlers of a stag beetle. As you moved them closer, one part passed inside the other. Every inward movement was attended by the click of a ratchet. The two parts went together, but wouldn't pull apart. The only way to get them back to their original position was to push them fully together, after which they continued freely back on themselves.

Appalled, I watched as Priscus pushed them together, and then spun them forward to push them together again. 'Such elegance of design!' he marvelled. 'You can adjust them to fit the largest or the tiniest of offending wrists.'

'How do you get them off again?' I asked. It was a stupid question. I'd already seen the answer. But there might be some hope that Priscus knew something I didn't.

No such luck. A gloating look spread over his face, and he turned away from me to show the slaves how the mechanism worked. Barbarians as they were, and ignorant of Latin, they knew the answer without having to ask.

'They don't come off, my darling,' he said at length. 'Not, that is, unless you cut them off. And, really, who would be wasteful enough to ruin workmanship of this quality? No, dear boy, once these things are on, it's amputation or nothing.

'The moment we're back in Constantinople, I'll be straight off to a workman I know. It may be a design that has somehow slipped the memory of man. You can be sure it's a design too simple and too useful to stay forgotten.' He giggled and shook the manacle again at the slaves. They shrank back. 'Do you remember what I said the other evening when you were spying on me about how fear magnifies pain? The moment you feel this bronze contraption clicking shut about your wrist, you know that, even if there is no physical pain, you are lost one way or another.' He giggled once more and kissed the tarnished bronze. He pulled on the chain. This also was of bronze, as were the clamps that held it to the wall. It was all as secure as on the day when some grinning devil had watched it being put together.

Priscus was right about the nature of invention. Century can follow century, and some truths can lie forgotten or undiscovered. Once revealed, they can be so simple that only luck can ensure they are forgotten again. Even if whatever was eating him from within took proper hold – even if his drugs failed him – the joy alone of presenting Heraclius with his own copy of this perverted ingenuity would keep him alive till we got home.

I leaned against the cold, crumbling bricks and took a deep breath. I'd not waste time on asking myself what these wretches might have done to bring this punishment on them. Nor would I think of their screams as the lights had been withdrawn and they'd heard the locking of the door above, or of how long they must have been alive down here before the end. I'd not even look again at the skeletons. As said, two of them were still in good order. Others within reach of these had been pulled about. I *wouldn't* speculate on whether some of the bones had tooth marks on them. I tried to think of Theodore and Maximin playing outside in the sunshine.

'Weren't the ancients just a splendid people?' Priscus cried in another ecstasy. 'You can forget those dumpy temples I saw you blubbering over. Their true genius lies fresh and undisturbed in every underground hideaway. If only I'd had this before me when Homer and Demosthenes were flogged into me – why, it might have made me as finicky about language as the most learned young Alaric!'

'If this place exists,' I said with icy control, 'we can be reasonably sure that there are other cellars.' I looked down at the floor. It might be worth asking if other cellars were as damp as this one. But it was a question of underground springs. Other cellars – especially elsewhere in the palace – might be bone dry.

'You must keep looking,' I said to the slaves. They bowed low. I hurried past them to the crumbling stairs. I'd need new shoes before I went out. The pity was I hadn't time for another bath.

40

As I'd expected, word hadn't got round that I was now the only authority in Athens. That meant no one tried to get past my armed slaves to badger me with petitions for favours or justice. For the moment, persons of quality just bowed and got out of my way. A gathering mob of the local trash had followed me right from the gates of the residency. They might know something about Nicephorus. If so, it would explain their tone and looks of displeasure. But I paid no attention to the low and sinister murmur from behind. The smell of their bodies, whenever the breeze shifted, was a different matter. Was it not partly for these occasions, though, that perfume was invented?

'Irene tells me there will be carrying slaves tomorrow,' Martin wheezed apologetically for the second time.

I nodded and continued looking down, so I could keep myself from stepping off the raised stones into the drying filth of the streets. I was down to my last pair of fine shoes.

'The Areopagus is nearly half a mile to walk,' he said, as if revealing we'd have to walk all the way to Corinth. 'It's then quite a bit up the hill.'

'You say it's been rebuilt and given a roof since ancient times?' I asked. I stopped and waited for him to catch up with me. I still hadn't got him fixed into any scheme of regular exercise. But, if walking the streets of Athens was better than nothing, it wouldn't do to have him fall into the mud. More to the point, the unarmed slaves were already overburdened with book rolls, and he was struggling along with all my writing materials. I pointed at what might have been the Colonnade of Nicias. 'Isn't that where Diogenes the Cynic lived in his wine vat?' I asked.

Martin shook his head. 'According to one of Aristotle's letters,' came the learned response, 'he lived just above the spring flood line of the river.'

I nodded and looked about. Apart from the smoke-blackened colonnade, we were now among the monumental buildings Justinian had paid for. They were smaller, of course, than in the centre of Constantinople. But this might have passed for one of the secondary districts of the Capital where it touched on the centre. There was no feeling, among these arched buildings and their many-coloured stones, of the real – or perhaps just the *old* – Athens. One more junction, though, and we'd be into the Areopagus district. Though not ancient, the buildings here were old enough to give an impression of authenticity.

From here, worse luck, it would be straight up to where every association – however old the stones might be – would be relentlessly modern.

I looked sideways at Martin. His face had taken on an abstracted look. 'Would you mind telling me,' I asked in Latin, 'what Sveta meant earlier about a *witch*?'

The answer I got was a tightening of his face and a deep blush. But I repeated the question. We still had a hundred yards to go, and there could be no escaping my direct question.

He swallowed and looked down at the dried mud of the street. 'Oh, you know what Sveta can be like,' he said. 'She's taken it into her head that the Lady Euphemia is the demon who's always lived in the residency. She's frightened for Theodore – and for you.' He trailed off with a mumbled apology.

I smiled. Yes, I knew Sveta very well. As for Euphemia, if those wild couplings did eventually kill me, I'd be in no mood to complain. 'Dearest Martin,' I said in a condescending voice, 'we both know that Euphemia came here three years ago with Theodore. You really should keep your wife under better control.'

Some hope of that, however! We walked on in silence.

The Bishop of Athens had finished preaching a sermon of the most astonishing perversity. Two of the Asiatic Greek bishops had even dared to walk out. The other Greek delegates had looked at each other and murmured with rising disgust. I could be glad that Martin had made it into something merely banal in Latin. But that was long over, and I was now deep into my opening speech. This was, I could see, going even better than I'd hoped. There had been no time for prior composition. But, if the real ancients – those, that is, for whom Greek wasn't essentially a foreign language to be got by rule, and never spoken without notes or fear of going wrong – could speak extempore, the learned young Alaric wouldn't be seen glancing down at a text. Though I had answers to every question that might be raised, it would be for the best if no one thought of these questions until after he was back home. And so I'd begun with lush flattery of all present, and had then moved to a passage that I'd intended to be of terrifying complexity, and that was running fast out of control.

I found myself straying into a morass of qualifying hypotheses. But, though stretched tighter than I'd ever have dared pen in hand, the thread of the whole sentence still hadn't snapped. So long as he kept the main subject of the whole period in mind, no one should have lost me in either language. But I was coming close to an embarrassing descent into chaos. Much more elaboration, and I'd lose sight myself of the structure I was raising, or I'd lose much of the audience. Each of the subordinate clauses still open, I made my decision and went straight into my descent. I glanced upward at the windows of the domed ceiling and imagined a blind coming down as I made one closure. Another blind came down in my head as, the sentence rhythm moving ever closer to its final upward lunge, I closed another. As I closed the third, and then the fourth, I could feel the tension in the room. I heard the strain in Martin's voice as he followed me in Latin and willed me not to fall over myself – not now, when a single slip would ruin the effect of the whole. I looked quickly about the room. The Bishop of Ephesus had given up his expression of sour disapproval, and was sitting with his mouth open. Martin was doing brilliantly in Latin, and had brought the same look to the face of the Bishop of Milan. Would I get there?

And I did. I closed the last subordination, and passed without drawing breath into the last half-dozen words to round off the whole. As I finished, fifty bishops and assorted clerics got off their wooden benches and cheered themselves black in the face. Between where I stood and the semicircle of delegates, the minute clerk threw down his stylus and waved a waxed tablet the size of a gaming board over his head. I smiled and bowed and took the waves of applause. Men cheered and touched their foreheads. They turned and hugged each other. Martin's hands shook as he lifted his cup of water. I allowed myself a brief and complacent look at my silver inkstand of office. Thirty pounds of pure silver it weighed. I'd paid for it myself when appointed to the Imperial Council, and specified that, between its three lion feet and its bowl in the shape of an old drinking cup, its long stem should imitate in small scale the serpent column set up in Delphi to commemorate the Persian defeat, and now moved to the Circus in Constantinople. I'd never yet fallen below its promise. I might now have exceeded a promise that perhaps only I could understand.

But the council was returning to order. I raised my arms for attention, and was straight back to business. 'It may be legitimate,' I allowed, 'to say that denying a Human Will to our Lord and Saviour will imply that He had not a complete Human as well as Divine Nature, so that He was not truly both man and God. Thus, to preserve the integrity of the Human Nature, it is possible that belief in a Double Will is orthodox of necessity. Now, it may be granted that such concern for the true humanity of Christ incarnate cannot be other than praised. The orthodox position is that we must take Christ to be both Human and Divine. At the same time, it can be asked if the possibility of a Single Will be inconsistent with a Human Nature.'

I looked round again. Everyone was still glowing with the recollection of my long and wonderful sentence – and pleased at his own ability to follow it in either language. Until that passed entirely, I could get away with this mass of gibberish. I smiled and raised my hands in pious supplication. 'Yet it may also seem to be doubted,' I took up in a tone of utter reasonableness, 'if the faculty of will belongs properly to a being's nature rather than to his person. A failure to conceive this doubt is surely why some of the most learned men of the past age could assert that the lack of any faculty of will to the Human Nature of Christ deprived him of a complete Human Nature. By contrast, however, it may be said that the will is a faculty of person, not of nature. It is persons who have free will and exercise it to choose this or that. If the Human Nature of Christ had its own proper will, so that Our Lord had literally two wills, then there would surely be two Persons, one Human and one Divine. But to assert this is to fall into the most damnable heresy of Nestorius, who divided Our Lord's Person into two. And can it be understood that the Human Nature of Christ could have its own Will, distinct from the Will of the Second Person of the Trinity, and not be a person?'

I paused for the ritual denunciations of Nestorius to echo round the hall. This gave me time to pull my thoughts together for the next and rather tricky point. 'The question, then,' I went smoothly on, 'is whether Our Lord and Saviour Jesus Christ can have one Will and yet two Natures. Or is it that a Single Will might imply the damnable heresy of the Monophysites – that He has but a Single Nature?' I stopped for Martin to catch up, and for the further cries of 'Anathema be upon them all!' Then I brought out what might be seen as a verbal trick, or as an escape from the whole circle in which men had been scurrying for ages past: 'The orthodox position, settled for once and all at the Council of Chalcedon, is that Christ has two Natures, Human and Divine. There can, of course, be no retreat from that position. Yet, while the doctrine of a Single Will follows necessarily from the heretical doctrine of a Single Nature – for, if there were but a Single Person and a Single Nature, how could men speak of a Second Will? – does the doctrine of a Single Nature itself follow necessarily from the doctrine of a Single Will? This is the question that we have been called here to consider.'

I stopped again, now for a sip of water and for a look about the hall. This penultimate sentence had been the critical one. I'd established that we could probably get enough of the Monophysites to agree that a Single Will was nothing more than a development from their notion of a Single Nature. But could we, at the same time, persuade the Greeks and Westerners to accept that a Single Will might follow from a Single Person, and not lead straight into the notion of a Single Nature? Get agreement on that, and we could square the circle. Priscus had put the whole thing more crudely over his stewed river frog: 'a flattening of two opposed formulations beneath a third on which both sides could agree'. But that was essentially what I was about.

There was no need, however, to let it sink in fully. I was here at the moment more to impress than to persuade. Suddenly aware of the water clock that was gurgling away beside the minute clerk, I stared down at the quotation from Pope Gregory of sainted memory. From a technical point of view, I'd have done better to quote Sophronius of Miletus. But, after all the foregoing, I needed something in Latin. Before we could reach out to the Syrians and Egyptians, we'd have to pull Greeks and Latins much closer together than they'd been in over a century.

Martin's voice had for a while been grating slightly from the strain of interpreting a message that had to be perfectly rendered in both substance and form from Greek into Latin. It would have been better for him if I had prepared a text in advance and let him work on it. But he'd get through my speech without serious trouble. We'd have to trust the local interpreters not to bugger up the rest of the council. It was a rest for both of us to do Gregory in Latin. It was simple work for Martin to put Latin into Greek. The mechanical act of reading gave me time to think of the next long sentence I had in mind. This one, I'd decided on the spot, would have a double subject, and I'd give each of them three levels of subordination.

And that's what I now brought out. It was not a total success in my own view. The idea had been to bring out two subjects that, like the Nature of Christ, would be both fused and distinct. Sadly, I threw in an adverbial phrase that I discovered almost too late was properly attached to neither subject. I rescued the slip with a separate clause that broke the iambic rhythm and had a rather alliterative and even a trashy sound. But Martin corrected this in his Latin version. The Greeks either didn't notice, or didn't feel inclined to notice. They went instead into another controlled riot of applause and led me into my final passage: 'And so, My Lords, I have, to the best of my ability, covered the issues that we have been called here to discuss. I must emphasise again that this is a *preparatory* council – in which the finest minds of the Church have been brought together not to reach a full conclusion, but instead to decide if these issues are worth putting before an ecumenical council to which the heretics will be invited. Of course, the Emperor has empowered you to reach a full conclusion in the negative sense. If you decide that there are no issues to discuss, years of theological speculation, directed by Caesar himself, must come to a sudden halt.'

My voice faltered slightly here. This hadn't been intended. I fought at first to control the slight break to the smooth flow of words. Then I realised what a good rhetorical device this would be. It might bring home to everyone the possible consequence of using the free judgement I was allowing them to reach an unwelcome decision. I stole a look at one of the Asiatic Greeks. Though he'd never been advanced beyond a decayed see in the middle of nowhere, he was probably the most brilliant living theologian in the Church as a whole. If he wanted, he could turn this council into a screaming mob. But he was looking back at me with courtly politeness. I made a note to offer him preferment to Halicarnassus. With his frenzied asceticism, the present Bishop there couldn't last much longer.

I took another deep breath and continued: 'But if it is your considered opinion that these issues deserve a full hearing, they will eventually be put to an ecumenical council . . .' I was now reaching the end. What I had to avoid was the clear implication that a 'yes' here would turn any main council into a formality. Everyone must have realised that this was the intention: after all, why call 'the finest minds' together simply to decide if the main question was fit to be picked over by all and sundry? But I wanted the option both of a done deal and of plausible deniability should our needs suddenly alter.

And now I was definitely finished. I sat down to another storm of applause. Men ran forward to embrace my knees. I nodded grandly at the shouted acclamations. Slumped over his own lectern, Martin had the look of a man who's just been acquitted in court of something horrid. Well he might. Well he might, indeed. His public duties could now be far gentler. A slave had come in to the room to reset the water clock. I glanced at the list of agreed speakers. Some of these had picked up enough of the superior gossip in Constantinople to have had some inkling of what I was about. For most of them, what I'd just said must have come like a thunderclap. What anyone would say between now and the final session was a mystery. But the main consult could now begin.

41

Thinking of Diogenes on my way here had called to mind one of those possible, if slightly improbable, stories of the old days. Apparently, Plato had set all his acolytes in a twitter with his definition of man as an 'unfeathered biped'. He was still basking at his next lecture at the applause this had got him when the naked and half-crazed cynic burst into the lecturing area with a plucked chicken. 'Look, Plato,' he called in a loud voice, waving the chicken over his head, 'look, I've found you a man!' Doubtless, he'd got himself straight on to the list of those who'd have to be clubbed to death in a cellar if ever Plato got his perfect society. The only public response, though, was an amendment of the definition of man to an 'unfeathered biped with broad toenails'.

I'd been presiding in this now baking hall for what seemed an age. My opening speech had been the high point in the day's proceedings. This over, we were soon into the hard grind of the other speeches.

When you're enthroned at almost Imperial height, and every speaker has to address himself to you from a position where everyone else in the room is looking at you, it puts nodding off out of the question. So I'd passed much of the morning and most of the afternoon thinking of Diogenes, and wishing he could burst in on us with any disruption – witty, profound, or merely obscene. I moved sweaty feet under my robe of office and stole a glance at the note I felt I'd made a month before. 'My Lord Bishop,' I said in a tone that evil old Phocas himself couldn't have found offensive, 'you have now been speaking for three hours of the water clock. There are seven other speakers on my list, and the sun is moving against us. Would it be possible for you to summarise your remarks?'

Gundovald of somewhere close by Marseilles looked up from his text and gave me the smile of an aged timewaster. 'Oh, but Your Magnificence,' he said in sweet rebuke, 'the citation from Pope Gregory of sainted memory is *wholly* appropriate. If I may continue with the second page—'

'But My Lord Bishop,' I hurried on with inflexible charm, 'I can promise the whole extract from his sermon will be inserted into the official record. Can I, however, draw your attention back to the matter we are currently supposed to be investigating? This is whether the ninety-fifth Canon of the Council of Agrigentum can be taken, in its Latin version, neither to imply nor discount a Single Will as well as a Single Nature for Our Lord and Saviour Jesus Christ?' I stopped for the interpreters to put this into Greek, and then for a mutter of answering prayers from the Greeks. I looked about the room. As I'd allowed, the Dispensator was seated right at the front of the gathering at bishop's height. He'd been following Gundovald with rapt attention – well he might, as it was a Pope being cited – and was now taking notes with such force that his stylus cut through the wax and was scratching loudly on the underlying wood. I let my eyes come to rest on an empty place a few yards to his left. I'd not bothered waiting for Simeon to put in an appearance. I'd not commented on his lack of so much as a written apology. I'd do more than slap the insulting old loon's face the next time we were alone. Transfer to a frontier monastery wouldn't be the half of what was waiting for him when he touched dock in Constantinople. He'd never set eyes again on that nice episcopal palace in Nicaea.

Gundovald was still looking for the right beginning to his answer. I thought round for some helpful prompt that couldn't be taken for a slight. Perhaps I should have let him run on. I could feel a slight but insistent buzzing in my loins. Of course, only Diogenes could have got away with active wanking in public: 'If I could but stop being hungry by rubbing my belly!' he'd famously responded to the complaints. But I was beginning to feel that I might take myself off without hands if I thought hard enough about Euphemia.

But why bother with Euphemia? If old Gundovald was a time-waster, his secretary was decidedly worth a second look. I'd been aware of him since the old man had walked creakily over to the speaking place. Like a focusing of eyes in the sunlight after a nap, I'd gradually realised how much the boy looked like a younger, smaller version of myself. Without any sense of a crossing point from one to the other, interest had ripened to lust. I might seduce him over the next few days, against the time when Euphemia would start using her time of month as an excuse for sleeping at night. In any event, he and she could now alternate in my thoughts till I'd brought myself quietly to boiling point. Then I could think of myself.

Yes, I decided, I'd give way to the old dear. I could then set my face like stone and keep myself occupied till the clock ran out of water again and I could call a break to proceedings.

I had my mouth open to speak when I felt a gentle plucking at my left sleeve. 'Your Magnificence,' a voice breathed in my ear, 'the Lord Priscus would ask a moment of your time.'

Typical of Priscus to piss all over my one bright patch in this horrid afternoon, I thought. I stood up. Forty-seven pairs of legs creaked as everyone else got slowly up and bowed. 'Gentlemen,' I said in Latin, 'this session is adjourned for one hour of the water clock.' I repeated myself in Greek. Without waiting for Martin to untangle himself from the mass of unrolled papyrus that now covered the bound volumes of earlier council proceedings, I stepped down from the platform and made for the exit.

I balanced on the topmost stones of the ruined wall and looked down from the Areopagus Hill. Part of the view was blocked by the still higher Acropolis. Otherwise, I had an unbroken view over Athens to its wall and beyond. I shaded my eyes and looked again.

'They must cover the ground as far as Piraeus,' I muttered in Latin. I turned and looked to my right. The sea of wagons and moving humanity stretched almost as far as I could see before the great single cloud of dust became impenetrable.

'Still not twenty million of the buggers,' Priscus said back at me.

'We can be sure of that. But I'd not try counting them.' He sniffed and clutched harder at the slave who'd been supporting him as we walked up the hill.

'I suppose they're here to demand food,' I said, keeping my voice low and neutral. 'The question, then, must be how long they can stay here before they run out of what food they have.'

'Spot on, dear boy,' came the reply. 'But it depends how much they managed to loot from Decelea. It also depends how much we have in the warehouses.' He nodded down at what now looked a pitifully insubstantial city wall. 'They've no talent for siege warfare. We held Thessalonica for three years with four hundred men. If they took Decelea, I don't imagine the walls were in better repair than when I last inspected them. So long as they don't realise they could batter parts of our wall down with a few hundred men in the right formation, I think we can sit this one out.'

Priscus let his face break out on a grin as he found himself a round stone of the right size and sat on it. I felt sweat running in a continual trickle down my back. I could try telling myself it was the effect of sunshine on several yards of quilted blue silk. But there had been too many moods of doubt or hypothesis in what he said. Outside Athens, there might be a whole people on the move. They were flowing about our wall like water round a stone. The wall enclosed an area perhaps three-quarters of a mile across at the widest. Even if it didn't fall inward at the first push, it was surely too long to hold if attacked at too many points. But the area it enclosed was too small for anything approaching defence in depth.

I jumped down and sat on another stone beside Priscus. I found myself looking over at the Acropolis. A thousand years before, the Persians had taken this. Back then, however, it had been guarded by a wooden palisade. Since then, it had been surrounded with proper walls. As originally built, the Propylaea had been a weak point. Since the first barbarian siege, though, this had been strengthened. Could we withdraw to the Acropolis and hold that? I wondered.

Priscus looked into my face and laughed. 'Good for a last stand,' he said, nodding over at the collection of white buildings. 'Unless it starts raining again, though, there's a problem of water.'

'You told me you provisioned the citadel of Trampolinea,' I said, 'by setting up a block and tackle to carry up water.'

He grinned and scratched under his cloak. 'We had regular soldiers there,' he said. 'That meant we could largely ignore public opinion. Athens will be defended by its own people. Show any lack of confidence about the walls, and you'll have the barbarians looking in at you, and rioting behind you.'

I changed the subject. 'We'll never get them to Corinth,' I said.

His face darkened as his mind came back to the obvious. Such danger as we might run personally was an occupational hazard. But how to keep everyone else safe?

I rubbed my eyes and looked back down the hill. Sure enough, there was Martin walking towards me, deep in conversation with the Dispensator.

'Don't look round please!' I urged inwardly. 'One look round, and you'll shit yourself in public.' I got up and readied myself to take Martin aside.

Priscus cleared his throat and spat. I looked thoughtfully at the bloody gob that had gathered in a bright ball on the dust. 'Sooner or later,' he said in the tone of one who labours against a coughing fit, 'someone will come forward for a parley. We'll try and organise it by the northern gate. The wall's at its strongest there.'

Martin didn't disgrace me. When he did eventually look round, he simply pulled a face and went into some patter about the Will of God.

Ignoring him, the Dispensator hurried forward and scowled at me. 'I regard this as an insult to His Holiness,' he announced.

I opened my eyes wide and looked at him. Then I realised he was referring to Simeon's absence.

'My Lord, if I might draw your attention to what is happening beyond the walls,' I began.

He darted a glance to where I was pointing and gave a longer inspection to the wall. He looked for a moment over the swirling masses of humanity and snorted. 'This is a matter for you in your secular capacity,' he said. 'Bearing in mind what I heard on my arrival here, I am not at all surprised if we are now under siege. My own concern, however, is how a council of the Greek and Latin Churches can proceed when the leading representative of the Greek Patriarch will not attend even its opening session. I feel increasingly that my time is being wasted, and am strongly inclined to say as much in my report to His Holiness.'

'I am myself puzzled by the Lord Bishop's absence,' I said with diplomatic concern. 'I am sure it has a good explanation, and I can promise that it will not be repeated. And I think his colleagues are all agreed on the value of what has been said today by their Latin brethren.'

The Dispensator scowled again and sat down on the stone I'd vacated. Having nothing else to do, he looked harder at the barbarian tide that surrounded Athens on every side. Somehow, the wall now seemed even longer, and its enclosed area even smaller. There was a distant sound of cheering to the north. A line of horsemen had emerged from the dust. They were carrying long pikes held upward, and were followed by half a dozen large wagons. I saw them bumping and pitching as they came off the road and made for an open space about a hundred yards from the wall. As they all came closer into view, I saw that each of the pikes was topped with a severed head.

'So these are the Avars,' the Dispensator said, now with mild interest. 'They attempted an invasion two years ago of Italy. It was serious enough for the Lombards to break off their siege of Rome, and for us to agree not to counter-attack while they marched north to resist the invasion.'

'We are fully aware of your dealings with the Lombards,' Priscus broke in. 'The Great Augustus does not always approve.' He'd made a vague effort at the menacing, but his main attention was now taken up with a large map of the city defences that he'd been given by someone who wore a cooking pot on his head in place of a helmet.

The Dispensator gave one of his chilly smiles and turned his inspection back to us. 'Be that as it may, My Lord Priscus,' he replied, 'the Lombards do occupy much of Italy, and we have given up any hope of Imperial help in removing them. Besides, even if enslaved to the damnable heresy of Arius, they are Christians. These people' – he waved a hand to the still gathering mass beyond the wall – 'are, excepting a few of their Slavic allies, heathens. When I negotiated his lifting of the siege, the Lombard King assured me they practised both human sacrifice and cannibalism.'

That was news to me. But there was no doubt the Avars were savages. By comparison, the Lombards were almost genteel. I gave a curt bow and went over to where Martin was looking glum.

'Get up,' I whispered, offering a hand. He looked up from where he was sitting on the ground. I did think of assuring him that we were all perfectly safe behind the city wall. But he knew me too well to believe anything I might say about that. 'I want you to hurry back to the residency,' I said. 'Take two of the armed slaves who came out with us. Do tell Sveta to stop her packing.' I looked carefully at him.

He swallowed and gave a slight bow.

'Also,' I went on, 'I want to make sure that the supplies we bought yesterday are properly stored.'

I watched his dithery progress down the hill. Show Martin a sword, and he might faint away with terror. Give him the job of producing order out of chaos, and he'd generally shine. I thought briefly about the thickness of our own main gate. I wondered yet again if the residency had any deep cellars, and if access to them might somehow be concealed from an armed break-in. But this was something best looked at in person, and while the light held up. As Martin went out of sight behind one of the monasteries, I turned back to the others.

More of the militia leaders had appeared, and Priscus was explaining something about the western gate. Their heads were coming closer and closer together over the map.

42

'I rather think the hour is up,' the Dispensator said, now beside me. 'Shall we not resume proceedings?'

I stared past him. 'I think His Grace the Bishop of Nicaea will now put in an appearance,' I said.

And Simeon it was. Dressed in his full clerical finery, he staggered in the heat and from the effort of running uphill. He stopped for a moment and waved his stick at a couple of small, very dark boys who'd got in his way. As they danced out of reach, he hurried forward again, and picked his way over the stones that littered the clearing at the top of the hill.

'The end is upon us!' he cried in shrill terror. 'The hour of repentance is come!' He tripped over a stone, but clambered straight up. He gave one look at the sight beyond the walls and raised his arms. '"For the great day of His wrath is come; and who shall be able to stand?"' he now squealed. He sat down heavily on the ground and poured a handful of dust over his head. It spoiled what was left of his hair styling, and settled on his face where the tears had been running.

I stood over him and glowered. 'And where, My Lord Bishop,' I asked with quiet menace, 'have you been all day?'

His answer was another desperate look at the gathering mass beyond the walls, and several more verses from Revelation.

I finally gathered that he'd been watching a continual stream of refugees, from round about and from Decelea, entering through both gates. It seemed, as he'd listened to the tale of horror that Decelea had become, that he'd lost all sense of time or of his duties. He'd now come up here, I gathered, because, unless he took the more punishing route up to the Acropolis, or grew a pair of wings, the Areopagus was the highest point in Athens.

The Dispensator gave him a very cold stare before looking away. 'There is, I believe,' he said to me, 'a most ingenious metaphor yet to be heard in Gundovald's speech. I am told he began work on the text in March. I can understand your concern at its lack of superficial relevance. But his kinsmen in the Frankish royal house would not be pleased to learn that it was never delivered in full.'

As good a reason as any, I thought, to get back under cover. There was sod all I could do out here. This was definitely a job for Priscus – and one he'd surely do to the best of his considerable ability.

But Simeon had now started a bubbling laugh. 'We're under siege,' he sobbed. 'You can't go on with the council.'

'I must remind you, My Lord Senator, that the hour is up,' the Dispensator said with flat finality. He gave Simeon a contemptuous sniff.

Simeon responded by bursting properly into tears. For once, they were making full sense to each other without any need for interpreters.

Behind me, I heard Priscus laugh. 'If you don't want a good, hard kicking, dear cousin,' he called over, 'you'll do as you're bleeding told. If Christ has a Single Will, the rest of us can at least agree on our duties.' He stood up and pointed at the old court building.

'My Lord Fortunatus,' I whispered, 'please take His Grace of Nicaea inside. Please also apologise for me over the continued delay. I will rejoin you as soon as I can.'

The Dispensator nodded.

I watched as he got Simeon over the stones and hurried him past the Monastery of Saint Dionysius the Areopagite. Outside the meeting hall, the street was crowded with a mob of bishops. I saw one of them climb into a carrying chair. Another was trying to pull his robes off. The Dispensator got to them before they could all run away. But I could doubt if even he would be able to get everyone back inside and seated in readiness for the session to resume.

I walked over to where Priscus had gone back to jabbing a finger at his map. His militia people bowed to me and stood respectfully back. 'So we definitely are working together again,' I said in Latin. I looked down at a chorus of screams beyond the walls. But the dust was now too general for me to see its cause. 'Can I take it that you switched last night, when you saw the flickering from Decelea?'

Priscus grinned back at me.

There was nothing new to be learned from putting this into words. But it was worth spelling out for the avoidance of any doubt. 'The deal now is,' I added, 'that I give you a free hand in the defence of Athens. You keep your nose out of Church business. If the walls don't give way, we can both go back to Constantinople covered in glory. The Great Augustus can forget all about whatever may have happened in Alexandria. That bag of eunuch shit can look on in helpless rage as a few palace trinkets get melted down to commemorate what we've achieved in Athens.'

Priscus smiled and gave me a gentle nod. 'We stand or fall together, dear boy,' he said.

If I hadn't known him better, I'd almost have believed him.

I looked down the hill again. The Dispensator still hadn't got everyone back inside. Instead, he was deep in conversation with Simeon through the Bishop of Athens. As I was about to go down towards them, the Dispensator took Simeon roughly by the arm and pointed up in my direction. I looked past them to the foot of the hill. My heart skipped a beat as I saw the dark and silent crowd pressing forward. At the least, it looked as if there would be yet another delay before Gundovald could get back into his interminable speech.

As convenor of a Church council, it just wouldn't have done to come out with a sword. Priscus was armed. So, after a fashion, were his militiamen. I had my own three guards who hadn't gone off with Martin. That didn't add up to much of a defence against a mob of several hundred of the Athenian lower classes.

But I made an effort to look confident. 'Be about your business,' I called out. 'The city defences are in good hands.'

There was a low muttering of anger. The crowd parted and someone stepped forward. 'You've brought them here,' he said in more or less comprehensible Greek. He pointed at me and then at Priscus. 'What have you done with the Boss?'

'If you are referring to His Excellency the Count of Athens,' I said very slowly, 'it is he who has withdrawn from his duties. If any of you have information as to his whereabouts, a reward will be paid. If you have nothing else to say, I do suggest you go back about whatever business occupies you by day.'

I paused to draw breath and for a shift of tone. 'But, men of Athens,' I now cried, 'the barbarians are at the very gates of your city. Both duty and interest surely require us to set all differences aside and work together for the common good. Let us—'

Any thoughts I might have had of repeating my oratorical triumph of the morning came to an end as a stone thudded hard into my chest and I found myself sitting in the dust. I sprawled left just in time to avoid another stone aimed at my head, and I heard it land somewhere behind me. Someone far back in the crowd laughed unpleasantly, and everyone took a step forward. I saw a man at the front bend to pick up another stone. I scrambled to my feet and hurried over to where the Dispensator was standing in the doorway of the court building.

'Best get everyone inside,' I said. 'I'll see what I can do out here.'

I might have sounded more in charge of things if I hadn't now tripped over one of the uneven steps and fallen straight into his arms. He steadied me and pushed me under cover. He gave me a funny look and walked into the street. Paying no attention to the stone that brushed the sleeve of his best robe, he raised both arms to the cowering bishops who hadn't already got themselves inside. I heard another stone slap against one of the walls. I heard another go high and rattle against the tiles of the roof. Sword out, Priscus had got himself and his men under cover of a bricked-up porch. What good they'd do against this lot I couldn't say. But one of the older bishops had dropped his walking stick. I bent and picked it up. It might be good for something.

'Get that door shut!' I called in Latin as yet another stone landed at my feet and I went over beside the Dispensator, who was looking annoyed at the further disruption. I was about to suggest a quick dash inside. If we barred the doors, the mob might eventually decide not to try breaking in after us.

But Priscus had now finished his conference with the militia heads. He stepped out from the porch, sword in one hand, my convenor's bell in the other. He stopped in the middle of the street and ignored the roof tile that landed at his feet. He turned and grinned at me. I wondered how he'd got the bell from where I'd left it. But he stepped a few paces towards the mob that was continuing to move steadily forward, clubs in hand, looks of twisted hate stamped on their faces. He laughed into the faces and began ringing the bell. It sounded loud in the still air of the afternoon, and the mob came to an uncertain halt. As I wondered if he'd gone raving mad, I heard a shuffling from up the hill. They came from the top of the hill, where I hadn't seen them. They came from the side streets, which is where they must have been sitting about all day. It looked at the time as if they really had emerged like armed men from the dragon's teeth in the legend of Jason. But, as the bell stopped ringing, and Priscus raised his sword, the several dozen armed men from the better classes of Athens formed a dense and organised mass in the street, and stood waiting for instructions.

'You have a choice,' Priscus cried at the mob. 'You can get back to your filthy burrows, and leave your lives to the defence of your betters. Or you can suffer the penalty of those who really piss off the Commander of the East.' He looked round at his men. Some of them had swords. Some had long, spiked clubs. Some had bows with arrows already in place. He looked back at the mob, which still hadn't come forward, but didn't look inclined to disperse. He laughed and put himself at the head of the militia. 'If these vermin really mean business,' he said, 'so do we! Keep together – no falling out for any purpose – but we go forward and kill until the streets are clear.'

The Dispensator took hold of my arm. 'I think we can leave things with the Lord Priscus,' he said.

As he drew me back inside, I continued looking at the opening moves of a street battle that, with Priscus on one side, could have only one outcome. The men right at the front of the mob did make some effort to stare back. But those behind were already making a quiet bolt for the side streets that radiated from the bottom of the hill. And then the front men themselves turned and ran.

And that was it. Priscus sheathed his sword and bowed in our direction. 'I can't answer for the enemy outside the walls,' he called out. 'But the enemy within should take no further interest in your exploration of the Nature of Our Lord and Saviour.'

His men put away their weapons and let up a happy cheer.

The Dispensator was plucking harder at my sleeve. 'My Lord Gundovald is ready to take up his speech again whenever you choose to reconvene the council,' he said.

I nodded and forced myself not to hurry forward as we walked back inside.

I should have expected there would be a trap. But the immense length and irrelevance of his text, combined with an inclination to dwell on external events, had left me unprepared for when Gundovald finally looked up and began to speak extempore. Much of this was as irrelevant as his text. Three sentences, however – uncharacteristically clear sentences, I might add – had skewered me on one of my weak points. Back in Constantinople, I'd dithered for months between making up a doctrine of a Single Will and making up a similar but separate doctrine of a Single Energy. I'd finally decided on a Single Will because it had a more logical neatness, and because it was better calculated to turn Monophysite heads. Now the old fool had raised the possibility of a Single Energy, and gone straight on to cite the Acts of two ecumenical councils against it. Luckily, without Martin there to assist, the duty interpreter had so mangled his words that the Greeks were unaware of what he'd really said. But the Latin delegates were beginning to look as if they might start thinking for themselves.

I was coming to the second half hour of the water clock in my speech of clarification. The interpreter was totally lost, and reduced several times to consulting with his colleague for the right words in Greek – and a fat lot of good that did him or his listeners: his stammered paraphrase was as wildly off mark as an arrow shot by a dying cripple. But I had to stamp out the fires of doubt among the Latins.

'You will find the same declared clearly in the eighth chapter of definitions to the Acts of the Council of Constantinople held in the reign of the Great Justinian of august memory.' Here, I shut my eyes and made my best job of translating the relevant passage from memory into Latin. 'Moreover, before coming to any conclusion about particular facts of orthodoxy, I would remind the most learned fathers here assembled of the rules by which orthodoxy is distinguished from heresy. A man may depart from orthodoxy in two ways. First, he may deny the Gospels outright. Second, he may deny those logical inferences from the Gospels to which he chooses not to submit. A heretic departs from orthodoxy in the second of these ways. As such, he remains within the True Faith, though in more or less grave error.

'I do venture here to correct a verbal slip of the most learned Bishop in his definition of apostasy. An apostate does not deviate from orthodoxy. Rather, he moves from a position of belief in the Gospels to a position of disbelief. Apostasy is further to be distinguished from heathenism and blasphemy. A heathen is one who has never believed in the Gospels. A blasphemer may or may not believe in the Gospels, but always treats them and all based upon them in a manner that causes deliberate scandal among the Faithful.'

There was a loud breaking of glass overhead, and a large stone crashed on to the floor a few feet to my left. A few shards of broken glass settled on my robe. I raised my arms to quell the rising panic within the hall and looked at the Dispensator. He shrugged and got up. Just before the main door, he turned and made a long bow to me. Listening in the silence that followed, I heard a shouted order that wasn't from Priscus, followed by a scream of pain. I swallowed and tried for a smile as I looked round the hall. The interpreter had vanished under his table, and the minute clerk had thrown down his stylus in despair. But the Dispensator was now back in the room. He shook his head and sat down again. Another moment, and he was scratching away with his stylus as if there had been no disturbance.

I looked at the water clock. This session had been prolonged far beyond what I'd expected. But I pulled my thoughts together and continued: 'If I may return to the main issue, a man can be a heretic either from ignorance or by act of the will – that is, he may be a material or a formal heretic. So far as material heresy is not an act of the will, it cannot be regarded as a sin. Therefore, the fanciful theology of women or of the lower classes should be corrected whenever encountered, but not punished. However, any person of intelligence and learning, who is made cognisant of his deviation from orthodoxy, and who persists in his deviation – he is rightly considered a formal heretic, and may anathema fall upon his head . . .'

So I spoke on in the still and heated air, to a rising chorus of shouting and screams from the street outside. There was a trumpet blast, and now the clatter of what may have been a single horse. From the intense look on his face, the Dispensator might never have been out of the room. Certainly, he'd not be followed by a hundred enraged and stinking beggars, come to beat us all to death. Even so, the Greeks, who now had not the smallest notion of what I was saying, sat looking nervously at each other. A few twisted their beards with the strain of all that had happened and was still happening. Others fell into various modes of silent prayer. But I had little doubt the militia was winning. If Priscus was right, and the barbarians wouldn't attack until at least the following day, this was just the right excuse for imposing order on the city. Once the barbarians did move against us, we couldn't afford a rising of the urban trash behind us. As I reached a dramatic pause in my discourse on the various meanings of 'Person', I looked again at the Dispensator. He caught my look, and stopped scratching away on his oversized wax tablet. He stared briefly back, one of those thin and mildly triumphant smiles on his face.

Someone at least was enjoying himself.

43

In its best age, I've already noted, the Athenian taste ran to buildings small but perfectly formed. The great Temple of Jupiter was an exception. Though not big at all by the standards of Rome or Constantinople, it was vast in Athenian terms. Its bulk loomed high over the wall that it nearly joined. Then again, it had been started by the tyrant Pisistratus as a symbol of his might. It had then been left unfinished by the democracy that followed the downfall of his son – too expensive and now too old-fashioned, I could suppose. After seven hundred years, it had been completed by Hadrian on his celebrated visit. No expense had been spared, I'd once read, and the archaic design had been followed as if all the improvements in construction of the intervening centuries hadn't taken place. Now, its outer colonnade had been bricked up on its conversion to some other use, and it was surrounded by other low buildings that made the original plan hard to follow.

'Oh, there is a sort of administration here that's independent of Nicephorus,' Priscus said with an airy wave. 'Don't ask me what it actually does. But we can be glad that, in the chaotic administration of the Empire, not every city council has been abolished.'

I nodded and bowed to avoid knocking my head on a low point in the ceiling. Normally, after four days in a city, I'd have made a full inspection of how it was administered. If I was still pretty much in the dark about Athens, this was the natural effect of having concentrated on religious affairs – and on staying alive.

There really was no point in wondering about the administration of Athens, nor in the internal geography of what was obviously its actual heart. As with parts of the residency, the interior of this building had been divided into a labyrinth of offices and narrow corridors. As in the residency, most of the offices appeared to be unused. But, unlike in the residency, some were still in use, and this was now the headquarters of such resistance Athens was likely to make in the event of any storming of the city wall.

Darkness hadn't yet fallen. But the sky was beginning to glow red through the single high window as I stepped into what may once have been the temple sanctuary. A hundred or so men, all dressed in various kinds of military clothing – most showing unmistakable Germanic or Slavic ancestry – got up from where they'd been sitting on the floor and bowed. I jumped lightly on to a platform that still had the remains of a few statue bases to make it irregular, and waited for Priscus to climb up beside me. He was now dressed in the full regalia of a Commander of the East, and was, I had to admit, a gorgeous and a reassuring sight.

'Gentlemen, this will not be a long meeting,' I began. 'My purpose in calling you together is to announce that, as Legate of the Emperor, clothed in full authority, I have formally dismissed Nicephorus as Count of Athens. I dismiss him on the grounds of desertion in the face of the enemy, and declare him an outlaw.' I looked about the room. If the lower classes had liked the man enough to riot in his defence, no one here seemed put out in the slightest. Their tight faces made perfect sense in terms of the immeasurable horde that had finally arrived, and was now held back by a wall that, every time I tried to imagine it, seemed more and more inadequate.

'Anyone who can give information that may lead to the former Count's arrest – or his conviction in any trial that I may allow him – is assured of full immunity, no matter what offence such information may indicate.' I stopped again. No one looked as if he'd step forward. I'd see if anyone made a private approach later on.

I chose my words carefully and tried for a neutral tone. 'I am aware that the former Count has, for the past several years, treasonably failed to collect taxes lawfully due to the Emperor.' I stopped yet again. This had got everyone looking at me. But I smiled. 'I have decided to absolve everyone but the former Count of blame for this treason. In due course, assessors will arrive here from Corinth. By the authority of my commission, however, I remit all arrears of tax up to and including the day when the barbarians shall be repulsed from our walls.'

I pretended not to notice the relieved looks and sagging of shoulders this concession had brought on. Barbarians prowling outside the walls were one horror. A mob inside the walls that had no visible inclination to do other than stab us all in the back was another. But at least there would be no third army of ravening tax-gatherers. And, if both mob and barbarians could be handled, given reasonable luck and reasonable judgement, tax-gatherers – everyone knew – could never be appeased.

'Now, gentlemen,' I started again, 'you and your sons and servants, and such other free persons as may be dependent upon you and whom you believe to be trustworthy, are the defenders of Athens. His Magnificence the Lord Senator Priscus, Commander of the East, I appoint as leader of the defence, giving him all such authority over life and property as may be required for an effective defence.'

And that was it. I'd assumed supreme authority, and straightway handed its substance over to Priscus. My job was now to seal the stack of proclamations Martin had been working like a slave to produce in appropriate form, and otherwise keep my council moving in the right direction. Without looking again at the gathered men of Athens, I jumped down from the table and walked quickly from the room. I stood a few moments outside the door. Priscus had gone straight into his plan of defence. Whether it had any chance of success was beyond me. But he sounded happy enough. As I'd got a few yards along the corridor, and had a hand on the door that led into the tiny room where wine had been set out, I even heard a little cheer.

I brought both fists crashing down on the table. Martin jumped several inches, and his tightened grip on the pen sent several drops of ink on to the papyrus sheet. I glared at Priscus, whose face was shining with sweat in the light of the single overhead lamp. This was an unplanned interrogation, and he was making a right mess of it. Since there was no question of threatening Euphemia with anything at all, I wished he'd kept his mouth shut.

'Let me say at once,' I grated, 'that, when they are in short supply, there is a natural tendency to join facts into chains that are unusual and generally useless. However' – I looked at Euphemia, who was still dabbing at her eyes – 'however,' I continued when she was looking properly in my direction, 'I must emphasise that Nicephorus and his present whereabouts are of double importance.'

I paused again and looked about the library. Irene had overseen heroic efforts of cleaning. It would still be days – possibly months – before the smell of damp and ancient dirt would disperse into the main courtyard from all the lower rooms. But everything smashed and otherwise ruined had been cleared out of the library. The remaining bookracks had been put back in place. There were even about a hundred book rolls shoved at random into the compartments. Replacement furniture had been rescued from other parts of the residency and arranged with some appearance of taste and comfort. Whole areas of mosaic had been swept away, or scraped away with shovels, and the floor was now firm, if mostly uneven concrete. It would never again look as I'd imagined it in my dream. But it was easily the best room we had.

I waited for Euphemia to stop snivelling, and gathered my thoughts to restate things in the clearest terms I could manage. I went over the importance of knowing anything at all about Nicephorus.

'I will leave aside the question of murder,' I continued after pausing for another burst of sobbing. 'The girl we found along the Piraeus road may no longer be of any importance in herself.' I stopped and looked carefully at Priscus. He stared back with an innocence so exaggerated, it set me wondering again. 'What does matter is that, this morning, Nicephorus was seen by a trustworthy witness forcing his way through a stream of incomers to get out of the city. The hooded man may have been a man called Balthazar. It is possible that the bag they were carrying contained a large sum of gold. If these surmises are also of no present importance, we do have reason to fear that the Lord Count will – deliberately or by misfortune – find himself in barbarian hands. We must also fear that the barbarians will soon be aware of certain facts about the condition of the walls.'

I now looked at Euphemia, who was wiping her nose and giving hurt looks at no one in particular. 'You must, then, appreciate the urgency of our questions about your late husband's brother,' I said, now gently. 'It seems that, before he took off yesterday morning, he burned or scraped clean nearly all his correspond-ence. What remains is of no importance.' I stopped again, and thought with a suppressed tremor of what those two letters might indicate.

'Because we have no further leads,' I ended, 'we have no choice but to look to you.' I smiled at Euphemia – not the smile of a lover, of course, but the smile of one who is trying to settle a crying child and find out something of desperate urgency. 'Is there anything you can tell me – anything at all – about his dealings with a man called Balthazar? We know they were partners in a scheme of at least double illegality. But did you see or hear anything of these dealings? Did you see Nicephorus in the company of men dressed all over in black?'

Euphemia wiped her eyes again, but didn't this time dissolve in tears. Nevertheless, I'd had no impact on her story: that she'd kept to her own part of the residency, seeing Nicephorus only for daily prayers and a trip every Sunday to the church inside the old Temple of Hephaestus. Her own life with Theodore had been entirely self-contained.

I stopped the nasty sentence Priscus was forming and leaned forward. I must say she was looking decidedly fetching. But this had to be set aside.

Euphemia sat up straight and stopped my own next question. 'What you claim to know is all very well,' she cried. 'But I tell you that Nicephorus is a good man. I've known him for three years. In all this time, I never had reason to suspect treason or sorcery or any other impropriety. He was always very correct in his behaviour.' She fell back in her chair. No longer verging on tears, she looked defiantly back at me.

I shrugged. She wasn't telling the truth – I could be sure of that. But I'd get nothing out of her in company. She might be more forthcoming in bed. I turned to Martin. 'Please speak to Irene,' I said. 'I want her to go through this whole building with a measuring rod. I want *every* room opened up. If it's been opened already, I want it opened again. I want a full search for any cellar that might be large enough to hold everyone in an emergency, and deep enough not to become an oven if the residency is set alight. I also want its entrance hidden again from even a thorough search.'

I waited for Martin to finish his note, and took a deep breath. 'I do apologise, Euphemia,' I said, now in a tone of finality, 'for any unpleasantness that you have suffered. But I do appreciate your frankness in answering our questions. Please do feel free to return to your quarters. I am sure you wish to speak with Theodore until he goes back into the library or off to sleep in the nursery.'

'She's lying through her teeth!' Priscus snarled once she was out of the door. 'If your brains weren't so obviously in your ballbag, you'd see that.'

'I know that,' I said. 'But since I can't guess what the truth may be, I see no reason yet for more questioning.' I took a sip of the good wine Martin had laid in and rubbed my nose. At last, the spots really were going, and there might not be a third. For that much I could be grateful. I waited for Priscus to finish snuffing up some aromatic powder from a small box, and for the resulting spasm of groans and beating of head on the table to moderate. Then: 'Can we turn to the matter of defence?' I asked.

Martin cleared his throat and shuffled with his heap of papyrus. 'The Lord Priscus asked me to investigate the city granaries,' he began. 'Because these are supervised by the Bishop of Athens, they have not been looted by the Count. The grain stored in them is of the lowest quality, and all seems to be very old. But I counted sixty thousand bushels.' He stopped and looked at me.

I ignored him and looked at Priscus, who'd come abruptly out of his fit and was now sitting with his mouth open. I put my stylus down and stared at the smooth yellow wax on the tablet before me. I'd been about to calculate, on the basis of a pound a day of grain per head, and an estimated population of twelve thousand, how long we might have. But sixty thousand bushels! Even if these might be bushels of some local standard, the grain ship Ludinus had sent had obviously been full. And the monasteries probably had their own stores – as might all but the lowest class of citizens.

'Can you enlighten us, Master Secretary, how Athens came to be so well-endowed with food?' Priscus asked heavily. He snatched at the notes. With shaking hand, he took up the nearest lamp on the table and squinted at the careful tabulations.

I listened as Martin explained how every monk in the city had been pressed into carrying the sacks up from Piraeus.

'A wise man proportions his belief to the evidence,' I said when I could trust my voice not to shake all over the place. 'It's enough to say that we're in better shape here than we were in Alexandria during the summer.'

Martin gave me a puzzled look. I smiled nervously back. Priscus had now sat up and was tracing letters on the table with a finger dipped in wine.

'Yes,' Martin said at last. 'But there isn't enough firewood to bake bread. That means milled grain only for the poor to make into porridge.'

I shrugged and came back to the matter in hand. Bread or porridge, we'd not be starved out. I'd seen a whole flock of sheep driven by farmers as they streamed in from the country. Add to this that the cisterns were full to overflowing, and we were better off than the barbarians must be.

'Alaric will need to sign a rationing order,' Priscus said. 'Given that the citizens are the garrison, we can dole it out free of charge.' He frowned at the random series of letters he'd now traced, then rubbed them all out carefully with the flat of his left hand. 'I left the militia in excellent cheer,' he went on in a more positive tone. 'The women will sit up all night, cutting off their hair to plait into bowstrings. We have one catapult that can be put into working order by noon tomorrow, and another piece of artillery that might fire metal bolts if it doesn't fall apart.'

'You are confident we can hold the walls?' I asked, trying not to sound anxious. I failed.

Priscus laughed and stretched lazily. 'So long as those fuckers don't find the one big weakness, and we aren't reduced to fighting inside the walls,' he said easily, 'I'd say it was a piece of piss. Barbarians don't know siege warfare. If they want to make a rush for the walls, we'll open the northern gate and hit them with a rain of arrows when they hurry forward. A few days of that – oh, and let's pray for more rain, and the onset of pestilence in those famished bodies – and I think you can lie as easy in your bed as our mutual friend will let you.'

'Then I think we can close this meeting,' I said hurriedly. From the laboured scratching of his pen, Martin was getting ready for an attack of the jitters. So, bearing in mind the laughter that had greeted my suggestion that help might eventually be sent over from Corinth, was I.

But Priscus hadn't finished. Now flushed and energetic from his drug, he grinned and reached for his water cup. 'When I speak about the militia,' he said, 'you will appreciate that this doesn't include the rabble. We'll keep them fed just enough to keep them quiet. But I don't fancy trusting them with arms – not after this afternoon's performance.'

I nodded. The militia had finally drawn proper blood that afternoon, and this may have explained the warm reception Priscus had got. But I'd come away from the council surrounded by another hundred of those dirty, chattering creatures. Turning their backs to me as I approached, they hadn't turned violent. But I had been more struck than before by their curious indifference to the growing mass of humanity outside the walls. Had they no conception of what would happen if the walls gave way? I'd been wondering if it wouldn't be a good idea to trick them close by one of the gates, and then push them all out. I was glad Priscus wouldn't be arming any of them.

'There is a further matter,' he said with a cold smile. 'I think your assumption is that the barbarians waited until the passes were clear. But this doesn't add up. The rains finished three days ago. From the reports I've had of the rain that fell, the passes must still be awash. This means that the people outside our walls must have been here all along. I'd like to know where they could have been in Attica without being noticed – and why they've now decided to turn up outside Athens.'

This was definitely unwelcome news. I dropped my stylus and, my own hands shaking, watched as it rolled across the table out of reach. I pushed my chair back and got to my feet. Trying not to rush like a frightened child, I walked down the room to stand before the bust of Polybius. The broken nose did give him a supercilious look. If I'd gone to him for guidance, I got none whatever. I'd never confess to anything but perfect self-control – not to Priscus, at least. And I saw no value in setting Martin off. But all this was getting to me, and I was ready to allow long chains of any nonsense to stand in place of reasoned hypothesis.

I turned and found Priscus standing behind me. 'If you go on to the roof of this building,' he said with false brightness, 'you can see right over the city walls. You may have other plans for the night. But I think I'll go and have a look at what we can expect for tomorrow.'

I did have other plans, and these did include Euphemia. At the same time, now that Corinth was off the agenda for the next day, there were some notes I needed to look over for the next session of the council. Instead, I found myself following Priscus over to the far door of the library.

44

'You do have the most awful taste in women,' Priscus said with another chuckle.

I stood beside him and looked miserably down to the city wall. Beyond it, almost as far as the eye could see, the campfires glimmered like the reflections of lamplight on polished marble. Far above us, the stars looked down. The moon was low behind us. Athens itself was in darkness.

I looked at the eastern horizon. Was that a little finger of cloud that might show a return of bad weather? Or was it smoke from the campfires? Hard to tell – though the slight breeze had shifted direction again, and I could smell the damp brushwood that had been set alight out there.

Priscus burped so loudly, it might have been heard by anyone beyond the walls who was still awake. Without bothering to look at him, I heard the opening of a lead box and was aware of a faintly aromatic smell. It didn't matter if he was listening to me, or focusing on the rush of whatever he'd chosen to alter his mood. If I went on, it was for my own benefit alone. 'If there are five hundred men we can rely on to hold the walls,' I said, 'I suppose we can rely on the monks for all ancillary parts of the defence. Even so, an attack at more than one spot . . .'

'My dearest Alaric,' came the smothered reply, 'if these animals *do* attack in more than one place, we'll be fucked. It's as simple as that. Our job is to make it look as if we have an adequate force inside the walls. That's why it's so essential to know where Nicephorus has gone. When I was last here, Balthazar was living in a cave near Eleusis. We can hope they've both taken refuge there.' He blew his nose and laughed bleakly. 'Isn't there something in Homer about campfires at night?' he asked with a shift of tone.

I looked out again over the constellation of flickering lights, and drew breath to recite:

> *. . . Fires round about them shined.*
> *As when about the silver moon, when air is free from wind.*
> *And stars shine clear, to whose sweet beams, high prospects, and*
> * the brows*
> *Of all steep hills and pinnacles, thrust up themselves for shows.*
> *And even the lowly valleys joy to glitter in their sight,*
> *When the unmeasured firmament bursts to disclose her light,*
> *And all the signs in heaven are seen that glad the shepherd's*
> * heart;*
> *So many fires disclosed their beams, made by the Trojan part,*
> *Before the face of Ilion, and her bright turrets showed.*
> *A thousand courts of guard kept fires, and every guard allowed*
> *Fifty stout men, by whom their horse ate oats and hard white*
> * corn.*
> *And all did wilfully expect the silver-throned morn.*

'Oh, well said!' he cried. 'Such memory – such careful distinction of long and short syllables! I never did get the whole of it flogged into me as a boy. Still, I suppose you had no choice but to memorise it all when you decided to pass yourself off as one of us.'

Any need for reply was cut off by a low murmuring from somewhere behind us. I turned and saw the glimmer of lights. I thought for a moment that someone had let the barbarians in, and that they'd set fire to Athens. But the low murmuring was the sound of a purely civil disturbance. I helped Priscus down from the raised part of the roof on which we were standing, and we hurried along another of those leaded passageways to the front portico of the residency. Even before I pulled myself up to lean on my elbows and look down into the big Forum of Hadrian, I'd seen that the light was only the glow of many torches. 'A couple of hundred men down there,' I said to Priscus, who was sitting on a stack of unused tiles.

'Well, dear boy,' he drawled, 'do you fancy shimmying up properly to ask what it is they want this time? I absolutely promise not to push you from behind.'

How many promises the man had broken in his sixty-odd years wasn't a subject I fancied considering. But I'd have to rely on his perception of his own interests and take the risk. I took hold of the smooth marble and pulled myself on to the apex of the portico. Just below me on a ledge that projected out was a mass of statuary that copied the old front pediment of the Temple of Athena. If I did pitch forward, I could trust in that to hold me until I could be recovered.

Testing my balance, I stood carefully up. I looked over the gathering crowd. As yet, no one had looked up to see me, though the moon must be shining on my white tunic as it did on the uncoloured marble of the statues. I clapped my hands loudly together and waited for every head to turn upward.

'Who dares disturb the counsels of their betters?' I shouted.

There was a long pause, broken only by a continued low muttering and a shaking of torches. Then someone shouted from the middle of the crowd: 'Give us back Nicephorus!' There was a ragged chorus of the name, and a rising babble of many other things that mixed together so I couldn't follow them.

Keeping my balance, I raised my arms again for silence. 'You produce Nicephorus if you can,' I shouted as loudly as I could. 'He has deserted all of us. As of this evening, Athens is under direct rule by the Emperor's Legate. And I tell you all again: there is an enemy at the gates of Athens that will make no distinction of rank or opinion if it manages to break in among us. I do not ask you to join in the defence of your lives and your homes. But I do suggest that you refrain from disturbing the counsels of those who are to defend you.'

I was drawing breath to bid them good night, when there was a sudden scream of horror, and the forest of torches moved sharply back to the middle of the big square. It was impossible to see past those flaring lights into the crowd beneath. But I could see that those nearest the residency were no longer looking up at me. Their heads were now turned to somewhere below me on the right. I wiped sweaty hands on my tunic and stretched carefully forward. Just before I thought I'd overbalance, I caught sight of Euphemia. She'd got herself on to a balcony that looked over the square, and was leaning forward to see all that was happening.

'For God's sake, woman,' I snarled softly, 'get inside.' If she'd heard me she didn't turn. I saw her put up a hand to her cheek and continue looking over the ever-growing mass of torches. 'Euphemia!' I shouted. She did look round. The left side of her face was hid in shadow. The right side shone utterly blank in the moonlight. I wanted to shout again, but felt my balance going out of control. I put my arms out and struggled not to fall backwards to where Priscus had for some reason given way to loud giggles.

As I finally steadied myself, I heard the dull noise of undrawn bolts from below me. I saw the glint of moonlight on swords as half a dozen armed slaves stood forward from the opened gate of the residency. 'Piss off, the lot of you,' I heard Irene shout in the shrill falsetto she used for repeating unobeyed orders. 'Piss off home, or it'll be the worse for you.'

'Get those gates shut, you stupid old bitch!' I shouted downwards. Even fully armed, twenty Slavs were no match for a determined rush. Little as I knew back then of siege warfare, I did know how the most apparently solid stone buildings could go up in fire, given the right determination.

But, even as I drew breath to shout again, there was another shouted order from Irene. This was followed by the whizz and fluttering of a dozen flaming arrows. They flew across the twenty-yard gap separating the mob from the front of the residency. As they struck home, there was a great wail of terror and of pain. I saw torches fall and go out. The whole mob fell back still further, and I could see that every arrow had struck home. Some gone out, some still burning, their bright shafts gleamed beside the huddled shapes of the fallen. There was another order, and another volley of arrows, and then another. None of the armed slaves I'd seen below moved forward, but stood with glittering swords on either side of the gate. There would be no attempt now to force the gate. But volley after volley of flickering lights darted across the square.

At last, I stood looking down over complete silence. The mob had dispersed. The breeze came softly from behind, and I could smell none of the smoke from the burning pitch of torches and of arrows. I was about to jump down beside Priscus and make my way to the gate, when there was yet another shrill order from Irene. It was now that the armed slaves hurried forward. They went from body to body. Sometimes, they kicked and moved on. More often, they stopped and bent low to cut the throats of those who'd survived the arrows. The bodies, I supposed, she'd leave to be collected come morning, and to stand as a warning against any further attempt on the residency.

I leaned carefully forward again. The balcony was now empty.

'Have you gone round the twist?' I snarled at the large shape under the bedclothes where Euphemia cowered. 'You could have got yourself killed. Without Irene, you might easily have sent the mob out of all control.' I sat down and drank more wine. I reached forward on the bed and poked what might have been her back.

She gave a little cry of fright and struggled to get her head free of the blankets.

'What could have possessed you to show yourself like that?' I asked, now gently. I looked into her tear-swollen face. As ever, one look at her set my loins twitching. But I put this aside and frowned. 'I don't want you ever to show yourself to the urban trash again,' I said firmly. 'Do you understand?'

She swallowed and tried for a nervous smile. 'They've always thought I was the witch who lurks in the residency and awaits her freedom at the hands of one who is without fear,' she said quickly.

I cut off her next remark with a loud snort. 'Euphemia,' I said with heavy emphasis, 'you have lived in this building for three years. I won't make myself look ridiculous by taking you through the undeniable evidence for this claim. But you are Euphemia of Tarsus, widow of some brother of Nicephorus whose name and business I've never troubled to ask you. In addition, you are the adoptive mother of Theodore. You came here in the last year of Phocas. Whatever may have happened in this building was a hundred years ago – maybe two or three hundred years ago. Now, I want you to repeat all this to yourself and come back to your senses.'

I waited. This time, she did manage a smile of sorts. 'You don't understand what it's like to be all alone in this place,' she said. 'There are whole days when I can barely remember what it was like to live in Tarsus. Have you never walked through this building as the dusk was falling, and heard voices in the shadows?'

'No,' I said, 'and neither have you!' I finished my wine and put the cup down on a table beside the bed. 'There are three court-yards in the residency. One of them is rather large, if not particularly scenic. You should try walking about it in the full light of day. Now that you have some, you might set those maidservants to work on digging out a few of the flower beds. We'll all be out of here long before they bloom. But even watching the work of others is all the medicine you need.'

I got up on my knees and pulled my tunic off. I threw it at a chair on the other side of the room. It fell short and landed beside my sandals. I laughed and lay back naked on the bed. I stretched my arms full out and then over my head. I arched my back and stared up at where the brightest of the lamps shone in its bracket. 'Talking of medicine,' I sighed, 'you'll not *believe* the day I've had!'

45

With a final smash of the crowbar, the lock disintegrated. I waited for the slaves to get out of the way and stepped into the cupboard. In my dream, the door had opened inward. I'd already guessed that it really opened outward. Now it was no longer secured, it had swung slightly out. I controlled myself and took hold of the door handle.

There was a murmur of disappointment behind me as I found myself looking at a sheet of smoothed rock. 'What a waste of fucking time!' one of the slaves muttered in Slavic. I pretended not to have understood him and rapped hard on the rock. It was real enough and solid. I turned and nodded at the slave who was holding a polished mirror in readiness. He moved it gently in his hands, and sent a shaft of reflected sunlight from the opened window overhead on to the rock. Keeping myself out of the light's path, I looked carefully round. Leave aside the question of why – there was nothing to suggest that a door had not been placed against solid rock and then locked shut.

'We continue looking for deep cellars,' I announced. There had to be something deeper than the ordinary storerooms and the dungeon Priscus had found. I'd never seen a palace yet without somewhere deep for storage of treasures or for the refuge of its owners. If this wasn't the entrance, Irene could carry on searching. Even a day and half a night of frantic activity had left much of the residency unexplored in detail.

'You do realise, dearie, all these men I sold you are Slavs?' Irene tittered beside me. 'Even if they don't turn against us when the city gates open, can you trust them not to winkle us all out of hiding?'

I led her over to a niche that had once contained a statue. The plinth remained. The statue itself must have been of bronze or even silver. This had been stripped out long before. So too the metallic letters of the inscription. 'Irene,' I said quietly, 'I don't expect you to know the politics of the northern tribes. But weren't these men sold to you by the Avars?'

She smiled and shook her head. 'Oh no, dearie.' She laughed. 'These ones sold themselves to me last month. They turned up asking for bread. Since no one else wouldn't do business with them, I had to take pity. I bought them all with a promise of food.' She patted the leather breastplate she'd put on in honour of the siege and gave a thoughtful look at one of the bigger Slavs.

This did put things in a different light. I'd have to see what steadying effect my own promise and their kiss of fealty might have. However it might be with the barbarians, there was no doubt any more of their loyalty against the Athenian lower classes.

I stepped out into the garden for a breath of fresh air. Blinking in the full light of morning, I was met by someone with a stack of letters. Two of these were from the Dispensator. In one of them, he was complaining about a slight from another of the Greek bishops. In the other, he'd posed a set of questions about the Will of Christ that would take me a whole day of sophistry to answer. These he'd coupled with a reminder of how my confirmation of the Pope's title was still outstanding. It was worth asking which of these he'd written first. The other letters were from locals – word had finally gone round that I ran Athens. I waved the messenger inside and continued across the hard mud to where Theodore was playing again with Maximin and with Martin's child. The nice thing about being a child, I thought to myself, is that you don't usually know until the last moment that someone is about to slit your belly open and pull out all your guts.

'Come to Daddy!' I cried with a passable smile. I picked the boy up and kissed him. Back in Alexandria, I'd noticed how he was growing with every day that passed to look like Priscus. This hadn't been lost on Priscus, who'd now managed to claim some avuncular status. He'd even muttered about changes to his will. I put this out of mind and buried my face in the heavy clothing that

Sveta had insisted he needed against the chill of an Athenian autumn. There was a faint smell of unchanged underclothes and of rather questionable dirt from the heaps left by all the cleaning.

'If My Lord pleases,' Theodore said beside me, 'my mother has allowed me to beg permission to sit in the council hall. Your secretary has assured me it is the greatest religious gathering of our age, and that it will remain famous in all future ages.'

I looked down at the boy. For all the sun was burning through my own tunic, Euphemia seemed to have the same idea of clothing as Sveta. If he'd been dressed like that ever since leaving Syria, no wonder he was sickly. Athens might have had a wretched summer. Even so, it was hardly some frigid desert of the north.

'You are welcome to come along to the council sessions,' I said grandly. I'd already established that he had no Latin. He'd be no danger to what I now had in mind. If he really believed this prolonged cloud of hot air would be so much as noticed by future historians, he had less faith than I in any recovery of the human understanding from its present low point.

I gave Maximin into Sveta's arms. Knowledge that we were under siege appeared to have settled her temper – or whatever time of month directed her moods may have altered in my favour. I thanked her and turned back to Theodore. 'I feel I should continue with making your acquaintance,' I said. That might take my own mind off the gathering horror beyond the walls.

He bowed gravely, and the sleeves of his tunic brushed the ground.

'Please do ask your mother if you can be allowed to join us for dinner. Afterwards, we can go up and sit in our much improved library until darkness calls you away to bed.'

He bowed again.

I nodded.

There were a few white puffs of cloud in the sky. I didn't suppose they would turn to rain. If they managed to cover the sun, however, it would make walking through Athens less sticky than it might otherwise be.

* * *

We took a wrong turn after I'd taken a sharp left to avoid some petitioners. If dilapidated and mostly unoccupied, the buildings that lay between the residency and the old Areopagus courthouse did give the impression of a reasonably large city. But it was an impression only maintained by keeping to the main street. I thought we'd be going across the little bridge over the Ilissus. Instead, we took another turn, and found ourselves looking at the confused jumble of masonry that had once been the Baths of Marcus Aurelius. Beyond them was a fifty-yard clearing terminated by the city wall. This was now filled with tents and the beginnings of stone shacks put up by the refugees from outside Athens. I swore at myself for getting lost, and wished I'd just told my guards to shove the petitioners aside. I motioned at a side street that would take us into a huddle of small houses, and probably to the foot of the Areopagus hill.

We'd barely set out along the street, though, when we came face to face with another gathering. This wasn't more petitioners. Nor, I could be grateful, was it anyone looking for trouble. It was just a funeral procession of the lower classes. The two women in front were making a feeble show of crying out and tearing at their clothes. The dozen old men who shuffled along behind had their heads covered and were looking grim. I stared at the swathed bundle they were carrying, and I took off my hat and prepared to bow. Instead of passing by, though, on their way to whatever church had been appointed for the burial, they stopped directly in my path. One of the old men came forward and stepped through my armed slaves. He jabbered something I didn't catch. He stamped his feet and pointed at me. Someone else pulled at the shroud covering the body. As it came off, the body itself was dumped without any respect on the ground, and everyone stood away from it.

I looked at the body of old Felix. His face still carried a look of surprise, or perhaps of faint alarm.

'Was he found in his bed?' I asked with the slow clarity you use when addressing barbarian slaves. The old man who'd already spoken began jabbering again. I was beginning to get inside the local dialect. So long as you put out of your mind that these were in any sense the posterity of the ancients, and so long as you didn't try to follow every single meaning, it was turning out easy enough. Certainly, it wasn't hard to gather that he had been found in his bed. But my vague supposition that he'd shut himself in with a smoking brazier was crossed out by the news that all his windows had been left wide open.

I bent down and stared at the withered corpse. There was a mottling on what I could see of the chest, and a smell of corruption that suggested the old man had been dead for at least a day and a night. I pulled at the smallest possible area of a stained sleeve. The arm moved easily. 'No stiffness of death,' I muttered. These things always depend on surrounding conditions. But if he'd lasted out the morning after we left him, it would have been a surprise. I'd assume it was a broken heart. There was no value in assuming otherwise. I looked again at the dead face and pursed my lips. 'There are mysteries in life,' I said in Latin, 'that are best overlooked.' I couldn't tell if Martin had understood my full meaning. But he bowed piously and, with Theodore, went back to praying over the dead interpreter.

It was shortly before noon when I caught up with Priscus on the southern wall. He'd been dictating in Latin to Gundovald's secretary. Head uncovered, the boy's hair shone very blond in the sunlight. I looked at him just a moment longer than I'd intended.

Priscus broke in with a cynical laugh. 'If you've come about the dawn attack,' he said, 'you can rest easy that it didn't get very far.'

'*A dawn attack?*' I asked, joining Priscus in Latin.

'Oh, don't look so scared, my pretty young man,' he replied in an easy drawl. 'Your face has gone a red that entirely obscures the leftovers of your wanking spot.' He laughed and made a crude gesture that provoked one of my darker scowls.

It didn't help that the blond boy behind me now let out an idiotic snigger.

'I wouldn't call it an attack, though,' Priscus explained. 'It was probably no more than an uninstructed attempt by a few dozen boys with more courage than sense.' He waved the blond boy out of hearing and leaned carefully against the topmost stones of the wall. The wooden platform shook under our combined weight. He shut his eyes, and, as if by effort of will alone, stood up. He put a hand on my shoulder and directed me to a small huddle of barbarians who stood behind the ruined wall of what had been a house.

'What is that?' I asked, nodding at the crude assembly of timbers. 'You did assure me,' I said when I knew I could keep my voice steady, 'that these people knew nothing of siege warfare.'

'My dear Alaric,' came the sneered reply, 'if barbarians are generally ignorant, most of them aren't stupid. Look at yourself.' He laughed unpleasantly as I couldn't keep a second blush from spreading over my face. 'Look at that gorgeous little thing over there,' he added with a nod at the boy. 'Never assume these people aren't capable of learning from their betters. If they really were dumb animals, we'd still have a governor in York, and the pair of you'd be running about some northern forest with your arses painted blue!'

He laughed again and went back to looking hard at what was undoubtedly a wheeled battering ram. It lacked only the covering of hides needed to protect it from fire and arrows. 'They were lining it up against just the right stretch of wall,' he said with an approving nod. 'If you'd come here earlier, you'd have seen those duffers now sheltering against our bowmen picking up their dead. We'll chase them properly off in a while. Then I'll send a few men down to set fire to that thing. They can also recover the arrows. We aren't exactly flush in that department.' He coughed and spat over the wall. 'It would help if the external ditch hadn't been allowed to fill up with rubbish,' he added with mild disgust.

He pointed at one of the bodies. 'You'd have imagined, with all the talk of famine,' he said thoughtfully, 'that these people would have looked a little more starved. I'll grant these were the young of the higher class. But, if the others look wasted, you can't set these numbers in motion when there's nothing at all to put in their bellies. A bit odd, don't you think, my dear?'

'You thought there would be a parley,' I said. 'Any indication of one yet?'

As I spoke, there was the sudden blast of a trumpet from the other side of a wall. As we'd been speaking, a small gaggle of men had come in sight. The trumpet went silent, and the smallest of the men stood forward.

'You will open the gates for the men of the Great Chief,' he squealed in Latin. 'You will let us take the food and precious things that may lie within your city. If not, we will break down your walls with overpowering force, and give your city over to burning and killing till not one stone stands upon another, and not one of you remains alive. We will do to you as we have done to the other cities. None shall help you.' He went off into a long enunciation of the horrors of a sack. Fortunately, there were only three of us in hearing able to follow its chilling promises of blood and fire.

The herald stopped and arranged his features into a smile. 'But the Great Kutbayan does not desire your lives,' he shrilled. 'He is ever merciful, ever forbearing to those who do his bidding. Open your gates and give what you have within them, and your lives will surely be spared.'

To my left, I heard the sudden whizz of a couple of arrows. One of these flew straight past the herald. Another brushed the neck of the trumpeter. I saw him fall to his knees, blood spraying from where the arrow had barely touched him. There was a burst of cheering from the archers as he clapped a hand over his severed blood vessel, and then fell straight forward on to an area of broken mosaic flooring.

Priscus darted along the rickety platform and slapped someone on the back. 'Good show!' he cried happily. He disappeared into a crowd of young tradesmen, and the choking sounds beyond the wall were smothered in cries of pleased enthusiasm. Another of the archers pulled his bow back to the chest and let fly. This time, the arrow missed by a foot. But the herald was already hurrying out of range.

'Did I hear the name *Kutbayan*?' I asked when Priscus was back beside me.

'Such sharp ears you have!' he said with a happy grin. 'Though I really did assume you'd guessed that much already. I don't think the Great Chief has caught up yet with his subjects. But I have no doubt he'll put in at least a brief appearance later today.' He caught the look on my face and gave a really nasty smile. 'Yes, it will be Kutbayan himself if I'm not mistaken – Kutbayan who fed every officer in that army we sent against him feet first into the cogs of a water mill; Kutbayan who placed thin boards over all the children of Pentapolis and made the parents dance until they were pulverised like grapes in a press.

'Do tell me, Alaric dearest, if you think suicide a really terrible sin,' he asked with another of his cheerful grins. 'Believe me that the fires of Hell might not compare with what the Great Chief has in mind for us. How you dispatch Martin and his family is for you to decide. But do leave little Maximin to me. I know so much about the infliction of pain, that I can make death gentler than a kiss good night.'

I gripped the rough stones of the wall and waited for the tremor in my knees to pass away. Pile horror high enough on horror, and anyone will buckle. 'I hear you had an argument with Irene,' I said, changing the subject.

'The old witch tried to change my defence orders for the residency,' he said, spitting over the wall again. 'She's useful to make sure that food and hot water come at the right time. But I'll take a cane to her if she tries acting the man in every respect.'

So much for her night defence! I thought.

Priscus let go of the wall and leaned closer. He contorted his features into a leer. 'By the way,' he said, now back in Greek, 'you'll never guess whose rooms I saw her leaving just before I came out for the dawn attack?'

I'd been wondering why Euphemia had been so eager to crawl out of my bed the night before.

But there was a scream from the other side of the wall. I turned and looked down. One of the barbarians had crept forward and tried to recover weapons from the dead. He was now flopping about not far from the dead trumpeter with an arrow in his belly.

Priscus was immediately back with his young men. A few of them stared over at me with happy, triumphant faces. It was only for a moment; then they were dancing eagerly about Priscus as he barked more of his soldierly praise. Where I was concerned, he might be a slimy, shifty Greekling – the Imperial Councillor fighting for his position in the sun even as the sky clouded over. To his men, he showed only his other face. For them, he was the greatest military commander in the Empire – the Heaven-sent one whose leadership would save Athens from falling as Decelea had.

Now at a safe distance, the herald had started calling out at us again. In response, two of the youngest defenders heaved a grotesque thing of pumpkins and cucumbers on to the top of the wall, and began shouting back in Greek that they'd taken the Great Chief prisoner. Shouting the name Kutbayan, they made the thing bob up and down, and, with shouts of laughter, sliced off half the cucumber that was doing service as a phallus. The herald fell silent, and there was a ripple of outrage that spread back through the crowd of barbarians who stood behind him.

'Pretty sick-making, wouldn't you agree?' Priscus jeered as he came back to me.

I didn't understand at first.

But he poked his tongue out and made a rapid licking motion. He'd have laughed, but for a sudden spasm that had him clutching with white knuckles at the stones of the wall.

'What women do with each other is nothing to us,' I said stiffly. And, if that was true, it still didn't settle the twitching in my lower chest. 'However,' I said, coming to the reason that had brought me to the walls, 'I have a favour I must ask of you.'

46

'Unless Simeon was deceived or lying,' I said, 'the man can't have been sighted inside the walls.' I finished my cup of the Dispensator's beer and looked morosely at the whitewashed wall of his office. He'd been right about its dirt and lack of amenity. By comparison, the residency when I'd first arrived there was almost salubrious.

'I'd put nothing past a man with so little presence of mind,' the Dispensator said with a sniff of contempt. 'But I do assure you that I saw the Count – rather, I saw the former Count – very clearly indeed. He was standing in the shade of an old building. There were two men with him dressed like the ones who attacked us the day before last.'

I'd believe the Dispensator in place of Simeon, or any other of the terrified Greeks who'd sat trembling through the morning session of the council. At the same time, it wasn't just Simeon who'd seen Nicephorus walk out of Athens. Had he come back in before the gates were closed and barred? Or was there some hidden breach in the walls? I'd raise this with Priscus when we reported back to each other at dinner.

I went back to the previous subject. 'The difficulty with any murder,' I explained, 'is finding connections. Find those, and it's only a matter of time before you find your man. I'm flattered that everyone is still talking about it. But the killing of the Duke's secretary in Rome was actually very easy to solve. The angle of the blow indicated the height of the killer. That being so, all I had to do was sort out chronologies and motives among a limited number of suspects. The confession helped, but I'd already got all the evidence we needed for the hanging.'

'Ah, but it was a stroke of genius to guess that all those nails found about the body had been set into a bar of river ice,' the Dispensator cried, now as happy as he'd ever let show. 'But for that, we'd still be looking for the weapon.'

I smiled complacently and waited for the Dispensator to refill my cup. I thought back to what now seemed golden days in Rome, when I was just an elegant ruffian with few other duties beyond self-enrichment in the markets. In that glow of nostalgia, even the Dispensator could have passed for an old friend.

'You will need to force the Greeks to attend the next session,' he said, coming back to a still earlier subject. 'We are most provoked by their lack of moral fibre.'

I nodded. I'd already torn strips off the Bishop of Ephesus. He'd pass my threats to the other Greeks, and they would surely all put on some show of interest in the afternoon session. This would be mostly taken up with the Dispensator's own explanation of the Papal will. Deciding I'd now got him in the right mood, and keeping a very straight face, I explained again the difficulties involved in his demand for two interpreters to call out his words in unison to the Greeks. Bearing in mind the quality of our inter-preters, I repeated, we'd have no choice but to reduce the whole speech to a theatrical performance – one clause of his own elabo-rate Latin read out from a prepared text, followed by another joint reading in Greek.

'Spontaneity is possible,' I insisted, 'but only with a single interpreter . . .'

'Such was done for the Great Constantine when he opened the Council of Nicaea,' he said firmly. 'No less can be demanded when I speak in the name of the Universal Bishop. There *must* be two interpreters.'

I was saved the trouble of a reply by a loud scraping of many feet in the monastery courtyard.

The Dispensator suddenly smiled and lifted his cup. 'I have already spoken with the Lord Priscus,' he went on in a different tone. 'Further to his fittingly humble request, I have given orders for every monk in the city to work under his directions for the building of a second wall behind the weak point in the fortifications.'

I decided not to try looking surprised. He smiled again. With luck, I really might have got him. Or was there something just a little too warm and knowing about that smile?

'The Commander of the East does not fall below his reputation,' he continued. 'His idea of creating a killing field within the walls is most ingenious. Like the drawing of blood from a diseased body, it will be used repeatedly to relax the pressure elsewhere.'

There was a knock on the door. Without bothering to wait, Irene walked in. 'You've got to come back with me to the residency, love,' she said in Greek. She looked at the Dispensator and bowed about half an inch.

'Go away!' I snapped. She was the last person I wanted to see. The Dispensator was already on his feet and looking outraged. 'You should know women can't just walk into a monastery.'

'Well, suit yourself, dearie,' she said with a shrug. She reached into her satchel. 'The slave who was clearing out the Count's office found these underneath the charcoals in one of the braziers.' She took out and untied two waxed tablets. Safe between them were a few scraps of charred papyrus. 'They might be important.'

I sighed. Whatever importance they had, I'd never get from here to the residency and then back to the Areopagus in time for the afternoon session. I'd see what she had. Unless they told me something of the utmost urgency, they'd have to wait till evening. I took the scraps and spread them carefully on the table.

'The very walls resound with evil,' I read with much squinting. 'I sit alone . . . The rats depart . . . The Dark One lays siege . . .' I looked up. 'These other words appear to be in Syriac writing,' I said. 'Are you able to tell me what they mean?'

'The Lady Euphemia don't read no Syriac,' she said with a loving smile. 'But that dear little boy of hers tells me it's some devotional hymn. It's about the ending of all space and time, though not the return of Jesus Christ.' She crossed herself and squinted at the Dispensator, who glowered back at her.

I looked again at the scraps. There were other words and phrases in both Greek and Syriac. But they were too fragmentary to make sense without a long inspection. It was all in the hand of a man unused to writing for himself. Even making this allowance, there was something unhinged about the shape and direction of the Greek letters. If Nicephorus had been writing with his left hand, they might have been formed with less appearance of some over-powering emotion.

'Is there more of this?' I asked.

Euphemia nodded. She added that the other scraps made no sense at all, but she'd had them set on a limestone table and covered over with large pieces of window glass.

I nodded my approval. I nodded again as she explained that she'd put the office off limits to further cleaning and had locked the door. I'd overlook that she was ploughing as hard as any woman could in my own furrow – there was no doubt she was a woman of sense in more than just business.

'My Lord will forgive me if I wear my plain robe for the speech,' the Dispensator broke in. 'His Holiness is Servant of the Servants of God. It would never do for his representative to address a council in a spirit of less than the meekest humility.'

Meek humility! I fixed my gaze on the icon of Saint Peter that was the one splash of colour on the otherwise bare walls, and tried desperately not to laugh. If he'd got himself up from head to toe in purple silk, but omitted that astonishing text I'd finally wheedled out of him, meekness and humility might have been a more appropriate description of what the Dispensator had in mind.

He looked carefully into my face. He smiled again – and, once again, it was suspiciously warm. 'The Lord Priscus may have his reasons,' he said lightly. 'But I fail to see why the Lord Bishop of Athens cannot attend this afternoon's session.'

'I understand that Priscus has need of him for dealing with the monks,' I said with what I hoped was a casual shrug. 'Several of the abbots have objected to the wholesale commandeering of so many of their men. But, since the common people of Athens won't lift a finger for the defence, the Lord Bishop is needed to explain the plenary nature of your instructions.'

'It is a shame,' he said with the mildest possible frown, 'that, apart from you and Martin, the Lord Bishop is the only one of us fluent in both Imperial languages. Without his presence, it seems the Greeks will have to rely wholly on the interpreters.'

I gave a regretful smile. I'd not have described the Bishop of Athens as 'fluent' in Latin – the best I could say was that it was slightly less eccentric than his Greek.

'Still,' the Dispensator said, 'the needs of defence must be respected.'

I stood up and watched as Irene finished putting the scraps away. Anything regarding Nicephorus was important. But this really would have to wait. 'It will be only fitting, My Lord,' I said, 'if I lead you with my own hands to the speaking lectern.'

'I tell you, he's gone out again looking for trouble!' Gundovald quavered from his bench in the street. He was still outside the meeting hall. So was everyone else. Leading them into battle outside the walls would have been easier than ushering them through that open door into the relative cool and darkness.

'My Lord Bishop,' I said impatiently, 'your secretary has been borrowed for the day by His Magnificence the Commander of the East. I understand he is needed for his – for his ability to take notes in Latin.' Why Priscus should want to make notes in Latin wasn't a matter I cared to discuss.

'Oh, but he's been back since then,' came the reply. 'If he's gone off again, it's in search of loose women.' He put his hands together and muttered something pious and disapproving. 'He's the son of the King's Mayor. I can't take him home covered in open sores.'

I called over one of my slaves. 'You've seen the boy,' I said. 'There can't be many like him in Athens. Take two of the younger men and make a search of the inns and brothels. If they're still closed, just walk in. When you lay hands on him, bring him straight back. Don't even bother getting him dressed.' I laughed at the thought of that small and unclothed figure – and it would be a diversion from the council to see it – and turned back to Gundovald. 'I'm having him brought here,' I said. 'Now, please – I do most earnestly beg of you – get inside that building. All else aside, you'll get sunstroke out here.'

I looked over the closed faces of the Greeks. 'The last one of you through that door,' I hissed, 'is no friend to me or the Lord Priscus.'

A few of them tried to stare back at me. But the last one to bolt for the door tripped over his robe and had to crawl the last few feet in the dust.

With a gentle splash, and then a gurgle before it settled down into a steady, regular dribble of water into the glass collecting bowl, the clock was put in motion. As Gundovald was finally prodded from behind into silence, I stood up from my chair and bowed. There was a rustling of cloth and some scraping of the chairs and benches, as everyone stood up and bowed at me. I'd sent Martin back with Irene on some made-up errand. I was, I could say with reasonable assurance, the only man present, aside from two heroically useless interpreters, fluent in both Greek and Latin. I smiled and stepped down off my platform. Ignoring the protocol, I walked into the semicircle of seats and opened in Latin.

'Reverend Fathers,' I called with a dramatic sweep of my arm, 'you will be aware of a possible difference between the Latin and the Greek branches of the Universal Church. While no Greek theologian of general note has definitely pronounced yet on the issue, the most learned Hilary of Milan is said to have declared that the faculty of willing is, by necessity, an aspect of Our Lord's Nature, and not of His Person. If this be the case, Jesus Christ may be said to possess a Human as well as a Divine Will – one for each part of His Nature.' I stopped beside a deacon who represented the Bishop of Constance, and tried not to scowl at him. If he'd been a Greek, I'd already have marked him down for a transfer to somewhere perfectly horrid for the trouble he'd managed to cause me. I stared up at the eye of the dome far overhead and at the dark blue of the sky far above that, and looked down again, a friendly smile now on my face.

'But I am familiar with the sermon preached by Hilary,' I started again very smoothly. I stopped again for the interpreter to come out of his stammering attack. As I'd expected, he was again putting me so badly into Greek that his grasp of Latin could easily be doubted. 'The sermon was not corrected by Hilary before he was called unto God by a visitation of the plague. It may, therefore, be doubted if so definite an opinion was ever truly in his mind.'

I was about to move to my last point, when there was a sudden noise outside. It began as a blare of distant horns that went on and on. As that came to a close, the thunderous cheering continued. It all underlined how close we were to every part of the walls, and of how utterly and deeply surrounded we were. The oldest and most doddery in my audience could have eased himself out of the hall and climbed on to one of the wooden platforms before the noise of the Great Chief's arrival had begun to die away.

But this was, in the immediate sense, a matter for Priscus. I stared about the room and waited for everyone to come back to order. Simeon had covered his eyes and was bobbing up and down in his place. One of the Latin bishops yawned and pulled a face at the Bishop of Ephesus, who was dabbing sweat from his forehead.

I held up both arms for attention. 'An opinion of far more decisive weight than some reported utterance,' I said with loud cheer, 'is that of the Universal Bishop, His Holiness of Rome.' Worse luck, the interpreter had got the hated – if possibly defective – title spot on in Greek. But I stared down the sour looks it produced, and went on with my introduction of the Dispensator. All the Western delegates nodded their approval. I'll swear the man himself purred, and I stepped over to him and, as promised, led him to the speaking place.

I went back to my chair. I bowed to the Dispensator. He bowed to me. He dumped a thick pile of very pale and uncurled papyrus on to the lectern and cleared his throat. Holding their own texts, the interpreters stood with their backs to him. I smiled and leaned forward in my place.

'If My Lord pleases,' I said . . .

47

I got back to the residency as the sun was lengthening all its shadows. As I'd commanded, the swimming pool placed in one of the secondary courtyards had been cleaned out and refilled. The bathhouse, I'd again been assured, would never do service in its present state of repair. But this would do in its place. I sent my guards off for beer with the other slaves and made my way to the pool. All alone, I threw my clothes off and jumped into the cool water. I swam fifty lengths and tried not to think of anything connected with Church or state. I climbed out and jumped back in. I swam down to the deepest point and tried to pick up what I'd thought was a coin. It was only a chip in the green tiles. I came up and did a back somersault. I let the air out of my lungs and sank back into the depths. The pool was about twelve feet deep in the centre, and I sank slowly. I felt the growing pressure of the water on my ears. I was aware of the cold silence about me. I felt my knees make contact with the bottom, and could feel my whole body settle slowly on the smooth tiles.

I opened my eyes and looked up at the shimmering surface. It wasn't quite the wildness and infinity of the sea off Richborough. But it was enough, so long as I kept my thoughts out of reach, to let me pretend for just a moment that I was still a boy in Kent – a boy with no other problem than how to fill his belly for dinner, and how to parse the Latin old Auxilius had earlier recited, clause by clause, into my head.

One look, as I resurfaced, at the still dazzling blue of the afternoon sky brought me out of that fantasy. But I did another back somersault and thought of something obscene from Aristophanes. That made me laugh so much, I breathed in a half lungful of water. I coughed it all out and took another deep breath. I went under again and swam over to the shaded end of the pool without coming up. I turned and kicked against the smooth wall and swam back. I'd have made it to the other end. But I was alone and had nothing to prove, and my head was beginning to feel light from the shortage of air.

As I came up, I realised I wasn't alone.

'Aelric,' a voice quavered from the far end of the pool.

I turned over on my back and watched Martin pick his way carefully along the age-pitted marble. He stopped at the nearest point to me and waited for me to swim the last few yards that separated us. As I looked up at him, the sun dipped behind his head.

'Do you suppose,' he asked, dropping his voice, 'the Dispensator noticed what you did with the Greek translation of his speech?'

I pulled a face at him and, with a great splash, kicked myself away from the side. Martin jumped back just a little too late to avoid getting soaked up to his knees. I laughed and did three back somersaults without stopping or bothering to draw breath. I came to rest floating on my back. I thought of asking what he'd found among those fragments of recovered papyrus.

But I took a deep breath and thought of the Dispensator's speech. It had gone exactly as planned. None of the Latins had followed a word of the Greek version I'd dictated to Martin. As for the Greeks, they'd scratched their heads a few times, but had followed my lead in the shouted approbations. The Dispensator – probably in sure and certain knowledge of what I'd done – had gone back to the chair in a blaze of self-congratulation and the cheers of everyone in the room. If they'd understood anything of what was really said, of course, every Greek in the room would have had a fit from the stark assertion of Papal supremacy over every priest and every communicant of the Eastern churches. Instead, they'd been treated to a discourse, cribbed from Gregory of Nyassa, on how the separate but incorporeal Persons of the Trinity did not need to occupy distinct positions in space, but could be both separate and distinct according to the requirements of the observer. What light this could shed on the wretched Hilary – who hadn't dissolved into stinking slime a day too soon in my view – was beside the point. And why should anyone ask for relevance? Apart from my own speeches, the nearest approach in two days to actual relevancy had come from that sodding deacon. The less of that we had, the better for everyone.

I swam back to the side. 'I'll take the Dispensator's actual speech as the playful warning he surely intended it to be,' I said. 'I think the Emperor's commission gives me power to clarify the Universal Bishop title. If it doesn't, we'll simply have to put our faith in general success. It's far too late for worrying about little details. If you can draw up a new patent in absolutely clear form, I'll seal it at the start of tomorrow's first session.'

He nodded uncertainly. He knew as well as I did that this would be wildly beyond the hardest stretching of my real authority. But letting the Dispensator wreck everything was a bigger risk than the possibility of a few strangled cries of outrage from Heraclius. Besides, if I won the argument here, there would be no outraged cry. If I lost, it hardly mattered what more that eunuch Ludinus could throw in my face.

I put both arms on the side of the pool and rested my chin on them. 'But Martin,' I said earnestly, 'I do apologise for splashing you. I shouldn't have done that, and I'm very sorry if I caused you any humiliation.'

He sat down before me and nodded. Just because you are able, when of my exalted status, to do anything you like with someone like Martin, is every reason in the world for not doing it.

'And, Martin,' I said, still very earnest, 'I now command you to take off those fine clothes and join me in the water. It is my command as your former master, and my urgent wish as a friend who has your health and fitness ever in his thoughts.' I put up a hand to silence his protest. 'There's no one else here to look at you. Come on in – I'll swim five lengths with you. Just five lengths – they will take away all the cares that surround you, and set you up for dinner.'

Martin looked dubiously about. I was right that we were alone.

No one else would have to see the shameful thing he'd made of his body. With a stern look on my face, I watched as he took off his outer cloak, and then his over tunic. He tried for another protest, but failed to shake my look of command. He squeezed himself out of his short under tunic. He fiddled a while with the knotted cord of his leggings, and soon stood in all his woeful glory in just a pair of absurd linen knickers. A few more words of playful nagging, and those came off as well. As the sun dipped finally below one of the corner towers of the palace, Martin stood, with low, saggy buttocks and wobbling belly, naked by the side of the pool. He leaned slowly down and put a toe into the water. He pulled it straight out and gave me the sort of look a dog gives when you take off your belt and promise a beating.

'Take a deep breath and pinch your nose,' I ordered. 'You know that it's better if you jump straight in.'

He shook his head and clutched desperately at his flabby breasts.

'Oh, Martin!' I laughed. 'Look up at the sky and think of all the martyrs whose blood has been the seed of the Church. Do you suppose they would have been scared of a little water?' As he looked involuntarily up, I lunged forward and got one of his arms. He hadn't time even to scream before I'd claimed him for the pool. I pulled him to the surface and waited for him to stop coughing and spluttering. More words of apology and a friendly hug. Then we were off on our first slow length.

It doesn't matter how eunuchs swell up – they always seem to make it to extreme old age. I'd been worried some while, however, about Martin. He'd started piling on the weight after murdering an old enemy in Constantinople. I've always enjoyed a drink after shedding blood, but he'd just eaten and eaten, until he looked like a pear on legs. Alexandria hadn't slimmed him. He'd left an ear in Egypt proper, but come out with a belly yet more enlarged. I'd now seen how blue his fingernails could go when I made him walk fast up the Areopagus. If he wouldn't take exercise, I'd have to make him. There are times, after all – and even I'll admit the fact – when friendship has to overbalance respect for autonomy.

'No, Martin,' I said firmly. I looked at him from behind. The lock of ginger hair he always arranged so carefully over his crown was now stuck to his left shoulder blade. It showed the sorry truth about the transience of an Irishman's hair. 'Now you're in, it would be a shame to get out again. I know what – you start for the far end. I'll give you a half length advantage. Then we'll race. If you win, I won't nag you out of a whole leg of goose in honey sauce for dinner. If I win . . .'

I got no further. Martin had suddenly turned. With a cry of terror, he clutched at my outstretched hand and pulled me under the water. As I came up spluttering, he seized hold of me by the hair and dragged me another few feet further into the pool. I'd already been aware of the sound of metal on stone. Even before I was able to turn and look back at the pool edge, I'd guessed right. With a shouted obscenity, the black-swathed figure was trying desperately not to overbalance into the water. He was grabbed from behind by one of his two accomplices and pulled back. They raised their dull swords in unison and looked at me though their leather masks.

Holding Martin by the hand, I waded as far toward the centre of the pool as we could both keep our footing. The men had swords only. One bow and a couple of arrows, and we'd have been dead men. So long as we stayed away from the edge, though, they'd surely not dare give up their advantage and jump in after us.

I drew a long breath and shouted for help. Martin joined in. One of the men looked nervously about and raised his sword. But we shouted and shouted, and still there was no help. If we were in no actual danger, there was also no escape. Even if I could get to one of the sides before any of the men could catch up with me, my sword was tangled up with my clothes another ten yards or so beyond the pool edge.

Martin took both arms from about me and whispered in Celtic: 'Look, Aelric, I'll go over to that side. When they all come for me, you get out and go for help.'

'Shut up!' I snapped. 'You'll do no such thing. We'll stay here together. Besides, they're not interested in you.' I had no faith in

Martin's ability to keep out of sword's reach. I did wonder briefly if I might swim for the edge myself, and let Martin run for help. You can be sure I'd keep far enough back not to rush into martyrdom. But I dismissed the idea. The steps were at the far end of the pool. Martin would never be able to pull himself out of the water. Even if he could, he'd never waddle away fast enough to get help – and that was supposing there weren't more of these creatures. 'Let's count to three and then cry for help again,' I said.

48

I was about to start the count, when the low and bitter debate at the end of the pool reached its end. Without bothering even to remove his sandals, the smallest of the masked and hooded men jumped in. The water came up only to his waist, though his black clothing billowed about him as if the ingrained filth on his body had all dissolved at once to form a cloud.

Martin stepped back, and then again, till he was treading water to keep from going under. 'Aelric, please come back out of his way,' he whispered in Celtic. 'Can't you see it's a trap?' he added in quiet despair.

I wondered very briefly if this wasn't a trap. But I couldn't see one. I ignored Martin and smiled, and I waded forward until the water came up to my chest.

'Come on, you dickless coward,' I sneered, 'come and try yourself with a real man.' With a great splash, I threw myself backwards in the water. I stood for a moment on my hands. In the time before I went fully under, I put up one hand and took hold of my privates. I shook them provocatively. I even managed to pull back the foreskin before my back brushed the bottom of the pool and I flipped back into a standing position.

In that short time, the man had hurried forward, sword raised above the pool surface, and was now only about six feet away. Letting out a stream of cheerful obscenity, I bounced up and down and splashed water at the man. The other two had followed him down the pool, and now were standing on either side. Each was fifteen feet away. Unless they wanted to give up all advantage – and, if they were thick enough to jump in as well, even Martin could make for safety – that was where, calling out encouragement, they'd have to stay.

The man came forward a couple of feet and slashed at me. I dropped under the water and jumped back out of reach. When I came up, he'd come forward again, the water now reaching to his upper chest.

'How does it feel, having to squat down for a piss?' I sneered again. 'Can you still come if you stick a bloody great dildo up your arse?'

I don't know if he understood my rapid Greek. But he raised his sword for another go at me. As the sword splashed into the water just a few inches from the obscene gesture I'd made with my outstretched left hand, I bent my knees and went right under. As my belly touched the rough tiles, I made a great sweeping movement with both arms and swam diagonally in his direction. I avoided the clumsy attempt at skewering me and got both his legs. How he'd got this deep in all that clothing was a credit to his stupidity. But I now had him fast.

I pulled him straight into the middle depths of the pool. I breathed out a stream of shining bubbles and got him briefly about the waist. I pulled myself further up his body and took hold of both his wrists, pulling his arms wide apart. He struggled with feeble desperation, and I felt his wrist flex as he tried to do something with his sword. But he had all my size and weight against him. So long as I kept that grip on him, the sword was useless. I shut my eyes and twisted down to head-butt him in his upper belly. I hit him again and again until I felt him sinking deeper, now under his own weight. I opened my eyes and looked at the stream of bubbles coming from all about the mask. I dug my fingernails into the gap between the bones in his sword wrist. I tightened and tightened my grip until I felt his hand open. I heard the sword land with a dull clatter eight feet or so below us. Still holding both his wrists, I pulled away from the man and curled into a ball. With all the force I could manage, I kicked him in the chest and let go of him.

I swam down and picked up the sword. I paid him no further attention as I passed him on the way back to the surface, and he continued his slow and silent descent.

I broke the surface with a great gasp and then a shout of joy.

The other two men were now running up and down the sides. I reared up and waved my sword with another shout of triumph. I stopped myself from going under again, and swam towards Martin. Now standing with my upper chest out of the water, I shouted more obscenities and tested the weight and balance of this decidedly trashy sword.

It was one down. But, if I now had a weapon, and there'd be no other straightforward attack, we were still trapped in the pool. Even if it was just two left, was I supposed to stand up to my neck with Martin as the sky turned first red and then to darkness?

But I now heard a familiar laugh behind me. 'Oh, dear – oh dear, dear me!' Priscus chortled. 'If it isn't Cupid and fucking Silenus!'

I turned. He was standing just by the entrance to the courtyard, with nothing on but a folded sheet about his waist. I looked at him briefly. If Martin was troubling me, it seemed that Priscus was growing smaller by the day. He'd padded himself out when clothed with layer after layer of black. But, now he'd decided on an evening dip, I could see the bony chest and the shrivelled folds of his belly. He'd taken his left arm out of its sling, and removed the dressing. If his wound was no longer bleeding, I couldn't see what good he was planning to do himself by getting it wet.

But, even as I looked, the two surviving attackers lifted their weapons and moved to close in on him. I pointed at my clothes heaped up on the stone bench. 'My sword's over there,' I shouted.

Priscus looked at the bench and smiled at the two killers. Before they could join each other at the end of the pool and turn on him, he'd already walked easily over and unsheathed my sword. He shook it and laughed again.

'Well, come on, then, my lovelies,' he called cheerfully. He walked round to the easiest point of escape from the courtyard and took up a fighting pose. I'd not have held out much chance for him. Without his clothes, he really was just a collection of bones, held in with wasted flesh and joined by a few sinews and scraps of muscle. His left arm hung useless. But he laughed again and stepped forward at the first of the killers to reach him.

I'll admit that my own advantage in any fight – at least until I'd reached extreme old age – lay always in superior size and weight. I only made it to extreme old age because I never had to face anyone bigger or heavier who possessed an ounce of intelligence or luck. I can't say that I recall any movement at all from Priscus. One moment, he was still testing the balance of my sword. The next, six inches of shining steel were projecting from the man's back.

Without any change from his easy tone, Priscus laughed again and pulled my sword out of the dead body. He raised it again and stepped forward. Then he stopped and went rigid. He sat down in a coughing fit that didn't look as if it would have an end.

But I'd now reached the side of the pool. Still holding the sword, I pulled myself out with my left arm and jumped to my feet. His own sword raised over his head, the one surviving killer was hurrying forward to go at Priscus. I swung with all my strength and got him just below the wrist. My own sword would have sliced the hand off as if it had been the end of a celery stick. This one might have been an iron bar for all its cutting force. Even so, you don't hit out with my strength and not feel at least the smashing of bones. The man screamed and dropped his sword. Nursing his ruined hand under his left arm, he darted back from me. I bent and recovered my own sword and stood in his path. To get away, he'd have to get past me. Or he'd have to run all round the pool. If he tried that, however, it was a matter for me of stepping back four or five yards, and I'd still be blocking his escape.

When attacked on the Piraeus road, I'd barely had time to draw breath and put every effort into fighting for my life. Here, I'd had plenty of time to gather my wits, and was still pleased with a very easy kill. I grinned and stepped forward a few paces. I swung at the man with an easy motion and crippled his left arm at the elbow. There'd be no stabbing now, of himself or anyone else. I stepped back and kept my sword outstretched. 'We'll start with a few easy questions,' I said lightly. 'If I don't like the answers, we'll see what the Lord Priscus can do to loosen that tongue of yours.'

Still coughing, Priscus was back on his feet. Holding one of the other swords, he moved forward and stood beside me. 'Get him on his back, dear boy,' he wheezed in Latin. 'I'll show you what miracles of pain can be achieved with just one good hand.'

But the man jumped back from me. He raised his face to the sky and laughed. He paid no attention as I jabbed him in the side. Instead, he let out something too rapid for me to catch, but that might have been a prayer. He turned his back to me, and put his head down. Like an enraged bull, he charged at the wall that divided pool from main courtyard. I heard the bright smack of bone on marble plating as he threw himself forward. I saw the dark patch that he left in the fading light, and the faint smear that followed his descent to a still, black huddle at the foot of the wall.

I looked at Martin, who'd managed to heave himself out of the pool, and had now covered his face with horror. Feeling less jaunty than I had, I took a step forward.

Priscus got there first. 'Not dead,' he said as he kicked the body over again. 'But he might as well be for all we'll get out of him.' He bent happily down and fiddled with the lower clothing. 'We really aren't having much luck in our interrogations are we?' he asked. If he was about to add another gold ring to his collection, he didn't get it. Instead, he gasped as another spasm of pain took hold, and he clutched at his side.

I just managed, before he pulled his sheet higher, to see the lump on his right hip. It had about the bigness of a bowl the doctors use for cupping blood. I saw it for barely an instant. But the tight and dappled skin told me all I needed.

Priscus laughed to draw off my attention. 'But what have we here?' he gloated with a finger pointed at the remains of my stiffy. 'If I'd known your real feelings for our tub of Celtic lard, I'd not have gone to such extremes to trick you into Egypt to get him back.' He laughed again and coughed. He did look set for another laugh, but had to stop and clutch at the right side of his chest.

I hadn't seen him in pain there before, I noted as I went through the motions of glaring at him. And, if its purpose hadn't been so clear, I'd have had excellent reason for sneering back at him.

Anyone who can't tell the difference between lust and the excitement of a good kill has no right to call himself a man.

But Priscus now got proper control of himself. 'Get dressed,' he said with quiet urgency. 'If there're three of them, there might be more.'

I shivered slightly in the decided cool of an autumn evening as I hurried over to where I'd left my clothes. Without bothering to dab off the water that hadn't already dried, I pulled on my under tunic and my shoes.

'Bring a sword with you,' I said to Martin when I'd finished nagging him into his own clothes. 'Be ready to expect the worst.'

He nodded and swallowed. Without any actual protest, he picked up one of the fallen swords.

I looked back at the black shape that lay in the deepest part of the pool. If a few drops of the blood shed by Priscus had found their way into the water, that was something I could overlook. The filthy body drifting gently across the bottom of the pool was a pollution that another day of cleaning and refilling might not efface.

49

I can't say often enough that the residency was a big place. Over by the pool, there had been a longish and thoroughly desperate struggle. I burst into the nursery, sword in hand, and nearly skewered Theodore as he wandered past me with a pan of milk. He only just avoided dropping it on the floor. I dodged the jug that Sveta threw at my head when I asked if all was well, and left Martin to deal with her screams of outrage and the wailing of two frightened children.

It was different where Euphemia had her rooms. For the first time since I'd met her, she was out in the light of a rapidly fading day. She sobbed and rocked back and forth as she held the dead Irene in her arms. One glance told me she'd been killed by a single stab to the throat. Two bodies dressed in black told me she'd only been got after a struggle that would have impressed even if she'd been a man. Throats cut, all three maidservants I'd given Euphemia lay in the dust.

'Are you hurt?' I asked Euphemia.

She looked up, blank misery on her face.

'Are you hurt?' I repeated.

She shook her head and went back to crying over the body of Irene.

I'd come back to her later. Five dead intruders didn't mean the residency was clear.

Priscus had already crossed to the other side of the main courtyard and was pulling at the locked door to the slave quarters. The door had been locked from the outside. So too the shutters. Using the apology for a sword Priscus had carried away from the pool, I smashed the lock and stood back for the scared and angry slaves to hurry out. Two of them had drunk poisoned beer, and might not get through the night. The others had their own swords at the ready, and were sent off, in groups of three, for a systematic hunt through every room in the residency.

Now recovered, Priscus rattled the lock on the main gate. 'I don't see how they could have got through this,' he said. 'Do you know of any other way in?'

I hadn't found one. Nor had anyone else. But it was unlikely the attackers had managed to creep in during the day – not with the kind of security Irene had now set up. 'Some hidden entrance?' I suggested weakly. As I thought of something more useful, one of the slaves hurried into the darkness of the arched gateway.

'Come and look at this, Master!' he barked like an excited dog.

Even before stepping into the dark cupboard, I could feel from the cool breeze that I'd no longer be reaching out to set hands on a sheet of rock. I stepped back out and took a wax candle from the slave. Cupping this in my hand against the breeze, I went in again. It was as if there never had been any rock there. I looked through the doorway into perfect blackness.

'Who or what is within?' I called in Latin to test the echo. Except for a slight deadness of the echo, it was like shouting into a deep well. I moved closer to the doorway. After a momentary pause, I stepped through.

As in my dream of four nights earlier, I found myself on a flight of steps. But these weren't straight or neatly cut. I held my candle up. Before it went out, I counted five crumbled and irregular steps down. After that, the shaft veered steadily to the left, and I saw no further.

'Many thanks,' I said to the slave who now handed me a lamp with a horn windshield. I stepped fully into the shaft and looked about. Again in my dream, the roof had been high enough for me not to notice it. Here, it was low enough for me to have to bend my head forward. Further evidence, I told myself, that dreams can suggest new trains of thought, but don't provide new information about the world. 'Here it is!' I said, again in Latin, pointing at – though making sure not to touch – a bronze lever that projected about a yard from one of the walls of roughly cut rock. 'There's some kind of balancing mechanism that allows a plug of apparently solid rock to slide in and out of place.'

I stepped out again and turned to look at the pale and frightened faces. Behind them, I could see Priscus. He'd gone back to his rooms and had returned with a small box. He somehow managed to combine a knowing smile with sniffing the entire contents of the box up his nose.

I fixed my attention on the nearest slave, and went into his own language. 'I want the top of that big table from down the corridor pushed into this gap,' I said. 'I don't want anyone to go through for any reason. But I want this cupboard, and all about it, searched for whatever can be used to open and close this entrance from our side.'

The slave bowed.

I gave him a curt nod and walked past him into the corridor. 'You will, of course, keep up your guard,' I added. 'You never know who might still be down there. You never know who might still be waiting to get back in there.'

We'd had one evening of proper lighting. Now, the corridors were back in darkness. This time, however, they were clean. Without looking round to see if Priscus was following, I hurried, shielded lamp still in hand, up to the library, and sat down in the most comfortable chair. I reached out for the wine jug that had been left on the nearest table. I had a sudden thought and sniffed doubtfully at the contents.

'It's all right, My Lord,' I heard Euphemia say behind me. 'I've just brought it in myself.'

I got up and turned. Though still looking scared and oddly aged, she'd managed to dry her eyes, and she was talking with reasonable firmness.

I pushed her into where I'd been sitting and pulled up another chair. 'Do tell me everything you can,' I said with gentle urgency. 'I need to know *everything*.'

Even down to her reticence about what she'd just finished doing with Irene when those dark figures had burst into the room, there was an inherent probability in all that she said. It didn't take me an inch, though, beyond what I'd already guessed. Irene had picked up a sword and forced the men down into the courtyard. Then they'd regrouped and gone on the attack. It explained all that I'd found and no more.

I offered her a cup of wine, then recalled that she had no taste for it. I put her cup on the tray and drained mine.

I heard Martin behind me. 'The big slave with the scar on his face begs to inform you that they can't find another lever,' he said.

I shrugged without turning. Doubtless, there had been a thorough search. That didn't mean there was nothing to be found. I'd go back down myself in a while and see what I could find. Unlike a few barbarian slaves, fresh from their first sale at market, I'd had plenty of experience of how cunning engineers could be. The Imperial Palace in Constantinople was riddled with secret passages, and some of the machinery that worked the doors was concealed with astonishing skill.

I heard a knowing and unpleasant laugh as Priscus came into the library. 'Any chance of sharing some of that wine?' he asked. Face flushed very dark from his drug, he hurried over to the window and threw himself into one of the chairs that had been placed there in the great reordering. He waited for Martin to go over, cup in hand, and settled himself to look out into the darkness. I watched as his body began to shake with silent laughter. I thought at first – no, I *hoped* at first – this was some reaction to all the killing and general excitement. But this was Priscus. He might double up every so often with the agony of whatever was consuming his flesh. But anything approaching normal human shock was as much beyond him as normal human pity or fear. He finished his wine and twisted round, a happy sneer on his face.

'I suppose, Euphemia, dearest, you've definitely found your means of exit from this God-forsaken hole,' he said, ending with a faint chuckle. 'You'll adore Constantinople,' he went on once his voice was steady again. 'I must say, though, that our young friend would really be better off if he stuck to boys.'

Euphemia's answer was to get up and go towards the far door that led to her own quarters. I did think to follow her out. But Priscus was now turned fully round to face me.

'It may be for the first time ever,' he said as the door closed, 'but do you suppose we should try to be honest with each other?'

I got up and pulled my under tunic into place. It was still slightly wet, and this had left a stain on the old leather of the chair. I went over to look at the mural of Athens. One of the more enthusiastic slaves had tried cleaning a few centuries of dirt off this. In places, he'd rubbed far too hard, and patches of bright freshness now contrasted with others of dull smudging.

'When I was a boy,' I began without bothering to turn, 'I was told how a fox gets rid of fleas. He hunts about until he finds a lock of wool, and then he takes it to the river, and holds it in his mouth. He now goes slowly into the water, and the fleas climb higher and higher up his body. At last they all run over the creature's nose into the wool, and then he dips his nose under and lets the wool go off with the stream.'

I did now turn round. My first sight was of a very puzzled Martin. I would have smiled at him, but Priscus put his head back and laughed.

'You really aren't as stupid as you look, dear boy,' he said. 'But would you forgive me if I said that I did see you in here the other night?' He pointed to the now cleared area of floor where I'd been crouching with Martin. Then he put both hands together and cracked his knuckles. 'You didn't get that pretty golden hair of yours sufficiently out of sight.' He sniggered softly and looked into what I hoped was a blank face. 'I do say this, dear boy, to demonstrate that whatever I may have said to Nicephorus was just my own little joke.'

This was something I'd mope over when I had the time. What I did now was to glare Priscus into silence and continue. 'Let's accept that Heraclius is fed up with the pair of us,' I said. 'Or let's accept that tubby Ludinus had told him to be fed up with us – it amounts to much the same thing. It may have been his own incompetence that lost us Cappadocia, but you were formally in charge of the army. My land reforms have already done something to steady our hold of the Asiatic provinces, and will do much eventually for the whole Empire. At the same time, I'll grant I've pissed off every rich nobleman in Constantinople. The cast of churchmen assembled here are nuisances in their own right. The Dispensator, to be sure, has been an annoyingly persistent suitor on behalf of the Pope.

'All this being so, why not have Ludinus call everyone to a city in the middle of nowhere, stuff it with food, and then draw the barbarians away from Thessalonica with fair promises of filled bellies? It would avoid all the fuss of striking us down as individuals. There wouldn't be any hard looks from friends and relatives – no chance of complaints from any branch of the Church.' I stopped and allowed myself a bitter laugh.

Priscus raised his cup in a mocking toast. Martin fell into a chair and covered his eyes with the horror of it all. And, if a little far-fetched for anyone but Ludinus, it did make sense in itself. Heraclius had never shown any interest in the ancient classics. If he thought at all of Athens, it must have been of a city that consumed rather than yielded revenue. The men in black remained outside this explanation. The only question outstanding was whether Nicephorus had been in the know. I had no doubt he'd be happy to take off and leave his family behind. After all, he'd probably killed a very pretty girl just after fucking her – or let her be killed. It didn't matter that he'd been having spells cast to keep the pair of us away from Athens. He'd probably assumed he could otherwise have passed out the whole food surplus and pleaded with the barbarians to go away.

'Talk of killing *two* birds with one stone!' Priscus tittered. 'One stone kills the whole bloody flock. Aren't you beginning to admire Ludinus? If only the Grand Chamberlain had spoken up for financial economy in the same degree!' He turned and looked again out of the window into darkness. 'Has My Lord Senator any idea of how to get out of this mess?'

On and off, I'd been racking my brains all day for an answer to that one. I'd still come up with nothing. 'We can try holding the walls,' I said uncertainly. 'If we can then avoid being murdered inside them, I really do think I can get the council to go along with the Single Will compromise. You know the Great Augustus is easily swayed. We could try turning up unannounced. A few bribes might get us past Ludinus. Alone with him, we could try telling Heraclius . . .'

Even as I spoke, I realised how unlikely it all was. We'd have enough trouble getting out of Athens alive. Getting past someone like Ludinus into the Emperor's presence wouldn't be easy if we made ourselves invisible. I looked at the stain on my chair and walked over to one of the more populated bookracks. I pulled out one of the unsheathed books at random and tried to keep my hands from shaking as I unrolled the brittle papyrus. I squinted to make sense of the unfamiliar script. It was the work in which Anaxagoras had argued that the sun was a mass of blazing matter larger than the whole Peloponnese. Bad luck I still hadn't found anything in the room that was actually rare. I let it roll shut again and pushed it back into place.

Priscus got up and came over to stand beside me. 'Looks as if we're both fucked, dear boy,' he said. 'Don't you think we should have a look in that tunnel? When the walls come down, we'll fall back and hold the Acropolis as long as possible. But, given our own numbers, I doubt it will be longer than a couple of days. We need to find *somewhere* to hide Maximin.'

'Then let's have dinner first,' I said. I'd already thought of the tunnel as the best hiding place we'd found. We'd see where the other end came out. Given luck, that also might be hidden. If so, we might have found at least a hideaway for the entire household. Once that lever was pushed back into place, whoever broke into the residency with murder in his heart would never find the entrance. Put enough food and water down there, and everyone might be able to shelter there until long after the barbarian horde had run out of food and vicious entertainment and gone off again. Doubtless, Nicephorus knew about the tunnel. But, if he'd been willing enough to abandon his family, would he make a positive effort to betray Euphemia and the boy?

'Of course,' Priscus said, now thoughtful, 'we have no duty to anyone in Athens. We could take shelter there ourselves. I've never given her much time. Now I think of it, though, dear Euphemia might have her uses in Constantinople. It would just need the right management.'

'And what is the meaning of that?' I asked stiffly. If he was planning to use her charms as a key to get past the Imperial Guard, it would be over my dead body.

The only answer I got was another chuckle and a suggestion that dinner would need to be specifically ordered, given the late hour and all other circumstances.

50

'You'll keep that table top where it is!' Sveta insisted in her own dialect of Slavic. The slaves dropped the sheet of wood and stood back. She glowered at me. 'If you're mad enough to go down there,' she said, now in Latin, 'you might as well have some way back out.'

I looked to Martin for support. Still tearful from my refusal to let him come along and 'stand' at my side, he said nothing. I could have tried a direct order to the wife of my freedman but, considering her likely response, I'd not risk humiliation in front of the slaves.

Trembling as he looked into the blackness, one of the slaves held out the crowbar and length of rope I'd asked for. I grunted and allowed Sveta to give me the lamp she'd carried over from the nursery. It had a windshield and a very large oil reservoir. We could walk to Piraeus and back before that gave out, I told myself.

I looked at Priscus. 'Do you really think you're up to this?' I whispered. Light as he was, if he fell down at the bottom of those steps, it would be a bugger of a job to get him out again. But his face turned grim. If I tried another argument, it would only end as it had in the library. 'Very well,' I said. 'We stand or fall together.' That got me the ghost of a smile. 'But you'll not object if I go first,' I declared.

He arched his eyebrows, and stood out of my way.

'Get back from him!' Sveta hissed in Greek. 'No one can hear you now coming down those steps. But you see if I'm frightened of you.'

I looked round and saw Euphemia stand back from the

cupboard. I smiled at her and blew a kiss. We'd already spoken. There was nothing more to say.

'Alaric, it's dangerous down there,' she whispered in a more complete terror than I'd yet seen her. 'Please, don't go down.' She turned to Sveta. 'Look, I don't care what you think about me,' she pleaded. 'But can't you talk sense into him? Down there is nothing but an ancient and terrible evil.'

Sveta glared back in silence. I got myself between them and gave what I hoped was a nonchalant laugh. Back in the nursery, I'd just had one of those occasional moments in which I could wonder how much I was actually hated by Martin's wife. I'd not put up with another in public.

I swallowed and tightened my grip on the lamp as I stepped though the door and this time walked all the way down to where the shaft veered left.

'It's doors within doors within *more* bastard doors in this place,' Priscus sighed wearily. If it hadn't been for the big lamp I carried, we might never have spotted it. My dream had been accurate so far as this was an underground chamber. It was certainly big enough for hiding everyone should the need arise. But it had seemed at first just to be a storage cellar. Of course, it had no boxes of treasure. The little door at the far end had been hidden by a heap of rotten furniture. Its iron bolts had long since rusted where they'd been drawn back, and the door hung slightly ajar.

'We'd better see where it leads,' I said firmly. 'We'd better see as well if anyone is still in there.'

Priscus put a hand on his sword and nodded.

I went back to the crumbled steps and looked up at the lights. 'There's another tunnel down here,' I shouted up. 'Remember my orders if we're gone a while – no one follows till morning.' I heard Martin's stammered objection. 'Those are my orders,' I snapped. I looked about the room again and smiled. It was *much* smaller than in my dream, and a different shape entirely. I thought for a moment of giving up for the night. Come the morning, and we could return with a few armed slaves for company. Then again, could I really bring myself to wait? This was an exciting find, and my blood was up. We'd survived a daring assault on the residency. You don't just turn in placidly for the night when something like this was found. Who could tell where this might lead? I ignored the whole babble of objections that had followed my last orders, and walked back over to where Priscus was still waiting.

'It looks very narrow in places,' he said with an excitement that matched my own. 'If I suggest that you go first, it really is because I'd not like to get stuck with you behind me.' He giggled and stepped out of my way.

I'd come to another of those narrow points where I thought I'd never get through. But I squeezed my shoulders together and felt my cloak scrape hard against both sides of the twisting passage through the rocks. What had started out as a reasonable tunnel cut into the rock was now a minimally smoothed-out fissure.

'It's rather like being buried alive, don't you think?' Priscus asked cheerfully from close behind me.

I grunted and bent down even lower to avoid knocking my head on a projection of rock no one had thought to hack away. We might have gone a hundred yards. Or it might have been a hundred feet. I'd already lost all sense of direction in these underground twists and turns.

'How do you suppose Euphemia would be useful to us in Constantinople?' I asked. I'd spoken more for the sake of hearing my own voice than in hope of any meaningful answer. But my voice came so loud and so flat in this enclosed place that I fell silent at once. I made myself go forward another couple of feet. I could now stand fully upright. I only felt the sides of the tunnel if I bothered to raise my elbows.

Priscus stopped behind me and slowly breathed in to savour the oppressively damp air. If I was fighting not to turn and push my way back to the residency, he was showing increasing signs of enjoyment. It was some while since he'd even coughed. 'I meant what I said, dear boy,' he said happily. 'It's obvious you get on extremely well. I've always thought the little sexpot was wasted here in Athens, but never liked her enough to think of unloosing her in the night lighting of Constantinople. Are you really thinking you can bear to fuck her into a quivering heap and then dump her like Ariadne on Naxos? You really are her one chance of getting out of the residency to anywhere at all. That's surely worth something to her.' He began one of his sniggering laughs and failed to avoid walking straight into another piece of low rock.

That shut him up and left me alone again with my own thoughts. He had a point. Three nights of passion hadn't dulled her charms. Unless I was stuck in Athens long enough to grow bored with her, it really was a matter of finding the right excuse to give Heraclius when I finally rolled up with a concubine. For all his other faults, old Phocas wouldn't have turned a hair if I'd taken her about in public. Heraclius took a sterner view of anything beyond the most private fornication. Regardless of my own affection for the dear thing, though, she might be useful in a city where everyone beautiful was either locked securely away or a common possession of the rich and lustful. I might have felt some degree of shame that I was thinking how most effectively to turn pimp. But, when you've spent as long as I had, trying to think of any escape from an impenetrable maze, where every apparent exit had been blocked up or shown itself to be a trap, you may understand that I was getting ready to abandon most sense of decency.

I had a further thought. 'You did meet her when you were last here?' I prompted. 'That was back in the days of Phocas, didn't you say?' But now I knocked my head, and all my thoughts were scrambled in a white blaze of pain and a string of obscenities.

'One might have hoped for a gallery hollowed out in the rock,' Priscus said when he'd finished laughing at me and shoving me forward. 'Much more of this, and we may have to regard where we are as more a means of escape than a place of refuge. Would you care to speculate on where it comes out?'

'Perhaps in one of the overgrown pits at the foot of the Acropolis,' I hazarded. 'I do think we're going into the centre of Athens.'

If Priscus had his own thoughts of distance and direction, he didn't share them with me. We pushed on, now in silence.

About a year back, an outbreak of influenza in Constantinople had required me to sit in judgement on a case of parricide. The young man I was trying almost certainly hadn't been a party to his brother's crime, but was proven by his conduct to be a knowing beneficiary. The abolition of the death penalty for his lesser offence wasn't to take effect until the Emperor's birthday, and I thought I was doing the boy a favour when I stretched the point and condemned him to the lead mines. I could now see why he'd broken down and begged for the ancient punishment of scourging to death. I hadn't been down here long at all, and it was hellish already. Only the knowledge that there must be at least two exits kept me from a panic attack that would have impressed Martin.

I was about to stop again to clench fingernails into the palms of my hands, when I felt a slight but joyous breeze. If it smelled faintly of death, that was nothing beside the movement and cold of the air.

'Well, come on, my brave young savage,' Priscus urged, giving me a hard shove. 'Some of us are getting desperate for a piss.'

I stumbled forward, now seeing how, in spite of its horn shield, the lamp flame was beginning to twist and flicker in the breeze.

But there was no exit. Instead, I pushed myself through what seemed an impassable narrowing of the rock, and fell into a reasonably wide and tall passageway. Its walls were of dressed stone that went all the way up to the vaulted ceiling. I could tell that it hadn't been a sewer, though what else it might have been – and how old – I certainly couldn't guess. All I could say was that someone, a few centuries before, had caused a tunnel to be hacked from underneath the residency to get access to wherever it might lead. I looked both ways along the passage. It ended a few yards to our left in a wall of smooth rock. To our right, it seemed to stretch far beyond the outermost pool of lamplight.

'What can you think of *this*, Alaric dear?' Priscus asked in a sibilant whisper.

I looked again and stiffened slightly. I turned and pushed my lamp back into the tunnel from which we'd just come and waited for my eyes to adjust. To my right, perhaps a dozen yards along, there was the faintest glimmering of another lamp.

'What is it?' Priscus asked, now very softly.

I saw him rub his eyes and try to see what I had. But either I'd been mistaken about that glow or his own eyes weren't up to seeing it. No, I hadn't made a mistake. I put a finger to my lips and quietly drew my sword.

'We can't wait here any longer!' I heard Nicephorus groan as if not for the first time.

I'd pushed our lamp still further into our own tunnel, and we'd crept slowly along in the darkness. The side opening through which the glimmer had come wasn't a direct entrance, but was another, narrower passage with a doorway into some kind of chamber about six feet along it. We now stood outside, trying to make sense of a conversation that had been going on for a while before we'd caught a single word.

'The Goddess never fails those pure in heart,' came the reassuring answer from Balthazar. 'We have three more nights till the day of utmost radiance dawns. No one shall stand in our way when the time comes of our utmost power.'

I relaxed my grip on my sword and flattened myself against the cold and slightly damp stones of the wall. I'd moved a few inches to the right, when Priscus took hold of my sleeve and pulled me back.

'Not with *your* colouring, fathead!' he whispered. He pushed me further along the wall and put his own head round the corner. He held it there for the tiniest moment before darting back. 'I don't think we'll be going to arrest them,' he whispered again. 'They've eight of those shitty acolytes about them.'

I breathed slowly out. I didn't fancy a battle in the dark against superior numbers. We could make our way back to the residency, though, and return with enough men to try for an arrest. It was beyond reasonable belief to think either Nicephorus or Balthazar would top themselves rather than be taken. I'd just have to hope the fight wouldn't be too chaotic when it came.

No luck! Even as I stretched over to Priscus to breathe in his ear, bloody Balthazar took it into his head to restart the conversation. 'I feel a disruption in the Force,' he cried. 'The instruments of evil are among us.'

Even before I could hear the scrape of shoes, Priscus was pushing me back into the main tunnel. 'Not that way!' he muttered, keeping hold of me as I tried to dash for the way we'd come. He was right – long before we could get to it, our lamp would be seen, and we'd never squeeze fast enough through the narrow points. We hurried onward into the total and unexplored blackness of the other direction. We'd covered about fifteen paces when Priscus began one of his spasms. He buried his face in his cloak, and I carried him, thrown over my shoulder, further into the dark.

'I see him as clearly as if by day,' I heard Balthazar say in his most thrilling voice. 'They go towards the house of death.'

I'm sure Nicephorus was impressed. I was too busy trying to creep along at speed to think anything at all. Of course, bearing in mind he'd said there was someone, and that he couldn't be seen going towards the glow of our own lamp, there was only one direction in which to look. And, if he really had been able to see in the dark, Balthazar would have seen two people, not one.

But none of this got round the fact that those dark and utterly ruthless assassins were padding after us, and I had no idea where we were heading. I hurried along in the darkness, Priscus thrown over one shoulder, my free arm held out in case we came to another dead end. After some unguessable time of hurrying forward, I nearly sprained my wrist on a wall. I felt about and made off along another tunnel. The air was now increasingly fresh and cold, and, more and more, the smell of death was overpowering.

Without realising its approach, I found myself running in only near-total darkness. Somewhere ahead, there was a reflected glow of moonlight. It wasn't enough to see anything clearly. But it was a welcome sign of some possible escape from those approaching footfalls one or two dozen yards behind us.

Yes, there *was* an exit. I came to it almost before I could see it.

Rather like the tunnel that had brought us from the residency, someone had cut another opening in the smooth stones lining the underground passageway. For all I could tell, the passageway itself continued for ever and ever. But this opening had a flight of more crumbled steps, leading up to a patch of light from a moon that shone directly in. I threw Priscus forward on to the steps and forced him to the top. I nearly vomited at the sudden blast of corruption as he fell forward on to a cold and slimy corpse. I clutched hold of it to avoid falling back down the steps and sent it slithering down to the bottom. I thought at first that the jagged hole through which the moonlight came was too small for me to get through. But it had been narrowed with loose bricks, and these just fell outwards as I shoved at them with both hands. For one horrifying instant, I found myself tangled in my own sword belt. Then, pulling Priscus heavily behind me, I fell out into the full soft glow of the moonlight.

I lifted Priscus bodily out of the way and dumped him in some brambles. Even as I tried to pull out my sword and take advantage of my position against anyone who tried following us out, I realised without any shock at all that we'd come out beside the tomb of Hierocles.

51

'I don't think they'll follow us here,' Priscus said with a long gasp. 'Even they aren't that suicidal.' He got up slowly and uncertainly and moved towards the road. Just before he got there, he sat down heavily. I thought he'd finally collapsed. But: 'Don't go on to the paving stones,' he said weakly. 'You'll show like a louse on white skin.' He was right.

Trying not to snag my clothing on the brambles, I sat down beside him. I listened carefully. There was a faint scraping from within the tomb, and a quiet noise of argument. I kept very quiet, sweaty hand clutching spasmodically on my sword grip. But there was no louder scraping – no reason to suppose we were to be followed out into the open.

We sat there for what may have been a long time. Gradually, Priscus came back to something close to normality. . 'Did I ever tell you how I got out of Trampolinea alive?' he wheezed.

'I think you've already given me two versions,' I said. 'Have you a third that involves an underground chase?'

His answer was a low wheezing laugh. He took hold of a relief on the front wall of the tomb and used it to help himself to his feet. He stood, still clutching the tomb for support and breathing with forced slowness. 'Do pull that hood over your head,' he groaned. 'We didn't come out dressed in black for no reason.'

Twenty yards beyond the far side of the road, there were the remains of a campfire.

'Not fifty men about that,' he giggled softly, 'not fifty men awake, at any rate.' He looked harder. 'But somewhat more than a thousand fires, we can be perfectly sure.'

From inside Athens, our wall had seemed ridiculously flimsy.

Seen from out here, it seemed quite otherwise. We were, I knew, about a quarter of a mile outside. The moon had gone behind some clouds, and there was nothing to be seen of Athens except a break in the vast mass of dying fires.

Priscus took me by the shoulder and turned me to the left. 'Over there,' he said, 'we'll find one of the corner towers. It should have a dozen guards on the night shift. If everyone there can be woken, we'll get ourselves pulled up on ropes.'

I didn't consider trying to go back directly the way we'd come. But there was the possibility of sitting here and waiting for the slaves to come after us. It would soon be morning, and my orders to stay put would lapse. They could cut their way through the men Balthazar had with him. Then, we'd be able to get back into the residency. Come the morning, I'd personally supervise the blocking off of that tomb from within. We really couldn't afford anyone to find so easy a way into Athens – not straight into the residency.

But Priscus had already thought ahead. 'The longer we're out here,' he said in a most reasonable tone, 'the greater the chance we'll be caught out by the dawn.'

I nodded and stood up. There was a loud crack as I stepped on a dead branch of something. Priscus muttered something contemptuous and pulled me further away from the road. His own eyes had been useless underground. Now, he seemed able to see everything about us. We set off across the sea of bushes and jagged stones that stretched far away on each side of the road.

Perhaps I'd trusted too much in Priscus and his night vision. Perhaps the path he'd charted through the wilderness was more circuitous than I'd thought it was. But long after we should, in my view, have stood calling softly up at the sleeping guards, we were still picking our way over broken ground. We hadn't even come to the ruined bathhouse that had been taken over by the barbarians as a covered position close by the tower Priscus had mentioned. I looked up at the clouded sky. Far over in the east, there was the slightest glow of the light before dawn. Not long now, and we'd be able to see where we were going. If anyone out here was up early, he'd be too busy shaking life back into his stiff and chilly limbs to bother looking at a couple of dark figures flitting about. We'd get ourselves back into Athens, and shock everyone in the residency by our loud banging on its gate . . .

There was a low and bitter laugh about a dozen feet behind me. 'Did you really think you could evade the gift of sight the Goddess has made me?' Balthazar asked. He grunted an order, and I heard the rasp of a drawn sword somewhere on my left.

I spun round and saw the movement of a darker blackness against the dark of the night. Almost without thinking, I'd got my own sword out and had lunged with it. There was a gasp of pain, and I felt my victim drop to the ground. I stood back and looked hurriedly about. Whoever else was out there had gone very still, and I could see no movement. But there was a faint sound of someone breathing, and it wasn't Priscus. Trying not to make any sound of boot leather on stone, I moved slowly in the direction of the breathing. At the very last moment, there was another flash of darkness within the dark, and Balthazar was laughing again.

'Don't think there is any escape,' he said, now conversational. 'Those who have done evil must themselves suffer evil.' I heard him breathe in and then cry out in a loud voice, 'Come, come, good beasts of the frozen north,' he shrilled in Greek. 'Come and see what golden prize I bestow upon your thrice-accursed souls.'

'Fuck you!' I snarled. Sword raised to strike him down, I rushed at where he must be standing. I crashed straight into Priscus, who was trying for the same. We fell down together in a heap. As we swore at each other and got up, Balthazar skipped out of reach and began more of his shouting. I grabbed at Priscus. There was still no light worth mentioning. But the great darkness of Athens was assuredly before us. 'Let's get out of here,' I hissed. But I now felt a hand brush against my face. I dropped Priscus and struck out hard with my right fist into nothingness.

'O Goddess, Goddess,' Balthazar cried in the great voice he used for impressing the gullible, 'now is the time to serve thy servant.' There was a response from a few yards away in a drowsy

Slavic, then an angry grunting from somewhere else. Balthazar was far behind me again, and was setting up an old invocation that might have woken the dead.

> O come with rosy fingers, Dawn,
> And gods and mortals show the morn.
> Yes, hither, hither come: reveal
> What evils might the night conceal ...

It would have been more dramatic if there had been some gradual fading in of light. But it was enough that just about everyone in hearing distance was coming out of his slumbers and beginning to feel about. I took hold of Priscus by his cloak and began pulling him forward. I stepped straight on to a hand. I silenced the shout of pain with a quick downward stab and carried on forward. I saw the big dark shape before it could see me, and rammed my sword into its middle with all my strength. The man went down without any sound. But there was now blood spurting all over me, and my hand slipped as I tried to pull my sword back out. As I tightened my grip and pulled hard, someone who'd been lying down put his arms about my legs, and I went straight down. I was up in a moment, but my sword was gone. I struck out with both fists at another lumbering shape and felt a giving way of jawbone beneath a great beard.

All this time, Balthazar hadn't let up his maniac invocation of a dawn that still hadn't come. I think I got someone on the nose with my elbow. Not caring how and where I landed, I jumped away from the arms that were trying again to lock about my legs. I did land on my feet. I bounded forward, but now tripped over a stone and fell into a pair of massive arms that tightened about my chest as if I'd been a child. I tried wildly for a head but I only found myself buried in the lower half of a large and stinking beard. Someone else had now thrown himself on to my back, and I was held fast.

There was a long and blundering shuffle, as the man beneath me got himself free and joined in holding me face down on the rough ground. I heard a shout of triumph and then the hard crack of one stone on another just above my head. I held my breath and went very still.

'Right, let's be looking at this fucker,' someone growled in Slavic. There was a tired laugh beside him.

I waited till there was no one on top of me, then jumped up with all my strength, ready to make a dash for it. But, if I'd been down for what had seemed the tiniest instant, there now *was* enough light for anyone to see round. I'd broken out of the main huddle. I was picking up speed – when a single massive hand took hold of me by the scruff of the neck and held me without any hope of escape. I was thrown down with force. Even now, I might have got up again. But my cloak was caught in more of those brambles, and I struggled just a moment too long. Before I could get clear, someone new had got me from behind, and was holding a knife hard against my throat.

'One move, you thieving shit, and you're dead,' he croaked with ill-natured menace.

'Please, please, good sir,' I called feebly in Slavic tinged with a Germanic accent, 'give food for the starving. You can do what you like with me after.' I stroked his leg with my one free hand. But the light was coming up fast. The time was already gone when I could try playing along with the most obvious suspicions. There was a great shout of rage from another man, and someone ripped the cloak straight off me. I rolled back in the brambles, showing a tunic of torn but very blue silk.

'We've got ourselves a fucking Greek!' came a voice from my right. There was a shouted laughter of three or four big men. I saw a hand reach over and press a knife back to my throat.

'Correction, my dear fellows,' I heard Priscus laugh from some-where behind me. 'You have caught yourselves the top man of King Heraclius himself!'

All hands were suddenly taken off my body, and I was able to sit up and look about me. The three or four men I'd guessed were in fact over a dozen. They sat, grinning uncertainly at me, knives still at the ready. One man holding a spear at him, Priscus was sitting on a large stone. He rubbed his head and smiled. He looked easily round and raised both hands.

'And I, who have brought him to you, am Priscus – the only general who has ever driven off your Great Chief in open battle.' He smiled again and nodded encouragement at the man who'd now stood back from him. He got up unsteadily and walked over to where I was still sitting in the brambles. 'One of us,' he said to me in Greek, 'had to shit on the other. The only reason I waited so long was that I was sure it wouldn't be you.'

He pointed at the man nearest to me and frowned. 'Get him bound and gagged,' he said. 'You really don't want to take any further chances with the little squirt.'

52

Though Athens lies on a wide plain, this itself is watered from three lowish sets of mountains. There is Aegaleos to the west, and Brilessus to the east. To the north is the Parnes chain. Decelea guards – rather, it *had* guarded – the easiest southern passes through this chain. I'd thought, the previous day, that the Great Chief had finally arrived outside Athens. No one bothered telling me anything at all as, bound and gagged, I was thrown across a small pony and taken north. But it was fair to assume that it would be somewhere close by the smoking ruins of what had been a town of about a thousand people that I'd be ushered into the presence of Kutbayan himself.

There is, I hope you'll agree, no such thing as luck. It is a most vulgar concept – much called on to explain facts that would make perfect sense if the long chains of cause and effect by which everything happens could only be made to reveal themselves. At the same time, I've never met anyone who failed to act but on the assumption that there is good luck and bad luck. As the sun rose higher in the sky, and I tried to slither into a less uncomfortable position on my pony, I had plenty of time to reflect on the really awful run of luck that had brought me here. I really should have taken one look into that blackness of the open tunnel and set myself to thinking how it could be sealed up again for good. Instead, I'd gone into it with Priscus of all people. Everything since that one choice had followed with an unbreakable run of the most rotten luck.

Once or twice, I heard Priscus raise his voice in a manly laugh as he discussed another of his interminable battles. It had been a surprise to learn that he'd ever won a single battle, let alone against the Avars. No one had spoken of this in Constantinople. Certainly, Priscus himself had never mentioned it. The impression I'd always had was of a Commander of the East promoted because there was no one else to put in the job, and because he did at least know how to retreat while his enemies wore themselves out.

We stopped for a while at noon. It was then that someone ungagged me and squirted water into my mouth. I made myself swallow every drop of the dark and brackish stuff, and tried to ignore the omnipresent smell of death. 'I want to speak with your head man,' I managed to croak. I didn't really believe I could talk my way out of the relative positions Priscus had managed to establish between us. But it was worth trying. It failed. The only answer I got was a light punch in my side and a hurried replacement of the gag. I could suppose it was a mercy that this was a proper slave gag – that is, it was one of those things that resemble a short strap-on dildo, and only keep you from speaking without stopping your breath.

Once we were moving again, and I'd got my tongue into the least awful position against the roll of much-employed leather, I managed to pull my head up long enough for a look round. I'd supposed the dead were human. In fact, it was herd after herd of cattle that had been killed and stripped and left to rot in the sun. I could see shrivelled women and children darting from one heap of bones to another, stuffing their mouths with whatever scraps of stinking offal had been left. I would have looked more. It was a change from looking down at the stones of a very bad road, but hardly pleasant enough to risk choking. I made myself go limp and went back to reflecting on the defects of an enquiring mind.

Before I could be trussed up like a beast to the slaughter, my tunic had been ripped down to my waist. I could feel the opening pains of sunburn on my back as the afternoon grew hotter and more oppressive. I had to fight like mad not to scream, and then start blubbering from the pain and horror of it all, when someone slapped me on the back at our next stop. This time, I drank what was given me and didn't try looking up.

It was only as I felt the power go out of the sun that the beast carrying me began to slow, and the continuous mumble of laughed conversation from behind me died gradually away. Someone held a knife before my face and giggled. Then he cut the leather straps that had kept me in place, and I slithered off to land on my back in the dust. A grinning red-bearded face looked down at me as I squirmed from the sudden pain and tried once more not to cry out. Still holding his knife, he bent slowly over me. I didn't suppose that, having been carried all the way here, I was to be done in by someone of such obviously low quality. More likely, he was trying to scare me. I looked steadily up at him as he moved his head to left and right, now blocking and now showing the sun. At last, he pulled a face and put his knife away. He stood up and stretched his arms with a loud cracking of sinews. When he bent forward again, it was to loosen my gag. I still couldn't speak, but there was no longer that leather stump jammed against my teeth.

'Get him on his feet, and get him washed,' I heard Priscus call from somewhere out of sight. 'You can take a comb while you're at it to that pretty hair of his. It's thick with dust.' He laughed and went into Greek. 'You'll surely allow,' he chuckled at me, 'that you look a proper sight.'

I don't know how long I'd been sitting, bent forward with my head on the ground. Because I hadn't slept in over a day, I might have nodded off for a while. If so, I'd only dreamed that I was sitting all alone in the middle of a wide ring of tents. Every so often, really or in my dream, dirty children came over and stared at me. An old man may have come over for a while and lectured me for a long time in the language of the Avars. What he said seemed full of meaning. But, since I had no Avar, and was in no position to try him in Slavic, his meaning was lost on me.

The light was fading when I was pulled back into full awareness by a gentle slap on my still exposed back. I sat up with a suppressed cry and tried to look round. 'I'm going to cut your hands free,' someone young said in passable Latin. 'If you try anything, I'll hurt you badly. Do you understand?'

I nodded. A moment later, and I was trying to rub feeling back into my swollen hands. My legs were tied so I could walk only with the limited movements of the very old. It was thus that I finally shuffled within the stinking interior of one of the larger tents.

'Oh, you still do look a sight, my poor dear boy,' Priscus cried with what anyone who didn't know him might have taken for genuine concern. 'Someone give the lad a drink.'

'I'll allow that you have indeed brought us the Lord Senator Alaric,' someone said from the other side of the tent. He spoke the good Greek of Constantinople, but was sitting on the far side of a ring of lamps, and I couldn't see him. But it was the voice of a eunuch. It may have been a eunuch of my own age. Or it may not. These creatures can sound young far into middle age. As I tried to look through the glare of the lamps, the eunuch sniggered. 'If you're trying to see who I am,' he said with evident glee, 'I see no point in disappointing you. It isn't, after all, that there's anyone you can grass me to.' He laughed again and got up.

'Oh, it's you!' I said with my best effort at contempt as he came over and stood before me. 'I'd never have guessed you would risk yourself in barbarian hands. But I'll finally grant that, whatever you are now, you were at least born into the male sex.' I smiled and repeated with the emphasis of insult, 'The *male* sex.' I tottered past Seraphius, eunuch of the third grade, and sat carefully in the chair beside Priscus. As I took the offered cup of beer, I heard another eunuch voice – this one from behind me.

'The lack of respect you show for your betters has once again been noted,' the voice said.

I looked up from my beer and sniffed. I'd been expecting all day to meet the Great Chief Kutbayan. Despite his alleged lack of humanity, I might have had some chance with him. As he came round and stood beside Seraphius, I looked into the grinning face of a bald and, if possible, a still more obscenely fat Ludinus. I knew then that I was lost.

'The most I'd expected when I came out here,' he said, falling into that slow and ceremonious eunuch drawl that was halfway to singing, 'was that I might be able to identify your body. I now see that I did very well indeed to assume personal supervision for the will of the Great Augustus.'

He stepped forward and slapped my face. He put a soft and slightly damp hand to my throat and leaned forward to see me properly in the light. I spat into his face and laughed as he stepped suddenly back. He put up a slightly stained sleeve to wipe away the gob, and I saw the glitter in the lamplight of his golden ring of office. It wasn't two years before that he'd been made Grand Chamberlain. But the ring Heraclius, against all urging, had pushed on to that bloated finger would never be slid off again.

'See, Ludinus,' Priscus interrupted, 'I told you it was young Alaric. And young Alaric it assuredly is. Hasn't our plot worked out just swimmingly?'

Ludinus turned his attention to Priscus, and his face took on the closed look of a eunuch who knows that he's winning. 'But, Priscus, my dear,' he cried with soft menace, 'I still haven't admitted that this is, in any sense, *our* plot!'

'Oh really, Ludinus,' came the answer in a voice just a little too easy to sound natural. Priscus stopped himself and looked thoughtfully in my direction. 'Do ask yourself what else could have got me out of Athens on the off-chance that I'd stay alive long enough to see you. I could have held even those walls for a month of Sundays, and your friends would have run out of food and patience long after they'd turned on you. Just believe that I'm acting under directions sent out from Constantinople by Heraclius himself. You know as well as I do how often he'll change his mind before the end of anything he orders. He may have turned against me and back again a dozen times since putting his seal on that letter. But there's no reasonable doubt that I have his letter safe in my baggage in the residency. You'd be a fool to do other than believe me.' He sat back and snapped his fingers at one of the armed barbarians behind us. He switched briefly into Slavic to thank the man who pressed a cup of beer into his hand.

Ludinus smiled greasily, while his eyes darted back and forth between us. I could have tried playing Priscus at his own game. But, even as I swallowed to get my voice working, Priscus reached quickly forward and pushed my gag back in. I tried to spit it out, but someone now tied it from behind.

'Sorry, dear boy,' he said in a pitying tone. 'You've had your only drinkie for tonight.'

He stood up and yawned. 'So the deal is that I take off pretty soon for Athens. Without Alaric to keep his beady eyes on me, I'll open the gate tomorrow night, and the looting and burning will get under way. No one will stop me when I take off on horseback. If you try anything underhand, the coded letter I've sent via the Governor of Corinth will be put into the hands of Sergius in Constantinople. What it says about you is quite damning. I do suggest you'll not wish ever to know its exact contents. But you know the Patriarch won't stand by when he learns that we've let all those bishops – not to mention his good friend Alaric – be put to the sword. You can bet the Great Augustus will treat my written word as the truth, and it won't look good for you.' He put his head back and roared with laughter. 'Oh, it won't look good for you at all – if it's ever read out in Council, you'd do better to stay here and look after the Great Chief's *harem!*'

Ludinus scowled and looked baffled. He bit his lip as he wondered, perhaps for the hundredth time, if Priscus really was telling the truth. When your entire life has been one gigantic plot, you lose sight of all common sense. He might have pulled my gag out again and questioned me alone. Then again, he'd only have assumed that I was lying too. When he did finally turn back to me, it was to slap my face again and then to walk round behind me and pour beer on to my peeled back. He recovered himself by sniggering over my muffled cry of pain.

'Get the blond animal out of here,' he trilled when he was back behind the lamps. 'I have old business with him that I'll finish when the time is right.' He waited for Seraphius to put his words into Slavic. As two set of arms reached forward to get me to my feet, he came forward again and gloated into my face. I can't say I blamed him. More than once in meetings of the Council, I'd given him the rough side of my tongue. No one would ever forget how I'd demolished his proposed scheme of currency debasement to make up for the shortfall in taxes. If anyone did, there were still my written objections to his further scheme of selling monopolies in oil and pork. As he described what he had in mind for me outside the walls of Athens, he hopped from foot to foot, and drool ran down his chin from between his rotten teeth. And he might have continued all night if the two men holding me hadn't run out of patience and dragged me with trailing feet from the tent into the gathering chill of the evening.

53

The celebrations might well have been on my account. I don't suppose any of the drink-sodden barbarians who broke off now and again from their feasting to come over and look at me understood either the concept of an Emperor's Legate, or of how anyone my age had been appointed. But they did understand that they'd not have to waste their lives in endless assaults on the walls of Athens. That alone would have justified the clatter of drinking horns and the loud and repeated bursts of joy. For all Ludinus had scared the shit out of me, will you credit how the smell of roasted ox had set off hunger pangs in my empty belly? I suppose you might. If so, you can take it further from me that anything you've read about the commonality of property among the barbarians is nothing more than worn-out rhetoric against civilisation. Those who had no sword, or no man with a sword, really had been left to hold back death with whatever filth wasn't actually poisonous. For those who had swords, the deal brought by Ludinus meant better food than ever.

I'd fallen into an exhausted doze in which I didn't even dream when I felt myself prodded awake. The big campfires were burning low, and there was a sensible diminution in the revelry. Were we coming to the midnight hour? I wondered as I opened my eyes and tried to focus on the dark figure who sat before me on a low stool. There was a dying fire behind him. But I knew, even before I had my eyes properly open, who it was.

'But why such melancholy in one so young and pretty?' Priscus cried softly. He chuckled low, and waited for me to focus on him. Then he turned for a look at the guard who'd been set over me. Snoring softly, he lay on the ground, an empty jug cuddled in his arms. Priscus turned back to me and spread his hands out before him.

'I'll be making off in a while,' he continued, now in Latin. 'Ludinus decided in the end not to accept the pack of lies I offered him. You'd have enjoyed the nasty turn our conversation took once he'd come to that conclusion. Luckily, though he used the guards to arrest me, he gave poor Seraphius the job of watching over me.

'Oh, poor little Seraphius!' he said after a long pause. He flexed his hands as if they were still about a throat, and laughed. He paused again, this time going stiff from the returned pain of whatever was consuming his flesh. He began to reach for his bag of drugs, then recalled he'd left it in the residency. He bit his lip as the want of something to shovel up his nose took hold within him. But the spasm didn't last, and he forced a smile back on his face. 'I did briefly wonder about taking you with me. But you're a big lad – you'd slow me down when I really do need a fast getaway.'

He stopped again and smiled sadly. He took out his knife and looked at the leather straps that held me tight. 'When the dawn comes up again, you'll be fed and given wine to drink. This will be to recover your strength for the journey back to Athens and to keep you alive through all that is planned for you there. The Avars and the Slavs they rule would get it over and done with in no time at all. But you can trust Ludinus to lay on a good show.

'Another reason I'm going to leave you here,' he went on, 'is because you are a bit of a liability. I will defend Athens as no one ever has in its long history.' He stopped for a gentle laugh, and counted on his fingers. 'The place fell to the Persians, and the Spartans, and to King Philip of Macedon, and to Sulla, and any number of times to the barbarians. I'm really not sure it has *ever* fought off a determined siege. Well, it will stand up to this siege with Uncle Priscus in charge of things. My reports are that your speeches to that council have been quite spell-binding. That, plus the horror of watching your slow death in front of the walls, will have all those priests marching back into their hall and voting without a single dissenting voice for the novel and probably heretical view that the Will of Christ is a single aspect of His undivided

Nature. So, between now and Christmas, I'll roll up on Constantinople and present the Great Augustus with a double triumph. You can be sure I'll fuck that bastard eunuch over before I'm finished. If he drags out the time left to him washing plates in a military brothel, I'll not have been the man I think I still am.'

He stopped again and put his knife away. He looked closely into my face. 'But, Alaric, I haven't come here just to make you feel bad. You must accept that I always have rather liked you. The other night, you heard me tell Nicephorus about the nature of pain. Believe me, it really does exist in two dimensions. There is the pain direct. Then, there's the real terror of pain which is the knowledge of what it does to the body. That's why execution by torture is always preceded by a tour of the instruments of pain and an explanation of their use. It's to break the will of a victim – so he's ready to start screaming and puking even as you lay hands on him.

'You have to believe me when I say that the first kind of pain you *can* deal with. It's simply a matter of giving up on the idea of any continuing existence for the body. Sooner or later, one of your vital organs will fail you – or whoever Ludinus is screeching at will take mercy on you and go just a little too far. Until then, what you have to do is go as deeply inside yourself as you can. When your seared and mangled privy parts are held up before your eyes, you try not to think of them as your own dearest possession. When you feel the hooked glove, glowing white from the brazier, drawn again and again over your body, and your fingers are nipped off at every joint, and your tongue is drawn out to unthinkable length before you feel the serrated shears pushed between your toothless jaws – don't think of that leaking, convulsing parody of the human form you have become as bearing any relation to the gloriously pretty thing I've been lusting over since we first met.

'Above all, dear boy,' he ended, 'do remember that we'll all be watching you from the safety of the walls and praying for your soul. You really won't be alone out there!' He stopped and got wearily to his feet, and went over to the dying fire behind him. He came back with a strip of parchment he'd set alight. He let it burn about a quarter of the way down, then blew it out. He giggled gently as he pushed its smoking end under my nose, and I shrank back from him with a gagged wail of despair.

For the first time ever, he'd managed to break me. Without that gag, I'd have been screeching prayers for mercy. As it was, I lost control of all bodily functions. It was only the sudden roaring in my ears that blotted out most of the soft laughter.

But Priscus had no time for the full enjoyment of his triumph. He got up again and reached for a little bag he'd left at his feet. 'If you were anyone else,' he said, 'I'd kill you here – not, mind you, because it would be a mercy, but because you do know all about that secret way into Athens.' He smiled and leaned down again and looked at me. 'But I do know exactly who you are. You're Alaric the Decent.' He stood back and his voice took on a bitter edge. 'You'd never betray those you loved – no, not even for the certainty of a clean death.' He settled his voice and smiled again. 'I suppose that will console you through the long ordeal that Ludinus is still elaborating in his filthy mind. I know you don't believe in God or any kind of Final Judgement. Even so, you can keep your mind from giving way entirely with the knowledge that you'll die as decently as you've lived.' He stopped. This time, he really had finished. Without looking back, he walked slowly out of sight, and left me alone in the growing silence of the night.

I do believe the convention, at this point in my story, is for me to explain how I gave way to despair – how I finally called on God for help, and how, when nothing happened, I wept the tears of the young and bright and beautiful who knows exactly what will be done to him. Perhaps I should also describe how I tried and failed to bite off part of my gag and choke myself on it. But, since you know that I'm sitting here in Canterbury, seventy-odd years after the event, in a good light and with a cup of strong French red beside me, would you really have me slow down what is already a somewhat protracted narrative? I think not. So, let's hurry over those sleepless and embarrassing hours that I passed between about midnight and shortly before the first light of another dawn, and move straight to the matter of my escape.

I thought at first the gentle sawing on the ropes that held my hands behind me was part of the torment. Ludinus was no match for Priscus when it came to breaking a man. But he'd certainly enjoy strutting about in front of me, promising to reconsider my end if I only sucked off my guards or whatever. But it was a child's hand that pushed my wrist out of the way as the knife cut deeper into the restraining knots.

The girl I'd fed beside the tomb of Hierocles now knelt before me to cut at the leather band that held in the gag. She put a finger to her lips as it came free. She pressed the knife into my hands and watched as I cut my legs free. She pointed over past the big tents. 'There are horses over there,' she whispered. 'There's only one man to look after them.' As silently as she'd come over to me, she stole back into the darkness, leaving me wholly alone in a camp where everyone who mattered was fumbling about pissy drunk where not already asleep.

The horses neighed with soft alarm as I turned over the dead body of the man who'd been supposed to guard them. Priscus must have got him from behind and snapped his neck before he was even aware of those strong and bony hands. He wasn't a big man, and his clothes were a tight fit on me. But I was already as filthy as any other barbarian, and I'd easily pass as one of the Germanics who'd taken service with the Avar horde. I looked for a while at the largest of the horses. If I set out now, I'd not be missed until I was nearly back under the walls of Athens. We must have come well past the ruins of Decelea. So far as I could tell, we were some way into the first of the mountain passes. But Athens could be no more than a few dozen miles back along the road.

I patted the horse and whispered something soothing. I looked up at the sky. It would be dawn soon enough. Then, the less utterly hung-over barbarians would be up and shambling about. Every time I let myself think where I was and what I still hadn't fully escaped, I'd give way to another attack of nerves. Even the very young don't bounce back at once from that. Then, as I was about to swing myself on to the horse and make my best getaway, I heard the unmistakable voice of Nicephorus.

It came clearly through the silence of the fading night. 'You *must* take me to the Great Chief,' he pleaded in Greek. 'I have information of the utmost importance.'

'Oh, shut the fuck up, you bastard Greekling!' came the answer in Slavic.

There was another babble in Greek, followed by the sound of a blow and then a squeal of pain.

If only I'd got straight on that bloody horse, I'd now be fifty yards beyond the camp, and I'd never have heard Nicephorus. You'll understand that I'd still have been shitting myself from terror, if only I'd had anything left inside me to void. If I shut my eyes, I could still see Ludinus gloating into my face, and Priscus finishing what he'd begun. But I stepped away from the horse and looked up again at the sky. If Aelric of Richborough would already have been out of the camp, the Lord Senator Alaric had been told of work that needed to be done. Even so, I stood a while longer beside the horse. Grinding my teeth with annoyance took my mind off the less creditable fact that I'd broken out all over in a sweat, and I was trembling almost beyond control. But I did eventually step away from the horse. What other answer can you give when duty calls this plainly?

54

'Who dares disturb the repose of the Grand Chamberlain?'
Ludinus called in his grandest voice. It was a wasted effort. The
barbarian who'd caught Nicephorus obviously hadn't a word of
Greek, and Seraphius, who did know Slavic, was lying dead somewhere out of sight. I stepped back out of the light of the
turned-down lamp and let the barbarian try explaining himself
now in broken Latin. Needless to say, the Grand Chamberlain
Ludinus had never soiled his ears or tongue by learning any of the
former Imperial language, and this wasn't a conversation that got
very far.

I'd already smeared dirt over my face, and, so long as I kept my
mouth shut, I'd just be accepted as another barbarian who was
tagging along beside the man who'd laid hands on the Count of
Athens. Nicephorus hadn't noticed me. Since he thought I was
trussed up and awaiting his further instructions, there was no
reason why Ludinus should give me any attention at all.

'I don't understand,' Nicephorus now broke in. 'Who are you?'
He pulled anxiously on his beard and looked round the parti-
tioned-off area of the big tent where the eunuch had been housed.
Like everything else in the camp, it was dirty and still clammy
from the endless rains. But those brightly coloured rugs and hang-
ings, and the profusion of glass bottles and the gold and ivory of
the furniture, spoke of something beyond the comprehension of
anyone who wasn't in on the secret. I had been wondering on and
off how much Nicephorus knew of what was happening. One
brief and sideways glance at him, and I could be sure that, whatever else might have been in those Imperial letters he'd burned, it
hadn't been news of this.

Nicephorus licked very dry lips and looked away from a jewelled icon of the Emperor that had claimed his attention. 'If you aren't Kutbayan,' he whispered, 'who are you?'

Ludinus sat up in his low bed and stared back at Nicephorus. 'A more appropriate question, my good fellow, is who are *you*?' he asked more grandly still. As the mumbled explanation started, and stopped, and started again, he fussed with his pillows and put on to his face the sort of friendly smile you only ever see in a court eunuch who has something nasty in his heart.

Suddenly, he sat forward, his mouth hanging open. He put up a hand for silence. 'You are telling me,' he asked, 'that there is a secret way into Athens?' He threw a suspicious look in our direction, and I stepped politely back deeper into the shadows. 'Who is that man behind you?' he asked us both in a clear but conversational tone. The barbarian nodded and bowed. I forced myself to keep looking down at the compacted dirt floor of the tent. Ludinus stared at us a little longer, then simply motioned us out.

'I don't think I've seen you before,' the barbarian said as we stood outside the tent. We were now deep into the first light of morning. I put my soft and manicured hands behind my back and smiled.

'We all came in the other day,' I said in a strong Lombardic accent. 'You don't keep us away when there's raping and burning and killing to be done.' We both laughed. Bearing in mind the vast numbers who'd come south, there was no reason why anyone should have seen me before. But I'd keep things vague. We fell silent, and I tried not to show how I was straining to hear the mostly whispered conversation a few feet away from us. If it was easy to guess its general nature, though, all I heard was a few cries of fright from Nicephorus, and a single burst of contemptuous laughter from Ludinus.

Now might have been the moment to jump the barbarian from behind, and to take his sword and go back in and settle those two bastards once and for all. But, if he chatted away easily enough about the joys he'd found in Decelea, the barbarian was standing back from me, and kept a hand near his sword.

I was about to suggest a quick search for beer among the dark and much smaller tents that surrounded us, when the leather flap went up, and Ludinus was blinking in the daylight. 'Hold this man fast,' he said in Greek. Neither of us moved. He sighed and muttered something about the missing Seraphius. 'We have immediate business with the Great Chief,' he added, still in Greek. This time, he spoke the name – 'Kutbayan! Kutbayan!' – and pointed to what I'd previously taken as the outer ring of tents, but that now showed itself as the nearest row in a great sea of tents that stretched into the unknown distance. And I'd thought it was all the barbarians under the walls of Athens. If not twenty million on the move, my own guessed figure had been childishly out.

I looked down again at the ground, and let the barbarian set hands on Nicephorus and shove him in the right direction. Ludinus looked angrily about – doubtless for Seraphius, but didn't shout for him. Instead, he snorted and muttered something under his breath. Leaving us to follow at a slight distance, he set off in his courtly hobble along a narrow path that led between the greater mass of tents.

The whole world over, barbarians are filthy and chaotic in their living arrangements. I can't say how long these had been camped here. But it was long enough for the surroundings to have been made into the usual sewer. We moved through hundreds – no, thousands of small tents. Most of these were still silent. Now and again, though, there was a woman or a few children trying to get a fire going. These were the lucky barbarians. Heaped up in the open, beyond the wide path through which we were moving, like logs stored for winter, what may have been thousands or tens of thousands of the thin and shrunken kept up as best they could the sleep that is the last refuge of the unhappy.

I could feel the opening heat of the sun behind me as we finally came to a wide avenue. There were no tents lining this, but rather a double row of bonfires, all dying low. Before each of these, I could see a huddle of stakes set into the ground. From each of these hung a scorched and naked body – men, women, sometimes a couple of children lashed together in a forced embrace. All were dead. From all about came the smell of roasted meat.

I didn't dare to look properly about. Ludinus, though, did. He came to a stop beside a clump of five children who might have been tied up beside their mother. He walked slowly round the group, tittering softly into a dirty napkin. 'Behold the justice of the Great Kutbayan!' he trilled to a very silent Nicephorus. I thought for a moment he was looking into my face. And he was – but only to see if I was as pleased by all this as he was.

'But, *why*?' was all Nicephorus could whisper by way of reply. It was as if he'd really thought the common people of Athens were the limits of human degradation. If so, he'd never seen barbarians in their natural state. You could easily see the realisation that, if he'd thought the Athenians were his friends, no one here was likely to harbour kind thoughts for him of any kind. 'What could they have done to deserve this?'

Ludinus smiled and stopped beside one of the largest of the slow-roasted bodies. 'Why?' he gloated. 'Because they were alive and in the way – and because power is nothing unless it is used.' He moved with surprising lightness of tread to another group of dead children. One of these had been torn apart by what may have been one of the braver wolves. They others were still tied in place, mouths open from their last piteous cries. 'You will be pleased to know, my dear little Count of Athens, that my last action before leaving Constantinople was to have the Patriarch himself and all his friends placed under house arrest. When I return, it will be with the heads of My Lords Priscus and Alaric – and I already have these in the bag, I can tell you.'

He giggled again, and now moved away from the bodies to push his face close to Nicephorus. 'Nothing will then stop me from reordering the whole Empire so it can shine once more in its ancient glory. I will myself take the field against the Persian savages, and hurl them all the way back to Ctesiphon. Do you remember how, back in the days of the Great Justinian, it was the eunuch Narses who led the armies to victory when the profes- sional generals had miserably failed? Be assured that the name of

Ludinus will be the latest and most glorious in the roll of honour. Ours shall be evermore known as the Age of Ludinus. Heraclius himself will be nothing beside that!' He stopped and stretched his arms out to the rising sun. He took out his napkin again and wiped away the drool that was running uncontrolled from between his flabby lips. 'Truly, there is room only for one sun in the heaven,' he added with a dramatic flourish of his hands.

To his credit, I saw Nicephorus shift nervously from one foot to the other. 'But, Your Magnificence,' he said, 'we did agree on the list of those who should be saved after the fall of Athens—'

He was interrupted by a long titter. 'We will bear your list in mind,' Ludinus said. 'But you shall certainly have your wish for Athens to be cleansed with fire. From what you tell me, fire is the least that it deserves!' He laughed again and hugged himself.

From what I could see of his back, Nicephorus was having second thoughts. But it was too late now to pull back. The big leather tent of Kutbayan was only a few dozen yards away, and the guards who stood before its closed flaps were casting looks of mild interest in our direction.

It was also too late for me to act as I'd been hoping I might. Except with the knife that girl had given me, I was still unarmed, and the barbarian was both huge and fully armed. I am sure that, if I could remember and then describe every step of the way between the two tents, we could agree that certain opportunities had arisen. But I was far from at my best. If I did, at the time, see a couple of opportunities, it was always after they'd passed. It was as much as I could do to resist the urge to run back to the horses and keep walking in the right direction. I'll say that I did find one possible opportunity as we approached the tent of Kutbayan. It was as the barbarian stopped and bent down to fiddle with the straps on his boots. I might then have got him from behind. Then, I could have butchered that piece of eunuch scum and offered Nicephorus his life if he'd make off with me. But it really was too late now. We were in full view, and I just couldn't bring myself to an attack that, even if successful, would amount to suicide.

Ludinus smoothed his robe where it had come up over his

thighs, and tottered forward to the big, heavily armed guards. 'I come on Caesar's behalf to address the Great Chief,' he called in Greek. He stopped and waved both arms dramatically at the guards.

They looked over at us, but didn't move.

55

I'd imagined Kutbayan would be a huge thing with a beard to match. I'd thought of him any number of times these past few days as a fiend, roaring drunk on the blood and fear of the conquered. Nothing had prepared me for the beardless and rather elderly man who sat in his tent between two unarmed young assistants. If you leave aside the lack of writing materials, and the pronounced slittiness of his eyes, this might have been one of our own generals, receiving and dictating messages in his tent. But even before my own image of him could dissolve and reform itself, I knew this was indeed the Great Chief of terrible reputation. You could see that from the hushed manner of his assistants – and from the cold glitter of his eyes.

His first words were to us in Avar. When these brought no response, he switched into very good Slavic. 'Where is the interpreter?' he asked. He leaned back in his chair and waited.

As if he'd guessed the meaning, Ludinus frowned and looked about the tent. 'I must speak urgently with the Great Chief,' he said loudly in Greek.

There were a few blank looks. Another of the attendants who stood behind Kutbayan left off scratching the scars that kept his beard from growing and shrugged.

Without moving, Kutbayan raised his voice in faint annoyance. 'Where is the unballed one who interprets?' he asked. He waited again. When there was still no answer, he got up from his chair and took a step towards us.

Except for the two Greeks, we all threw ourselves to the ground. Without looking to see what everyone else was doing, I tried to blend in with a feeble attempt at a prostration. I looked round only when I could hear everyone else getting up. I was last back on my feet, and stood, looking firmly down at beaten earth that had smelled of blood.

I now heard Kutbayan draw breath. 'I want someone here *now* who understands the language of the Greeks,' he said in what didn't rise above the sound of a polite conversation. One of his assistants leaned forward, and I caught a low whisper as to the whereabouts of a certain Kollo, who might still be drunk. Kutbayan frowned. 'Now, get this pair of time-wasters out of my tent,' he said. 'They can come back when there's someone to interpret.' He sat down and pointed at the assistant who'd been relaying a message when we entered. He thought again, and raised a hand to cancel the instruction. He looked briefly at me, but then pointed at the man who'd led us to the tent. 'You go and get him,' he said.

The man bowed and nearly tripped over a stool as he hurried out into the fresh air.

I've said I hadn't been able to bring myself to a suicide attack. But this was merely a calculated risk that bordered on the lunatic. I cleared my throat and didn't bother with a foreign accent as I spoke in Slavic: 'O, Great Chief, Leader of Men and Lord of All Creation,' I said, 'I know the language of these Greeklings from the time I spent among the Lombards.'

Nicephorus was first to speak. 'Alaric!' he croaked. 'What are you doing here?' He stared into my face with uncomprehending horror.

His face turning what may have been puce, Ludinus gave me the look of a man who's just seen a ghost.

I reached forward and struck Nicephorus so hard across the face that he fell to his knees. 'The Greekling, O Lord of All Creation, shows insufficient respect,' I explained with a low bow at Kutbayan. 'I heard them talking together as they came here.' I stopped and went into a tremble that was entirely unacted. 'They have news that will surely anger My Lord.' I swallowed and stared up. 'Will My Lord pardon me for conveying the filthiness that is within their black hearts?'

'Speak freely, young Germanic, and freely have my pardon,'

came the formulaic reply. Kutbayan sat back in his chair and pressed his fingers together, a thin smile on his face.

I turned and faced Ludinus, who was now about to recover the use of his voice. 'What have you to say before I get you tied over one of the livelier bonfires?' I asked in a Greek that – just to be on the safe side – I made sure to stumble over a few times.

His answer was a shove into my chest so hard, I almost fell sprawling on to the ground. He stepped past me and made a low bow. 'Kutbayan! Kutbayan!' he cried in his most imploring voice. He smiled and reached out at the Great Chief to pluck the hem of his jacket. He pointed at me and shook his head. 'Kollo – where is Kollo?' he asked with desperate emphasis on the name.

He was interrupted by Nicephorus, who was now up on his knees and starting a babbled plea for mercy.

Ludinus twisted round to look at him. 'Shut up!' he hissed. He silenced the pleas with a sharp kick. 'Keep your mouth shut if you don't want to play this chancer at his own game.' He turned back and would have started calling out again for the Great Chief's own interpreter, when Kutbayan held up his own arms for silence. Ludinus stopped in mid-flow, and even let himself be pushed over to the wall of the tent by a couple of the assistants. One of them put a knife to his throat, and that was an end to his interruptions for the time being.

'What are they saying?' Kutbayan asked with a look into my face that nearly brought on a fart of terror. He got up again from his chair. He glanced over to where Ludinus was still trying to smile and gesticulate for attention. He raised a hand for silence, and the knife pressed harder into the eunuch's throat. When all was silent, he turned back to me.

I stared into what might have been the eyes of a snake. The problem with these remote barbarians is that you can never guess what they are thinking. At any moment, Kutbayan might have me dragged out for execution. Just as likely, he might embrace me. 'The fat one is blaming the other for talking in front of me about their plans,' I explained.

Kutbayan looked away for a moment to glare once more at

Ludinus until he'd stopped trying to wave his arms for attention. He turned to me again. 'And what will you tell me of these "plans"?' he asked very softly.

'They were talking to each other, O Great Chief,' I whispered with faint horror, 'about how King Heraclius has sent orders for you to depart from his realms – to depart or face the wrath of his soldiers.' That was all I'd have dared say. But Nicephorus now came back into the conversation with an unstoppable flood of denunciations of me. I turned this neatly into a threat of what Heraclius would do if the 'worthless old fool' Kutbayan didn't head back at once into the zone of starvation. I even used the endless pointing at me to advantage by talking of the Western barbarians – all as big as me – who were marching towards us with the Exarch of Ravenna at their head.

Kutbayan really wasn't at all as Priscus had let me think him. He didn't lose his temper. He didn't reach for the nearest weapon or set about the grovelling Count or the now silent Ludinus with a whip. He wasn't in any sense your normal barbarian. He certainly was no fool. He waited as I ran out of inspiration and fell silent. He listened to the continuing babble of Nicephorus and looked at a desperately thoughtful Ludinus. He also was no fool. Unless I could bring this to a rapid end, he'd find some way of getting his point across; that, or Kollo would stumble in with enough Greek to push me out of the conversation.

I tried another wild throw of the dice. 'O Lord,' I cried out indignantly, 'the bearded one is saying that the treasures brought to you by the fat one were washed in the blood of slaughtered prisoners, and cursed by the great priest of the cross-worshippers so that whoever touches them becomes as unmanly as the fat one.' I dropped my voice to a scared whisper. 'The other unballed one who speaks Slavic is even now passing this about the camp.'

There was a murmur of outrage from the assistants. Kutbayan didn't so much as blink. 'Who are you?' he asked. He stared once more into my face, now seeming to look straight through its covering of dirt, now fixing himself on my eyes. 'What is your name? Who are your people?'

'I am Aelric,' I blurted out. 'I'm from a place in the furthermost west called England.'

'Well, I don't think I trust you,' he said, not once taking his eyes off mine. He gave a thin and very suspicious smile.

He and Priscus would have got on with each other no end. My stomach turned over a dozen times in the space of a single heart-beat, and I pulled my eyes free and looked silently down. How much longer could I keep this going?

'Go and find Kollo,' he said, still facing me. Someone behind him bowed and made for the exit. 'You,' he said to me, 'go and stand beside the fat one.'

I looked back at him. 'I speak truly, O Great Chief,' I said firmly. 'But let me question the bearded one again.' Without waiting for a repeat of his order to join Ludinus, I went and stood over Nicephorus, who'd now fallen on to his belly and was rubbing his face in the dirt. 'Listen, you bag of shit,' I said in a questioning tone. 'His Nibs will give you both a fair chance. Whichever one of you gets first to the nearest set of bodies outside this tent can stay alive. If you don't want to be rolled about in a nail-studded barrel, I suggest you get moving.'

Ignoring the knife that was still pressed against his throat, Ludinus now pushed forward. 'Don't move, you bloody fool!' he urged Nicephorus. He sidled away from the armed assistant with a move that showed his origins as a dancing boy, and stepped suddenly forward. He knocked me aside and stood again before Kutbayan. He pointed at me and put a hand over his mouth. He made a quick gesture of a throat being cut and shook his head. He smiled and pointed at me again.

But I'd judged Nicephorus right. Even as Ludinus seemed about to bring everything back to order, the Count got up with a strangled scream and made a dash for the exit. I heard the rasp of a sword outside and a brief and bubbling scream. As Kutbayan swore loudly and hurried out of the tent, I let my shoulders sag.

I turned to Ludinus. 'I'll bet he didn't trust you with the details of the secret way into Athens,' I whispered.

'Then it must be you to give those details,' came the snarled reply. He gave me another big push in the chest, and made for the tent flaps.

I'll say again that suicide was no part of this admittedly mad plan. Even as Ludinus was beside Kutbayan, who was now frigid with anger, and going into a speech so emollient no Greek was needed to understand that something had gone wrong, I took a very deep breath. 'The fat one has a knife!' I shouted. 'He's gone out to strike the Great Chief from behind!' I pushed past the scrum of barbarians who'd got out before me and were piling on to Ludinus, and managing to fall on top of Kutbayan in their eagerness. I raised my voice and bellowed for assistance. I darted away from the tent, and tripped straight over Nicephorus. I landed with both knees on his belly, and his mouth opened and a loud burp came out. I thought for a moment he was only wounded. But wide, staring eyes that didn't move told me he was dead. I scrambled up and shouted a call of alarm at the man who was coming at me with a sword. I pointed back at the tent and got out of his way. There were other men hurrying forward, all with drawn swords. But these weren't interested in me. Without another look back, I ran as if I were trying to win some ancient foot race towards where I'd found the horses.

56

I'll pass over the details of my escape from the camp. I may have got to the horses in a state of advanced terror. The dead and naked barbarian may already have been found. But I was able to start a cry that Kutbayan had been killed, and that Greek soldiers were already fighting their way into the camp. I got on to the first horse I could touch once everyone was hurrying off to get armed, and didn't look round till I must have covered a mile on the road back to Athens.

When I did look back, it was in the sure and certain knowledge that a hundred barbarians were riding me down – all of them mad with anger, and with Kutbayan in front. In fact, I was the only man in sight with a horse. I forced myself to slow from the irregular canter that was the best I'd been able to get from the horse over these worn paving stones and tried to look important as I was carried slowly past the unordered crowds who seemed to be wandering without purpose up and down the road.

I stopped at the second of the rain-swollen streams that I passed. I watered the horse and scrubbed all the dirt I could from my face and hands. I hadn't eaten in over a day. But I drank until I thought my stomach would burst. As I passed over another little bridge that kept the road going without break across the flat plain of Attica, I found myself among a few dozen men of my own colouring. They shouted cheerfully up at me in one of the most northerly dialects of Lombardic. Not fancying a long conversation, I answered in English, and managed to get away with a halting exchange about the weather. I did overhear a few comments suggesting that this gigantic raid south had taken all pressure off Thessalonica and the remaining walled cities that guarded the approaches to Constantinople itself. But that much I'd already guessed for myself. The next crowd I passed all had the squat, yellow appearance of barbarians from the furthest reaches of Scythia. They parted in silence as I approached them from behind and let me ride through.

I passed through crowds of the starving. They held up imploring but weak hands as I pushed my way through. I passed by trains of well-guarded pack animals, all loaded with what must have been food. As the sun reached towards its noonday zenith, I passed by what had been the ruins of Decelea. There were fires here and there that were still burning from the fast and over-powering attack. Every gust of breeze carried over the stomach-turning smell of corruption. If I listened hard, I could just make out the buzzing of a million flies. But you'd never have guessed otherwise from the heaps of stone that began fifty yards from the road that this had only recently been a place of civilised habitation.

I was approaching the first of the tombs that began to line every road to Athens from a few miles out, when I heard the first sound of violence. I'd come to another stream. Even in spring, this one was too small to be worth a formal bridge. Instead, the stream where it cut the road had been filled with big stones that let water pass through underneath, while allowing men and beasts to cross with reasonable care. I thought at first the noise I'd heard was just an effect of water as it rushed through the stones. But, as I reached the crossing, there was the definite sound of a cry.

I reached nervously for my little knife as someone dressed in black reeled out and stood before me, sword in hand. The horse was tired, and it hadn't been fed. But I was ready to try making a dash forward.

'Well, dearie me,' the man cried in Greek. 'But who's been the luckiest little bugger that ever was?'

I steadied myself on the horse and tried to glare at Priscus. I thought of getting down and beating him to a mound of red pulp. Then I thought of telling him he was under arrest for treason, or whatever else would most conveniently justify sticking his head on a spike somewhere inside Athens. But he was the one with a sword, and I just wanted to get back inside the walls. 'Nicephorus tried to betray us all,' I said quietly. 'I got him killed outside Kutbayan's tent.'

Priscus lowered his bloody sword. 'And Ludinus?' he asked.

I shook my head. He might have been butchered like Nicephorus. More likely, he'd crawled out from under a dozen armed barbarians and stayed alive long enough for Kutbayan to call everyone back to order.

Priscus smiled and sheathed his sword. 'I, of course, would have got him as well – and the Great Chief into the bargain. Did I ever tell you how I got out of Trampolinea alive?'

'I don't suppose the real truth does you any credit,' I answered.

He laughed and helped me down from the horse. He laughed again as my legs gave way and I ended on my back.

'You still can't ride to save your life,' he sneered. He reached down and pulled me to my feet.

'Your friend over there – he *is* dead?' I asked with a nod to where I'd heard the scream.

Priscus gave a sniff of tired scorn and sat down on a stone beside the road. 'You may think yourself entitled to say otherwise, dear boy,' he said with a trace of embarrassment. 'But there really is much to be said for our previous agreement about standing or falling together.'

I did look about for the appropriate reply. But, as I arranged myself on another big stone, I yawned and stretched – and, then, without any feeling of what was about to happen, began to cry. I tried to stop. I put up my hands and tried to pretend I was wiping sweat off my face. I could tell myself with perfect internal calm that this was as disastrous in its own way as it would have been if Ludinus had found a couple of words in Slavic. It had no effect. My body shook with bigger and bigger sobs, and I found myself rocking back and forth on that stone as if I'd been poor Martin after any of the bigger frights I'd led him into.

I felt something hit me in the lap. I opened my eyes and looked down at a small satchel.

'If you can forget about the smell, my fine, young barbarian,' Priscus said, 'there's about half a pound of dried beef in this. It's putrid stuff, but you'll feel better with something to weigh your stomach down.' He got up and went over to the horse, which had been edging slowly away from us. He took its reins and led it back to where he'd been sitting. 'Oh, come on, cry-baby Alaric,' he said with mock impatience. 'When I was your age, Imperial Legates had much less mobile upper lips.'

I looked up again at the sun. This time, I sneezed. By the time I'd finished blowing my nose, the sobbing fit was over as quickly as it had come on. I looked back along the road. There might have been a very distant column of dust. It might have been the after-noon heat haze. It was hard to say – though I could feel the start of another jittery turn.

Priscus watched me and gave a pitying laugh. 'Just noticed, I see, that we shan't be alone,' he said. 'Did your barbarian ances-tors really kick us out of Britain? Or did they just creep in behind those who did the fighting?' He pulled me to my feet again, and laughed as I found myself unable to move. He sat down beside me. 'Do explain, dear boy,' he asked in a conversational tone, 'why you responded so harshly to our fat friend's scheme of increasing the coinage. We really are short of cash, you know.'

My legs were beginning to shake, and I thought I'd start crying again. But I put my thoughts into order and looked away from the distant but now unmistakable cloud of dust. 'You can take in one hundred solidi,' I said, 'mix in a quarter of base metal, and reissue a hundred and twenty-five. It doesn't actually increase the number of things you can buy with them.'

Priscus smiled. 'Ah, but surely whoever issues them can buy more of what is available?' he asked.

I thought again, trying to remember what I'd said in my long memorandum to Heraclius. 'I'll grant that whoever spends them first has an advantage,' I said. 'In the short term, though, you simply rob the last people to receive the debased coins, as they pay higher prices for things – and these are usually the poorest. In the longer term, you disorder all the exchanges, and destroy confidence in the Imperial money. It's better to spend more on the military by cutting all other expenses.'

But Priscus had got me back in order, and was no longer interested in the finer points of coin debasement. He was instead looking at the approaching cloud of dust. 'I hope you'll not object to sitting behind me on your horse. To be sure, it's the only way you'll ever see Athens again from inside its walls.' He grinned and gave the horse a comforting pat. He pulled me once more to my feet. This time, I could move.

I shivered again in the dank, underground chill, and looked at the fresh brickwork. 'Martin begged me not to have the opening sealed up,' the Dispensator explained. 'However, I felt I had no choice.'

I nodded.

'We can be relieved that you ensured the death of the Count of Athens before he could betray us all. At the same time, the man called Balthazar remains at large, and we cannot afford the danger of even a hidden entrance into the city.'

I nodded again. There was no need to go on about the bricking up of the opening in the tomb, or the mass of earth and rubble packed behind this wall that sealed the opening from the big tunnel. I turned away and looked along the tunnel. In the dark, it had, the night before last, seemed endless in itself, and part of something much larger. The lamps carried down with us showed that, whatever function it once had served – and I was no wiser about this – it was no labyrinth at all. Between the opening forced from the residency to the opening forced from the tomb of Hierocles, it was very long indeed. But it was only a single tunnel, with one sharp turn and with a few chambers leading off. Now I'd been from one end to the other, I could see there was no other means of access. Had it been an ancient tomb? In the absence of any inscription or other evidence, it was worthless to speculate.

The Dispensator stood back from his own pleased inspection of the brickwork. 'I don't know how long Martin waited beside that doorway in the rock,' he went on, finally turning to the first questions I'd asked him. 'But you really are a fool if you think he'd have followed your stupid orders. He dithered. He prayed. He dithered again. Long before the dawn, he and his wife were shouting for admission outside my monastery. They'd left every armed slave to watch for your return, and had taken their chance alone in the streets of Athens. It was Sveta who eventually took over the job of explaining to me what had happened.'

I looked away from the withering stare and walked beside him back along the tunnel. A bath and some wondrously clean clothes had restored me to an outward semblance of order. Martin had nursed me through another sobbing attack, and the Dispensator had shown enough tact to take Priscus out of my office to explain the defence orders he'd given in our absence. Why I'd been brought down here I couldn't say. But it saved me the embarrassment of joining Priscus on the walls, where he must, even at this moment, be feeding his vanity on the shouted welcome back of the whole militia.

There was a loud scraping behind us as someone finished pushing his way down here from the residency. The Dispensator took the half sheet of papyrus from the silent monk and moved closer to one of the lamps. Now there was no draught of air through the tomb of Hierocles, it was increasingly stuffy down here. I could see the point of sealing the only other exit. But this did make the place distinctly less welcoming as a place of refuge for the entire household. It wasn't my eyes – the lamps had burned distinctly lower ever since they'd been placed in the wall niches.

The Dispensator grunted and held the message out for me to read. I took it into hands that, try as I might, still wouldn't stop shaking, and translated: 'The mob is trying to break into the main granary. The monks of Saint John beg to be dispensed from their obligation not to draw blood.' Either they hadn't noticed that Priscus was back, or they'd chosen to stay under Church control.

I handed the sheet back and straightened up. 'Give me one of your pens,' I demanded of the secretary. After a nod from the Dispensator, I scribbled the required permission on the back of the sheet and watched as the secretary squeezed himself back into the fissure that led to the residency.

'So you think Nicephorus and Balthazar weren't just using the place as a convenient means of access?' I asked with a return of my own to some earlier stage in our long and disordered conversation. 'You think they were running things from down here?'

The Dispensator looked back along the tunnel. 'While searching for you and Priscus,' he said, 'I made a full inspection of this place. I cannot say that I was pleased by what I found.' He put up a hand to silence any questions. 'I have been in Athens just fifteen days, and have been mostly unable to follow anything said in my presence. But I have now had the chance to speak properly with His Grace the Bishop of Athens, and with Martin. I do not like *anything* that I have heard. And I think little of you for your stupidity. I might have hoped that even you would not be so blinded by lust.'

'Where is Euphemia?' I broke in. I was silenced by a cold look. I stepped back from him and waited obediently for him to continue.

'The creature of whom you speak has withdrawn herself from the residency,' the Dispensator said with quiet emphasis. 'You may be assured that I have neither seen not set hands on her. Where she has gone is her business, and I do not suggest that you should make enquiries of her whereabouts. To be sure, no one whom you may command to begin a search will obey you. I have now moved into the residency, and I propose to ensure that you concentrate on your proper duties, which are to complete your chairing of the council and to assist in the defence of Athens.'

I let him go first through the narrow opening towards the residency. The tunnel itself had been transformed by a few dozen lamps. This long fissure was as horrid now as when I'd first pushed through it with Priscus behind me. But I kept my nerve by explaining in full the equal but different horror of our position: how we'd all been marked down by Heraclius himself for destruction, and how there was no certainty that any degree of success in Athens would change his mind.

The Dispensator was still questioning me about probable events in Constantinople when I stepped, right behind him, into the residency cellar and came face to face with Martin.

There was still a tremor in his voice. But he did manage to control himself. He looked at the Dispensator. 'The Lord Priscus sends greetings, and begs that you may join him on the walls to discuss a matter of some delicacy.' He gave me a despairing look, before handing me a stack of documents for my immediate attention. The top one was an order for looters to be summarily hanged. I'd seal this in my office. Together, we'd all of us hold the walls somehow. What happened after that could be faced as and when.

I lay back and waited for the long and luxuriant glow of another orgasm to reach its end. At last, I sat up and pulled Euphemia towards me. I tried to look into the faint outline of her face. 'I can hide you for the time being,' I said with slow emphasis. 'Tomorrow, or the next day, however, I must insist on your reappearance in this building. Then, we will go together out into the sunlight, and you'll stop behaving like some Syrian monk who's been too long on the top of his pillar.' I shut off her objections with a gentle slap to the face. As agreed, she had slipped away the moment I was through that doorway. Where she'd hidden herself I didn't think to ask. But I had to stop a lunacy that was sending even the Dispensator into holy terrors. It would get her killed. It would bring me into scandal.

'Your name is Euphemia of Tarsus,' I went on. 'You arrived here at the invitation of Nicephorus. You have a child to look after. If you want to see Constantinople, you'll be well advised to put all these childish fancies aside. *Do you understand me?*'

'And is My Lord proposing to make me his wife?' she asked with an apparent burst of sanity.

I looked harder at her in the gloom. I'd not answer that I had higher ambitions, when I eventually did marry, than a provincial widow – even if the sex was heavenly. But it was a reassuringly female question. I was thinking of what answer to give when I heard another long and muffled roar of collective anger from somewhere outside the building.

'I think it is the common people again,' Euphemia said. 'They spent all night trying to burn down the houses of everyone who is defending the walls. It may be that they have again found someone to kill.'

I reached out for where I'd left my wine cup and took a long sip. I got on to my knees and pulled her towards me again. There was time yet before she had to go back into hiding, and I was uneasy from thoughts of what might so easily have already been my fate before the walls of Athens.

57

As the sun rose on my eighth day since stepping ashore at Piraeus, I made my way to a resumed council through streets that were littered with uncollected bodies. If it hadn't been for the grim-faced monks and the few armed civilians who'd been taken away from holding the walls, I might have thought Athens had already fallen to the barbarians. But I'd just walked the whole circuit of the walls with Martin, and watched the masses of armed men who were now coming together in loose formations outside the range of our arrows.

'The Lord Priscus expects an attack before noon,' the Dispensator had said when he could spare time from fussing over the placing of an aged catapult that might have done us better service by being set alight and thrown on to the heads of any attackers. 'We can agree that there will be no attempt at a parley by Kutbayan. His instructions are to break in and destroy us all. But, so long as we can keep the barbarians from setting hands on this stretch of the wall, Priscus believes we may be able to repel an attack in not more than two other places.' The Dispensator had then allowed himself a long inspection of the gathering masses, before changing the subject to a reminder of the Pope's right to his title.

That had been right after the dawn. I now stood with Martin in the shadow of an equestrian statue, and waited for the monks to pull away the bodies that choked the entrance to the narrow street we had to enter. Every one of them clubbed to death in a manner that avoided any shedding of blood, there were enough bodies for the smell of corruption that already came from each to justify a napkin soaked in my strongest perfume.

'I've counted a hundred and fifty,' I said with a wave at the handcart that had now been produced. 'Assuming an even distribution of bodies across the city, it looks as if Athens will be in need of a new lower class.' It was a feeble and a wasted joke.

Martin swallowed and looked without answer at the two armed slaves I'd brought with us. 'The Bishop of Athens told me many things yesterday morning,' he said in a nervous whisper. 'He said the common people are persuaded that any breach of the city walls will bring all the statues in Athens to life. These will then repel the attack without any effort on their part.'

There was no answer needed to that. I waited for the handcart to be pushed aside, and led the way in silence.

Except for the shouted acclamations in two languages, my two-day horror among the barbarians might have been a dream. There was the minute clerk with his stack of waxed tablets, there the assembled churchmen, each in his accustomed place. In my absence, the Dispensator had taken charge of the council, only to adjourn it till further notice. Now it was back to business. I held up my hands for silence and looked again at the list of questions that had been written in many hands on the sheet of papyrus Martin had given me.

'Reverend Fathers,' I cried in Greek – and Martin was now interpreting – 'let me begin with the question of Nature and Persons and Will and Substance.' I looked about the room. There was the buzz of just one fly in the still air. Sooner or later, this too would go out for the richer pickings to be had in the streets. I smiled easily and fixed a look on the pale and very troubled face of old Gundovald. He was still fussing over his lost boy, and looked set to start another burst of weeping. I looked instead at Simeon. After his first day of terror, he'd settled down rather well. So far as I could tell, he'd made no further trouble of any kind. There's much to be said for a barbarian siege when you have a Church council to manage. I took a deep breath and prepared to outdo all my previous addresses to the council.

What I said is of little importance. Indeed, I said nothing I hadn't said once or twice already. What was important was that I was back, and that I was now making every effort to keep my well-trained flock from straying.

I'd got to the second refill of the water clock when the sounds of battle that came through the high windows from all about suddenly rose in volume. I stopped in mid-sentence and glared at the Bishop of Ephesus as he got up from his place and hurried from the room. I'd barely resumed the thread of my argument than he was back.

'The barbarians are within the walls!' he cried. He fell down beside the minute clerk and pulled his robe over his head. Though it had been in Greek, the Dispensator had followed that meaning well enough. He sighed and put his stylus down.

I stepped forward into the space before the semicircle of seats and held up both hands for attention. 'Reverend Fathers,' I cried. The screams and clash of arms were undeniably coming closer, and I had to shout again for attention. 'Reverend Fathers!' I roared. This time, every face in the room turned back to me. I smiled weakly and cleared my throat. 'Keep interpreting a phrase at a time,' I whispered to Martin, who had covered both his eyes and was beginning to rock back and forth. 'The residency slaves have their orders. The most we can do here is our duty.' I stepped closer to the four dozen scared churchmen and continued in Greek.

'You will all have read in your schooldays of how, in ancient times, when Rome was still a republic, its days of empire still in the future, the Gauls burst into the Senate House. Remember, then, how the Conscript Fathers faced the barbarians – sitting calmly, like statues, despising the violation of their proceedings.' You can be sure I added nothing about the massacre that followed this. The Latins mostly scowled back at me. They might have blamed me as representative of an Emperor who'd called them into danger. But this sort of thing was, for most of them, an occupational hazard. To do them justice, the Greeks at least stayed in their seats.

Trying not to look at the closed door, I listened as the sounds of desperate battle came closer and closer. Then, as I took up my speech again – this time in a shout that would, before long, give me a sore throat – the noise began to recede.

This might have been the end of the scare. Even Martin was getting his voice in order as I elaborated on one of the supplemental decrees of the Council of Chalcedon. But, as I paused to unpick the tangled syntax of an unexpectedly long sentence, the door flew open, and an enormous barbarian swaggered into the room. He was followed by another who was nowhere near his size. He lowered his sword and looked about the now absolutely still and silent room.

'Well, well, fucking well!' he roared in Slavic. 'What have we here?' He tipped his great bearded face back and roared with laughter.

Over on my left, I saw the Dispensator tighten his grip on his stylus. Whatever his clerical vows, he'd not go down without a fight. But I was completely unarmed. I'd left my sword hanging in the room outside with my cloak and outer shoes. I looked quickly at the open door. For the moment, it was just these two.

I stood up and pointed calmly at the big man. 'Get out of here!' I said quietly in Slavic. 'You are interrupting a council of Holy Mother Church.' For a moment, I thought I'd got the man by surprise, and that he might even go away.

But Simeon broke the long silence that followed my words with a cry that fell somewhere between a squawk and a babble and pointed at the two armed men. And now the spell was broken. The big man laughed again, and waved his sword at Simeon, who threw himself forward on his hands and knees and tried to crawl under his chair.

I looked desperately about for anything I could use as a weapon. The jewelled crucifix set up behind me would never do. All else I could see was my big silver inkstand. I looked about once more – anything but this object of great beauty and great value. But it really was – unless I fancied going at two armed men with my own stylus – the only object readily to hand. While the big man was still teasing Simeon with his sword, I jumped forward from my chair and grabbed the inkstand with my right hand. I staggered from its weight, but managed to swing its yard length over my head. The big man saw me too late. He tried to move out of my path, but only fell against one of the more solid chairs. I nearly toppled sideways as the big end of the inkstand made contact with his right shoulder. With a shout of pain and surprise, he went down like a stricken beast. Not bothering to see if he could get up again, I bent and took his sword from where it had fallen. Before he could get out of the way, I lunged at the smaller man and got him straight in the belly. It was hardly an elegant blow. But I silenced his long scream with a kick to the head that broke his neck.

The room was silent again. Every face was turned in my direction. I saw that Martin had taken young Theodore by the shoulder, and got him safe behind the water clock. The bishops remained mostly in their places.

'No others,' the Dispensator said in a voice that even he couldn't keep from shaking. He'd kept enough presence of mind to hurry over to the door and look out into the entrance hall. 'It looks as if they were strays.'

Not answering, I pushed past him and we went together out into the hot sunshine. He was right. I could see that the tide of battle had rolled forward through Athens, all the way to the foot of the Areopagus. Now, it had receded, leaving a few bloody corpses. Apart from those still heaps, it might now have been business as usual. I looked around carefully. Somewhere, behind the shabby buildings that blocked my view, the battle was still raging with terrible intensity, and I felt a stab of shame that I'd left its conduct to others. I looked briefly at my bloody sword, and then at the Dispensator's drawn face, and hurried back into the main hall.

The shock had now passed, and men were on their feet. A crowd of bishops had gathered about the fallen barbarian, and they were doing their best to kick him to death. Everyone fell back as I approached.

I stared down at the man. He'd landed badly on the floor, and looked as if he'd broken his left arm. His right shoulder I'd smashed beyond healing with my inkstand. 'You can get outside and die like the others,' I snarled in Slavic. 'Show some respect for your betters!' I gave the fallen man a vicious kick of my own, and watched as he began to push himself obediently towards the door. I glanced down at my velvet shoe. The man was leaving a trail of blood as he moved. But there was no stain on the bright yellow of my shoes.

I looked up at the high ceiling and tried to think if there was anything still to be said about the relationship between Nature and Substance. There must have been plenty. But none of it came to mind, and there were no questions from my little senate. I bowed to Simeon, who was clutching the back of his chair, and returned to my own place. The sounds of battle really had receded, and we could try to go back to our own work. The main sound in the hall was the clatter of wood as the minute clerk finished covering one of his waxed tablets and reached behind him for another. Now, almost as if it had been no more than notice of refreshments that had interrupted the proceedings, Martin even managed to interpret the last part of my previous sentence.

We might actually have gone back to work. Since I hadn't run off in search of the battle, I could think of nothing else to do. I looked away from the corpse that no one had thought to clear away, and thought of a point arising from one of my earlier definitions. But, as I leaned forward to clear my throat and start another speech, the door opened again, and one of the militia leaders ran in.

He bowed to me and then to the assembly. He realised he was standing in the pool of blood that had oozed from the smaller barbarian, and stepped back with another bow. 'My Lord,' he cried in a strangled voice, 'I must inform you that Priscus is dying, and he asks that you and the Lord Fortunatus of Rome should take over the defence of Athens.'

I got up and swallowed. I raised my hands again for silence. This time, no one paid attention. Everyone was on his feet and running about as if the building were on fire.

A grim look on his face, the Dispensator was beside me. 'I think I got the meaning of that,' he whispered into my ear. I nodded. 'If it hasn't been done already, we really must get the western gate closed. The plan is to concentrate forces where the main street is narrowed by the big statue of Hadrian. If we can hold the line there, the rooftop archers should be able to . . .'

He trailed off as the Bishop of Iconium pushed his way between us and screamed something about getting ourselves over to the Acropolis. I reached forward and slapped his face twice. He stopped screaming, and it gave me time to get my own thoughts properly in order. I took the Dispensator by the sleeve and began to shove people out of the way as we made for the door.

'It may already be too late,' he shouted. 'But we can still do our best.' I waited by the door while he pushed his way back into the wild panic to get the little barbarian's sword.

As I waited, I saw Martin and Theodore at the far end of the room. The Bishop of Athens was beside them. If I'd known more about the barbarian thrust into Athens, I'd have sent them back to the residency. As it was, I'd have to trust in the judgement of His Grace of Athens.

58

Priscus opened his eyes and focused dreamily on my face. The doctor had now taken a candle to both his arms, and the room was filled with the smell of scorched flesh as well as vomit and other bodily excretions. I watched as, from both wrists right up to the elbow, the doctor set about scraping away the blistered skin and painting on still more opium juice to quell the pain in that drug-hardened body. It needed a double coat of the dark and oily liquid before Priscus came out of his latest spasm and was able to look up at me. I stared back into the now tiny black dots within his eyes.

'So, you repelled the attack?' he was finally able to gasp.

'Yes,' I said. I fell silent again.

And we had got through it. Somehow, with me to lead men into the actual fighting, and the Dispensator to direct movement of our catapult from one part of the fray to another, we'd held the city. Without him there to manage it, the plan that Priscus had laid a few days earlier had almost gone wrong. As thousands of men were thrown against the wall, the weakest gate had been opened, and, as expected, the main attack was then diverted. It was now, though, that Priscus had gone down – not wounded by the enemy, mind you, but floored by a fit of internal spasms that not even his iron will had been able to bring under control. It had been almost too late to tighten the noose – thousands more than expected had swarmed through the opened gate, and their assault had reached even to where we debated on the Areopagus. But almost too late wasn't the same as too late. The Dispensator and I had been just in time to close the gate and seal off the multitude in the streets, and then stamp on the trapped men as if they'd been ants. We'd done it, and the main attack had collapsed into a chaotic retreat from the walls that our own archers were able to make still more utterly humiliating to the enemy.

Priscus was still looking up at me. I suppose he expected a better explanation of what we'd managed than 'Yes.' At the least, he was probably expecting me to tell him whether any of the blood that was still splashed all over me was my own. But I said nothing. He drew his tongue over parched lips and tried for a laugh. 'Don't try telling me otherwise, dearest Alaric,' he now said in a distant, vastly weary Latin. 'But I know that you've got her hidden away in this building. And don't tell me that you still deny the evidence of your senses.' He looked past me at the lamp that hung over his bed and swallowed a few times.

I looked at the doctor, who shook his head and moved the water jug out of sight.

Priscus managed a weak smile. 'Oh, but you do deny it, don't you?' he went on. 'If you want to believe that she's just barking mad from having to share this place with Nicephorus, you really are a fool. Even I gave up on seducing her once I realised what she really was.' He now did manage a wheezing laugh and fell silent.

'And I suppose everyone else believes this?' I asked.

He shut his eyes and his breathing became slow but regular. I thought he'd drifted into unconsciousness. But he opened his eyes again and, though without success, tried to focus.

'You know she came here just a few years ago with Theodore,' I said. 'She's no more a witch than I am. You're the fool if you believe other than that.'

With a great effort of will, he raised a hand and waved his forefinger slowly from side to side. 'My dear boy,' he whispered, 'that tunnel we found is only the beginning of what lies under Athens. The whole city throbs with evil, and you must be the only man in the Empire who can't feel it. Did your clerical friend tell you how many human remains he found stuffed into that tomb?' I tried not to step back. He noticed and laughed softly. 'I don't suppose he did. After all, since you don't believe anything, there's no point even telling you about it. But this isn't what's important. Wait till she reappears, and then keep hold of her. You really will find her useful in Constantinople. Just make sure to keep her out of the sun till she's done her work.'

He shifted again on his bed and tried to keep his focus on me. 'But tell me,' he croaked, now uneasy through the rising waves of oblivion, 'what do *you* think happens after death? Do you believe in a Final Judgement? Or do you really believe that death is the end of all things?'

I thought hard. I'd decided at once what he didn't want to hear. The real question was how bastardly I felt about his own perform-ance in the barbarian camp. The answer was *very*. I settled my face into a look of vague piety. 'We are assured, both by Scripture and by the teachings of Holy Mother Church,' I said, 'that death is but the passage to a new and eternal life. Perhaps not now, but eventually, your eyes will close one last time on the world that you have done so much to make into a nightmare. You may then sleep a few days, or a hundred years, or a hundred thousand years. It will all be nothing to you. Finally, though, when the Seven Angels have sounded their seven trumpets, and the Tribulation is passed, Christ will come back in glory, and every tomb will give up its dead. Then, as naked as the day you were born, you will stand before the Throne of God, and you will be judged for every one of your sins. I know you have no doubt that you will be judged truly, and that your resurrected body will be handed over for everlasting punishments beside which all that you have ever done to others will be as the brush of one of the flies that now crawl on your flesh.'

Yes, it *was* a bastard thing to do, and I'll make no excuse. I didn't even feel the joy he would have felt as I looked down into that white and terrified face. But I guessed that I'd got him at just the right moment. In a while, he'd drift away into dreams that would be of the only hellfire he'd ever know. Between then and his slow return to waking, I had little doubt that he'd pass through every semblance of infinity. Yes, I knew the effects of opium – and I knew why, of all the drugs in his wooden box, opium wasn't among them.

I stood up and nodded to the doctor, who bowed respectfully.

'Will he recover?' I asked, now in Greek.

He pulled a face and shrugged. The Lord Commander, he told me with the endless equivocating of his profession, might be on his feet again within a couple of days, and, with increasingly frequent relapses, last another few years. He might, on the other hand, not see out the night. It all depended on the hidden progress of his consumption. He waved vaguely at the icon of Saint Luke that had been placed above the bed.

I looked about the untidy room. I could have sent the doctor out and begun a search for any secret documents. But I really doubted if there was anything at all to find that I didn't already know. I was still looking at the door of a small cupboard when I remembered there was real work to be done. I tried to brush away a lock of my hair that was covering one of my eyes. The blood that had soaked into it was now set like something a hairdresser would have envied.

'Tell me if there's any change,' I said to the doctor. He bowed low as I walked out of the room. There was still work to be done – and it could start with a bath.

The long day of battle was fading into the west when I caught up with the Dispensator. He was overseeing some hesitant repairs to our one piece of long-range artillery. This was the machine that fired the six-foot bolts. It had broken down long before the attack was over, and didn't strike me as likely to see action again. We climbed up the ladder and stood together on the wooden rampart, and looked down from the walls over the carpet of still uncleared death that stretched before us.

'Aren't those the bodies of rioters killed inside the walls?' I asked, staring harder into the lengthening shadows. 'Why are they all naked?'

The Dispensator nodded absent-mindedly. 'I read of this in one of the ancient histories,' he finally said. 'The barbarians thought we were throwing plague victims at them, and this is what eventually broke their attack.' He stopped and crossed himself, and began a whispered prayer for his endangered soul.

But he stood back from the wall and looked at me. 'I did watch you leading your men into the charge,' he said. 'I hope you will not be offended if I say that a professional would have divided his forces, and might have taken fewer losses. Even so, it was most welcoming to the men to see you laughing and shouting at their head. You did well.'

I must say that I had no recollection of any laughing or shouting. I could remember biting my lip as I ran forward, and raising a very heavy and unfamiliar sword. I could remember a vague satisfaction as I got someone in the neck and went forward into a shower of blood. Beyond that, it was all broken fragments, and these mostly included the moments of relative calm in the slaughter. But, if the Dispensator wanted to think me a hero, I'd not complain.

'If you can spare a few moments tomorrow morning,' I said, recalling why I was here, 'I've decided to take the sense of the council. It might come to a vote, but I'm pretty sure I'll carry the majority of the Greeks.'

The Dispensator looked up at the brighter stars that were coming out, one at a time, in the furthest east. 'And I suppose you look to me, young man, to save you from the trouble of a vote by directing our own people to shout out as you desire?' He looked in silence at the sheet of rolled-up parchment that I now held out to him.

Without the barbarian attack, without confirmation of what was happening far off in Constantinople, it had been my intention to strike a ruthless bargain. But we were now where we were. There is a time for haggling and a time for giving way gracefully to the inevitable. I did hope for a certain gracefulness as I handed over the sheet. Such a pity the drugs I'd taken after the battle to keep going had put a visible tremor into my hands.

He looked up from his long and silent inspection of the Latin text. 'And this is a fully accurate translation of the Greek?' he asked. He brushed a dirty finger over the text in both languages that Martin had written out in his neatest chancery hand. He stroked the wax seal that I'd myself attached with silken threads.

I nodded and swallowed to try to get some moisture into my mouth. 'It is an absolutely unambiguous fresh grant,' I said. 'You can keep the grant that Phocas made in his last days and I purported to confirm. After all, you never know what force my own grant will have. But, so long as Heraclius hasn't already sacked me in my absence, His Holiness must, from today, be regarded throughout the Empire as the Universal Bishop.'

'Then we can take the matter as settled,' he said, keeping his voice neutral. 'We make no comment on the orthodoxy of your propositions – and will add this to whatever resolution you put before us. Nevertheless, we are persuaded that the propositions in themselves deserve to be considered by a full and ecumenical council of the Church.'

There was the sudden crack of an arrow that fell short and broke itself on the wall. I stepped behind a wooden screen that had been put up to shelter the defenders.

Without moving from where he was standing, the Dispensator pursed his lips and rolled the parchment shut and replaced it within the ivory ring that Martin had found in one of the abandoned offices in the residency. 'So, My Lord Alaric, we have a deal,' he said. 'I do appreciate the difficulties you may still face with the Emperor. But this has, all considered, been a most smooth and predictable transaction. I will take this with me on the ferry to Corinth next Monday. Once back in Rome, I shall await news of your reception in Constantinople.'

He followed my astonished look over the walls and smiled. 'I am reliably informed that the Great Chief will make another appearance tomorrow morning. This time, he will call a parley. I will go out and meet him and negotiate his withdrawal. You know that I have negotiated an end to five sieges of Rome by the Lombards.'

Even to Priscus, I might have suggested that a personal meeting with Kutbayan didn't sound advisable. But this was the Dispensator. I nodded and made a note to myself that everyone would need to be informed of the further adjournment. I'd reconvene the day after next. That would bring us to Saturday – which was about what I'd imagined in the first place. I was hovering between thoughts of my closing speech to the council, and whether I'd wear the green or the yellow, when I heard the thud of another arrow, this time into the other side of the wooden screen. I stepped hurriedly back behind its cover again, and watched as the Dispensator set off on his continued inspection of the city defences.

He turned back after a few yards and smiled. 'I believe the Lord Priscus will eventually take over the defence again,' he said.

If he really believed that, he hadn't just come from the man. But I said nothing.

'However, I do think it appropriate if I am the one who negotiates the withdrawal. Several wives of the Great Chief are of the Faith, and I am confident that he will be more easily persuaded by me than by a Greek whose warlike skill and personal courage are more than compensated by his reputation for double-dealing. Our garrison is exhausted. We cannot rely on keeping the ordinary people quiet. A second attack – this time with all the Great Chief's force – will not be so easily repelled.'

'So, you'll empty the granaries into his lap?' I asked.

The Dispensator smiled again. 'Cast thy bread upon the waters: for thou shalt find it after many days,' was his only response.

59

Simeon waited till Martin had finished interpreting before snorting with disgust. But the Dispensator had made his intention plain from the beginning. After a long preparatory stage, in which their main symptoms had been palpitations and sweating attacks, my drugs had now settled down to a steady glow. I sprawled on the biggest couch in the library, and looked complacently at my slippered right foot. I heard Simeon put his wine cup down with a sound of scraping on the surface of our one decent table.

'If you believe you can make any sort of deal with that creature, you're absolutely mad,' he said. 'Open those gates, and it will be the end for all of us.' Sooner or later, he'd go back to being as scared as he had been when the barbarians broke in on the council – or as he'd been once everyone the Dispensator and I had left behind were exposed to the taunts and petty thieving of the urban mob. For the moment, he was just angry.

'My Lord Bishop,' I said, keeping as diplomatic as anyone might have managed at the end of this ghastly day, 'we didn't ask you here this evening to discuss the military situation. That is now in the hands of His Excellency the Dispensator. I need your undertaking that you will ensure the unanimous assent of the Greek bishops the day after tomorrow, and that you will countersign my report to Caesar as I have explained it to you.'

No good. The man was now on his feet and walking towards the bust of Polybius. Between stuffing food and weapons through the reopened door within the cupboard, the slaves had found time to bring in enough lamps and candles to light the room almost as well as it was by day. There was none of the gloom here you'd associate with the midnight hour. He stepped sideways to avoid a heap of books that hadn't fitted into any of the racks. Then I saw him stop and put his face close to the damaged bust. There was another snort, and he was coming back.

He stopped beside one of the larger tables that covered the worst patch of the ruined floor, and took up the casualty list. I'd prepared this in Latin for the Dispensator. But its meaning was clear enough. 'How did you manage to lose so many men beside the gate?' he asked with an ill-natured look in my direction. 'Priscus did tell me he was planning to avoid a direct encounter. From what I hear, you fought with all the skill of a drunken savage. Little wonder you've persuaded yourself that opening the gate is our only choice.' He pulled a very sour face and sat down again in his chair.

I swung my legs off the couch and sat up. 'Simeon,' I began again, still smooth, 'we did have an agreement . . .'

'*Agreement*, eh?' came the sneered reply. 'You buggered up everything in Egypt good and proper. Don't suppose bullying us into admitting that black may, after all, be white will make up for that. Don't ever suppose letting this tonsured barbarian risk getting all our throats cut will put everything right with Heraclius.

'As for these vicious accusations you and Priscus made the other evening – oh, do me a favour!' He trailed off for a long and bitter laugh of triumph. 'My dear and soon to be *late* cousin might have got somewhere with those. Even supposing they are true, a piece of dirt like you will never get close enough to the Emperor to repeat them. So you go ahead, and get your savages to stand up in their clerical finery and agree that black is white. It's the Greek bishops who really matter in Constantinople. And you'll get nothing out of us!'

I pretended to ignore this last burst of ill-humour, and got up and went over to look at the mural. I could see I'd missed a fine chance earlier in the day. I should have waited till Simeon had been skewered by that barbarian before going into action. But that's life for you – it's often a catalogue of missed opportunities. Still, I'd not miss out on this one. Behind me, the Dispensator breathed out impatiently, and I heard him whisper to Martin for an explanation of what was being said.

Still looking at the wall painting of Athens, I told myself that it must show the city as it had been in the time of Demosthenes. According to what I'd read in Dexippus, the colonnade that fringed the whole of the main market place was decisive evidence. As if for the first time, I saw how so much of what was shown here was now just heaps of rubble beyond the modern wall.

'I suggest we should check that they really have withdrawn before we send anyone down to Piraeus to see if the Corinth ferry will come,' I said in Latin.

The Dispensator said nothing, and I took this as a provisional assent. If possible, I'd seen more barbarians than ever outside the walls. I'd stood there with the Dispensator until long after darkness had come. Until the light went altogether, we'd seen the irregular columns of men as they came over from the main camp north of Decelea. Even after that, we'd seen the flaring torches as others beyond counting had joined them. More than ever, we were as surrounded as one of those artificial mounds in Egypt that rise above the Nile flood. But the mere knowledge of the coming parley with Kutbayan was turning every mind in the room but one to the matter of how and when we'd be leaving Athens.

'Simeon, has it ever crossed your mind,' I asked, switching back into Greek, 'how desperately short we are of money in Constantinople? You can't fight off the Persians without soldiers, and you can't employ soldiers unless you have the money to pay them. Now, His Holiness the Universal Bishop has decided to present the Great Augustus with a gift of twelve hundred pounds of gold. The former Western Provinces are not notable for their riches – but the Western Church is very rich. As is proper in these cases, it will be a free gift. There will be no conditions attached. However . . .' I stepped closer to the painting and didn't care if anyone watching me might guess that I was smiling. I'd suddenly realised that the mural showed the Temple of Athena with two extra columns on its front portico. I leaned forward and stared at the carefully depicted inaccuracy.

I turned and gave Simeon a bright smile. 'You know, My Lord Bishop,' I continued, looking carefully into his still snarling face, 'you did call the Pope's right-hand man a "gross and vulgar barbarian". Of course, you did this only to me, and I'm sure you have no fear of what I might say against you. But you did also insult your Latin Brother in Christ – and to his face, and with the Bishop of Ephesus as a witness. A complaint from His Holiness about your behaviour is unlikely to be ignored by the Emperor. Where do you think he'll send you – a mountain or a desert monastery? If you like, I could put in a word for you. The former British provinces have a most bracing combination of cold and rain.'

I could have stood there all night, watching the subtle changes of colour and expression in Simeon's face. But some threats are best unelaborated – not least when the facts on which they are based are neither wholly nor partially true. I left him in his chair and went over to the window, and looked out into the utter darkness of the midnight hour.

'Have you made notes of your closing speech?' Martin asked me.

I hadn't, but I assured him that it would be very simple. Whether I made it in Greek or Latin, it would take no effort to put it into the other language. Even here, the tension was perceptibly relaxing.

'I have no idea what orders the captain of our own galley was given,' I said in Latin, turning back to face everyone. 'But, if he does put in on Monday – or is still in Corinth – I'll somehow get him to take us to Constantinople. If we can work the rowers at full strength, we should see the Senatorial Dock days and days before a *certain other person* can be carried back along the main road. I'm assuming, of course, he will be carried. Then again, I don't assume there will be any horse able to carry his bulk. So long as we can get back in time, I do suspect we can talk Our Lord and Master into a better view of his interests.'

I fell silent. Through all I'd just said, Simeon had been trying to follow its meaning – as if you can understand an unknown language by looking intently at how a speaker moves his lips. Awareness of his desperate concentration had kept me from realising how depressed I'd suddenly begun to feel. Perhaps the stimulant was starting to fade. More likely, this was one of those times when putting thoughts into words shows them as the wishful thinking they probably are. With Sergius under house arrest, and all the palace eunuchs running wild against me, who could tell if I could even get into the Imperial Presence? Unless I could bribe someone to open one of the gates, and then force my way into the Presence, the white, thirty-foot-high walls of the palace were as impregnable as Constantinople itself. If Heraclius was resolved not to see me, it would be as much as I could do to avoid being torn apart by the city mob. I thought again of Martin's private urging to make a dash to the West before word could drift back that we'd lifted the siege.

I changed the subject. 'What happened with the body of Irene?' I asked.

'I had her buried in the Church of Saint Eutropius the Lesser,' the Dispensator said. 'My secretary has taken over the running of this household. And I must apologise on his behalf for the extreme lateness of dinner.' He walked over to one of the long windows and looked out into the darkness. 'I did suggest boiled mutton. But we shall have to see what the slaves could manage.'

Euphemia didn't come to me that night. After a day of hard killing, I might have fancied her attentions. But I didn't miss her. Instead, for the first time in days and days, I fell straight into a long and exhausted sleep. I dreamed I was back in the barbarian camp, with Priscus and Ludinus both gloating down at me. But it was one of those indistinct dreams, in which you feel no terror. Though I could taste the full sourness of my replaced gag, I stared serenely back at the twisted faces, and heard nothing of what was said to me.

The dreams shifted, and I was now beside the tomb of Hierocles. The dead girl stood there, smiling wantonly and offering herself. Even before I could step backward on to the road, however, she was gone, and I had retraced both space and time to be once again in Richborough. I stood up to my waist in the chilly, grey sea water and looked out to where mist blotted out the horizon.

Behind me, on the beach, there was something I didn't care to turn and look at. I took a step further into the water, and then another, until the waters came up to my neck. With another step, they closed over my head, and I opened my mouth and breathed them into my lungs.

Even before I could realise what I'd done, the dream shifted yet again, and I was grovelling before Heraclius. I couldn't say where I was. When I looked up, I didn't see anything beyond his very still purple boots. I stretched forward again, and adored the Great Majesty for ages and ages. As I lay there, I could feel my body shrinking and withering with age. When I managed to look up again, there were the same purple boots, though I now had the sense that they covered other feet. Still, they didn't move.

So the dreams tumbled through my head in a riot of muted colours and faint sounds. Perhaps they continued all night. Perhaps they were all crowded into the few moments before I opened my eyes and blinked in the morning sun that streamed through the uncovered window. But it was some while after I'd woken and looked about in vain for water in which to wash before I could shake off the feeling of vast and inconsolable sadness that had tinged every dream I could recall.

60

As if nothing at all had happened, or was happening, Theodore was pushing Maximin in his swing. The sun had gone in behind one of the slightly grey clouds that were scudding across the sky, and Sveta stood beside me with her arms folded.

'He will be coming back with us,' she said in Slavic. She nodded at Theodore. When I said nothing back, she asked if I'd be adopting him as well.

'You did well to go for the Dispensator,' I said. I made an effort to look her in the eye. 'Thank you,' I eventually said in place of the more elaborate speech I'd had in mind.

Unblinking, she stared back at me. 'One of these days, you'll get us all killed,' she said. 'You know my great booby of a husband worships you and prays nightly for your safety?'

Having no answer in mind, I shrugged.

Without another word, she walked past me to where Theodore had now lost his hat. The sun would soon be out again. Whatever she thought of the boy's adoptive mother, she was entirely at one with Euphemia on the danger this might pose even to the slightly sallow skin of a Syrian.

I heard a voice behind me in Latin. 'Alaric,' the Dispensator said, 'I have prayed all night before the relic of Saint George. I am perfectly assured that God will bless our efforts.'

I leaned closer to Sveta. 'Get enough water into that cellar to last five days,' I whispered. 'Take a couple of picks too. If you can make anyone go down there again, have the slaves dig out the blocked exit through the tomb.'

She nodded, then looked steadily back at me.

Before hurrying away, I glanced quickly about. A couple of

the slaves had continued clearing rubbish off one of the old lawns. It had no grass, of course, but looked as it if might by the next spring.

The midday hour had come and gone, and still I stood beside Martin, looking in silence from the walls of Athens. One at a time, we'd been joined by what must have been the whole surviving militia, and then by a multitude of grim and hooded monks. At first, the wooden platform had shaken as every new arrival had stepped from the rickety ladder that led up from the cleared ground behind us. By now, there were so many of us that the platform had the deceptive solidity of something that might give way at any moment.

Before the sun was fully up, the nearest gate had opened, and out, all alone, had walked the Dispensator. 'Don't be ridiculous, Alaric,' he'd snapped at me before then. 'Do you suppose your presence will add an ounce of persuasive force? At the very best, you'll only upset the man.' And so, with one of his thinnest smiles yet, he'd looked upwards for a guidance that I, of course, didn't see, and had stepped firmly on to the long Piraeus road. He'd been greeted by a little monk, and, I supposed, by Kollo who'd finally been sobered up to interpret between Greek and Latin and between Latin and whatever the Great Chief might choose to speak for this conference. Ludinus had been nowhere in sight. Perhaps he was somewhere in the dense crowd from which Kutbayan had stepped to greet the Dispensator.

That had been hours before, and the Dispensator was still deep in conversation with Kutbayan, who sat opposite him at a small table that had been brought out and set with wine cups. They sat just out of arrow shot. I could have given orders for one of our working pieces of artillery to be brought over. A volley of six-foot arrows might have got the old monster, and rid the Empire of its most deadly enemy after the Great King of Persia himself. Oh, I might have given these orders and more. But no one would have obeyed me. Without the Dispensator to give them, everyone beside me was taking orders now from the Bishop of Athens. He stood a few yards from my left and looked on without moving. I might be the Emperor's Legate. Up here, I was just another spectator. Though I'd put on a thin tunic, the clouds were gone, and, with every shift of the breeze, I could feel the chill of sweaty silk as often as it brushed against the small of my back.

There was another burst of laughter from the armed men behind Kutbayan, and another clashing of swords on shields. I squinted to look harder into the sun. Kutbayan himself hadn't moved, though the Dispensator now stood up and walked a few yards in our direction. He turned back to Kutbayan and raised a hand behind him to point at something above our own heads. There was more clashing of arms. But now Kutbayan was on his feet. I saw him walk forward to the Dispensator and lead him back to the table.

I felt Martin shift slightly. He ran his tongue over very dry lips. 'Do you remember,' he whispered, 'how Pope Leo of sainted memory went out of Rome in ancient times to a conference with King Attila?' he asked.

I nodded. I could have observed that a century and a half wasn't quite ancient times. But, with the Emperor safe behind the marshes that stretched far about Ravenna, and the few soldiers left in Italy there to guard him, it had, sure enough, been the Pope who'd gone out to plead with the Huns when nothing else could have stopped them from smashing down the walls of Rome. Whether Saints Peter and Paul really had hovered a few feet above his head, whether it had been threats of hellfire – or whether it had been the mass of gold he'd squeezed out of the Senators – Leo had performed the saving miracle of turning Attila back from Rome. And, since Kutbayan still hadn't lost his temper and called an end to this conference, it looked pretty much as if the Dispensator was about to repeat the miracle for Athens.

'At least someone's had a good time in Athens,' I sighed when I could think of any reply. Martin looked quizzically at me, and then turned to where something was now definitely happening.

I'd been looking miserably down at what had been the ditch, so had missed the dramatic moment when Kutbayan threw both arms about the Dispensator. But I did look up in time to see the immense crowd part and the pair of them step within it. Arm-in-arm, they walked slowly back towards the now visible tent, and a great roar went up on all sides and spread with gathering volume through the whole of the multitude that surrounded Athens. You can forget the triumphant cheers of a packed Circus in Constantinople. This was far greater. It went on and on – a steady roar of approbation, and little eddies here and there of ecstatic battle cries.

As the two men stepped together into the tent, the noise gradu-ally faded away, and there was a renewed and very long silence. On each side of the wall, we waited and held our silence. For all I could tell of what was going on inside that tent, they might have been eating lunch together. Then, just as I was about to think the tension could last no longer, the tent flaps rose again and they stepped back out. Now, Kutbayan had put off his armour and was dressed in a robe of shimmering purple. He turned back to his nobles and said something that I was too far away to catch. Then a herald appeared beside him and shouted out in Avar. The Dispensator leading him by the hand, Kutbayan took a step towards Athens.

I stood back from the wall and stretched. 'It's all agreed,' I said flatly. I turned to one of the militia leaders. 'Have the gate opened.' Without looking in any direction, I raised my voice. 'Any man who so much as shows a sword,' I cried, 'I'll kill with my own hands.' I did think of reminding everyone what horrors had now been avoided. But my voice was now lost in another roar that was joined from within the walls of Athens.

'If she wants to pray in the big church on the hill, that is where she *will* pray.' Though on his best behaviour, there was an edge in Kutbayan's voice that didn't ask for continued objection.

I nodded, and the Dispensator gave another respectful bow.

It was all over now. The grain would be carried out in sacks to the waiting carriages. In the meantime, I was, as agreed, giving Kutbayan a more informative tour of Athens than Nicephorus had managed for me. Keeping him as far as I could from any inspection of the walls, I'd shown him the dye works and the Church of a Thousand Relics. I'd presented every bishop to him who could stand without voiding his bowels. We'd drunk wine in the residency, and I'd let him try the now cleaned-out latrines. At last, we were standing in the shade of what may once have been another memorial to victory in the Persian War.

Kutbayan reached up and touched the lower part of a relief in which some youths were leading a couple of bulls to sacrifice. 'You seriously tell me,' he sneered, 'that a race of naked boys fought off the Great King of Persia?'

'United under the Great Alexander, the Greeks as a whole conquered the Persians,' I said, not bothering to keep the pride out of my voice.

His answer was a sniff. Keeping silent, he stood on tiptoe and touched one of the perfectly shaped thighs. Then he turned and looked up at the Acropolis.

'The priest you sent out did a good job,' he said at length. 'But I'd already promised to spare the big church on the hill.' He looked down at the dark patch in the dust where one of his men had fallen in the attack. He laughed unpleasantly and pushed his face close to mine. 'I'm given to understand that my men were turned back yesterday by an elderly priest and a stupid boy from a place called England.'

I smiled back nervously. His face was turning an ugly colour, and I hoped desperately Priscus had been wrong about his sense of propriety.

But he laughed a little less unpleasantly, and he looked again at the Acropolis. 'You know that I was supposed to *take* the food you've been good enough to promise?' he asked, now looking hard into my face.

I resisted the urge to step back. 'This way, we've agreed, we all get something of what we want,' I said evenly. Of course, we were speaking in Slavic, and the crowd about us could only guess from the tone what was being said. I noticed a few scared looks, but put everyone back at ease by joining in the man's renewed laughter.

Kutbayan wiped his sweaty brow and looked at the hushed and respectful crowd. These were mostly the militia men, and I hoped they were keeping to the agreement and had left their weapons beside the walls. 'I suppose we all do get something of what we want,' he agreed. 'Even you, Aelric of England, shan't miss out on the blessings of peace.' He showed his blackened teeth as I couldn't resist stiffening at the mention of my real name. The man did have a good memory. I thought he'd had much else on his mind when I'd let the truth slip out in his tent. 'I've sent your fat friend back to King Heraclius,' he added. 'He'll be home long before you get there.' He stepped out of the sun that had now moved from where it was hiding behind the monument. He blinked for a moment and looked closer still into my face.

Then he relaxed and laughed, now almost pleasantly. 'Most of him will be back before you,' he added. He reached into a leather pouch that hung from his neck and pulled out a bundle of stained silk.

I took it from him. The moment I had it in the palm of my hand, I'd guessed what it had to be. But I undid it and stared for a long time at the podgy blue finger. The ring of a Grand Chamberlain was still set into the flesh.

'If you are at all the man your priest says you are,' he said, 'this will put you back into the favour of the worthless effeminate the Greeks have set up as their King.'

And it would. Whatever he might have ordered in private, Heraclius would never admit to sanctioning what, even for an Emperor, amounted to treason and blasphemy. Ludinus couldn't wriggle free from the blame of having set the Avars on a city that, even now, was holy to every civilised man – a city, mind you, stuffed with bishops, and Western bishops too. I wrapped the finger very carefully and bowed.

He looked up again at the Acropolis. 'Women always take their time,' he sighed. 'But I think I can trust your people to keep her safe. If you want me to lift the siege before this day is out, I have things to do. I've had my fill of a city filled at best with worn-out glories. There really is nothing here to burn, and hardly anyone worth killing.'

Just before passing back through the wide-open gate, he stopped for the customary embrace. As was only proper, I had mine after the Dispensator, and mine was considerably less warm. 'Aelric of England,' he said, 'you may think you had the better of me in my tent.' He smiled and took one of my hands between his own. He stroked the smooth and very soft flesh of my palm. 'I was aware that you had been taken,' he said with another smile. 'I guessed who you were before you even opened your mouth. No Greekling would ever have done anything so utterly mad for his people. You really are wasted among them. Come and see me if you ever get sick of your Great Augustus.'

Just beyond the gate, he stopped again and turned back. 'And do give my best wishes to Priscus. I was hoping to see him, but appreciate that he's still feeling poorly. Tell him even he can't imagine the death I'll give him when he's finally brought before me as a prisoner.'

I watched as Kutbayan walked briskly out to his waiting people. The gate still wide open, I turned and went back inside Athens. A few of the lower classes were shambling about from wherever they'd been driven under cover for the visit. They capered in front of me, uttering cheerful obscenities and making still more obscene gestures with their hands. I paid them no attention. They'd be smiling on the other sides of their horrid faces when it sank in that bugger all of the food Kutbayan had left inside the walls would be doled out to them. It would be a long and deservedly cheerless winter for them.

61

The light was fading as I got back to the residency. There was still a mountain of work to be scaled before I could give the orders to pack. There was the final vote of the council to be managed. I didn't suppose this would be more than a formality. But it would take the better part of the next morning, with all the praying and formal acclamations that I'd have to sit through. Then there was the matter of how we were all to get back to Constantinople. I'd assumed that our Imperial galley was still waiting in Corinth. Even if it was there, I might have trouble with the Governor of Corinth. The only matter now settled was that we weren't to have the barbarian multitudes roll over us.

But that, let's face it, seemed quite enough to me. The tension that had been only briefly lifted on my journey up from Piraeus, and then come back with still more crushing weight, was now lifted. Beside that, the further business that I've mentioned was nothing. Even the still doubtful reception I could face in Constantinople was something I'd think about when I had to, and not until then. I felt like a boy at the beginning of a school holiday.

I knocked hard on the big wooden gate of the residency, and smiled at the grim slave who observed that I'd been going about unguarded. I peeled off my sweaty outer robe and dumped it into his arms. Martin, I was sure, would still be praying in the chapel – that, or Sveta would have carried him off to dinner in the nursery. I thought briefly of joining them. But I looked about the bare entrance hall, and wondered at how a change in my own mood could brighten what I'd come to think an oppressively dark and unwelcoming place. I passed quickly through it and passed through what had once been other grand rooms – rooms that also now seemed nearly as grand as in the old days. Even the labyrinth of dank corridors that stretched beyond seemed lighter and more airy.

I bounded up the spotlessly clean steps and into the library. I hurried through it, not stopping, but still noticing how cheerful it seemed. I passed along the neatly swept corridors, and nodded a greeting to the silent statue of Demosthenes. Just before reaching the silent courtroom, I took a left into a small sitting room that had once been where the judge rested between sessions, and stepped behind the bookrack that obscured the far wall. I knocked three times on the door that no one else had so far managed to notice. 'You can come out now,' I said happily. 'Everything is sorted.'

I paused and knocked again. Now, I snorted and pushed the door open. I looked about the empty room that had no windows. Even in the darkness, I knew it was empty. There was no smell of a lamp that had gone out. For all I could tell, it had been empty all day. 'Back in her own rooms,' I muttered.

But she wasn't there – not, at least, unless she'd managed to turn herself to mist and seep under the door that was still closed with the Dispensator's seal on its lock. I shrugged and thought of my own bedroom. I brightened again. Yes, I thought – where else could be more appropriate?

As I was taking the steps down from the library, two at a time, I heard a muffled shout, as if of fear or pain. As I stopped, it stopped, and I stood for a moment, not breathing in, but wondering if I'd been mistaken. I was at the foot of the steps when I heard a babble of distant voices, and now another shrill and horrified scream. Even on my ninth day since first stepping through the gate, noises in the residency could still confuse me. Had these come from the corridors leading to my own rooms? Had they come from the grand room? Had they even come from behind the far door in the library?

But there was now a loud crash of something falling, or being broken apart, and this noise definitely came from the ground floor of the library block. It was beside or past those big arched supports I'd seen only once. I took a left at the bottom of the library steps.

The door leading to the row of arched supports was ajar. As I pushed it open and stepped into one of the many areas that I'd left off the cleaning schedule, I heard yet another scream, this one much closer. I could have sworn it came from the slave dungeon where I'd stood with Priscus. I stood still and listened. Then I heard another crash as if of breaking wood, and, in a familiar voice, the cry: 'Back, spawn of Satan! Who will save you now?'

Most scenes can be described with very few words. Even moments of high drama normally take place against a background familiar enough to be alluded to and not closely described. What I'd now stumbled across, however, has no familiar elements, and I must struggle to avoid the prolixity of a submission at law.

I was halfway down the stairs into that room filled with skeletons. These were now completely disarranged in what looked like some vague effort at clearing the place. Or there might have been a long struggle. The room was brightly lit from the flames of two torches set into the wall brackets. But I could give only a passing look at the evidence of past atrocities. All my attention was focused on the here and now.

Her clothing smeared with dark gobbets of what could only be congealed blood, Euphemia had one of those manacles about her left wrist. She'd pressed herself against the wall, and was holding up a severed head in both hands. As I looked on in silence, she took it away from her face. She saw me, and spat out a mouthful of dark jelly. It fell on to her breast, then continued on to the floor with a quiet splash.

'Alaric,' she cried in a choking voice, 'help me!'

Balthazar wheeled round and gave me a stare of utter madness. 'Don't go near her!' he shrieked. 'This is her time of weakness! The Goddess is strong within me!'

I saw the bloody knife that he held in his right hand. I saw the smashed wooden box at his feet, about the size of a coffin. I saw the naked body from which the head had just been cut. I looked back at the head that Euphemia now threw into the middle of the room. It was the blond boy that old Gundovald had been fussing about for the past four days. I forced myself not to look into the dull eyes and looked back at Euphemia.

'Thank God it's you, Alaric,' she cried, now with a smile that sent another gobbet of dark jelly on to her chin. 'He was trying to kill me.'

I hurried down the crumbling steps and moved towards her.

'Oh, please, Alaric,' she implored, holding out both arms, 'please, get me out of here. It's *horrible*.'

Balthazar rushed at me and put up his hands to push me back. 'Keep away!' he shouted. 'Don't let her touch you!'

Theodore might have had more strength in his body to restrain me. I pushed Balthazar hard in the chest, and he crashed head first against the wall. He slid down on to the floor and started a long coughing attack. Then he groaned and pitched forward into a silence in which only his shuddering breaths showed that he was still alive. I blinked and looked about me again. I stepped back and tried frantically to make sense of what I was seeing.

'He sacrificed the boy before my very eyes,' Euphemia whimpered. 'He forced me to do such *horrible* things. Will I ever be clean again?' She burped and more of that disgusting jelly leaked out on to her chin. She smiled suddenly and reached out her arms again. I heard the short chain rattle that held her to the wall. 'Get this off me, Alaric,' she said, her voice now taking on a low, husky quality. 'Let's just get out of here into the daylight.'

I bent forward and made myself touch the headless corpse. I straightened up and looked again at Balthazar. He was only stunned. In a few moments, he'd come back to life. I pointed at one of the manacles that now hung loose on the wall. 'Get that about one of his wrists,' I commanded.

She stretched forward as far as she could manage and grabbed at Balthazar, and fiddled ineffectually at first with the bracelet of dark bronze. At last, though, she had it about him. She got to her feet and came forward to the point where the chain stretched tight.

I ignored the new flood of pleading and endearments and bent down to touch the dead boy.

I stood up and wiped my hand on the lower part of my tunic. 'You say the boy has just been killed?' I asked in the neutral tone I'd learned to use when sitting in court.

She nodded eagerly, and moved her arms again so that the chain gave another of its dull rattles.

'I'd say he's been dead for days.' I stood back and sat carefully on one of the lower steps that led down from the referred light of the long passageway outside the arch. 'Tell me, Euphemia, what *really* happened.'

She tried to smile and repeated what could only be a pack of lies. Every elaboration of the story had to be another lie. I gave up on following the incidental details and looked over at the body where it sprawled in the remains of the cobwebs. It must have been carried down in the long wooden box that lay smashed on the far side of the room. I couldn't explain the three sets of footprints in the room. None of them was mine. Probably the body had been taken from the box and somehow guided rather than dragged across the room. All I could say for sure was that Balthazar could never have carried the box down here by himself – nor have lifted the body from it. Doubtless, he'd cut off the head. Beyond that, the explanation of present facts was blurred by a dawning realisation of others.

'You helped kill that girl – didn't you?' I asked suddenly.

A proper denial would have been all the answer I needed – all the answer I *wanted*. The brief look that flashed across her face was the equivalent of any confession that might have emerged from the longest cross-examination.

I leaned forward and put my head in both hands. 'There's no point asking for reasons of those who are mad,' I said. 'It's enough that the pair of you have been in this together – even if you both might claim somehow to have been working against each other.' All the woman had to do was give me a few words of decent explanation. Instead, I looked straight away from where she'd pulled up her clothing to show her thighs and the middle parts of her body. I looked away from her lush, voluptuous smile. I took a deep breath, then made myself stare at her again.

'How many have you sacrificed in the past few years?' I asked. 'What did you do with the blood? Don't tell me you were drinking it.' I thought of a sorcery scandal back in Constantinople that had sent Heraclius into a frenzy. 'Were you bathing in it? Is that why the latrines stank to high heaven?' I had a further thought. 'Why did you kill Irene?' I asked. 'Why the maids?'

Oh – if only she'd found the presence of mind to jump in and stop this entire train of questioning! It wouldn't have taken much, after all. I *wanted* to believe I was talking nonsense. But she only simpered and pulled her clothes up to her neck. She spread her legs where she sat in the filth of centuries and groaned with simulated lust.

She heard the scrape of my sandals as I got up, and struggled to get her face clear of the clothing. 'Get me out of this, Alaric,' she pleaded, holding up her left wrist. 'We can go out into the light together, just as you said we would. It will be you and me and little Theodore. We can all go to Constantinople together. It will be just as you've always wanted.'

I stared down at her through slitted eyes. The lawyers admit there are classes of madness that absolve from any guilt. But she'd known enough of what she was doing to hide it from the world. Even if she really was what she plainly believed she was, her actions would still have been wrong. Murder is murder, and justice must always be done.

'If you look properly at your manacle,' I said in my coldest and most judicial voice, 'you will see that it was made *not* to come off.' I turned and willed myself to blot out those horrified screams as I made my way carefully back to the top of the steps. The wooden door was inches thick, and pushing it shut muffled the worst of the screams. I tried and tried to push the bolts into place. But ages of rust had caused them to swell and seize, and I found myself twisting them to no effect.

It was now that my legs gave way, and I fell sobbing to the floor – sobbing with the horror of all I'd seen, and with the horror of what I was now doing. I might have pulled the door open again and gone back down. Even before the faint cries from within

433

began to fade, I'd found myself starting all over again to tremble with lust. If I shut my eyes, all I could now see was how she'd spread her legs in the filth. It was suddenly as arousing as it had been disgusting. I do think I was about to scramble back to my feet, when I heard a quiet chuckle behind me.

'It needs more than main force to get those things back in,' Priscus said.

I twisted round and looked into the pale and ghastly face. His arms bandaged from the application of the opium, his whole body trembling with the strain of standing upright, he still managed a long and wheezing laugh as he gloated down at me.

'Get up,' he ordered in a surprisingly firm voice. 'Push the door as hard as you can. Try to lift it slightly in its hinges.'

I did as I was told, and he took over fiddling with the bolts. At last, there was a sharp grating as first one and then the other was pushed back more or less as they'd been found five days before. I flopped back to the floor, and would have begun crying in earnest.

But Priscus kicked me hard in my side. 'If a job is worth doing at all, my dear boy, it's worth doing well,' he sneered. 'There's the other door yet to be closed. Come on, get to your feet. Do as Uncle Priscus directs.' He wheezed out another laugh. 'Yes, come on, my pretty. Let's be out of this gloom. Can you believe there are times when even I want to be in the light?'

The slaves had left the key in the outer door. Once I'd pushed and pulled until the lock fell back into place, and we were into a silence broken only by his ragged breathing and my continuing sobs, Priscus kicked me again. He kicked me until I got back up from where I'd sat down. He struck me lightly on the cheek. I then had to catch him as he staggered backwards, and almost carry him back to the main part of the residency. I looked at the door that closed off the whole block from which we'd come. Priscus held up the key that I knew would also lock this one, but shook his head.

'I'll give orders later for the door to the arch to be bricked over,' he said. 'A coat of rendering over it all, and no one will ever know about the door.' He clutched tightly on the key and let me carry him out into the increasingly dim light of the main courtyard.

434

'How much did you hear?' I asked as I looked up at the still bright sky.

'Enough to let me guess everything else,' he said. 'Don't allow it to get you down, though. Even if living here with Nicephorus for company turned her wits, she really was a bad sort. Since no one else dared tell you about it, I thought I'd let you find out for yourself. As for Balthazar, he did have it coming.' He paused. 'I wonder who'll eat whom?' he asked without looking down at me.

I said nothing.

He smiled and sat slowly down beside me. 'I may have an odd way of showing it sometimes,' he went on. 'But you really must believe, darling Alaric, that I do like you very much. If you choose never to discuss this matter again, I promise not to raise it of my own motion.'

I said nothing, and we sat together in silence as the sky turned dark, and, one by one, the stars began to come out. The wild flowers were turning pale in the dusk, and I could tell it would be a chilly evening, when Priscus finally told me to help him up, and we turned to go in and see what progress Sveta had made with the packing.

'I don't think I can be blamed for any dereliction of duty,' Priscus opened as we passed into one of the lit areas of the residency. 'I can still regret, though, that I wasn't able to direct things yesterday as they reached their crisis. I have no doubt, however, your report to Heraclius will narrate things not as they were, but as they should have been.' He stopped and looked slyly into my face. 'After all, my dearest of friends, we do stand or fall together.' He leaned against the wall for support and giggled.

I said nothing, but looked into a bronze mirror someone had hung on the wall to reflect daylight along the corridor. So far as I could tell in the gathering darkness, even the dull red mark of my spots had now faded. It was as if they'd never been there. I stared long at the smooth and supremely beautiful face in the mirror. And still I said nothing.

EPILOGUE

Canterbury, Wednesday, 10 June 688

Oh, what a great heap of papyrus I've made again! And how my wrist aches from the burden of covering it all in my spidery Greek handwriting. I do allow there is more that I ought to say. I have stopped almost still in the middle of things. But this is as much as I feel inclined to say.

Well, there is a little more that I need to say. I did get my unanimous vote, and I even went back home in a triumph that Heraclius didn't choose to piss all over – not, at least, in the short term, and not deliberately. Yes, I'd done what anyone might have thought the impossible, and got provisional agreement on the doctrine of a Single Will for Christ. We did nothing with it at first. There was still a long war to fight and win. But, once the Persians had been driven back and utterly destroyed, Sergius and the Emperor brought all sides together in our long-promised ecumenical council, and it seemed that agreement had been reached. I stepped modestly back and let others take the credit, but I had finally settled the Monophysite heresy on terms that both sides could reasonably call a victory for their own position.

Or so I was able to think for a couple of years. Sadly, the Church authorities in Rome eventually decided that the Sergian Compromise was itself heretical, and anathematised it under the new name of the Monothelite heresy. By then, however, it no longer mattered. The Empire had put forward what was nearly its last effort to regain Egypt and Syria from the Persians. We had nothing left when the Saracens popped out of nowhere to take them away from us again. It was rotten luck, everyone agreed, and it meant that Heraclius ended his reign on a disastrous note that even I couldn't avoid for him.

As said, though, the new dispute no longer mattered. The loss of the Monophysite areas was a military and strategic disaster, but removed all need for theological compromise, and the Empire was easily brought back to orthodoxy as it was maintained by Rome. His Grace Theodore, even before he was made Bishop of Canterbury, was of critical importance in all communications between Rome and Constantinople; and it was due largely to his own efforts that the dispute was settled as it was.

It could have been different, mind you. We can blame the Saracens all we like. But they'd have got nowhere if the Syrians and Egyptians hadn't been so utterly disenchanted with the victorious and restored Empire. As ever, it was that bloody fool Heraclius who was the real villain. If only he'd left things with Sergius and me, the Pope himself would have lain down with the followers of Eutyches. Instead, he'd had to keep telling everyone he was the Emperor, and that all should believe as he directed. Then there was the army of tax-gatherers he set loose on provinces that were already bled white by the Persians. No wonder it all went tits up.

But it was such a very long time ago, and it does me no good to set myself brooding over it again. What does matter is how fat Sophronius will take my story. He came in and stood over me the other day, clucking over how much longer I'd take. He told me then he'd brought in a couple of monks from France who could translate my Greek into Latin. He'll scream blue murder if he ever gets to read the unvarnished truth about the Little Council of Athens. It may not show a Pope as directly in error. It doesn't say much good, though, about Saint Fortunatus of the Lateran – whose dying breath, sealed in a vessel of many-coloured crystal, has worked so many undoubted and miraculous cures of the feeble-minded.

But it's always *if*, isn't it? Sophronius would scream blue murder if he were ever to read my manuscript. But there are fifteen stairs to the room where I'm now sitting. I've counted them many times for myself. Many more the times I've counted the heavy tread of Sophronius as he's passed up and down them. Later today, as he passes down them with my immense heap of papyrus in a box that I know he will insist on carrying by himself, he will reach the seventh stair. When I've pulled hard on the length of twine that snakes so unobtrusively from the stairs into this room, I promise that he will never set foot on the eighth. Two really can keep a secret, if one be dead.

I haven't seen my dear, young Theodore in over a month. But, when I stand behind him at the funeral, whispering into his ear, will he really be able to resist the matchless eloquence of the Magnificent Alaric, his adoptive though somewhat estranged father? I'll lay a bet with you, gentle reader – the next chapter of my story *will* be written in Jarrow.

Oh, you just wait and see!

Richard Blake

The Sword of Damascus

686 AD.

The Byzantine Empire is a shattered rump.
The armies of Arabia have overrun its African
and Syrian provinces. Meekal the
Magnificent, the Greek turncoat who rules
Damascus, dreams of conquering
Constantinople itself.

Far off in the wastes of Jarrow, old Aelric
writes his memoirs and waits for death. Little
does he expect a double siege, a kidnapping,
a near-fatal chase through the ravaged
Mediterranean and a confrontation at the end
of this that will settle the future of mankind.

Will age have robbed Aelric of his charm, his
intelligence, his resourcefulness, or of his
talent for cold and homicidal duplicity?

HODDER

Richard Blake

The Blood of Alexandria

612 AD.

Egypt, the jewel of the Roman Empire,
seethes with unrest, as bread runs short in the
slums of Alexandria and the Persians plot an
invasion. The mummy of Alexander the
Great, dead for nine hundred years, can still
calm the mob – or inflame it.

Aelric, the young British clerk who has
become a senator and the henchman of
Emperor Heraclius, has come to Egypt to
force the unwilling viceroy to give its land to
the peasants. But the city – with its factions
and conspirators – thwarts him at every turn.
And when an old enemy from Constantinople
arrives, supposedly on a quest for a religious
relic that could turn the course of the Persian
war, he will have to use all his cunning, his
charm and his talent for violence to survive.

HODDER